A SONG OF MAGIC

CAROLINA CASTILLO

CREATIVELY UNWRITTEN LLC

Published by Creatively Unwritten LLC

First Edition: February 2022

Second Edition: February 2023

To Zoey—my favorite person

CONTENT WARNING

A Song of Magic has content that could be triggering to some readers, such as:

- Death of a parent
- Emotional and psychological abuse
- Corporal punishment
- Open door sex scenes
- Drug use

Please read with caution and take good care of yourself.

For any more information on this book, as well as Carolina's playlists, please visit https://carolinacastilloauthor.com

A NOTE TO GET YOU STARTED

This edition of A Song of Magic came because I, like the smart planner I am, decided to write a second novel in this world. I adore these characters, and when Sophia's sister wouldn't stop talking to me, I chose to write her story. If you've read a previous version of this book, you will find that some things are different in this edition—like a certain character's name (hint: it's Jay; he's now Lucas).

If this is your first time reading, thank you so much for being here. I really hope you enjoy this story and its characters.

Love, Carolina

1

There was something calming about the moments before someone did magic. The air softened and became thinner, anticipating the rush of power that would hang invisible like an electric current.

Sophia Candela wasn't a witch, and she could do no such thing as make magic. It didn't stop her from pretending to be one, though.

She stood serenely on top of a balcony as she observed the main floor of her club, Nowhere.

It was bursting with excitement, and the ecstatic energy of it hummed under her skin. Her hand was on the iron railing of the balcony, which adorned the staircase all the way to the floor. The house band played a sultry song, something they often played to begin shows. Shows they strived to make the best in the city. They happened every weekend of the year, unless a holiday happened to fall on one.

Sophia was dressed in full witch garb, a modern, sexy kind—the way she had always imagined witches to be. Not like in some of those older movies where witches were evil, and therefore, ugly.

She adjusted the little crown of black crystals resting on her dark brown hair, which reached just past her waist in its natural mix of curls and waves. The jewelry around her neck, wrists, and fingers all matched the crown, and they glittered in the colorful overhead lights.

Made of silk and lace, her black dress fitted itself perfectly to her body, cinched at the waist, and flared at the hip. A deep slit opened up to her thigh, and the neckline came up to the little dimple where bones met, to surround the sensitive skin of her neck, and sleeves ran down to circle her wrists.

She had pulled on a pair of patterned lacy tights, because why not, and her heels were too high and far too uncomfortable. Not the most practical, but they only added to the witchy persona, even if her toes screamed for relief. She would put up with a few minutes of discomfort to look her best for the show. She'd change them after, as she often did.

Sophia didn't sing at the club often, but when she did, the effort showed.

She imagined a real witch would wear more practical, comfortable clothing, but costumes were supposed to look pretty, not be functional.

She leaned against the railing and listened to the music, now animated and rhythmic, heavy on the brass. The tables on the second level were shrouded in darkness, for those patrons who preferred the privacy. It had been the idea of her best friend and business partner, Victoria, and the patrons couldn't have received it any better. It created an environment of privacy people were desperate for, in Sophia's experience.

Victoria had outdone herself with the décor. That was where Victoria excelled, and where Sophia did not. Every table had a lacy table-cloth. The centerpieces consisted of black, battery-operated candles inside a circlet of black flowers, cobwebs, and plastic thorns on some tables, potion bottles that looked aged and poisonous in others, small cauldrons with dry ice blowing smoke into the air, and crystal balls with swirling colors within.

There weren't any patrons up here yet, as a show was about to begin on the level below. The bar was stocked and the bartender was setting up for the evening. Sophia waved at the dark-skinned woman, who grinned and waved back. She was also dressed like a witch, but her braids were messy, as was her makeup. She looked like a pirate witch, if that was a thing.

Sophia smiled to herself, glad her sisters and Victoria had always obliged her in her silly games, even now as adults.

Growing up, they had all spent a big chunk of their days running around pretending to turn each other into toads. Now, Victoria and Sophia were still dressing up to give customers a unique, immersive experience. Back then, Sophia's mom had often said that turning people into toads was not what witches did, but Sophia had always believed she could if she really wanted to.

One whispered spell was all it took because the breeze could pick it up and take it to the ears of one who always listened. Even if sometimes her imagination tried to convince her that she had, in fact, turned a houseplant into a small frog. No matter how old she got, she would never pretend she didn't find the idea of it utterly exhilarating.

Of course, reality inevitably came knocking, and she would remind herself that people didn't do things like that. That if magic existed, it had eluded her.

But sometimes, the image was so clear, she could have described it to a sketch artist and gotten a picture. At other times, it felt like a fleeting dream. The aftertaste of a memory.

At twenty-nine years old, there were days when she still wanted to believe the only reason she couldn't turn her ex-boyfriend into a toad was because she had forgotten how to and just needed practice. What did her mom know about being a witch anyway?

A flash of memory told a different story, but it was gone before she could grasp the tail-end of it, like silk caught in a windstorm. She shook her head to clear the images. She didn't have time for this. Complete mental presence was crucial in the moments before she got on stage. Singing at the club was a regular occurrence, though each time she stood under the bright lights, anxiety threatened to consume her whole.

She could see the stage from where she stood as the band wrapped up the song they'd been playing.

As soon as the song ended, Evan, the band leader, put down his guitar, unhooking the colorful strap from his leather-clad shoulder. He set it on the stand next to the drum set.

The other musicians remained where they were, looking up the sheet music for the next set. The woman at the drums, a curvy blonde with more energy than anyone Sophia had ever known, laughed at something one of the trumpet players said to her.

Evan took the mic he'd been singing into from its stand. His chest was bare, except for the black leather jacket. He had dark skinny jeans on, riding low on his toned hips. Almost every inch of exposed skin was tattooed, save his face and head.

"Good evening, Witches and Gentlepeople," Evan said, and cheers erupted around them.

The moment he spoke, Sophia's stomach clenched with nerves. Anticipation rolled over her body, and she pressed a hand to her stomach, hoping to settle it a little. It didn't work. Neither did the deep breaths.

Evan opened his arms to the cheers, smiling widely. He was the center of admiration from both men and women who came into the club. Sadly for all of them, Evan had just gotten married to his partner of ten years, the lovely, reserved, dark-skinned man behind the keyboards, who was beaming.

"Thank you for coming tonight to Witches' Night Out at Nowhere," Evan said. More cheers erupted, louder this time. "Tonight, you all have the honor of hearing our special guest sing for you. The voice of an angel..." He looked around the room, his pretty bright eyes narrowed as he added, "A very sexy angel."

Laughter erupted. Sophia wanted to laugh, but she was too nauseated for that. She might throw up. The microphone waited for her on one of the tables. She didn't turn it on. She wasn't opening the show, but it gave her hands something to do, so she didn't fidget.

The lights began to change for the show, the excitement palpable now. Sophia let it wash over her, grinning widely as the lights turned very low and only one spotlight remained where Evan stood. The stage opened wide to the band's left, where she would soon stand and sing, and where their dancers performed their impressive routines.

"Thank you for coming tonight," Evan continued. "This special night of charms, spells, and potions will serve our great city by helping the unhoused and those in need. Your contributions mean the world to us at Nowhere." More applause and cheers. "Eat, drink your potions, mingle, and enjoy Nowhere's own Dancing Witches and the lovely Sophia Candela."

Cheers exploded as the lights went out again. Evan went back to the band on the side of the stage, strapped on his guitar, and the music started.

The stage curtains opened. They were heavy, dark velvet, and they gathered at the sides as a dancer, the fabulous Lisa, took the stage. Lisa dragged a chair toward the center of the shiny stage, the lights low and cool. They cast her in shadow, so her silhouette was all they could see at first. The lights came on as she began to move with the music. Lisa was barefoot, wearing a little sheath of a dress that appeared to be entirely made out of black pearls. She was tiny, a mass of lean muscles, and her dark hair, which contrasted with pale skin, was bound back in a low bun. She let her body move to the music, an instrumental with a slower rhythm, her movements fluid, which reminded Sophia of how water moved in the ocean.

After the first number, two dancers came on stage. Their choreography was perfect as they moved in unison in back-bending abilities that had the crowd gasping and cheering. Their execution was impressive, graceful, and perfectly in-sync.

For a moment, Sophia regretted not taking dance lessons when she was younger until she remembered she had two left feet and no amount of instruction could change that.

It was a shame since she was Latina on her mom's side, so one would think it was in the genes. At least, as far as Sophia was concerned, the dance gene simply skipped her since her sisters were lovely dancers. The last note hit, and the dancers froze, posing for the final time before moving off the stage as the crowd went wild with cheers.

One more set of dancers and Sophia had to grip the mic to keep her hands from trembling. They shook anyway.

She stepped onto the top stair and waited for her cue. She didn't even see the last act. She was far too nervous now as the moment approached. It didn't matter how much she sang, how many times she stood on that stage, or how many hours of practice she put in. She would always get nervous. Something about singing in front of people made a person feel vulnerable in ways nothing else could.

She breathed in, held it for a moment, the shivering inside her out of control. She could feel it in her knees, which had become jelly. Their patrons came to the club for this. For the music, the live singing, the dancing, the atmosphere of camaraderie. And Sophia loved music like she loved little else. Music did something to her that she didn't understand and truly wanted to. It was a love she'd inherited from her mom, who'd been a brilliant musician.

The lights changed to darker jewel tones as the electric guitar screamed. She felt the string's vibrations somewhere in her bowels. A spotlight moved slowly across the floor as Sophia brought the mic to her red lips and the first notes left her mouth. Guests turned in their chairs to face behind them. She held on to the railing, and for the first part of the song, she did not move, afraid that she was going to fall on her face. After the first verse, though, as notes left her mouth flawlessly, she felt brave enough to take the steps slowly down. Once she hit the main floor, she made her way through the tables, and shivered with the knowledge that every eye in the house was on her. The melody seeped into her skin, and it wasn't her singing anymore, but the version of her that lived in the music. That version stopped from time to time to gaze sultrily at a grinning patron, and she also paused and leaned on tables, allowing the slit of her dress to open even more. People wanted a show, and she gave them one.

Every eye was on her as she made her way up to the stage, and when she saw that the patrons were under her spell, she allowed herself to relax. As one song ended, the next began without pause, and the crowd, enamored, drank it all in.

It started with a keyboard, notes crisp. She sang before other instruments joined in and the song swelled. Sophia's entire body erupted in chills, and she swore the lights brightened around the audience. And it had nothing to do with the lights above their heads.

There it is, she thought—the reason why she loved singing, why she adored music so much. She closed her eyes, allowed the music to envelop her. She knew the moment it happened, when she was no longer in control of it, when she simply became a vessel, an artery through which the music flowed and allowed those listening to *feel*.

She almost expected it, as if her body knew it was about to happen.

She hit a high note, a pretty one that was rounded at the edges and tasted like chocolate almost. A faraway taste that existed in a place between the seen and the unseen. And when she opened her eyes, color exploded around her.

They didn't show up every time, the rainbows. There were a handful of songs Sophia felt deeper than most, and that's when they came, but she had to be fully in tune with them. The experience usually stayed with her for weeks, inside her veins, humming right below the surface. She had only seen something like this when her mom had been alive, when Sophia was a little girl. Her mom would sit at the piano, the keys making music no one had ever heard before, and made the air move in a way Sophia could see it in ribbons of color.

Thinking of her mom brought a stab of pain, and she pushed it away as she sang. It was difficult, when the music made her feel so much all at once. She almost didn't have the strength to let it go. Something in her wanted to bask in the sadness, but she didn't. Couldn't.

Sophia felt her skin bead as if she were standing outside in the rain. Her skin felt tight, as if it didn't belong to her, and as she sang the last note and prepared to sing her last, everything brightened before it dissipated into the air like smoke. The colors were the first to go, dimming before they were gone, but the air shivered for a while after, even as she began the next song. She felt a little breathless throughout the last song, waited eagerly, but the color did not return as she so desperately wanted it to.

She bowed when she finished, her body a little sluggish. People smiled up at her in delight as they clapped. She barely heard any of it. Had anyone else seen it, or had she been the only one again? So far, she'd never heard anyone else talk about seeing things like she did, or hearing them. But then again, she never spoke about it either. For a long time, she thought she had synesthesia, but she knew better now.

She grinned at the crowd one last time, and indulged in the weirdness of it all as the shivering in the air disappeared. Everything looked normal again, but the walls seemed to breathe still, and would for a while after.

Sophia thanked her audience, and made her way backstage. Once behind the curtains, she finally breathed and allowed herself a moment of delayed panic. Her breath was hard for a while before she was able to calm herself.

"Amazing as always, boss." One of the acrobats grinned as she went toward the stage. Sophia smiled at her and said something like 'good luck' but she couldn't be sure that her vocal cords were even working. She greeted

Other performers that were still waiting to go on. Some were regulars of the club; others came in from time to time, depending on what Sophia and Victoria had available for shows, and what they needed. Nowhere had gotten popular enough that they had requests instead of needing to seek out performers.

Shivers ran down her spine, adrenaline coursing through her trembling body. Inside the dressing rooms, lockers lined a long wall, and across from it, a wall of mirrors sat with bright lights above them, and cushioned seats in front of a counter. The tabletops were scattered with makeup, hair products, sequins, clothes, but the room was empty otherwise.

The strong smell of cosmetics was oddly calming as Sophia went into the adjoining bathroom. She looked at herself in the mirror as she pressed a hand to her churning stomach. Her hazel eyes were a little wide and glassy, but otherwise, she looked good. She had even pulled off a cat eye with her eyeliner, which didn't happen often—she always messed it up somehow. She washed her hands with cold water, and it anchored her. With the same paper towel she dried her hands with, she wiped at her sweaty neck.

There was music playing still, cheers and applause, and all over merriment, which she loved.

Taking a deep breath to finish calming her wayward heart, she smoothed down her clothes and headed out toward the floor. Not before she switched out her shoes for something a little less painful, though. Now in low-heeled black boots that made her feel significantly less sexy, Sophia took the long, narrow hallway that connected the employee areas and office to the main floor. There were posters all along the dark gray wall—portraits of every employee of Nowhere, as well as special guests. The idea had come to Sophia before bed one night, and the employees had loved it when she floated the idea of fun photoshoots.

Her steps clicked on the floor pleasantly as she went. When she opened the door and entered the noise of the house, she looked for Victoria in the crowd.

She greeted guests, thanked them when they congratulated her on the performance. She recognized some faces, as they had a lot of repeat customers. It brought her joy to see almost everyone dressed up. It didn't have to be Halloween for people to get into the spirit of things.

She found Victoria by the bar, on a barstool. The one next to her friend was empty, so Sophia started making her way to it.

Her best friend's dark skin was like velvet in the low light, smooth, perfect. She was always glowing, makeup or no, which seemed unfair somehow.

Shimmering eyeshadows were expertly applied to her lids, and they made her bright green eyes almost glow. The intense cat-eye made them pop more than normal, making her look ethereal.

Victoria was tall, willowy, and her curly hair was, as always, reaching for her shoulders in perfect black ringlets. Sophia stood by the bar as Victoria adjusted the see-through wings strapped to her back. She was, obviously, a fairy.

"You outdid yourself," Sophia said as she took her seat on the stool, grateful to be off her feet. They were pounding still, which was pretty typical for her. She always chose the most uncomfortable shoes she could find. She was like a magnet for them. Didn't even have to try.

"I really did," Victoria said, a smile stretching her full lips as she admired her work. Her long nails were painted black, and she had a glass in her hand with a cocktail that was half gone. "And so did you," she added as the band transitioned seamlessly into another song. "Your singing was beautiful as always."

Sophia smiled proudly. "I did do a good job."

The bartender placed a drink in front of Sophia. An Old Fashioned —one of her favorites. She sipped as Evan began to sing again, his voice so smooth, Sophia was sure angels had blessed his vocal cords.

The current song reminded her of something, the violin drawing notes that Sophia felt deep inside her gut, but an image didn't even have time to form before it was gone.

That happened often, especially lately. She needed a multivitamin or something for brain function at the very least.

"How did we get so lucky?" Victoria asked, gesturing toward Evan with her glass.

"I have no idea." Sophia grinned, the music sending waves of vitality through her. The guitar, the drums, the keyboard. It was her happy place—loud music, happy people sharing an experience with each other.

Now that her singing was out of the way, she could relax, and it felt nice not to be wound so tight she felt like she would snap. She sipped her drink as her mind went back to the colors. Where did it come from? And why was she the only one who could see them? Maybe she did have synesthesia. Sophia's sisters certainly didn't see anything, as far as she knew.

"Did you see what happened before?" Sophia asked Victoria, who faced her quizzically.

"What do you mean?"

"When I sang. You saw it, right?" Sophia had no idea how to put it where she didn't sound like she was losing her mind.

"The performance? Yeah, it was amazing."

Sophia battled the disappointment. Of course, Victoria hadn't seen it. No one ever saw it but her.

"Are you all right?" Victoria questioned, and Sophia smiled.

"Of course. It's a lovely night."

Victoria was approached by the manager they'd hired a few months before, Hayley. She was great at her job and a great asset to have around. As Victoria left, Sophia sipped her drink, her mind still back at the swirling rainbows. She finished her drink and gestured to the bartender for another.

"That was interesting."

The voice was deep, a warm bass that resonated inside her own chest. She turned on the stool, found herself looking into a solid, expansive, hard chest. She looked up and up and up.

The first thing that struck her was his eyes and how they were probably the product of a pair of great contact lenses because no one had eyes that blue. He had a straight nose, a tiny gold hoop glinting on one nostril, which was terribly appealing if she was honest. That and the hair that reached his broad shoulders in messy dark waves made him, quite possibly, the sexiest man she had ever seen in her club. Ever.

Or possibly the sexiest man she'd ever seen anywhere.

"Whatever do you mean?" she said, studying the hollows under his high cheekbones.

He studied her quietly for a moment, and she got the distinct impression he didn't believe her. Eventually, his lips stretched lightly into a lopsided smile.

Her stomach shivered. It was the weirdest sensation.

"You sure you don't know?" he asked in that unsettling bass, and leaned just a tad closer. Not enough to be in her bubble, though, she noted. Her eyes slid to the spot where he had left a button undone in his dark, fitted, button-down shirt. A smattering of dark hair peeked through the top, and he had the sleeves rolled up to his elbows.

"I haven't seen you around here before," she said, ignoring his question as she realized that he looked slightly familiar. She was sure she had never seen him before, but that also didn't make much sense somehow. It was a peculiar feeling, knowing and not knowing at the same time. Like how she could see his eyes were blue, but in her mind, they should be brown.

"No, this is my first time here. Great place."

She wanted to say something witty, graceful, but words failed her. She felt awkward, nervous, all of a sudden.

His fingers were long and graceful around the glass he held, the liquid amber within it almost gone. She bit back an unholy noise at the sharp pain at the back of her arm, and she turned to see Victoria right behind her. She offered her hand to the beautiful man.

"Hi, forgive my friend's manners," Victoria said, as they shook hands. She turned and briefly looked at Sophia like she was crazy before she pasted a smile on her face for the stranger. "I'm Victoria Williams, and this is Sophia Candela. Welcome to our joint."

This time, he really smiled. When a dimple appeared on his cheek, Sophia could have died a happy woman.

God, he was adorable.

"Grey," he said, then turned back to Sophia and offered his hand. Sophia took it as his name echoed in the most peculiar way in her head, and when they touched, a bolt of electricity ran up and down her arm, like she'd hit her funny bone repeatedly. She yanked her hand away as surprise widened his eyes.

"Interesting," he said softly as he reached into the pocket of his gray slacks and pulled a small square. He pressed it to her palm. Eyes flashed in her memory, a pretty golden brown, and something squeezed inside her. When she looked back up at his face, she saw that he wasn't as cool as he wanted to seem. He was no longer smiling, and there was a tiny twitch around the corners of his lips.

"How do I know you?" Sophia whispered. She ignored Victoria, who looked from one to the other, her brows raised almost to her hairline.

"I don't know," he said, but the words didn't ring true. "Maybe from another life."

Sophia closed her hand over the little card as his fingers deliberately grazed the skin of her palm, sending shivers down her back.

"Call me if it turns out to be true," he said before he let go of her hand. She watched his back retreat toward the exit, frozen. Even when he disappeared through the curtains that led to the lobby, Sophia sat there as if rooted to the cushioned stool.

"What was that?" Victoria whispered as Sophia looked down at the little black square in her hands. It was a good quality card, thick. And there was nothing written on it. Mouth slightly agape, she turned it over, and found the other side equally blank.

"I have no idea." She frowned, turning the card a couple more times before she looked up at Victoria. She briefly wondered if someone was pulling a joke on her. "That was the weirdest meeting I've ever had in my entire life."

"Yes, it was," Victoria said, raising her brows again. "You've never been a big flirt, but that was painful to watch."

Sophia felt her frown deepen. "I wasn't flirting with him."

"Why the hell not?" Victoria demanded.

Sophia blinked at her friend. "Are you crazy?"

"Did you see the man?" Victoria gestured wildly, her voice rising a few notches.

Sophia's eyes widened in warning. "Would you keep down your voice?" She gritted through her teeth as she looked around to make sure no one was listening in to their very private, public conversation. No one was paying them any attention, as if Sophia's world hadn't just gotten twirly and weird.

"He's really hot," Victoria pointed out, quieter now.

Sophia's shoulders sagged. "So hot. Did you see the nose ring?"

Victoria bit her lip and crossed her eyes, making Sophia sputter with laughter.

"Calm down," Sophia said. "I don't think Thomas would appreciate that."

"He wouldn't appreciate me appreciating beauty?" Victoria's smile was smug. "We've been together for two years. Thomas knows exactly who sleeps next to him."

"I hate you two cute idiots in love."

Victoria and Thomas had the kind of relationship Sophia would want if she wanted a relationship at all, but after her previous experience, she was in no rush to be with anyone.

"We really are cute idiots in love." Victoria waggled her brows and sang, "You could have it too."

"Yes, I know, but I don't want it."

"Fair enough. As long as you don't backslide, we're good."

An involuntary shiver ran up and down Sophia's back.

"God, no," she said. There was no way she was going to make *that* mistake again. Her ex, Aric, had made her life a living hell for four years. Needless to say, Victoria was not a fan, and neither was Sophia, for that matter.

"Maybe a fling is in order?" Victoria suggested.

"You mean with the stranger I met for five minutes at my club? I hardly think that was a meet-cute."

"The super-hot stranger," Victoria reminded her. "Also, and correct me if I'm wrong on this one, but you don't need a meet-cute to have a fling." She rolled her eyes dramatically. "You really need more game."

Sophia laughed. "Maybe you should teach me, oh flirty wise one."

"You did pretty good during your set. Bring some of that energy into your non-singing hours, and you're golden." When Sophia laughed, she expected Victoria to join her, but she didn't. Instead, she looked thoughtful. "He looked familiar, didn't he? Grey the gorgeous," she added as she took Sophia's brief silence to mean Sophia was confused.

"You thought so too?"

"For sure," Victoria said. "Mostly because when would we have known a man who looks like that and then have the ovaries to forget him?"

Sophia would have laughed again, but Victoria had a point. There was something about the beautiful stranger that wanted to trigger a memory long buried. Grey with his blank business card, his deep voice, and a face she felt that she, in fact, knew from another lifetime.

o o o

GREY WALKED OUT OF NOWHERE ON SHAKY KNEES. HIS ARM still smarted from that electric current.

What the hell was that?

He'd gotten what he needed from the visit, and stepping away from the loudness of the music allowed him to think clearly again. He wasn't a big fan of crowds or noisy places. He could handle it from time to time, but it drained him to be around many people.

His hand was inside his pocket, and he rubbed a small smooth stone between his fingers. It was more a self-soothing gesture than anything else, but the black jade was a powerful amulet against negative energies and people. He carried it with him at all times.

A man couldn't be too careful when so many knew the things he did.

It misted as he stepped out into the cold. His skin beaded instantly. He had a bad habit of not wearing a coat since he didn't spend much time outside anyway.

The parking lot was dead, as everyone in the city seemed to be inside Nowhere. It was an impressive place. Good music, good service, delicious liquor. And a beautiful owner he had no business looking at for too long.

Seeing Sophia Candela in the flesh was, in an inadequate word, surreal.

Yes, several of his latest spells had led him straight to her, and though he didn't understand why yet, the magic had not been wrong. What he hadn't expected was what happened when he got there.

The explosion of color when she sang had been confirmation enough, not to mention the actual electricity between them when they touched. He had never seen anyone do what she did when she sang. Except for himself when he played certain songs on the piano.

She had seen them too. That much was obvious to him. He had seen the look in her eye, the sparkle that came into the hazel depths, the knowing smile as she continued to sing, every single note lovely and decadent, like chocolate.

And the way she moved. His head nearly fell off when he she glided down the stairs in those sexy kitten heels that looked like they could kill a man. They almost killed him. Everything about her was alluring. He didn't like it.

A shadowy figure approached him from around a corner as he reached his sleek, black sedan.

Helena was dressed a lot like the people inside the club, except that she didn't dress that way ironically. Her dress was long and it floated around her as she approached him. The sky-high heels made a satisfying click on the ground with every one of her steps, and her icy shade of blonde hair was a pretty halo of waves around her equally pretty face.

"So?" she asked him quietly when they were inside the car.

He put the car into gear, and it moved forward, utterly silent as he pulled onto the road.

"Seems like the magic was right," he murmured. "Now I just have to find out why her."

"She has a beautiful singing voice," Helena said. She was also a singer and had a successful online presence with her music, which was mostly covers of other people's songs. Helena often said that when she was ready for something else, she would do that, but she would meanwhile continue to do what she had been doing for years and had worked so well. She often collaborated with other online artists, which she loved most of all, and had even roped Grey into doing a song or two, though he preferred playing to singing. Only she could convince him to sing in front of a camera.

"She does," he said, his voice even. He thought back on how it had been when Sophia had sung that specific note, close to a whistle tone, just not quite. She had held it exquisitely, her eyes closed, her red lips curved ever-so-slightly. And then she'd opened her eyes, and he would have a hard time ever forgetting what that made him feel. Shock at first, elation at her talent, but something else too. And the colors...

"And..." Helena said patiently. "You have to give me more than that, Greyson."

"And I don't know what role she will play." It was the truth, but it was also a shit answer. Grey threw her a sideways glance.

"The eyes still freak me out," she told him with a cocked brow.

He rolled his eyes, but waved his hand anyway and felt his eyes turn from blue to their natural brown with a flash of warmth.

"Happy?" he inquired drolly.

"Very much." She grinned. "Tell me more about Miss Sophia Candela."

"She owns Nowhere with another woman, a Victoria Williams."

"I know *that*."

He shot her a look of surprise. "How?"

"They're women of color running a business successfully and keeping their employees and their clientele happy. I'm all over that," Helena said. He should have known she'd be familiar. "Besides, Nowhere is the hottest club in the city."

"I've never heard of it," he mumbled, a little chagrined for some reason.

"That's because you're a sweet, introverted, little weirdo."

He scoffed but felt a smile tug at his lips.

"Look, the truth is I have no idea what's going on and why the spell we cast brought me to Sophia Candela, but when she sang, it was evident we were in the right place."

Helena curled her lip in an expression of regret. "I wish I could have seen it."

"I know." He patted her knee lightly. "I'm already brewing more."

The knowing potion, a recipe Grey had found while rummaging through his late father's magic journals, allowed him to see and hear more than what was usual. When he took it, everything around him breathed, moved, was more colorful and brilliant. The biggest thing for him, when he took it, was how the music was almost solid. How it moved and flowed. Not every song was the same; they all looked different, made him feel different. So when Sophia Candela, of all people, had sung and he had seen those colors, he'd felt like he hit a jackpot. He hadn't even had to take the potion, and he had seen her music so clearly, he could have convinced himself he had taken the potion and had just forgotten.

"Sign me up for a bottle of it and a couple of the others," Helena said as she looked out the window, suddenly pensive.

Grey looked out at the road. Helena presented a side of herself that everyone wanted to see. The beautiful, bubbly thirty-year-old with exceptional vocal ability. But in reality, she hid a secret. A debilitating illness that had appeared one day out of nowhere. A disease Grey had been watching for years, trying to concoct a cure for it.

No other witch had been successful in finding a cure, though many had tried.

His heart squeezed.

"I got you," he said quietly, but added nothing else, because he knew she would appreciate it. He'd spend the rest of his life searching for a way to help her, experimenting with new ingredients. So far, all his potions had done was mitigate the symptoms. At least his potions had stopped her debilitating headaches, the terrible bruising all over her skin, and the hair loss. But she needed more than that, he knew. Taking care of symptoms wouldn't stop the disease, one witches called the void, from eating away at her mind until noting was left. Only a semblance of the person. And that was for people who were not magical. For witches, such as Helena and himself, the loss of faculties led them to do horrible things to other witches. The void ate away at a witch's power, until nothing was left, and their mind gone, the witch spent the rest of the time they had left seeking power in any way they could. Usually, that meant other witches got seriously hurt, or killed.

It was horrible to watch it happen, and for it to happen to Helena… He couldn't conceive of a world without her, so he didn't let his mind go there.

"How do you feel?" Helena turned on the seat to look at him, her eyes shrewd. "Seeing Sophia Candela."

His brows twitched. "It's not like I know her."

"Don't you?"

He took a shaky breath. He could try to bullshit himself out of that one, but he couldn't do it with Helena. She was too sharp and had little patience for it, which she showed him when her eyes narrowed, then rolled.

"She seemed familiar, and that was it. I'm more interested in her magic."

"Right." She observed him for a while longer. Her gaze was like a laser on his side, but he didn't want to talk about it.

She sat forward again and pulled out her phone.

"When you're ready to talk about it, let me know." She was busy on her phone after that, and that was just as well. Grey didn't want to talk about why Sophia Candela had made his body react the way it did. Heart rate increased, sweaty palms, and too much saliva pooled in his mouth. He felt like a dumb teenager.

Sophia was a beautiful woman, all curves and lovely golden skin, but that wasn't the reason for his reaction. At least not all of it. He enjoyed looking at a beautiful woman as much as the next guy.

It was the fact that she was the daughter of the woman who had ruined his family. His father's lover, who he was running away with when they got into a car accident and died.

2

Sophia stood in the middle of the attic of her childhood home. It was a small space, and though her mom seemed to have a lot of stuff in it, it didn't feel cramped.

Sophia's feet were bare against the cool hardwood floor as she took in the room. There were two windows, and under one, a narrow table held items Sophia had always found fascinating. A large colorful shell, rough on the outside, smooth and pearlescent on the inside. In it, a bundle of green herbs her mom liked to burn. Sophia remembered how she whispered things into every corner of the house.

Her father hated the smell and always complained about it, so her mom started only doing it when he was at work. Next to the shell, a simple wooden holder held a stick that had smoke curling into the air, pure white in the sunlight. In the corner pretty rocks caught the glint of the sun, and Sophia picked up a pale pink one, a little jagged around the edges, and put it in her dress pocket like she had seen her mom do. She ran the tip of a finger on the old wood table. The smells of herbs burning were familiar and comforting.

Her mom spent most of her time up here when she wasn't doing mom things. When she was still around.

A heaviness descended over Sophia. It was difficult being up here. Being reminded of her mom hurt too much.

The light was soft from the sheer white curtains on the windows. Every panel was a different style and fabric, and Sophia liked that. Something only a fascinating, special person would do. There was something beautiful in the imperfect.

Her mom was special. She was lovely and soft-spoken, a smile always on her face. She loved white, wore it almost always when she was up here, making magic. She locked herself in this room a lot and always came out of it glowing, her eyes deeper, as if she could see and hear things others could not. At least that's how it felt to Sophia.

She turned slowly, a haze coming over the room. Her mom was suddenly in the center, where plants hung low from the ceiling.

She was lovely.

Her hair was curly and long, and she always kept it away from her face, just like Sophia did. There was a flower stuck in the pile of hair atop her head, and her full lips were painted deep red. It was striking against her deeply tanned skin.

She was wearing a long, loose, white dress that reached all the way down to the floor, and when she turned to smile softly at Sophia, her brown eyes warmed, Sophia felt a pang somewhere in her heart.

Mom was holding a leather-bound book in her arms, pressed to her chest.

"It's the intention, Sophie Darling," she said, her voice sounding strangely muffled as if she were speaking through a pillow. Sophia frowned.

"Where's the music, Mom?" she asked in a near-whisper. Her mom never came up here without the music she had recorded. It was always playing. Sophia suspected her mom was a fairy, that she could turn tiny, no bigger than Sophia's own hand, at will.

Sophia had never seen her mother turn into a fairy, but she imagined it was so when she was alone in her bedroom as lights and fractals danced around her when her mom made music upstairs. It was Sophia's favorite part. It made her happy, gave her a lightness that she didn't know how to name.

"You have it," Mom answered, still smiling, but her smile slipped suddenly, and her eyes turned sad.

Sophia could feel the sadness in the air, like a heavy weight that moved and breathed. There was no heavier feeling to her.

What do I have? Sophia couldn't voice the question out loud. It was as if she had a gag on her throat. Her mom turned around, going to a plant hanging by another window. She whispered under her breath, but Sophia couldn't hear anything now. The room started getting darker, then disappeared altogether. Images swirled in the air like the smoke of the incense her mom had been burning.

o o o

SOPHIA ONLY HAD A VAGUE MEMORY OF THE DREAM WHEN she was woken up by her ringing phone. She looked at it, her eyes bleary, gasping when she noticed the time.

How the hell had this happened?

"Oh God," she groaned. She was late. She hated being late. "Dad, hi," she said when she accepted the call as she jumped up from the bed, throwing her turquoise comforter aside and heading to the walk-in. She had slept through three alarms.

"Good morning, sweetheart," came her dad's voice. He was having a good day, clearly, because he sounded cheerful. "How did you sleep?"

She put the phone down on the dresser, picking up a pair of jeans from the hamper and pulling them on, jumping up and down while she pulled the tight material over her hips. Maybe she needed to go up a size, she thought as she buttoned it and slid up the zipper.

"I honestly have no idea," she said as she took off the t-shirt she'd worn to bed and replaced it with a sweater with a famous rock band name in the front. She realized she didn't put on a bra immediately, but she refused to wear one if she didn't have to, so she moved on quickly from that.

"You have to sleep, Sophia."

"Thanks, Dad, I know." She pulled on boots, sitting on the floor.

"And yet you sleep less and less every day," he said. "You know, sleeping helps with aging."

"I am deeply unconcerned about aging," she said as she rushed out of her room, her phone in one hand, a bag in the other, and her keys dangling off her finger. The house was brightly lit from several tall windows in the living area. She loved the view of the city and the water in the distance, but it was a bitch to heat and cool. Everything had a downside, even beautiful places in prime locations. Not that she had room to complain.

The house was tidy, simple in its decor, the walls a very light gray, but complemented by jewel-toned pieces on the side and coffee tables, as well as several small plants, most of them fake. She had a knack for killing every living plant she'd ever gotten. Her mom would have been disappointed, as she had been amazing with plants.

Going through the living room, she stopped at the coffee table. Her ear, a different part of it, one that heard differently than her normal ear, opened as her eyes landed on the little money tree that she kept on the coffee table. She had put it there to remind herself to take care of it but had obviously failed. The leaves were yellow and falling onto the marble table, and there was barely any sound coming from it. Since she was very young, she remembered being able to hear special music coming from plants. She had never told anyone, save her oldest sister, who had looked at her as if she was crazy, so Sophia had kept it to herself ever since.

"Oh no," she whispered, touching the wilted leaves, her heart hurting for it. How many times had she wished she had the same talent and dedication her mom had for plants when she was alive? Her mom had been able to care for just about anything, going as far as murmuring to them softly, playing music, and telling Sophia that it made the plants grow faster and stronger.

Her dad's voice droned on about skincare and feeling younger as he got older, and she leaned forward, almost touching her lips to the tiny leaves. She put the phone down.

"I'm so sorry," she whispered. "I wish I was good with plants like my mom was, so I could bring you back to be as healthy and lovely as the cactuses I haven't managed to kill yet."

She kept one of those cactuses in the kitchen and the other in her office at the club, and had been reading up on the care of house plants, but kept killing them anyway. Upsetting at best. Her mother's voice almost echoed around her, telling her that it was the intention that mattered.

She'd say, "it's the intention that matters, Sophie Darling," and Sophia had no idea what she had meant back then. Now, she knew that intention had nothing to do with it. Intention wasn't watering the plants when Sophia forgot.

Her heart hurt for the plant as she turned and walked past the archway to the kitchen, which had a couple of short cabinets at the top, where she kept her vases. She grabbed a banana from the fruit bowl on the dark counter, putting her phone at her ear again to hear that her father was still droning about skincare and skin procedures.

"You know, getting work done is perfectly normal," he was saying. He was moving around, probably getting ready to go to the office. He lived at the office, a true workaholic. "Have you been meditating?"

She walked out the side door and into the garage, where she got into her car, a dark red SUV.

"I meditate." She put her purse on the passenger seat.

"I meant if you're doing it like I told you to."

"No, Dad. I haven't meditated every day like you told me to." He seemed to think she had more time on her hands than she actually did.

"If you'd only listen, then you'd be fine. Mornings are best. I can hang up if you want to get one in."

She stopped as she waited for the garage door to slide up and out of her way.

"I don't have time for that this morning. I have several shipments and a lot of paperwork to do at the club."

"If you just went to bed at a reasonable hour—"

"Dad, I'm the owner of a nightclub," she said as she began pulling out of the garage. "Late nights are going to happen from time to time. And don't worry about my skincare. I have been double-cleansing and everything." Not thanks to him, but she wasn't going to tell him that.

She placed the phone on the cradle attached to a vent as it connected to the Bluetooth. A message popped up, joining several from Victoria, Hayley, Evan, and the group message she had with her sisters. This one, however, was from Jeanette, Victoria's mom and the only mother-figure Sophia had when her own mother had died.

JEANETTE: I HAD A PECULIAR CARD SHOW UP
THIS MORNING AND YOU CAME TO MY MIND.

She wasn't surprised to see the message. It was almost as if she had been waiting for it, in a sense. Those feelings came often, but she was good at ignoring them. She stopped on the driveway, watching the road on either side of her, but picked up the phone as her father continued to drone about meditation and skincare.

For as long as Sophia could remember, Jeanette had been intuitive to the point where sometimes it felt like she could read Sophia's mind. Sophia clicked to reply, a wave of love going through her as she thought of Jeanette with her beautiful dark skin, those green eyes that saw so much, Sophia had never been able to keep anything from her. Victoria was the living image of Jeanette, which was eerie and endearing all at once. Victoria wasn't into the supernatural stuff, and it wasn't like Sophia was, but she did find it fascinating.

SOPHIA: WHAT WAS IT?

A picture came through with a bright green dragon in mid-flight.

SOPHIA: WHAT DOES IT MEAN?

JEANETTE: DRAGONS ARE MESSENGERS OF
SIGNIFICANT CHANGE.

SOPHIA: WHAT KIND OF CHANGE?

JEANETTE: I'M NOT SURE, LOVE. I CAN PULL A
FEW CARDS WHEN I GET BACK FROM THE
HOSPITAL AND LET YOU KNOW WHAT
COMES UP.

She agreed, typed a quick message, and pulled out onto the road.

"Sophia, are you still there?" her father said, and she realized he had said something and was waiting for a response.

"I'm here, sorry," she said, shook her head once. "I'm just distracted. Listen, Dad, I have to go to the club now. I'll call you later."

She hung up. Her father wouldn't take kindly to that response and being cut off earlier than he wanted in conversations, but she didn't have time today, and she did not have the patience either.

As she got to the club, a delivery truck pulled in. She reached into her purse to get out her keys, realized she'd forgotten a jacket. At least she didn't have to be outside much. Seattle was beautiful, and Sophia loved the moodiness of the rain and cloudy weather, but it did get bitterly cold sometimes.

When she dug into her bag, the little black card sat inside a pocket, the material smooth but heavy, and blank. She pulled it out alongside the club keys. She would just throw it away, as he was obviously playing a prank on her. She got out of the car, walking toward the back door, a heavy iron. A cheerful greeting for the delivery guy, and she opened the door, the card now forgotten in a pocket of her bag.

When Sophia had received all the deliveries, she busied herself with payroll, her least favorite thing to do. She punched in numbers, and as she went to dig into a drawer for a pen, her eyes landed on the cactus on the desk beside hers.

The cactus, which last time she had looked at it had been perfectly fine, was yellowing and drooping to one side, deflated like a week-old helium balloon.

"Why?" she said out loud, standing to walk to it and listening for the faint music. It sounded like a muted guitar that was severely out of tune. She touched the soil, noticed it felt fine, not too dry because it had been watered a couple of days before. It was all it needed. "I followed every rule."

What did she have to do to keep one plant alive?

Buy fake ones, apparently.

"First the one at home and now you?" she said to it. "Help me out here."

Back on her laptop, she searched for articles on plant care, her thoughts inevitably back on her mother. Plants and Silvana Candela was almost synonymous, as if one couldn't exist without the other, and it was like every plant was a baby and her mom knew every cry. And here was Sophia, listening in and getting nothing. There were no cries. More like a whimper of despair, pathetic and limp.

"I'm losing my mind," she said into the empty room. There were no cries, and there was no music. But there was music last night, and that had definitely been out of the norm. A human shouldn't be able to see music the way she did. But she did. And so did the beautiful stranger the previous night.

She reached into her bag again, digging for the little square card, turning it in her fingers as she leaned back on her chair. It mocked her with its blank sides, and she put it down on the desk, annoyance stabbing through her. He probably thought he was funny, giving her a piece of black cardboard and confusing her. Prick.

But was he playing a joke on her? He had seen... or had he?

She wanted to talk to him, demand that he answer every one of her questions. Maybe he could explain what was happening to her.

She returned to the computer screen, updated numbers and hours, and when she was done, she looked at the card.

"What in the hell?" She muttered and picked it up.

A name, *Grey Constantine*, was scrawled in silver across the black background. Her stomach clenched at the name. It was unpleasant, unlike the way it had felt to hear his deep voice.

How could it be? She thought as a phone number appeared right underneath, as if it bled from the back of the card.

Her mouth opened and closed, then opened again, her heart now racing and a bead of sweat sliding down her back. Her trembling hand slowly set the card on the desk, as if it would explode. Or worse, jump up and bite her or something bizarre like that.

Sophia picked up her phone, her eyes darting back to the card as she pulled up a text conversation.

> SOPHIA: YOU'RE A DOCTOR, RIGHT?
>
> JEANETTE: LAST I CHECKED.
>
> SOPHIA: IS IT POSSIBLE FOR ME TO HAVE
> EARLY-ONSET ALZHEIMER'S OR DEMENTIA?

Jeanette called her instead of answering with a text, as Sophia knew she would. The question was strange enough, she supposed, that it warranted a call.

"Unlikely," Jeanette said as soon as Sophia accepted the call. "Why do you ask?"

"My mind is playing some curious tricks on me," Sophia said as she got on her feet and walked out of the office to pace up and down the long narrow hallway, with its dark walls and paper portraits.

"Tell me more. Maybe I can help."

Sophia opened her mouth to answer, but nothing came out. She didn't really know, did she? How could she explain something like this?

She went back into the office and looked at the card on the corner of her desk.

"I think I'm being pranked," she said, huffing out a breath. She wanted to tell Jeanette, but they didn't really talk about Sophia's mom very often. Sophia found it hard to think about her. "I'm being ridiculous. I killed another two plants and I'm not handling it well."

"You might be overwatering."

"That's the thing, I haven't."

"Under-watering?"

"Ah, yes, that could be it." Sophia sighed. It was no use even wondering what she'd done wrong at this point.

"Are you struggling?" Jeanette asked, and Sophia instantly knew what they were now talking about.

"I've thought about her a lot in the last couple of days," Sophia told her, dropping onto the chair, wishing these things didn't hurt still. That it wasn't always right there under the surface. But time hadn't helped at all, not when Sophia dreamt of her so often. Not when she was reminded so much of how her mom had died. Running away with her lover, a man who was also married at the time. "I don't know why."

"Because she was your mother. You loved her."

"Yes, I did, but it's more complicated, I think," she said, thinking of Grey Constantine, his weird card, the music. The fact that his last name was the same as the man her mom had run off with. How much of that was a coincidence?

Suddenly anxious, she wanted nothing more than to think about anything else. "I will have to call you when I'm not at work. Maybe I need one of those cleansing rituals you keep telling me about."

"Alright, Sophie Darling," Jeanette said, using the term of endearment that had caught on early in Sophia's life. "Come by soon. I love you."

"Love you too."

Sophia hung up as Victoria walked in, dressed casually and looking rested and glowing like her skin was made of porcelain. Her mass of curls was gathered at the top of her head.

"God, I hate you," Sophia said as Victoria hung her purse behind the door. "How can anyone look this good at this time of day?"

"What a slap in the face when I come bearing life juice." Victoria handed her a paper coffee cup, which Sophia accepted with a grin and a blown kiss. "And it's all about the strict skincare routine."

"Not you too," Sophia groaned. "My dad went on and on about it this morning."

"He's not wrong," Victoria said. "But also, the incredible sex."

"Oh look, a catch," Sophia muttered and took a sip of her coffee. It tasted like vanilla and cinnamon and just a little bit bitter. "Doesn't the honeymoon phase end after a few months?" She grumbled, looking at the cactus. Was it even yellower and deader than when she got there, or was she going to need to be committed?

"It will go away someday, but for now, I am going to enjoy it." Victoria grinned, her full lips a pretty soft brown, shiny. "Did you call that beautiful man from last night yet? That could be what you need to do to get the sex part of beautiful skin. The skincare I can help with."

Sophia couldn't help but look at the card again. It judged her from where it lay on the desk. What the hell did Grey Constantine want? How was he related to her mom's secret lover? The name couldn't be a coincidence. Will Constantine had a son, if she recalled correctly, but unlike her older sister, Sophia didn't go digging into people's lives.

"I have not called him," she responded when she realized she hadn't spoken in a while.

"Are you going to?"

"Maybe," she said, but she very well knew she would. There were so many questions.

Was it about his last name? The music thing? That weird-ass card? Business cards didn't behave like that. What kind of new technology was that?

Maybe she needed a therapist again.

Could be trauma, she considered. She'd dealt with a lot of that, and therapy had worked.

But then she remembered the jolt of electricity that ran up and down her arm when their hands had touched. That was harder to explain. Had it been static? She doubted that.

Ugh.

Sophia picked up her phone and typed the number in, almost hearing how his name sounded when it was spoken. There was a rhythm to it, like a song that you couldn't get out of your head. She'd always hated when that happened to her, so she was after getting rid of it. It didn't matter how adorable he was with his dumbass nose ring and the hair and the forearms and the voice...

She typed the text before her thoughts could get derailed even more, or before she convinced herself to let it go and move on with her life.

> SOPHIA: YOUR BUSINESS CARD IS WEIRD.

She didn't identify herself because he would know, unless he gave a card like that to every woman in Seattle. Though she imagined a man who looked like him was probably very busy.

His response came only minutes later, as she was going through the schedule one last time, as Victoria had sent it to her to make sure it was correct. She uploaded it onto the application she'd had made for the staff, where they could check payroll, schedule, and contact them if needed.

> GREY: WHAT MADE YOU TEXT ME NOW?
>
> SOPHIA: YOUR CARD FREAKED ME OUT.
>
> GREY: IS THAT ALL?

She frowned down at her phone.

Victoria smirked from her chair, a laptop open on her lap.

"What did he say?"

"Nothing interesting yet." The truth, but also, she wanted to keep this close for a while until she got some answers. No need to rile people up over something that could very well turn out to be nothing.

Yeah right.

> SOPHIA: CURIOSITY, PERHAPS.
>
> GREY: CURIOSITY ISN'T A BAD THING, IN MY EXPERIENCE.
>
> SOPHIA: ISN'T IT? WHAT WAS IT THAT HAPPENED TO THE CAT?
>
> GREY: IT LIVED A FULFILLED LIFE. IT WAS CURIOUS; IT ACTED; IT LEARNED.

What kinds of things did it learn, she wanted to ask, but refrained. She was pretty sure she didn't really want to hear the answer to that. Or maybe she did. Then his next message came in and she sat perplexed by it, before she realized how much it bothered her.

> GREY: I ONLY GIVE MY CARD TO THOSE I KNOW
> WILL DISCOVER THE NUMBER WITHIN IT, IF
> YOU WERE WONDERING.

What a stupidly obscure thing to say.

> SOPHIA: AND HOW DOES THAT WORK,
> EXACTLY?

> GREY: MAYBE I WILL HAVE TO SHOW YOU
> SOMETIME.

She raised a brow, the beginnings of a smile making her lips twitch. What a line.
"I see you smiling over there," Victoria said.
Sophia rolled her eyes, but her smile grew a little.

> SOPHIA: MAYBE YOU SHOULD.

The smile wiped away. Sophia wanted to say she didn't sit there waiting for his response to come through, but she would be a filthy liar. Her heart began to race, and she had no idea where she got the guts to type another message. This time, she would get a reaction, and she wasn't even sure why she asked it.

> SOPHIA: WHAT'S THE REASON YOU CAME TO
> MY CLUB?

> GREY: YOU SURE YOU DON'T KNOW?

> SOPHIA: I DON'T DO RIDDLES; TALK TO ME
> STRAIGHT.

> GREY: OK.

She watched the three dots appear and disappear several times before the message came through.

> GREY: I CAME TO YOUR CLUB BECAUSE I
> NEEDED TO MEET YOU.

Her heart dropped. Red. Flag.

And here she thought he was cute. Sometimes the cutest ones were the biggest creeps.

> SOPHIA: WEIRD TO HAVE AN ADMIRER LIKE THIS.

> GREY: A CURIOUS CAT, IF THAT MAKES YOU FEEL BETTER.

She paused, heart thumping, her stomach very tight and churning hotly. Maybe a part of her didn't want to know, but another much curiouser part asked anyway, because why wouldn't she. She *loved* getting herself in situations where she was uncomfortable, clearly.

Sophia typed the message and sent it without proof-reading it so she didn't lose her nerve.

> SOPHIA: HOW ARE YOU RELATED TO WILL CONSTANTINE?

3

After he got her message, Grey stared at his phone for a while. He wasn't sure how to respond. Did something happen to his insides the moment her text came through? Yes, it did. Was he a little nervous? More than a little, actually. She was obviously not going to pull any punches, and he both respected it and was terrified by it.

How did he tell her about the way touching her hand had felt? How it sent shocks up and down his arm, down to his feet. Or how when he saw her, he knew he'd known her before. He just couldn't remember when or where. How her hazel eyes were so intriguingly familiar and for more reasons than the fact that she looked just like her mother?

He was standing in his bright kitchen, where sunshine streamed through a giant window by the bar he kept well-stocked in the corner. The dining room, which was adjacent to the kitchen, had a sliding glass door that led out to a balcony. He liked to spend time with a good book or his guitar out there.

An old, heavy, leather-bound book with his most used potion recipes lay open on the kitchen island. Next to it were several vials in different shapes and sizes, as he found many of his bottles in craft and thrift stores. Some were still empty; some were filled with a dark blue liquid. The big pewter cauldron was still on the stove, cooling off before he made a batch of a different brew.

Dried herbs hung from the ceiling in a corner of the kitchen, by the door to the pantry, and books about potion-making sat on a shelf on top of the stove that also housed a few cookbooks.

He had many other potions, but those he kept inside the pantry, neatly arranged for easy access. He'd had the original pantry extended when he bought the house. It was spacious, with room for not just his potions but all ingredients, cauldrons and other witchy materials, as well as food and your run-of-the-mill kitchen appliances.

His phone felt like a ten-pound weight in his hand.

The card he had made behaved that way because of a special ink infused with a disappearing potion. It only worked once, as he had placed a simple spell on it. The only reason she could see it was because she had every intention to talk to him. Otherwise, it wouldn't show her. It was one of his favorite parlor tricks. The other question... well, that question was a lot simpler.

GREY: YOU KNOW HOW I'M RELATED TO HIM...

He deleted it and started again. How did anyone have this conversation?

GREY: MAYBE WE CAN SIT AND TALK
SOMETIME.

He sent it and tapped his fingers on the counter as he waited for her response.

SOPHIA: MAYBE WE SHOULD.

GREY: JUST SAY WHEN AND WHERE.

SOPHIA: MY CLUB. TONIGHT.

A place where she was around people, where she felt safe. Yes, he would see her there. He texted a time, and when she agreed, he put it in his calendar. As if he wouldn't be thinking about it all day.

And then what? They would most likely speak about their parents' affair with each other, pretend that they were over it. But what happened after? Would he show her what he could do? How did he find out how she was connected to his magic?

Grey shook his head. He didn't have time for this. He had many other things to do before the next full moon, like acquiring ingredients for his next batch of potions.

He went into the pantry. The potions were in neat rows, all clearly labeled. In one of the shelves, he had a round, glass storage container stuffed with a mixture of herbs, salt, and other ingredients, and a piece of paper with a quick spell. Back in the kitchen, he set down his items, ready to meet with people, as he did when he had enough requests for potions. The kitchen had always been the best place for this kind of work, so it had become habit, and he'd found no need to change it.

Grey removed the lid from the bowl and pinched some of the powder within. He drew a nearly perfect circle on the white marbled counter. Next to it, a smaller circle for payment packages.

"Communicationis apertas," he murmured as he set the bowl down by the stove. The circle glowed brightly for a split second, then simmered like dying coal.

It wasn't long before the first person came through. The man's head floated in midair like a mylar balloon.

"Mr. Smith," Grey said with an incline of his head.

"Constantine," said Mr. Smith. He was a regular but never lingered, always serious and direct. He had salted, dark-blonde hair, a similarly-colored mustache, and dark eyes.

"How can I help you today?"

"I need," Mr. Smith looked down, as if reading something, "twenty-four Simple Pain, four Health Fortification, seven Energy Boost."

Grey kept a mental note.

"You know what happens after taking Energy Boost," he said with an inquiring expression. The energy crashes from taking the Energy Boost Potion were almost not worth it. They could be good in specific situations, but Grey always advised against them when possible.

"I do," Mr. Smith said.

Grey nodded and went to pick up the potions Smith asked for. He packaged everything into a small, matte black box and came back to the kitchen. He waved his hand at a small book he kept with client information.

He rattled off an address to Mr. Smith. "Still at this address?"

"Not gonna change any time soon," the older man said.

"Please make your trade," he said, and Mr. Smith nodded.

A few seconds later, a pouch appeared on the counter inside the smaller circle. Grey checked the loot, and satisfied with the ingredients Mr. Smith exchanged, he sent the small box.

Mr. Smith thanked him and disappeared.

The rest of the afternoon went similarly. Some orders were more extensive than others; some were special requests, and people came to him for potions because Grey was good at making them. And besides, the ingredients he got as trades were invaluable to him since many potion ingredients could be difficult to source ethically. This job afforded Grey relationships with people, and it made said job that much easier. That was unless he'd had to do one of his in-person visits.

A shudder fluttered over him. He couldn't think about those visits. Not now, or ever, really. He didn't know how he'd come to do that kind of job, or why there was nothing he could do to separate himself.

What kind of a man did it make him?

Grey shook his head sharply, scattering those thoughts away. There would have to be time for it later, but now he had other things to do. He had to keep a clear head for his meeting with Sophia Candela. The conflicting feelings that plagued him about her made his skin vibrate. Like when he'd touched her skin and memories had sparked somewhere in faraway corners in his mind. Memories that had little to do with the way he felt about her mother.

As his last client's head disappeared, he murmured, "finis communicationis," and cleaned up both circles, putting the powder back into its container.

Helena appeared around a corner when he was coming out of the pantry.

She wore a silky, pink robe, her blonde hair pulled up at the back of her head. Her eyes were a little red-rimmed, and she looked pale and tired. She'd looked much better the previous day, probably due to some sort of charm to fix her appearance. He knew how much she hated to not look her best. It led people to ask questions she didn't want to answer.

"You look like hell," he said as she tightened the robe around her. She appreciated not being coddled, but his heart cracked a little at the sight of her. So fragile-looking when she was such a powerful woman. Helena had a special kind of magic. One that helped anyone in her vicinity to be calm and relaxed. It was how she captivated audiences who listened to her singing, which was beautiful in its own right.

"I feel like hell," she said and stepped forward to put her arms around his middle. He hugged her back tightly, kissed the top of her head, before she pushed away.

"I need a few things," she said and pulled out a small pouch from the pocket of her robe. She placed it on the counter.

Grey simply gestured to the pantry, and she disappeared through the door, and he heard the clinking of vials as she put things into another pouch. She was always conservative with what she took, though she knew everything in there was hers if she needed it.

"Your recording is almost finished," he told her. She had recently sent him a song she'd recorded, asking for editing for a new release she had soon. As an official job, Grey mixed music and also composed tunes for video games and shows. Sometimes a jingle here and there.

"I could barely control my breathing, and that was after taking a Health Boosting potion." Her voice was a little muffled before she came back with her pouch hanging off her wrist. In her other hand, she a pink Health Boosting, which she drank in one gulp. The color returned to her face almost instantly.

"This is not going to work forever," she muttered.

"It's all we have for now," he said, his heart dropping. Ever since Helena had started getting sick, paralysis had taken over him, as if all the years of research and attempts at a cure had been for nothing. He'd watched the illness as a little boy, and had been obsessed with a cure ever since. Doctors called it the Violet Death, due to the bruising on patients' bodies. Witches called it the void.

"I'll have more soon, after the full moon in a couple of days," he said.

She smiled but with a little bit of regret. "I didn't mean it that way."

"I know," he assured her. "I'm sorry I can't do more."

"You do enough, believe me." She lifted the little pouch. "Thank you."

"Thanks for the ingredients." He breathed easier because she looked so much better. Her skin became more plush, youthful.

"Stop doing that," she said, and he met her blue gaze.

"I'm not doing anything."

"Bullshit." She put the potions into her pocket. "I know you, remember?"

"I'm going to worry about you," he told her, and she pressed her lips together, her eyes turning sad. "You can't control that."

She sighed. "You know, after I messed up our relationship, I didn't think you'd ever be able to look me in the eye. But here you are."

"You're a much better friend than you were a girlfriend."

She narrowed her eyes. "I'm aware of that, but hearing it still stings."

"Should have been a better girlfriend," he quipped. She punched his shoulder. The pain was dull.

"Maybe you're just dumb."

He chuckled, and she joined him.

"Listen, I have to go. I have a bath and a good spooky novel waiting for me at home."

"Spooky season is over," he said as she walked away toward the entryway.

"It's always spooky season in my house," she called, her voice an echo through the house.

He spread his hands in defeat as she disappeared, then patted his pockets for his personal potions. The screen of his phone told him it was about time to meet Sophia. It was always a good idea to carry a couple of potions that could get you out of a sticky situation. His fingers reached for the little crystal resting at his chest, inside his shirt.

He pulled on dark tennis shoes, checked himself to make sure he looked all right. Gray jeans, a black t-shirt, and a black sweatshirt would have to do.

He visualized where he had to go. The alleyway behind Nowhere was a narrow cut-through alley, and it would be dark. It was the perfect place to port. He could drive, but he didn't feel like dealing with Seattle traffic.

He rubbed his fingers together to ease the familiar travel anxiety, and his body tingled as it disintegrated from his kitchen, disappearing into the air with a small gust of cold wind.

His skin chilled as he ported. It was never the most pleasant thing to do, as it felt as if his cells separated and came back together. He felt weightless like he was being held as he floated in the air. He reappeared in the alley and looked both ways to make sure no one had seen. He didn't want to have to modify someone's memory. It felt wrong to do so. He allowed himself a moment for his head to stop swimming before he took the narrow passage toward the street. It was sprinkling lightly. People were starting to walk into Nowhere already, waiting in the lobby to be taken back to their reserved tables.

The decor had already changed. Last night when he had come, the decor had indeed been spooky. Cobwebs in corners, bats hanging from the ceiling, candles that looked like they floated in midair. Now, everything was almost set up like a 1920s style bar, a speakeasy of sorts.

How charming. Impressive with how much work the previous decor must have taken. And as far as he'd heard from Helena, they did that often.

"Welcome to Nowhere," a young man said in a pleasant tone. He was dressed in a pin-striped suit and a hat on his blonde head. "Do you have a reservation, sir?"

Grey opened his mouth to answer, but before he could, a door opened on the bookcase behind the young man, and Sophia came out.

She wore a suit too. It was black, and it was fitted to her every curve. Under the suit jacket, a red scrap of lace and sparkle left part of her waist bare. As it had been the previous night, her hair was curly, but tonight it was pulled back into a high ponytail.

"He's here for me, Jack," she said to the young man, who smiled and gestured for Grey to go on in behind Sophia. She looked apprehensive, and he couldn't say he blamed her at all. Now that he was in front of her, he had to tap his fingers to his thigh to keep from fidgeting.

She smiled uncomfortably. "This doesn't have to be weird, right?"

"I guess." He doubted it.

She turned and led him into the club. The band was not playing, but there was music coming from the speakers. He followed her to the stairs, up to the second story, keeping his eyes firmly at his feet, though he had to admit it was hard when she was shaped the way she was. There was a second bar up here and several round tables. The tables were a lot more private. She led him to one tucked in a corner by the railing, overlooking the rest of the bar and stage.

There was only one other table occupied, by two people very much immersed in each other. He waited until she was seated before he took his seat—his mom had taught him manners.

She cleared her throat. "I think we're going to need a drink."

"Yeah," he chuckled, and a server came up to them.

"Hey, boss," the pretty blonde woman said with a huge smile and a southern twang. "Old Fashioned?"

Sophia smiled at her, and he found himself dazzled by her smile. It lit up her eyes, and she looked up at the server.

"Yes, thank you, Tina," she said and looked at Grey with raised brows. "You?"

He looked up at Tina.

"Same, thank you."

"Coming right up," Tina said as she turned around and went up to the bar.

Sophia looked down at the bottom floor a little awkwardly.

"I'm sorry," he said, placed his hands flat on the wooden table. There was an electric candle lit between them. "This is awkward, and you're right; it doesn't need to be."

She looked back at him, her hazel eyes curious.

"Yes, but last night wasn't normal, was it?" She said. "Naturally, things will be odd. And not just because of last night."

He frowned. She had a point.

Damn it.

"I don't know that I have anything to explain away," he said but realized he was absolutely full of it. Of course he had to explain to her why he was being cryptic.

She raised her brows cynically.

"Alright, fine," he said. "Ask me anything you want to know."

She observed him quietly for a moment as the server came back with their drinks. Sophia sipped before she said anything.

"How could you see?"

"See what?"

"You know what I mean." She leaned forward a bit. "Are you a witch?"

He could feel his face drain of color, so he drank half his cocktail to buy himself a little bit of time.

"That's a pretty specific and strange question," he said, discomfort making him wish he was at home in his studio, playing something instead of being here. This was why he liked being on his own, to avoid uncomfortable situations. Even if he was the one to get himself in it.

"You can just say no," she said with a bit of a smile, a sparkle in her eye. It was when he realized she was making fun of him.

He could play at that game, too, though the thought of it had anxiety surging through his entire body.

"What if the answer isn't no?" He murmured, and her mischievous smile disappeared. She simply looked at him with her eyes a little wide, and when her mouth opened and snapped shut without a sound, he chuckled.

He wondered if she knew how appealing she was, with her pretty hair and those arched brows over the unique color of her eyes.

Then it dawned on her. Her face was so expressive Grey saw every emotion that went through her. He fully laughed this time.

"Oh, you think you're funny." She rolled her eyes, but there was a small smile playing around her lips.

"Not even a little," he said. It wasn't a lie or him trying to be modest. He was not very funny, but mostly because he couldn't think of anything on the fly. He was more creative when he had some time to formulate a thought. "Do you believe in magic?"

"Maybe," she said but didn't add anything else.

"And yet you asked if I'm a witch." He drank again, draining the rest of his drink in one gulp. "Are you?"

She snorted. "Sure am."

"Well, in this day and age, a lot of people call themselves witches," he said. "All it takes is a few crystals and moon-bathing naked."

"Really?" Her brows shot up again. "So that's what you do?"

He appreciated her quick wit, and he was about to respond with what he would have hoped was a witty comeback when he met her eyes. Something flashed through his memory. Later summer afternoon, a swing, sweet smiles between friends, and shared secrets.

"You look so familiar," he said, rubbing his fingers together underneath the table. A small zap of energy rang through his hand. It grounded him, made him feel less crazy.

Serious, she sat back.

"Could it be because of our shared history?" she asked evenly. "I'm not sure I ever met you before last night."

"Yeah."

She brought her glass to her lips. His eyes followed.

"And I was right," she murmured and when he raised his brows, added, "You have brown eyes."

He blinked, confused for a moment until he remembered the charm he had used the previous night. He had found it in one of his dad's grimoires and used it from time to time if only to experience what it was like to have different colored eyes.

"Right. And how did you know I had brown eyes?"

"Because no one has eyes that shade of blue. I'd bet my club on it."

"You're very sure of yourself."

"Why wouldn't I be?" Her head was cocked to the side.

He shrugged. He was enjoying himself way too much. So much that he had almost forgotten why he was here.

"What if I told you that what you did last night was special?" He said, keeping his voice even, and leaned forward to rest his arms on the table. As if he was the other end of a magnet, she leaned forward as well.

"Well, yes, it is," she said, watching him squarely. "The question remains how you saw it too."

"If you can see it, then it would make sense that someone else in the world would be able to, as well," he pointed out.

"Yes, with seven-plus billion people in the world, I would assume so." She narrowed her eyes. "But no one else around me can see it, and then you show up. With our shared history, I would think it was about that. But it's not, is it?"

His jaw clenched with nerves, but he forced himself to relax by taking a deep breath. He shook his head.

"How are you related to Will Constantine?" she inquired, but he could see in her eyes that she knew. By the simple mention of his father's name, he knew she knew.

Around them, the tables began to fill as the band could be heard doing a quick soundcheck downstairs. Grey didn't look toward the stage. His eyes stayed on her as if glued there.

"He was my dad," Grey said and swallowed heavily. He didn't like talking about it. His father had been a good man. A good, flawed man who'd died while running away with his mistress.

Her face became solemn then, and she did look down toward the stage on the main floor.

"She was my mom," she said, but he already knew that. It wasn't like you came across many people with the Candela name in Seattle, especially connected to a family as powerful as the Montgomerys. He had it burned in his mind since he was a little boy and had found out what happened.

He didn't know what to say.

Finally, she turned back to face him.

"So if you're not here for that, then what are you here for?"

"I was led here." By magic, he added silently. He put his hand forward, palm up. She instinctively put hers in it, and he flipped it so her palm was up. Her hand was soft and warm, her nails short, unpainted. With one of his fingers, he traced a line on her palm. He felt her shiver once, then again when he hummed.

"You have a lot of discipline in you," he told her, allowing the many lines of her hand to tell him what he needed to know. "Independent."

She looked a little skeptical. "Anyone can be those things," she said.

"Not everyone is disciplined and independent." Her hand was warm in his. "But you are."

"I think that's a given," she said.

His lips twitched. A few days ago, he would have never been able to say that he would be enjoying his time with one of the daughters of the woman who ruined his childhood, yet here he was.

He looked into her hand again, seeing all the lines there. So many lines, so many crossroads. So much life. And a lot of passion.

"A bit of a temper," he said and her lips twitched as she held back a smile. "I see travel to a lot of different places, and that doesn't just mean the kind you can get on a plane for." That was interesting. "And a fair amount of confusion about a big aspect of your life."

Her fingers twitched as she sucked in a breath, but said nothing.

"Also, a strong sense of empathy."

"I'm a human being, of course I have empathy for others."

"There's more to yours."

"How so?"

"I'm not sure," he said. Sometimes not knowing was just as powerful as knowing, in his experience.

He let go of her hand, and she retracted it right away, as if he had burned her. They were connected somehow, and not only because of what they both saw when she'd sung.

"Look, there isn't much I can show you in front of your patrons." He leaned closer, kept his voice low. "But I can assure you that I saw what you did with your songs last night, and I was led here to find you for a reason."

Her expression was one of confusion and concern.

"If you want to know more, call me anytime."

On a whim, he reached into his pocket and pulled out a small crystal. It was clear, for the most part, but particles in rainbow colors glimmered in the center as if it had liquid moving inside. It was attached with black wire to a thin black string with a silver clasp. She took it and looked at him with her brow raised.

"Jewelry? Isn't it a little early for that?"

He laughed and she did too, which broke the tension that had hovered over them from the moment he arrived. Something tugged at him, deep inside, like a string was hiding behind his navel. He couldn't place the feeling. It was something utterly unfamiliar.

"It's an amulet," he told her. "For protection."

"Protection from what?"

He stood and so did she. Curious, a little peaked, he moved closer to her, and she didn't move away. She had a daring glint in her eye.

"Whatever you need protecting from."

Her lips parted a little.

"Touch it until it warms." He stepped back.

Her wide eyes stayed on his the whole time. He could almost see the wheels turning in her head.

"You'll know if you do. Reach out if you have questions. Or if something weird happens."

"Weird how?" Her voice was a little breathless. He felt it more than he heard it, even as the band played a song that was soft and whimsical.

"Things you can't explain logically."

His navel tugged again, and he fought the little bit of lightheadedness that remained. He nodded his goodbye. He had to get away. Something was off with him and he had to find out what it was.

4

When Grey's back disappeared through the doors, Sophia sat at the table for a while. She was aware that she was doing that thing where she dissociated and her mind wandered way too far. Hard not to let it.

She looked down at the pretty crystal, cylindrical and angular, the sparkles within it glowing like rainbows, even in the darkness of the club. Her thumb ran over the smooth surface.

Sophia knew about crystals, just not enough to understand what Grey meant by using them as protection. She knew they could have healing properties, thanks to Jeanette's explanations, though Jeanette was more skeptical about crystals than most since she was a doctor.

Just in case, and because she had seen crystals like these in her mom's attic, she slipped it over her head, letting it rest between her breasts. It was cool against her skin, and she found an odd sort of comfort from having it close. It probably didn't do much—she suspected it was a placebo effect more than anything else—but it wouldn't hurt to have it close anyway.

Sophia looked down at the lines intersecting her palm. How the hell had he known those things about her, though? Maybe he'd done a search online? Or had her investigated?

Before that train of thought got away from her, she rolled her eyes at herself. This wasn't a movie, and Grey Constantine probably knew things about her because of their shared past. It most likely had nothing to do with anything sinister.

That, or he could be a con artist. A magician?

She frowned. It was true that she was disciplined, but one could say that to many people and it would be true for half of them.

It was like throwing noodles at the wall. One was bound to stick.

Or all of them, in Grey's case.

That part made no sense. If Grey was a charlatan, how could he have unsettled her so much? He had sparked so many strange feelings and near-memories, she was left reeling. She had no idea what to think of it all. Shaking her head, she suddenly had the need to be where it was quieter, where she could think clearly. Things felt foggy, and there was a pressure in her chest she couldn't quite get rid of. It didn't matter how much she breathed or how deeply, it stayed with her until she clocked out of her shift later that night. Fortunately, everything had gone well and there had been no fires in need of putting out because she would have failed spectacularly at being anything but a hot mess.

Even later, she tossed and turned, unable to sleep. Each time she closed her eyes, she could hear every little sound, felt every slight shift of the house. Like the ghosts that existed somewhere in between worlds were more awake and therefore louder.

There was music playing somewhere, and she wondered who the hell would have music playing in the wee hours of the morning. How inconsiderate. At least it was far enough that it wasn't more than a murmur in the distance, but she was tired and cranky enough to decide to be pissed about it.

Another couple of hours of flitting in and out of sleep, and finally, Sophia got out of bed with a heavy sigh. The weekly brunch tradition with her sisters was going to be rough this morning.

The tradition had stayed with Sophia and her sisters after their mom had died. Every Sunday, their mom would dress in her prettiest dresses, and would take Sophia, her sisters Roselyn, Julia, and a baby Amy to a little place in the city. It was their special girl time, and they had continued going with their paternal grandmother after the death of their mom. Sophia suspected her grandmother felt bad for the four of them being orphaned at such a young age. And when Roselyn had died shortly after their mother, the blow had been too painful to continue in any traditions. Until Sophia, her conscience eating at her, had called up her sisters when she was in college and begged them to start going to Sunday brunch together. They'd agreed, and they had been doing it every week since then.

And there was nowhere she'd rather be on a moody Sunday, despite the exhaustion coursing through her.

Jean-clad, an oversized t-shirt and a coat in various shades of black, Sophia drove through the cloudy city, numb to the traffic, and fifteen minutes later, she pulled up to Sutton Place. The first parking spot she saw, she took, paid the fee, and began the block-long walk toward the little cafe. A fine mist fell around her, typical of the city at this time of year. The low heels of her boots clicked pleasantly on the sidewalk, but she stopped suddenly. Her legs simply refused to move. The back of her neck prickled, and she looked behind her. The chill that ran up and down her body wasn't just about the brisk morning air, something told her, and she hugged herself as she hurried down the sidewalk.

When she got to the front of the cafe, its pretty blue and white awning familiar and comforting, she was greeted by one of the newer hostesses, who smiled and waved her back as she picked up the ringing phone.

Sophia couldn't help the small smile that came to her face, seeing her sisters sitting together at a small round table by a large window that overlooked the street. Her sisters looked so similar, their skin a light shade of brown, so much that they were mostly passing. Lighter than Sophia, who was more tanned, having taken to their mom more, down to the texture of their hair.

Julia wore a pretty red top with long, lacy sleeves and dark jeans. Her short dark hair, which barely brushed her slim shoulders, was sleek and shiny, in a very Julia fashion. Amy wore tennis attire, and her long hair, a fiery shade of red for the past two months, was pulled back into a high ponytail and left wavy, in its natural state. The juxtaposition of the two was so sharp then—Julia's rigidity and Amy's carefree aura.

Sophia thought of Roselyn. What would it have been like if Roselyn was still around? If she had been sitting there too, waiting for Sophia to arrive for their tradition that hadn't lasted long enough. What if her mom had been there too?

She snapped back to the present, watched Julia watching her from the other side of the glass, and pasted a smile on her face. Inside, she took the third chair on the same table they had sat at almost every time they came.

"I am exactly on time," she said as she took the seat. Julia liked punctuality and Sophia always made sure she was time.

"You sure are. What were you doing out there?" Julia asked and took a drink of what looked like cranberry juice. Her nails were short, filed so the corners were wounded, and painted a pale pink.

"Being a creep," Amy said, but grinned when Sophia stuck her tongue out at her.

"What a horrible thing to say," Sophia said as she poured hot water into a teacup, which had been waiting at the table.

"Amy's never been known for her tact," Julia said. "Since she was a baby, she was a little semi-truck."

Absolute truth.

"How was the show the other night?" Amy asked, ignoring the comments pointedly.

"It was really good," Sophia said, the words inadequate. She didn't even know what words existed to explain what had been going on since that night. Of course, she wouldn't tell her sisters about Grey—that would require an incredible amount of whisky. Or tequila. Most likely both.

"I want to come see you next time," Amy said, clearly unaware of the kind of turmoil in Sophia's head.

"You should come to the next celebration," Sophia said. It would be a Latin celebration of everything spooky and superstitious. Okay, so she had inherited her love for the weird and the occult. Big deal.

"We should have a girls' night." Amy played with her mimosa glass, a tall crystal flute. "Lord knows I need one."

Julia's thin, arched brows rose over her dark eyes. "Why? Stressed?"

"Always," Amy said, as if it was perfectly obvious. "Do you guys understand what it's like to be a young entrepreneur?"

Someone who didn't know Amy could fully believe she was serious when she said that, but Sophia and Julia knew better, so they just rolled their eyes at their youngest sister, and moved on.

"How's it been?" Sophia asked. Recently, Amy had started an online boutique with her own designs, which were nothing if not incredible, and it had blown up overnight because of social media. Which Amy was also very good at.

"Fine, but it's driving me nuts. I am always in front of the computer. I've become Julia." Amy's eyes were comically wide.

Julia smirked. "Let me know if you need any help with it," she said. "You know, since I actually went to college for business management."

"You would throw that in my face," Amy scoffed.

Sophia and Julia laughed.

"In all seriousness," Julia said, "you're doing great. I'm proud of you."

Amy only smiled a little, but her skin beamed, and Sophia saw every bit of herself in that expression. That need to make sure Julia knew how well they were doing because Julia worked so hard to help when their mom died. Sophia didn't know what she would have done without Julia.

"And how is work at the office?" Sophia asked Julia, who clenched her jaw.

"I told you working for dad was going to come back and bite you in the ass," Amy said before Julia could respond. "But did you listen?"

"I did not listen, and you were right. The man's ruthless," Julia said but did not elaborate. No one asked anyway because even if Julia wanted to say something else on the matter, she still wouldn't. Loyal to a fault, Julia. Unless you fucked with her and then you'd know her ire.

"Dad's nothing if not a consummate workaholic," Sophia said. Which was why she had refused on going into the family business and opened her club instead. Lucky to have received an inheritance when her mother died, she had been able to open the club with Victoria without needing financing from a bank or help from her wealthy father.

"Is that cute dancer going to be there?" Amy asked, as if the conversation had never shifted. Sophia would have laughed if it hadn't taken her by such surprise.

"What cute dancer?" Julia asked.

"I can't remember her name, to be honest." Amy sipped her tea.

"Could be anyone, really." Amy didn't discriminate when it came to attractive people. "Still, come to the club next week for the Latin Spooky, which we're calling Espuki because it's stupid and funny."

That earned a twitch of Julia's lips and Amy's confused frown.

"Don't really get it, but don't you worry, I will be there for the half-naked dancers." Amy wiggled her brows and nodded slowly before she tipped her glass and finished her mimosa.

Sophia threw her a narrowed look. "Objectifying my dancers won't go well for you, doll," Sophia said. "You could get kicked. You might want to slow down with those mimosas."

"Why? This is my way of getting out of my indoor tennis lesson."

"Why don't you just cancel the damn thing? And why are you still taking lessons?" Julia said as the server came back to take orders. When they had ordered (Amy another mimosa), and the server was gone, Amy said,

"Because my instructor is Tom."

"Who is Tom?" Julia blinked incredulously at Amy.

"Oh, just a new flame," Sophia said, and Amy rolled her eyes.

"He's the guy I've been seeing. I met him at the country club."

"And what happened to..." Julia tapped her temple with a delicate finger. How could anyone be that perfect?

"Josh?" Amy shrugged. "We broke up."

"Why? I liked Josh," Julia said.

"Then you date him."

"I'll remind you I'm a married lady."

"Yes, I haven't forgotten," Amy muttered, bringing a glass of water to her mouth to cover her grimace.

Julia only rolled her eyes. It had never been a secret that Amy did not like Julia's husband, Harold. And to be fair, neither did Sophia. Harold was controlling and kind of a prick all around. The type of guy who would get a server fired for bringing out the wrong order. Julia was the only one to keep him in line, and even then, he was close to unbearable.

"And how about you, Sophia?" Amy said to break the tension.

"Oh, we are not going to talk about my love life." She drew the line at that. "How is everything else going?"

"I bought a plant, and it already died, poor thing," Amy said. Sophia loved her for changing the subject, and she expressed it by tapping Amy's ankle with her foot. Julia seemed oblivious across from Sophia.

"Meditate and manifest it," Julia said, smirking at Sophia in that annoying way that made Sophia want to throw a roll at her or something. Anything esoteric in nature, Julia made fun of. It was annoying, but Sophia had often wondered if maybe Julia only acted that way because she could and not because she felt that way.

"Hasn't worked for me," Sophia said, thinking of her plants. Both dead. She groaned, then, as if her hand was magnetically attracted to it, her fingers grazed the amulet resting between her breasts. She had forgotten it was there. It warmed gently under her fingers, so she let it drop, a little put off and nauseated. Her phone vibrated in her pocket.

She looked at it, her stomach rolling a little.

GREY: THANK YOU FOR SEEING ME LAST NIGHT.

Seeing him... neat way of putting it since she was the one who was seen in ways she hadn't felt seen in a long time. If she was completely honest, in ways she had never been seen, in fact. Her fingers itched to type a message to ask him what the hell it was he wanted from her.

"Who is that?" Amy asked as she leaned over to peek.

"Definitely none of your business." Sophia moved the screen away to block it from view.

Amy acted shocked. "How dare you?"

"Now I want to know even more," Julia said.

Sophia sighed and put her phone away before her sisters could reach for it.

"It's nothing," Sophia said with finality and a little bit louder than she needed to. Both her sisters stared at her with wide eyes.

"Defensive, defensive," Amy said slowly, then smirked at Julia. "I guess it's important enough to keep a secret. Can't wait to hear about it."

Sophia sighed. She was so tightly wound, her neck tense. "I'm sorry," she said. "I haven't been sleeping well."

"Why not?" Julia sat up a little straighter, but only a little bit. More like a shift in the air around her than a physical thing. "Anything bothering you?

A little close. Damn.

"I've been busy with the club, mostly," Sophia said. Not a lie, but not a full truth either. "I've been dreaming about mom a lot."

Julia's face barely changed, but Sophia regretted saying anything anyway. Of the three of them, Julia probably had the most complicated feelings about their mother. Not that Sophia didn't have those too.

She sighed. "That was a text from a guy I met at the club two nights ago."

Amy squealed. "Tell me more. Is he cute?"

Oh, he was cute, Sophia thought. Really, really cute.

Fucking hell.

"Yeah, I guess," she said and immediately felt like a damned fraud. "He felt a little familiar."

"Familiar how?" Julia asked, instantly suspicious.

"I don't know. Like I've met him before," Sophia said and briefly considered telling her sisters the connection between them and Grey Constantine. She shook her head when the fog hit her again.

Sophia smiled at the server when she returned with coffee for the table and more water, but it felt tight on her face.

"Maybe one of those coincidences," Amy said. "Or, maybe it's the universe trying to talk to you."

Julia seemed to hold an exasperated sigh, just as Sophia's phone buzzed.

GREY: ARE YOU FEELING ALRIGHT?

Sophia opened the phone and tapped a message.

SOPHIA: NOT SURE HOW I'M FEELING, TO BE HONEST.

"Do you have a picture of this man?" Amy asked.

"I do not, as I don't go around taking pictures of perfect strangers."

"I have some memories like that," Julia said, getting the other two's attention, which Sophia clung on to so they didn't have to talk about Grey anymore. He unsettled her too much. "The kinds that feel like déjà vu but a lot stronger. I figure it's just growing older. You forget things more easily."

"You're two years older than me, so I'm going to ask you to relax about being old," Sophia said as the sever came back with their food.

They ate in relative silence, the topic of Grey thankfully forgotten.

"Do you ever recall mom talking to her plants?" Sophia asked her sisters, wishing she had words for what she actually wanted to ask. Do you see the music too? Do you dream of things that don't make any sense?

"Oh yes, she talked to them all the time," Julia said, but Amy made a face that was gone quickly. Of course, she would not remember much since she had been only six when their mom died, so her memories were a lot more fractured.

"I kind of remember," Amy said. "Hard to tell if it's real or if I'm just remembering what you've said about her."

Sophia hadn't considered that. How someone's words about an event could mar your perception of it.

"She used to play music to them too," Julia said. "I always thought it was strange, but not in the context of our mom. It was so like her to do things that seemed weird from the outside."

"I wish I remembered more," Amy said, her voice losing some of its brightness.

"Me too," said Sophia and put down her fork, her appetite suddenly gone. She echoed Amy's reasons for wanting to remember and whatever else was going on with her. Their mom had seemed to understand the whole thing with the plants; Sophia was sure of it, though her memories were so foggy, she couldn't tell up from down. Everything up until her mom died seemed to blur together.

"And her green thumb did not pass down to me," Amy said, eyes widening. "I can't keep them alive to save my own life."

"I know," Sophia said. "I killed a cactus, of all things."

"Even I can keep a cactus alive," Amy said, and Julia laughed but said nothing. She was good enough with plants, but she didn't have a lot of time to care for them, with how demanding her job was. And besides, Sophia had the inkling that Julia had a hard time enjoying the things their mom once did, due to the circumstances of her death.

They sat together for a while, talking about inconsequential things when Sophia's neck prickled again, and she found herself looking out the big window by their table. Across the street, a person stood with a black hoodie over their head. She could barely see features, but she could tell it was a man, and when she had stared at him long enough, he turned and walked away. Sophia's eyes followed him until she could no longer see him, and shivering, she turned back to her sisters and continued their conversation.

5

Sophia had every intention to go home after brunch, but only briefly. Instead, she got on the freeway and went the opposite way, toward her father's house. It was hard keeping her eyes from going to her rearview mirror to make sure no one had followed her, her skin crawling.

The house of her childhood was just outside the city. It had been in her family, on her father's side, for generations, and Sophia's grandparents had gifted it to her mom and dad as a wedding present. Often, she thought about that and how extravagant of a gift it was. The house wasn't a mansion, but it certainly wasn't quaint either. It sat withing a gated community set up in such a way that you never saw your neighbors if you didn't want to. Which they never really did when Sophia was little. The other wealthy inhabitants of the neighborhood had been older, so there weren't many kids to play with anyway. Besides, Sophia liked that in their childhood, she'd had Victoria and her sisters. It was all she had needed.

A pang went through her as her mind did that thing again. That flip, like something wanted to come forward in her memory but couldn't. She was getting real tired of it.

At the big iron gates, she gave her name and code to the security guy before being allowed in. Her eyes slid to the rearview mirror again, breathing a sigh of relief when no one followed her into the complex. Nerves vibrated under her skin, even as she felt the relief spread through her, leaving her suddenly exhausted.

The driveway that separated her father's property from the main road was long, just wide enough to allow two cars to drive at the same time on it. It was almost half a mile of paved driveway, the sides perfectly manicured and lined with tall evergreens, which formed a canopy above her that made her feel sheltered from the rest of the world.

A feeling of melancholy, more pronounced than ever these days, spread through her like warm honey. It could have been anything: missing the simplicity of childhood, that time that she'd never get back. A time where she'd had no clue her mom had nearly abandoned her and her sisters, including a sick Roselyn.

Breathing through the shimmer of anger in her stomach, she pulled into the circular driveway in front of the house. An oversized garage was to her left, where her father kept more cars than one person needed. There was a fountain in the center of the large circle, which Sophia thought was pretty over the top, but such was her father. A little bit too much. Kind of endearing at this point, since the old man was set on his way, as he liked to remind Sophia and her sisters. The fountain was empty, and the flowers that usually bloomed around it were dead from the season. The fountain hadn't been there when Sophia was a kid, but her father had updated the home a couple of times in the past twenty years.

It seemed to be a favorite thing of his, finding something he didn't like, changing them just to change them again in three or four years.

As she got out of the car, she took a deep breath. The air smelled different up here. Crisp and clean. Lighter.

Keys in her pocket, she trudged up to the front door as a cold breeze made her shiver.

The house was stately, attractive in its pretty dark blue, gray, and white façade. A tall front door sat on a porch that extended all the way around the house, where a swinging bench sat overlooking the vast land that had never been used for anything other than just being there. Empty. Such a waste.

The front door had frosted glass on the top half, and it was painted a dark blue to match the rest of the outside. Back when she was little, the wood had been a pretty blonde, and the glass a little less sleek than the current one.

There were typically planters hanging from the white banister, but they were put away for the winter, giving the house a look of emptiness that clawed at her. What would have her mother done had she been alive? Maybe she would have taken the plants down too, but Sophia suspected she would have put them in a greenhouse. Or brought them into the house to care for until it warmed up again.

Her father, on the other hand, was a man who liked things to be a little sleeker, less cluttered because he was a 'civilized man' as he liked to proclaim. What about having a bunch of plants in the house make you uncivilized, she wanted to ask, but never had the guts to. He was a business man. A shark. Someone who knew what he wanted and went for it. Never mind his privilege... but no one would say anything about that out loud.

Sophia knocked a couple of times and tried the doorknob. It was unlocked, so she pushed the door open and stepped inside. The house was quiet, and there was no movement. It was Sunday, so her father should be home, though she wouldn't put it past him to be working anyway. The man was a workaholic if Sophia had ever seen one. A trait she had inherited and had tried very hard to do away with.

Sophia loved this home, with its tall, narrow windows overlooking the big yard in the back and trees surrounding the property, a covered pool that made no sense to have if her dad was never there anyway. She had played in that yard so much when she was a kid. It brought a smile to her face to see that the swings she'd played on were still there, covered in a vine that was dying in the cold. It would be back in the spring, the vines growing lovely red flowers and almost surrounded the whole frame with color and life. Her dad had often said he kept them because he wanted his grandchildren to one day play on them too.

It would have been sweet if Sophia had planned on having kids, but she was not. Maybe Julia and Amy would give him that someday. Or maybe she would, but that would be in her own time.

Her footsteps quiet on the wooden floor, she walked through a wooden archway, elegant and ornate, and headed toward the sunroom. Her mother had kept an impressive number of plants in there, converting it into more of a greenhouse than a sunroom back then.

The plants love this room, her mother had often said in that soft voice she had. Sophia could almost see her dancing around the room, a long skirt flowing around her ankles, watering and whispering sweet nothings into the ether. *Look how happy they are, Sophie darling. Can you hear their chatter?* Sophia would smile because she could hear the plants talking amongst each other about how happy they were, especially on watering day.

The room was circular, with a skylight that had also been updated, letting even more light in. And where before there had been lovely living plants, now, the place only held a brown coffee table in the center of the room. It had an oversized picture book with famous bridges from around the world and a vase of silk flowers next to it. The mantle was clean of clutter. No knickknacks or crystals, or vases with flowers...

She wondered what her father had done with her mom's patchwork chair, where she would sit and read or write into one of those notebooks she liked to carry around. There was a tall vase instead, with a geometric design.

There was not one moat of dust in the room, though she doubted her father spent any time in it.

"Sophia?"

She turned to her father's voice, finding him standing by the archway to the sunroom. She hadn't realized she had come into the room so far that she was almost by the spot where her mom's chair used to be. She shook her head to clear it and pasted a smile on her face, though it felt stiff. He was smiling, wearing dark jeans and a white polo shirt.

Conrad Montgomery was a tall man, a little thick around the middle as he aged, with light-colored hair salted with the passing years. His blue eyes were still sharp underneath softly arched brows, his nose straight.

She went and hugged him when he opened his arms to her. He smelled like coffee.

"Sorry for coming unannounced," she said as she stepped back and looked up at him.

"Honey, you are welcome here any time; no announcement necessary. How was your brunch?"

"Great as always," she said.

"And how is Amy? She's not answering my calls." He seemed annoyed by that, but only mildly. Sophia had noticed a change in him as the years passed. He seemed more calm, a lot less prone to angry outbursts these days.

"Amy's fine. Busy with her store."

"I told her to hire people from the start, but did she listen?"

"Does Amy ever listen to anyone?" Sophia asked and he nodded and laughed a little.

"You're right. Your sister has never been one to take advice from her old man."

From anyone, corrected Sophia, but kept it to herself. Amy definitely danced to her own tune, and both Sophia and Julia had always admired that about her.

"So..." her father said. "I'm going to guess you're not just here because you really wanted to see your dear old dad."

"It was," she told him, though she'd never tell him it was about way more than that. "And also, I wanted to ask you about Mom."

He blinked as if surprised about the topic.

"About what?"

He led her to the sofa and they sat together, facing each other.

"Well, I have been having some dreams about her and I was curious," she began, unsure of how to continue. "She used to have a lot of plants."

"So many!" His eyes widened slightly as he recalled. "This room was filled with them. She had so many varieties, things that were not easy to care for, but she always had a special touch."

"She did," Sophia said, but again, she lacked the words to speak what she wanted to say. "I just always wondered how."

"How she was so good at it?"

Sophia nodded, and he shrugged.

"I honestly don't know. I know she talked about her mom also loving plants and growing up caring for them, so I guess that's how she got good. Generational thing."

Her grandmother, Evelyn, who Sophia had been middle-named after. Sophia never knew her, as she had died when Sophia's mom was young.

"That must be it," Sophia said, disappointed. "Did you keep any of her notebooks?"

He looked confused, but only for a moment, before he shrugged again. "If we have anything, it would be upstairs in the attic. A lot of her things were taken away after she..."

When he trailed off, her heart jolted and began beating faster. She hated the attic, though she couldn't explain why. It was kind of creepy, though it hadn't been when she was younger. Her mom spent most of her time up there.

"Would you mind if I took a look?" she asked.

His brow remained slightly furrowed. "Why do you want to look through all that old stuff?"

She wanted to tell him about all her dreams involving her mom. But when she opened her mouth, it wasn't that she said.

"I'm curious about her plant logs," she said and surprised even herself. "Julia said mom used to write about their care in those notebooks she liked to carry around."

Her father's nod was slow, as if he had no idea what she was talking about. "Alright. Do you want me to help?"

"No, no." She wanted nothing less at the moment. "I won't be long."

She got on her feet before he could say anything else, and soon, she was upstairs. Where the hell had that come from? She didn't often lie to anyone, least of all her own father, but that lie had been automatic. No thought behind it.

A headache began to settle somewhere behind her sinuses, so she pinched the bridge of her nose as she climbed up the narrow staircase. The bedrooms, including her old one, was up in the second level. Except for her fathers, which was on the main level. A second set of stairs at the end of the hallway led to the attic. She could see its open banister gleaming from where she stood, rich and dark in color. Something fluttered in her stomach as she took the steps up, the third stair creaking, as it had when she was a young child.

She wondered why her dad hadn't updated that. Maybe he didn't come up here at all. A shiver ran up and down her back as she passed a bit of a cold spot when she reached the landing with the door. It was brown and wooden, unassuming. The brass doorknob was warmer than she had anticipated, and when she went to turn it, it did not budge. It used to get stuck when she was a kid too, but it was still surprising her father hadn't replaced it. She wondered why, and the thought made her a little sad when she realized this could be painful for her father. He hadn't married after her mom died, even when Sophia and her sisters had pushed him to.

"Come on," she said under her breath, pushing with all her weight behind it. The doorknob was twisting, so it wasn't locked. Next, she tried putting her weight into it, pushing with her shoulder, only to wince in pain as it shot down her arm.

She pressed her forehead against the wood, thinking of how every other door in this house opened perfectly fine with barely any noise, and the one she needed wouldn't. And wasn't that how life worked? Can't always get what you want, or some shit like that.

"Come on," she whispered again and had to quickly hold herself up, her heart jumping to her throat, as the door flew open and hit the wall behind it. Sophia froze at the threshold, a hand over her wildly beating heart.

Her knees wobbled as she stepped through the threshold. And in a moment of hazy recollection, she could almost see Sunshine, her mom's Norwegian Forest cat, trail in front of her, its bushy tail in the air. Sunshine had always walked into rooms first, as Sophia recalled. She had been the most peculiar cat—and very protective

Of Sophia's mom, her eyes green like moss and so knowing they almost looked human at times. When her mom had died, Sunshine had attached itself to Roselyn, and when she'd succumbed to her childhood cancer, Sunshine disappeared. It was as if all traces of her mother had started dissipating into the cosmos, one by one, until nothing was left behind for those who loved her.

Sophia didn't close the door when she entered the room, afraid she would get stuck up there. The thought made panic rise up to grab her by the throat, even as she stood in the center of the room. It looked so different than what she remembered. There had once been a macrame holder by the window, which had held many plants and herbs. Her mom often tore leaves off those plants and put them in a small pot she'd kept in a corner. None of that stuff was there anymore.

Even the mismatched curtains on the windows were gone, hopefully packed away. It was a square room, almost perfectly so, with an attached closet big enough to walk into. It had an adjoining bathroom with the prettiest claw-footed tub Sophia had ever seen, in which Sophia had witnessed her mother pour flowers and little bottles of colorful liquids before she submerged herself into the warm depths.

The room used to have a bed underneath the window too, but it was also gone now, along with a patchwork quilt in various shades of green Sophia remembered smelled like the earth right after a good rain. And did she smell that now? Briefly, before she became dizzy with the memory.

She walked over to the closet and realized how much the wooden floor creaked up here. The little bronze knob twisted without problems, and the door opened to reveal several white boxes stacked on top of each other. Sophia pulled out one of the boxes, set it on the floor. It wasn't labeled, and neither were any of the others when she started pulling them all out.

There were albums, neatly arranged on their sides, the spines showing date ranges, most from when Sophia was a kid. She opened one, finding baby pictures of her and her three sisters. Did her father know these were up here? She imagined he'd want them somewhere he could see them if he wanted to or would have given them to Sophia and her sisters. Maybe he hadn't looked through these boxes, but what did she know? Her father barely ever mentioned her mother. Sophia couldn't say she blamed him after what happened.

Sophia flipped through the album, then picked up a second one labeled with her mother's name. The name was written on the spine on a long white sticker. The handwriting was so obviously her mother's, Sophia smiled. It was a lovely penmanship; long, sweeping curves and loops, and letters so even, they could have been digital.

She opened it, finding pictures of when her mom was little and living in the Dominican Republic, but those were few. She looked the same when she was young as when she was older, her features simply maturing, her tanned skin so smooth and silky, and her hair dark and curly and long. There were a lot of other pictures with her mom as a preteen and as a teenager. Some were of her mom with a group of friends, at the beach with a guitar over her knee, her eyes closed, and her mouth opened in song. She looked so happy and focused, Sophia could almost hear the song distantly. She smiled, finding another photo. In this one, her mom was a teen, and she stood next to a tall, lanky boy with white skin and dark hair, smiling for the camera. He was so cute, his eyes a lovely mossy green. Something about him felt familiar, but that could just be because she was so desperate to remember something about her childhood that didn't feel weird.

"Who are you?" she said out loud as if the room could answer her. There was so much she didn't know.

She tried taking the picture out of the album, but was unable to as the photo was stuck. She left it alone, not wanting to destroy it. She knew this box would be coming home with her, so she could spend more time looking through those albums, but she closed the box and moved on to another. This one had little trinkets, old bottles in varying shapes with the dried remnants of liquid inside them. She seemed to remember these sitting on shelves on the wall and wondered what they were. She smelled one, but it didn't really smell like anything other than dust.

Sophia set the box with the albums aside, then looked into another one, and then another, trying to find... what? What was it she was looking for? Proof that she wasn't actually crazy? That maybe Grey Constantine reading her hand was just a parlor trick... Or worse, that it was real?

She shook her head with a laugh, but the laughter died. The way she could see so much, the lights and the colors. How she could sing some songs into lights...

Some time passed as Sophia looked through many of the boxes, got distracted with several. There were sealed envelopes with her mom's handwriting on the outside, and some with handwriting Sophia didn't recognize. There were hundreds of the little bottles, notes scribbled on the margins of books in a tight script that matched some of the envelopes, and they brought up so many questions, Sophia finally put the lid on the final box and huffed out a frustrated breath. Why in the world would her mom have sealed envelopes put away, without ever opening them to see the contents?

Was Sophia going to open them? Hell yes, she would. Just not now. She was looking for the notebooks. One final lid came off a box. The final one, she promised herself, as her eyes were bleary from the headache that now pounded against her skull. Nausea rolled in her stomach, but she set it aside. She didn't have time for that.

Then, she sat back from where she was kneeling, her feet numb, when she noticed all the notebooks stacked neatly inside the box. There were dozens, in many sizes. But when Sophia opened one, it was completely blank.

"No." She frowned down at the blank pages, flipped them over and over, until she confirmed it was entirely empty.

Sophia opened another notebook, then another after that, and another.

"It doesn't make sense," she said into the room and her words were loud to her ears, as if they had echoed. A chill overcame her, and a sigh made her shiver until she realized it was her own. Then, at the bottom of the box, three brown leather tomes sat. Yes, she remembered these too. Her mom rarely didn't have these with her. When Sophia had asked, curious like only children could be curious, her mom had often smiled and said she would tell Sophia everything when she was grown.

Well, I'm grown now, Mom.

She opened one, then the second, then the third. The lids were soft under her hands, like velvet. They were also blank.

Back on her shaky legs, she took a box down and met with her dad at the bottom of the stairs. He looked like he had been about to go up there. To see her? She didn't care.

She heard herself ask him to help her load the boxes into her car, his brief protest before he helped her load as many as she could fit in the trunk, back seats, and even the front passenger seat. He didn't understand why she wanted to take all that old stuff with her, he said, but she was only half listening as she hugged him and got into her car.

No, her memory wasn't failing her. She had seen her mother writing into those leather tomes, and she was going to figure out why the hell they were empty now, when it didn't make any sense for them to be.

That morning, when she'd made her way to her dad's house, she hadn't been expecting to find anything, but one thing she hadn't expected at all was to find blank pages.

6

When Grey was a young boy, his entire existence had become consumed with finding a cure. He clearly remembered the moment he realized there was an illness, though the details surrounding it were lost somewhere in his childhood. Pretty typical.

But he did remember making potions with his dad, right there in the kitchen of their home. Grey's mom hadn't been keen on it, but it was a small house and his father always said you had to do what you had to do. Then his dad died, and Grey had lost the motivation to figuring it out. He was a kid after all. What could he really do without his one and only teacher of magic.

As a teen, when he had found his will for magic again, when he played music and it did that thing it did, he'd found his fire again, but every potion he had made since then had only worked to a certain point. They seemed to slow down the progress of the void, but never fully cured it.

Sometimes, a cure felt so close, he could almost touch it. His current recipe was the best in the potions market, did the most, but it was still not close enough. Because now, as an adult with much experience in the realm of magic as he had, Grey was forced to do things he had never fathomed as a bright-eyed child. Things that no matter how many times he did them—and he had done them plenty—left a trace of bitterness behind that was difficult to swallow.

He stood, paralyzed, in front of a shelf of potions he loathed with everything in him. The pouch where he would put the concoction sat empty on the shelf. Beside Grey, Juan Jacobo Dolores, Lucas for short, best friend and fellow witch, stood in silence, waiting patiently.

"You want me to get them for you?" There was not an ounce of sarcasm in Lucas's heavily accented tone. Grey turned his head to look at his friend. Tall and reedy, Lucas was a solid mass of lean muscle. Grey was fit, liked to go on regular runs and picked up the weights several times a week, but Lucas was another story. He had darker skin and eyes that were like pure whisky, surrounded by impossibly long lashes. His smooth black hair was kept longer at the top, and the beard and mustache were neatly groomed. Tonight, he wore a pair of dark slacks, typical for him, with thin red suspenders over a blue button-up. A tattoo peeked out from his neckline. Unlike Grey, who wore his usual dark jeans and black button-up, the sleeves rolled up to the elbows.

On his side, Lucas had strapped a leather pouch for potions, like a holster to dangerous weapons. And weren't they? Potions were amazing tools, but also deadly. Funny how that worked.

Grey grimaced and reached for the potions he needed.

"You alright?" Lucas asked as he zipped the pouch on his side.

"No," Grey said. Of course he wasn't alright. Not even a little.

"Want to talk about it?" Lucas's voice was quiet, his accent thick and confused between all the languages he spoke. With Spanish being his first, he knew five others, last time Grey checked, though he wouldn't put it past Lucas to have picked up another.

"Not yet," Grey said, realizing he had been quiet for too long, staring at a spot by Lucas's ear.

Lucas nodded. "Whenever you're ready." As a therapist, Lucas had always been available for a talk. At first, unofficial, as they were good friends and that was a big no-no in Lucas's professional career. Now, as Lucas had shifted to a less formal way of therapy, one that was a lot more magical, Grey did see him often when his thoughts were too much to handle.

"You know," Lucas said, "it occurs to me that maybe we should dress for what we do."

"And how is that?" Grey asked. "A robe and a scythe, perhaps?" He pulled back his hair, tied it with an elastic, and faced his friend.

Lucas raised his brows, unimpressed. "You do that and tell me how it goes."

Grey could have laughed, but he didn't really feel like laughing. It would have felt like a travesty.

"Are you ready?" Grey asked quietly.

"Never."

Fair point.

Grey reached for his phone to find the address where the witch was being kept from hurting others, then put out his arm for Lucas to take it. When Lucas did, placing his hand on Grey's forearm, they disappeared together. The family had taken down their wards, the protection crystals and spells to protect the house from intruders, to allow them to reappear straight into the house. And good thing, because otherwise, Grey and Lucas would have had to scour maps and find places where they could port to without being seen.

When the two reappeared right inside the doorway of the home, Grey glanced out the small window next to the door. It was dark outside in England. There was no one outside, as the late hour had forced everyone into the safety of their homes. Inside the house, it was quiet and a little cool in temperature.

Lucas immediately reached into the pouch at his side for a defensive potion, just in case. Not that they expected any problems.

The entryway opened into a sitting room, which was small. Two love seats were close together, with a small square table in front of them. Across from the sitting area was a stone fireplace that had picture frames on the mantle. A blond man and dark-skin woman through the years, along with a young girl who managed to resemble both of them perfectly. On the wall, there were photos of the child growing up, other family members, and maybe friends.

Grey hadn't heard any names when he'd received the urgent call earlier, and he would not ask for them either. It was easier that way. He never wanted to get alerted of a witch's suffering. He never wanted to be the one to have to deal with it. But he was, and he coped in the best way he could.

They heard soft voices coming from the back.

His cheeks puffed out slightly as Grey blew out a breath, taking the first steps forward, Lucas a couple of steps behind.

"Hello?" Lucas called out, announcing their presence, and the woman from the photos, short and plump, came walking through what seemed to be a hallway, just off a small dining room and kitchen combination. Her smooth face was grief-stricken and became even more so when she saw Grey. Her hair was straight and smooth down her back.

"You're here already." She froze in place and her voice wobbled when she spoke.

Grey and Lucas also did not move, waiting for her permission to enter the house further. As if by standing still for those short moments could delay everything until they were all ready.

"Could you lead us to them?" Lucas asked and the woman nodded with apprehension that was so heavy, it felt solid.

"She's in the bedroom," she said. She looked to be in her late thirties, but her skin was lined with grief. "She's waiting for you."

Grey, his heart beginning to race, followed her.

They entered the room where the young witch was chatting quietly with her father. Her youthful skin made Grey halt mid-step. His heart sank even further. It was especially difficult when it was someone so young suffering from that horrible illness. It didn't seem fair. She had brilliant brown eyes and hair exactly like her mother's.

A red checkered blanket lay haphazardly on her, as she reclined on a pile of pillows against her tufted headboard. There was a tapestry behind her bed, enormous, which covered the entire wall. It had depictions of the world on it. Mountains, rivers, oceans, animals, and the stars in the cosmos. On the wall adjacent to the bed, a short bookshelf held what looked like sketchbooks. There was a single side table with a burning candle, which smelled of pine and cinnamon. The overhead lights were low.

The father looked wearily at Grey.

"Thank you for coming." He looked away as he said it.

Grey couldn't take offense. He'd be weird too, if someone came into his home to kill his daughter.

"Wow," the girl said with a small smile, the circles under her eyes dark. "You are so much better looking than I imagined." But she was looking at Lucas, who simply inclined his head toward her. "Mr. Constantine," she added. "I guess you're not so bad either."

Despite his mood, Grey felt his lips twitch.

"Don't worry," she said, "I won't tell you my name."

Grey's brows pinched closer together. Why did he feel horrible about that all of a sudden? What could he say to her? He stood like an idiot for a while, silent, deeply upset, nauseated.

"Does it hurt?" she asked, quieter now, and he didn't know what was worse. Not being able to respond about the name thing, or having to tell her what it would feel like to die.

He caught the mother's eye, and she looked away quickly, her chin trembling.

"It doesn't hurt," Grey told the girl, knowing that to be the truth, due to the potions he had created. It would be as simple and soft as falling asleep.

She nodded but continued to look more serious than any girl her age should. He took a hesitant step forward.

"I have to ask you for permission to give you these potions," he said and cleared his throat when it snagged.

"Granted," she said and smiled again. "I'm ready. I don't want to prolong this and risk hurting someone else."

"Someone else?" Lucas asked, instantly alert.

The girl looked at her dad, who turned his head to show Grey the bruises blooming on his jaw and cheek. And it would get more volatile as the illness progressed, Grey knew. He didn't have to say it to them. They knew it too. It was the reason he was here in the first place.

Grey wondered how long she'd been ill. If it had progressed faster because she was young, or if it was the opposite. It was hard to say.

"I'm not scared," she added. Everyone looked at her. She didn't look away, and certainly didn't look scared. "It sucks that I have to be done with this life now, but maybe I get to live longer in the next one."

The heaviness that had plagued him only grew with her words, as if it should have been possible.

Even when he tried to be detached, it punched him in the gut and threatened to swallow him whole. It was never easy, but when the witch was so young—barely eighteen, he thought—it was much more difficult.

He reached into the pouch on his side, the triangular shape of the vial so familiar, it made his stomach roll with nausea. He pulled the first one out, walking toward the bed. The girl's mother had sat on the other side of the bed, crying softly, tears dripping off her chin.

He handed the girl the potion, a dark blue that looked like galaxies swirled inside it. She took it, her fingers trembling a little, and blew out a breath before she took it, making a face. Grey knew it wasn't the most pleasant of potions, though it was beautiful and smelled like it should taste great. Like those bottles of all-purpose cleaner that looked like forbidden juice.

The parents sniffled beside the girl, close but not touching her at all.

Just taking that potion wouldn't do much more than make someone tired after a few minutes, as it was the combination of the three that did the job.

The girl nodded at Grey, and he could see that the nerves were, in fact, settling in now, as she swallowed and her eyes were a little misty. He pulled out the second vial, almost identical to the first but bright green instead.

She drank it fast, and when Grey would have handed her the third, she took a breath and looked up at her dad.

"Daddy, I'm going to be alright." Her voice was rushed, as if she knew that she was running out of time to say the things she wanted to say. "I promise. I know magic is hard for you, especially after all of this."

The father took her hand, gripped it tightly.

"But being a witch was wonderful, and getting this illness was eye-opening in so many ways."

Grey turned around to give them a semblance of privacy and saw that Lucas had stepped forward a little, the potion he had held in his hand put away. His eyes were darker than normal, and they met Grey's, but only for a brief moment. It had also never been easy for Lucas, and

Grey wondered if he did something to cope. Did it make him a terrible friend that he hadn't asked?

"I'm ready," the girl said.

Grey turned back to her, giving her the last of the vials, a clear potion that looked like there was not much to it, like spring water.

She would have a little while, maybe an hour or two to be with her family, before she would fall asleep and drift away.

"Child of the universe, may Mother's arms welcome you home," Grey whispered sadly as the color came back to her face for her final moments.

He tried to swallow, but his throat was too tight.

They didn't wait around for the final moments, as that only belonged to the young witch and those who loved her the most. So, Grey turned around, grabbed Lucas's arm, and ported back to Lucas's, before going to his own house.

With the heaviness of solitude as his only companion, Grey sat at the piano, and he played into the night.

7

Sophia's mind remained with the boxes she had left at home. She'd spent the entire day looking through them, only pausing for food and bathroom breaks.

She'd undoubtedly become obsessed.

Every box had contained photo albums, sealed envelopes, dozens of blank journals, and hundreds of little bottles with dried remnants of liquids at the bottom. And for some reason, she'd had a hard time opening the envelopes. It was as if her nervous system knew she'd find things there she wasn't ready to deal with. Or she was just anxious. Or she was still confused why there were sealed envelopes and her dad never got curious about it.

None of it made any sense, and every time she looked through the journals, as if looking one more time would magically make them fill up, something scratched at her memory. It was a puzzle that had only the edges filled in.

Now, she was at the club, and it was the last place she wanted to be. She had never felt like that about her own place. They were closed, but prepped for the rest of the week on Mondays. Schedules were discussed, reorders were made, and they cleaned, restocked, and redecorated for whatever show they had that weekend.

Everyone was dressed casually, which was always a little weird since Sophia was so used to seeing them dressed up for work. Sophia wore the same loose jeans as she had the previous day, but she had changed the top to a blue tank top, under a hoodie, which she pulled off when she got too hot as she moved around.

The anxiety remained with her the whole time they worked, even as she fell into easy banter with employees.

Everyone worked together well, and her nerves didn't stop her from having a moment of pride that they had fostered a healthy work environment. Though they could not control some people not loving each other, for the most part, everyone got along, and that was enough. And complaints about work had remained to a minimum as they reached their fourth year of being open.

She was helping stock the bar when there was a noise from the door, which Victoria went over to deal with, though Sophia's heart immediately jumped to her throat. She'd been extra jumpy since brunch with her sisters. Nothing she did helped. Victoria was back quickly and said someone was asking if the club was open.

Obviously not a regular, or someone who paid attention, because they had a sign with their hours right on the front doors. But all the same, Sophia swallowed. There was no need to be anxious, for her mouth to become dry as sand, but she was. Grey Constantine was making her jumpy. Damn the man. Coming into her life and discombobulating everything.

"Soph, are you alright?" Victoria asked as she approached Sophia after she finished decorating the stage. Victoria looked relaxed in red sweatpants and a long-sleeve shirt.

"I'm fine," Sophia said as she put the last bottle on the wall in the downstairs bar. "Why do you ask?"

"You're not being yourself." Victoria crossed her arms.

Sophia fidgeted a little. She didn't want to talk about this right now, but Victoria grabbed her hand and led her to the office. She closed the door and stood right against it, facing Sophia.

"Spill it," Victoria said without preamble as laughter rose from somewhere in the club, where music was playing as everyone worked.

Sophia looked at her purse, sitting on the desk, where Grey's amulet lay at the bottom. She'd decided that wearing his jewelry was too weird. But now, she wondered about what he said about it protecting her if she needed. It was hard not to roll her eyes at her own subconscious. She didn't need protection in her own club.

"It's nothing," Sophia tried to sound like she was relaxed but she could hear the tension in her own voice.

Victoria's eyes bore into her. "Are you kidding me right now?"

"I'm so tired," Sophia whined. She was so, so tired. She could lay on the floor and sleep. Maybe cry a little too.

Victoria sighed, her posture relaxing.

"You need to take time off," she said. "Some time to refresh."

"I can't take time off, there's so much to do."

"When was the last time you took a day off?" Victoria demanded.

"I don't know," Sophia responded, a little defensively. "You haven't taken any time off."

"No, but I'm fine. You look like you're going to collapse." Victoria pushed away from the door. "You want to tell me what is actually going on?"

Sophia felt her shoulders slump in defeat. Of course, she would tell Victoria what was going on. She didn't keep secrets from her best friend in the world.

"I found a bunch of boxes that belonged to my mom," she said and recounted everything she had seen so far. "It's just so strange, seeing her things. And what's even weirder is that I had distinct memories of seeing her writing into those notebooks and the leather-bound books, but they're all blank."

Victoria stood frozen while she processed what Sophia told her.

"My mom had books like that too, I think," she said. "Maybe talk to her about it?"

"Maybe I should." Sophia sighed deeply, the exhaustion settling in, bone-deep and achy. "But meanwhile, we have work to do. I don't have time for this right now. I promise I'll tell you everything when I'm sure I won't have a mental breakdown."

"If you say so," Victoria said as she opened the door. "I'm not done talking about taking time off."

Thankfully, they were busy enough that Victoria didn't mention it again, and after everything was done, Sophia bid goodbye to everyone as she closed up the club. It was dark out by the time everyone trickled out one by one, but Sophia still lingered behind for a bit longer. A habit she'd picked up, to make sure everyone was safe, especially dancers. There had been a few incidents with handsy customers in the past, and she took those seriously. They had good security, but you never knew who would come back to demand inappropriate things from performers, or do worse.

Sophia turned off every light on her way out, grabbed her purse, and caught the tail of Victoria's white sedan as she turned onto the road. The heavy black door slammed closed behind her. She turned and locked it, all alarms set inside, and headed toward her car. It was misting, and Sophia shivered with cold.

"I'd like a word with you, miss."

Sophia stopped and looked back. She turned to face a tall man with a reddish, patchy beard. He had dark shadows under his eyes and angry red splotches all over the exposed skin of his face, neck, and hands.

He moved forward, and she instantly took a step back. It was automatic, without a thought behind it other than that she wanted to get the hell away.

"I just need to talk to you," he said.

"I'm not interested," she said, but her heart leaped as he came closer. "Stay away," she snapped, holding her keys between her fingers, her thumb frantically searching for the small trigger for the pepper spray on the keychain.

"You know Grey Constantine," the man said, and her eyes snapped up to his. There was a whirring in her ears, like a laptop fan. "I just want to know what he wants with you."

"I said stay away," she stammered, her eyes becoming hot, and entire body trembling uncontrollably.

The man walked closer, but Sophia took another quick step back and a look toward her car, only paces away. Her hair, which was up, was getting matted from the fine rain, and she her entire body shivered. Whether that was in fear or cold, she couldn't tell. Her fingers continued searching for the tiny bottle, surreptitiously hidden in the keys, as the man's pace quickened.

"All I want to know is what Grey Constantine was doing here," the man continued, his voice rushed, and she heard an accent, though it was faint. "Why was he here? Is it because you can help me? I can sense it in you."

"Stay away!" She screamed, startled when he reached for her arm. Instinctively, she pulled away, collided with the side of her car, and her breath sobbed out of her as her thumb found the small trigger, and she pressed it, spraying him. He screamed but didn't let go on her arm. Instead, he shook her hard against the car and she found herself on the floor, dazed. Her keys fell out of her hand and slid away. Her eyes filled with furious and terrified tears. Of course she'd drop her stupid keys. She clawed at the man's arm, drew blood, and he yelped. He swore and pushed her hard. When she hit the ground, her breath swooshed out of her, and she had no idea which way was up for a few interminable seconds.

She thought of the crystal inside her purse, the one Grey had given her, wanted to kick herself that she hadn't worn it like he'd told her to. She managed to get on her feet, threw a kick and connected with something fleshy. The man gasped, and she dove to her purse, sticking her hand into the pocket. Her phone immediately went off, ringing incessantly.

All at once, everything went fast and slow, and just as bony hands grabbed her again, something happened that she couldn't explain.

There was a shout and a bright light exploded in the night, making it almost seem like daylight for one split second. Then, Grey Constantine himself was beside her, helping her to her feet.

"Hold on to me," he murmured in that deep voice of his, and she did, right before the world spun.

It was the weirdest sensation. Something came over her body, a lightness she had never felt before. Her body was weightless, pressed against Grey. There was no sound; everything was eerily quiet after that, except for a tinkling of piano keys. Or perhaps she had imagined it, as she surely imagined the fact that she was no longer in the parking lot of her club.

She stumbled into the strange living room, and his hands gripped her arms to stop her from falling. It was semi-dark, only a lamp on a small side table giving light.

"Are you hurt?" Grey asked her urgently as she tried in vain to make sense of what just happened. Her grip was so tight around the strap of her purse, her fingers hurt. A blankness overtook her, everything going fuzzy, and she looked up at him as an overhead light came on. His hair was pulled back and the little stone glinting on his nostril was clear this time.

"Am I hurt?" she said, not recognizing her own voice. Why did the words themselves not make any sense? She didn't feel anything, but her entire body was shaking violently. "I could throw up."

"Bathroom? Bucket?"

"I need to sit down," she said instead. He led her to a sofa in a rich shade of blue. It was soft under her, and she allowed herself to sink into the cushions as her head righted itself. He crouched in front of her, a glass of water suddenly in his hand.

"When?" She looked down at the clear water inside the glass. "How did you..."

"Drink," he insisted, and placed the glass in her hands.

She drank. The coolness of the water was a welcome sensation against her burning throat. She downed the entire glass in one long gulp, not stopping for a breath.

He took the glass when she finished, even before she offered it back

"How did you do that?" she asked him and met his dark gaze. He didn't answer right away. As if he was trying to figure out what he could say, and anger boiled inside her.

"Why did three men just attack me outside of my club, Grey?" she said, every word becoming louder than the last. "They asked why you were interested in me, and I need you to tell me what in the fuck you're into."

Now, she felt hysterical, wanted to rage, and scream into the void. But he looked troubled, a line between his brows, as if he had been frowning all day. Or all his life, perhaps.

"You're bleeding," he said, pointing to her shoulder. The burn came as soon as she looked down at the wound, and in other places where she had hit the ground. She would bruise, of course. She bruised like a mushroom.

"How did you know?" How did you come to me and how did you get there? Were you close? Did you see it happen?" But something in her answered that question, even though it didn't make sense. No, he hadn't been close. She couldn't explain it, and she wouldn't even try to.

He looked up at her from his crouching position.

"The amulet," he said.

She blinked at him and waited for him to explain, but his eyes flickered to her purse, and when she looked, she gasped. There was a faint light coming from inside. She reached inside, and with two fingers, picked out the amulet and dangled it between the two of them. It was, indeed, glowing.

Sophia didn't think she had ever been that close to fainting in her entire life. Thank God she was sitting.

"This?" she inquired numbly. "What the hell is this thing?" She held it out away from her body, as if it was a snake ready to strike. And maybe it was. There was no way of knowing for sure.

"I told you it would protect you," he simply said, as if that explained everything away.

The sudden rise of nausea made her pause. Oh, she was going to throw up on him. This was it. The most humiliating moment of her life.

"How?" she gasped, but she knew. None of this had been a coincidence, not today, and not when he showed up at the club that first night.

"Sophia," he said, his voice calm. His hands were in front of him in a slightly defensive gesture, as if he was trying to appease her. Like she was a wild animal. Or maybe it was to let her know he wasn't going to touch her, which was more likely. Something about it made her want to commit violence against this man. Her eyes were gritty and dry as she nodded instead.

"Tell me what happened," he asked. She noticed he was wearing all black. Was that all he wore?

"I already did," she snapped. "What the hell happened?"

"I don't know if I can explain that yet, but I will."

She searched his face for the lie, for something that told her how much shit he was trying to pull on her, but got nothing. No shifty glances and no blushing. Either he was a great liar, or he was being honest. Annoying.

"You show up in my life out of nowhere," she said, her voice far too steady, given how shaky she felt all over. "You are the son of the man my mom was having an affair with, and you came to my club being all weird and cryptic. And now strange men are showing up at my club, asking about you and me."

She didn't know Grey Constantine. He could be a serial killer, or a drug lord, or something that would only bring her trouble. It already was.

But her breath began to settle, and the burning that had plagued her shoulder numbed, along with the rest. She looked at the glass he still had in his hand, wanted to ask if he had put something in it, but decided she did not want to know. She wanted to go home.

"Is there someone I can call for you?" Their gazes met. "I would offer for you to stay here, but I don't think that's what you need at the moment."

"You don't know me," she snapped. "You don't get to tell me what I need when you won't answer my goddamned questions."

"I know." His voice was so calm, so lacking in defensiveness or aggression, that she deflated. She wanted to burst out crying. Because she felt the tears starting to well, she reached into her purse for her phone. Her sisters and Victoria would come get her, no questions asked. She chose the latter. Victoria would wait to ask questions, as long as she knew that Sophia was okay. Julia, on the other hand, would not, and Sophia didn't want to have to explain to her why she was in Grey Constantine's company.

He stood. "I'm going to go get a first aid kit and take care of your cuts, okay?"

She nodded without looking up at him.

When he was gone, she allowed herself to look at the place. The sitting room was not large by any means, and it had many windows looking out into the night. It was tastefully decorated. Simple, but cohesive, in a charming sort of way. The sapphire sofa where she sat was under a set of windows, and the chairs across from it were both emerald green. There was one bright yellow pillow on one, but the other had a book opened upside down. She couldn't see the title, but it had a colorful cover.

She could see a dining table just off the sitting room, and even parts of the kitchen, but she couldn't even muster energy to snoop. That's how she knew she was in shock.

She remembered her phone in her hand and pulled up her conversation with Victoria.

> SOPHIA: I CAN'T EXPLAIN ANYTHING RIGHT
> NOW, BUT CAN YOU COME GET ME?

She shared a pin with her location. Victoria's answer came only seconds later.

> VICTORIA: WE WILL BE THERE IN FORTY
> MINUTES, ACCORDING TO THE MAP.

Sophia had expected nothing less because that was the kind of friend Victoria was. No questions asked, no excuses.

Grey returned with a clear plastic box and sat on the coffee table again. She watched his fingers move, graceful and long. She pulled off her sweater to give him access to the scrapes. There was blood on the sweater, though not much. She watched him pull out a tiny clear vial from the first aid kit, and she had the thought that she had never seen a first aid kit like it before.

Instead of the typical antiseptics, it was filled with little crystal bottles, some gauze, cotton, and little pots with screw-on lids and powders within them. All labels were written in neat block handwriting.

She wondered if it was his handwriting.

Her heart pounded as he gently cleaned the shoulder. She felt no sting, no dull pain. Nothing.

Maybe it was the shock.

The smells of the balms and liquids were familiar and comforting somehow, and her eyes filled before she pushed it all down. She was not going to cry in front of this perfect stranger.

"What are these?" Her voice was thick. She knew the answer deep down, but she didn't want to dig in there. Not right now.

"Just home remedies," he said simply and quietly.

Right. No doubt that it was much more complicated than his words suggested.

"I'm going to make this right," he added as he secured a bandage on the scrape.

"How?" As she asked the question, it struck her that she wasn't sure she wanted to know the answer.

"By protecting you," he murmured, still cleaning the scrape.

"I sprayed him with pepper spray," she told him because he needed him to know that she was no damsel in distress, even though he had come to her rescue, for which she was grateful, even if it didn't look like she was. But she knew how it sounded, like she was a little girl seeking approval. She could have kicked herself.

"Good," he simply replied.

"Do they want to hurt you?"

"I doubt it," he said but nothing more. His lips pressed together rather tightly. It was when she noticed how pale he looked, how there were lines of worry, or perhaps something else, in his face.

"Victoria will be here soon," she told him.

He closed the lid to the kit when he was done, but didn't move away.

"I'm sorry this happened."

She had no words for him, so she only nodded once. Maybe it sucked to blame him entirely, but how could she not? He showed up at her club with his cryptic messages and suddenly she was being attacked by people asking about him. She had no one else to blame.

He made her tea as she waited for Victoria, who must have been speeding like a hellion because she showed up only thirty minutes later. Victoria's knocks were loud and insistent. Sophia got on her feet when she heard them, following Grey when he opened the door. Victoria immediately crossed the threshold and hugged Sophia tightly, her eyes trained on Grey with suspicion.

"I trust you didn't hurt my friend, because if you did, I hope you know I would scalp you alive," Victoria told Grey, never moving her eyes off his. She obviously meant every word.

"I see the truth in your words," Grey said.

"I'm okay," Sophia said, pulling back to see Thomas right outside the door. He was wearing nothing more than a t-shirt and gray pajama pants. His almond-shaped eyes were dark and eyeing Grey neutrally, black hair mussed, sticking up at odd angles.

"Grey didn't do anything," she told them, though the rest she'd have to explain when she understood it, if the day ever came. "He helped me tonight, I fact."

"Helped how?" Thomas asked.

"I'll explain on the way home," Sophia told him, squeezing his arm lightly. To Grey, she said, "I will see you around."

"I'll call you as soon as I know anything."

She followed Thomas and Victoria to the car and got in the back seat, which Victoria also got into.

"Sophia Evelyn Candela Montgomery, what the hell is going on?" Victoria immediately shouted when they were on their way. "You text me that cryptic, bullshit text and nearly give me a heart attack. I just left you at the club—"

"I know, but I couldn't tell you all of it before seeing you, or you'd be having a panic attack before you could even get in the car."

"She nearly had a panic attack anyway, Soph," Thomas said as he got onto the main road, toward the freeway.

Victoria huffed out a breath. "Explain it now," she said. "What happened?"

Sophia nodded and took a shaky breath.

"I was attacked outside the club as I was leaving tonight."

Both Victoria and Thomas went into a flurry of questions, and Sophia told them both what happened as they drove down the dark, wet freeway. Except for the part where Grey showed up and she was suddenly in his house without explanation or logic.

"We have to call the cops," Victoria said when Sophia was done. "Sophia, this is not a joke. What if he comes back? You could have been seriously hurt."

"I know and I will call them. Promise."

"And how is Grey involved in this?" Thomas asked, looking at her through the rearview mirror.

Sophia hesitated, weary of bringing danger to their doorstep the way it came to hers.

"He was around."

Victoria turned in her seat. "He was just there? Why?"

Her stomach seized. "Can we talk about all this another time? When I'm not freaking out."

Victoria's gaze lingered, and Sophia suspected her sharp friend knew she was deflecting. This is what Grey Constantine had done, coming into her life.

She would kill him.

Thomas pulled up to the house he shared with Victoria as she was still pestering Sophia with questions about everything that had happened.

The house was pretty, painted a dark gray with white accents and a cheerful orange door. The small front porch had two rocking chairs, which was so cute, Sophia wanted to cry. She really didn't want a relationship, but seeing those rocking chairs made a yearning awaken that she wasn't prepared for. She was fine on her own. Had been fine for so long, since her terrible last relationship. It had to be the shock.

Another voice, one that sounded terribly like her mother's, told her that wanting the closeness of a partner had nothing to do with being an independent woman. Both could be true at once, right?

Thomas pulled into the garage and they all got out.

"You could have dropped me off at home," she said, but didn't mean it. "Thank you for picking me up, though."

"I'm not dropping you off at home after all this," Thomas said as he opened the door to the house. He stepped aside and Victoria walked in first, babbling about food. When Sophia went to step through, Thomas pulled her in for a hug. It was tight and warm, and she felt loved and protected. She pressed her ear to his chest, her arms around his narrow waist.

"I love you," he said softly. "I'm glad you're safe."

"I love you too," she said, sniffled, then had to fight back the tears, so she held on to him even tighter and swallowed them.

"Are you hungry?" Victoria asked gently. "We made Thomas's family's special kimchi recipe and it's ready."

"I would love some kimchi," she squealed pathetically, then immediately dissolved into tears. "I'm sorry, I'm a mess."

"You're allowed to be a mess," Thomas said. "Let's get you some food. Mom always says food can fix anything. The woman is pretty much never wrong.

Thomas led her to the counter, where she sat on a barstool. Their kitchen was pretty, bright with its white and blue backsplash and equally white cabinets. And it was, as always, meticulously clean without much clutter.

Thomas busied himself getting the rice while Victoria pulled out three shallow bowls.

They were so in sync, knowing every movement the other was making. It was like they were dancing, throwing each other little looks and sweet smiles, and Sophia wanted to cry even more. She could say she didn't want that all day, and yet in that moment, when things were weird and upside down, she wished she did. Tears leaked without any semblance of control as she was handed chopsticks.

It was the shock, she told herself. It wasn't about them being cute at all.

She hadn't had that with Aric, her former fiancé and most disastrous relations she had ever had. In the four years they were together, she had never felt this easy sort of connection, where no words were needed. Thomas and Victoria were so aware of each other, it made Sophia ache for something like that. It made her wish it so hard and deeply.

Victoria set a bowl in front of her.

"Eat," she said. "You've been through a lot tonight."

So they ate together at the counter, and when they were done, Thomas left them to talk.

"You want to tell me how tall, mysterious, and gorgeous is related to this?"

Sophia fought against the spike in anxiety the question brought her.

"I told you," she said, pushing rice around her bowl. "He helped me."

"And you ended up at his house twenty minutes away from the club, opposite your house."

Sophia shrugged, deeply aware of what a bad liar she was, unable to open her mouth to say more.

"Have you gotten closer to him than you've told me?" Victoria asked.

"What? No," Sophia said. "You would be the first to know if something like that happened, you know that."

"I do, but I'm so confused."

"Don't worry, so am I," Sophia admitted before Victoria suggested going to bed.

Installed in the guest room, wearing Victoria's shorts and tank top, which were too tight on her, Sophia lay under the covers. She was trying to shut her brain down, no matter how many different techniques she tried.

She was almost relieved when her phone buzzed on the nightstand.

GREY: I'M HAVING EVERYTHING TAKEN
CARE OF.

Not knowing what that meant didn't make her want to ask more questions he wouldn't answer, so she set the phone upside down on the table, and turned on her side the other way. But she would be remiss to not admit that his words gave her a weird level of comfort that she clung to.

Her eyes closed, now heavy, thankfully. An image filled her head, of pretty eyes looking into hers as she whispered secrets she couldn't recall. There was a smattering of freckles on his little nose, and she itched to touch them as if they were little constellations.

She brought her hand to her chest, feeling the sputtering of her heart and the way the warmth of the memory crept up and filled her closed eyelids. She lay on her back, opening her eyes, and the tears finally streamed down her temples and into her hair. She couldn't remember anyone who looked like that from her childhood, but something about it felt so right and so familiar and so confusing. She shook in the dark, let the tears soak her hair. And when she had nothing left, she finally fell asleep.

In the wee hours of the morning, as everyone slumbered, a set of keys appeared on the nightstand with a faint flash of light.

8

Sophia woke up to an insulated mug on the nightstand. She picked it up and took off the lid to smell the coffee, closed her eyes in pure bliss before she took a sip. There was nothing better than that first sip at the beginning of the day. Coffee in bed? Heaven.

Looking for the time, she picked up her phone and found she had dozens of texts from her sisters and Victoria, and three missed calls from her father. And it was eleven in the morning. She paused. When was the last time she'd slept that late?

She opened her text messages from Victoria and Thomas, sent in a group they had together.

> VICTORIA: I DIDN'T WANT TO WAKE YOU, BUT THERE'S OATMEAL IN THE SMALL RED POT ON THE STOVE. FRUIT IN THE FRIDGE. BUT YOU ALREADY KNOW THAT.

> THOMAS: THE OATMEAL IS SUPERB, IF I SAY SO MYSELF.

> VICTORIA: ALSO, DO NOT COME TO WORK, UNLESS IT'S TO CALL THE AUTHORITIES AND LOOK AT THE VIDEOS FROM THE SECURITY CAMERAS.

Sophia had no intention of working that day, anyway. Next, she opened a message from Grey, her heart immediately racing.

> GREY: I HAVE TAKEN STEPS TO PROTECT YOUR
> CLUB. I HOPE YOU AT LEAST GOT SOME SLEEP.

Then another, about two hours after the first.

> GREY: I HAVE A LEAD ON THE MEN WHO
> ATTACKED YOU. CAN YOU COME TO MY HOUSE
> TODAY?

He added his address underneath.

Sophia knew, even before she gave it much more consideration, that she would go see him. She lingered in bed for a while, before she had to get out of bed to take care of things. The previous night felt so far away in the light of day. Strange things happened to her from time to time, dreams that sometimes felt like more than just dreams. An interaction with a stranger that made her feel weird, or an amulet that called a man who whirled her away in seconds...

The amulet was somewhere in her purse, waiting for her to slip it on, and she would do that before she left. Just in case. She typed a quick message to Grey, ignoring the rest of the messages coming in.

> SOPHIA: I CAN BE THERE IN AN HOUR.

She sent it and got up to get dressed in yesterday's clothes, cleaned herself up as much as she could, and picked up her purse before she realized she didn't drive here.

That's when she saw the keys on the nightstand.

"How in the world?" she murmured.

Had Victoria and Thomas gotten them for her? But how? And when? They hadn't gone out after they'd all arrived the previous night. And they didn't say anything on the texts.

What was she thinking? She knew the answer to that. Grey. Why was he involved in everything now? It was like frequency illusion, but worse.

She headed out, keys in hand, to find her car parked at the very front of the house. There were a few other cars parked on the road, but most were on driveways. It was heavily clouded as she got in behind the wheel, finding everything exactly as she had left it, down to the hair tie she kept around the shifter.

She took her time, sipped the coffee as she turned the ignition on. Once the car was purring, she set the heat to blasting, as she had left her sweater at his house the previous night.

When she got to his house, she parked on the road and admired her surroundings. There were two other houses on the dead-end road, all stately on the hillside, overlooking the water.

The driveway to the house was on a hill, and the front door was at the top of the winding path and stair combination. She'd walked down this path the previous night, she recalled, though she had seen nothing. And not just because she had been in shock. Trees and bushes lined the path, and other plants on the small side yard that were losing their battle with the season.

Hugging herself against the chill, Sophia got out of her car and wished she'd looked through Victoria's stuff for a sweater. She walked through a small canopy of trees that made her feel like she was walking in a well-manicured forest, if for only a moment. What was it like in the summer when everything was vibrant and loud? Right now, the music was faint, so much that she could barely hear it.

At the very end of the driveway, a set of stairs led to a covered porch, and on it was a lovely mahogany door. On her right, a porch opened into a wide circular area overlooking the Pacific in the distance. There was a sofa and a small table, and she imagined that would be a lovely place to sit and watch a storm.

She was reaching for the doorbell when the door opened, and one of the most beautiful men she had ever seen smiled down at her. He was dressed in dark slacks and a light button-up, feet bare. His skin was dark and smooth, his black hair sleeked back, and a beard that was groomed perfectly.

"I'm guessing you're Sophia," he said, his accented voice soft and smooth.

"I am," she said, stepping into the entryway when he moved aside, offering her hand. "And you are?"

"Lucas," he said, gripping her hand briefly and firmly. "I work with Grey."

He led her through an arch in the entryway, which opened to last night's sitting room with a big window overlooking the street below, where her car was parked. It was shocking how much she had forgotten from the previous night. Perhaps it was that she hadn't noticed in her panic.

Grey was a no-fuss kind of person, she noted. His furniture was cozy and colorful, and there were plants everywhere.

"What kind of work do you do with Grey?" she asked Lucas as Grey came down a staircase, dressed in blue jeans and a black sweater, his hair pulled back. He was also barefoot.

"Thank you for coming," Grey said as Lucas stepped away quietly, and disappeared through another door.

"You said you have a lead, and I want to know what that is." And maybe she would start getting actual answers.

He nodded as he stood in front of her. He smelled like soap.

"Well, then follow me to my office," he said and led her the way she had come in, to a room just to the right of the entryway. There was a sliding glass door to the balcony, which was bigger than she had seen when she'd arrived. The view was lovely, and she imagined if she lived in this house, she would spend most of her time out in the balcony or in this room. The office was pretty bare, but for a sleek desk with buttons on the side, and a computer on top. Two bookcases on the other side of the room held tomes with nothing on the spines, which instantly intrigued her.

Lucas was sitting in front of the computer, and he pulled up a video player, where she saw herself be grabbed by last night's man. There was no sound, but the video was clear enough to see everything. She watched herself spray the man, then be thrown to the ground as she reached for her bag. Lucas stopped the video then. Sophia wanted to see how Grey had shown up, though she knew.

"How did you get this?" she asked to neither in particular.

Lucas sat back on the office chair, throwing Grey a brief look.

"I have friends in important places," Grey said, then pointed at the man she'd sprayed. "See this man? I know him from a community I... volunteer with."

The pause wasn't lost on her and she felt her insides shiver, wondering what in the world this man was into.

"Well, can you help me locate him?" she said instead.

"We can try." Grey and Lucas looked at each other again, so briefly, she almost missed it.

"You're going to have to stop that," she told them, and they both looked at her. "What's with the secret looks?"

They didn't answer her, and she found herself staring from one to the other.

"This is ridiculous," she muttered, wanting to be anywhere but there if they weren't going to tell her anything anyway. She wasn't fond of wasting her time.

"I know it's all confusing and I want to tell you everything," Grey said, but Sophia certainly didn't believe a word he said. "I just have to be careful."

"Oh, now you want to be careful," she demanded. "Seems to me like you've been pretty reckless."

Lucas lifted his brows and cringed. "She's got a valid point."

Grey threw him a dirty look.

Something about their interaction both angered and fascinated her. Assholes.

"I honestly don't understand why you called me here if you're not going to tell me shit," she said acidly. "Can I at least get my sweater back?"

Grey blinked, as if he had just noticed that she was only wearing a tank top.

"Of course," he said so politely she wanted to smack him. She followed him to the kitchen, through a couple of archways in the living and dining rooms. The counters were light and shiny, and her sweater sat on it, folded neatly, and clean. She grabbed it, refusing to be impressed by how clean and organized his house was. Not that she had expected him to be a slob, but there had to be something wrong with him. The way he made her antsy was about more than their weird, fucked up, shared history. It had something to do with the nose ring and the hair, she was sure. And the body.

When the scent on the sweater hit her, she fought every urge to bury her nose into it and sniff it like a lunatic. It smelled like spring. Like him.

"Thank you." She avoided his gaze.

"You're welcome." He stuck his hands into his pockets, as if he was feeling awkward, which she thought was a little cute. But just a little.

"How did you get my car to Victoria's?" She realized what she had just said, so she added, "And on that note, how did you know where Victoria lives?"

"Lucas helped me," he said, a little chagrined.

"Lucas seems to help you do a lot of things."

"He's my right-hand man," he explained, but offered nothing else.

"And since you trust him, I should, too," she said tightly.

She expected a smirk of annoyance, but didn't get that at all. He pressed his lips together for a moment.

"You don't have to worry about your safety with us," he said quietly.

"Isn't that what dangerous people usually say?"

"Are you around a lot of dangerous people?" he countered, and her lips tugged, but she gritted her teeth to stop herself from smiling.

"Not typically," she said, looking into his pretty face, wondering what it was about him. "If we're done here, I should probably go."

He inclined his head. "Did you get to rest?"

Her stomach warmed, and something in her purred. She really needed to get a hold of herself around this man. The bare minimum shouldn't be something she celebrated on a virtual stranger. Especially one who had put her in the position he had.

She found she had to swallow tightly before she could answer him.

"I did." She paused and her eyes slid up to his. God, he was pretty. "I'm a little freaked out, you know."

His lips pressed into a line. "I know, I'm sorry."

He looked it, certainly. Was he really always this soft-spoken and agreeable or was it an act? And how much like his father was he? Was it this kind of demeanor that had gotten her mom entangled with the other man? Sophia wanted to believe that Grey was simply that nice, but she didn't really have any way of knowing that, unless she spent more time with him.

She was being ridiculous. Someone cleared their throat, and she wasn't sure if it was him or her, but she couldn't stop basking in the way he smelled, like soap and spring mornings. Her sweater now smelled like that.

"I'm going to make it right," he said, his tone reassuring.

"You say that," she replied, watching his face, but his expression remained impassive. She wanted to know what he was thinking, if it annoyed him that he had to help her of all people. "Doesn't it bother you that it's me?"

Even asking the question made her inside shiver, the overachiever in her wanting to assure him that she was perfectly capable of taking care of herself. That she was only letting him because he had been the one to put her in this position.

"This has nothing to do with our parents," he said, his eyes darkening, trapping her within them. "I may have feelings about all of this—" he swiveled his hand back and forth between the two of them. "—but I would never turn my back on someone who needed my help."

It hit her how easily she believed what he said. How she just had to look into his brown eyes to know he was speaking truth. That, or she was utterly delirious.

She reached for the amulet, raised it to eye level.

"Is this how you'll protect me?" she asked him as the crystal spun gently.

"That won't work forever." He touched the pointed bottom of the crystal with a long finger.

She stared at him. "You care to explain why? Given how I'm new at all this."

"They need to be recharged."

She blinked, sure he had to be kidding.

"You mean like a battery?" She deadpanned, the sudden urge to laugh so overwhelming, her lip trembled.

"Kind of." His lip twitched, as if picking up on her energy. "You can put it up by a window and let the full moon recharge it."

A giggle burst out of her lips, and hastily, she pressed her hand to her mouth.

"I seriously can't tell if you're joking or not." Her throat became hot and her eyes watered with the effort. "What am I saying? Of course you're not joking." What did a person believe? That Grey Constantine was a witch and he did magic? Or that she was maybe in a coma and this was all in her head.

"I know how it sounds, but since I was reckless and brought people to you that could harm you, I'm going to need you to trust me."

Trust him? Her first instinct was to scoff at the mere consideration. But he looked at her with those warm dark eyes, and something in her reached toward him. It was annoying, the magnetism he carried around like it was nothing. How he didn't have to say much to get her to forget that he was the son of the man who'd stolen her mom away. Finally, what made her laughter fall away was the feeling that came every time she thought of her mother. Something caught between annoyance and exhaustion.

"You're going to have to do better than that to earn my trust," she said, sounding like she had something caught in her throat. Or maybe it just felt that way.

The energy shifted instantly. He crossed his arms across his broad chest, as if he was bracing himself.

"It's obvious to me that something bigger than I could ever imagine is going on. I'm hesitant to be a part of it because, let me tell you, not impressed, so far."

"I just need some time." His tone didn't change much, and her exhaustion won.

She took a deep breath and held it for a few moments. She didn't think she had the capacity to argue, so she said, "Fine."

He at least had the grace to look chagrined.

"I'd like to give you some things," he said and walked off to what she assumed was a pantry.

She followed. "You're giving me snacks for the road?" she said and heard him chuckle from inside the pantry.

His kitchen was interesting. Clean counters, though not entirely free of clutter. He had a large black cauldron by the stove and herbs hanging from the ceiling, all dry. A flash of memory made her heart jump. She remembered her mom's attic, filled with herbs like these. He had colorful, opaque jars on the counters, as well as bundles of dried herbs and little bottles in the sink. And a black label maker, which made her want to smile because it felt so normal.

She heard him rummaging in the pantry, so she busied herself looking at his cookbooks, thought they were amusing. Not like any cookbooks she had ever seen. Curious, she walked around the kitchen, and from the corner of her eyes, a tome caught her attention from the small bar just off the kitchen. Snooping wasn't polite, she told herself, but found herself checking to see if Grey was still in the pantry, and crossed the space toward the bar.

It was large, its brown leather cover old and worn and she touched its softness, feeling the embossed designs, curled lines that spread on the entire surface, like vines. Her heart was somewhere in her throat now, a rushing in her ears, and she knew deep inside that if she opened this, she would see her mother's handwriting.

She felt it so deeply, she couldn't have been wrong. Just as she had been convinced that the books she'd found in her mom's stuff would be full of interesting notes. Maybe a secret or two. Answers to so many questions Sophia had for so long.

But no, this was different. This time, she *knew* it. Sophia had seen her mom write into this very book. Her fingers shook as she slowly opened the lid, and she had flipped several pages before the adrenaline whooshed out of her, leaving her suddenly drained and shakier than before.

The pages were completely blank.

She was breathing hard as she dropped the lid and it plopped onto the pages. Intense disappointment ran through her. It made her want to cry, so she pressed her hands to her eyes.

"It doesn't make sense," she whispered, breathless.

She swallowed a knot in her throat. Were there really coincidences in life, or did things happen through fate? Sophia had never believed in coincidences. Grey Constantine, the son of her mom's lover, did not show up in her club by coincidence. And Sophia hadn't been attacked by it either.

"Find something interesting?"

She turned too fast. The blood rushed out of her head, leaving her momentarily blind with dizziness, panic in her chest. She braced her hand against the smooth surface of the bar top and faced Grey.

"I didn't mean to snoop." Her voice was pathetically weak. She chalked it up to her wildly beating heart.

"Snooping would imply seeing something you shouldn't," he said. There was a black velvet pouch in his hand.

Sophia met his eyes, confused at his words. She wanted to say something else, maybe something witty or funny, but she felt drained. Throughout everything she had seen—or rather not seen—she hadn't realized how much she wanted to see her mom's handwriting on them. Something that was so personal to those departed, that held so much of who they were.

But that made no sense. Grey wouldn't have something written by her mom in his house.

She let out a shuddering breath.

"You alright?" he asked, coming even closer.

"Yeah." But she didn't elaborate. She couldn't let this sense of familiarity cloud the fact that she did not know this man. They were just two people who had been screwed over by each other's parent. "I should go home."

He nodded and handed her the pouch. Pulling on the drawstring, she peeked inside. It seemed to all be colorful jewelry.

"What's this?" She pulled one out. It was long, the string made of a soft material, and the tiny little jewels strung through it were bright and colorful. It almost looked like a bracelet.

"Hang them in your house, at points of entry," he explained. "It will protect your house from anyone entering without your permission."

She looked at the crystals, then up at him. Sure.

"So no one can come inside unless I let them." The words tasted strange. "Like vampires."

The corners of his eyes crinkled slightly, as if her words were amusing to him. "Somewhat like it, now that I think of it," he said. "If you don't want someone in your house, you can revoke permission and they won't be able to step inside."

"I need this for my club." She dropped the amulet into the bag. It would save her bouncers a lot of time and energy.

He smiled and held her gaze. His eyes became more and more intense as she looked into them, but she couldn't look away. She had missed it before, but his eyes were a pure velvety brown. No flecks of other colors in them.

They were like the earth itself. It was mesmerizing.

"There are a few bottles in there," he said, and she jumped at the chance of being able to look away.

"What are they for?" she asked as she picked one tiny vial and held it up. It had a clear liquid, and was long and thin as her index finger.

"If you ever get attacked again, use one."

"How?" She asked, afraid to hear the answer. But then again, everything seemed discombobulated and strange now. Anything he said could no longer surprise her.

"Throw it on the ground and it will... help you get away." He cleared his throat.

"Cut the crap," she snapped, sick and tired of the cryptic sentences and messages. "What does it do?"

He took what seemed to be an encouraging breath.

"They are potions."

"Like poison?"

"More like a tiny explosion in a bottle."

She raised a brow, trying to look skeptical, but held the little vial away from her anyway.

"It won't just explode," he said, reading her expression. He looked like he was trying not to laugh, which irked her even more. Still, when she put the potion back into the pouch, she did so gently.

"Just carry them on you and use only if you need it."

"I feel like I'm having a fever dream. Nothing like this had ever happened to me before," she mumbled, then swallowed the lie. Strange things happened to her all the time. She heard music in plants, for heaven's sake. She saw the music when she sang. "I'm going to ask one more time."

After a long pause, he assented.

"Why did you come to my club?"

He was quiet for a moment, looking out the window, and she thought he might not respond.

"I felt drawn to your club," he said.

"By what?"

As he briefly pressed his lips together, Sophia wondered where his friend went? Suddenly, she wanted nothing more than to get the hell out of there.

"You," he breathed.

It was then that she saw it. How uncomfortable he was. How much he hated it was her on the other side of whatever had drawn him to her club. That this was also weird for him, as cool and collected as he wanted to come across.

"And why is it me?" Her arms crossed. The pouch dangled from her fingers. "How much of a coincidence is it that we're connected the way we are?"

When his eyes found hers again, her stomach dropped and became liquid. There were storms in there. She'd hit a nerve.

"Look, I don't get it either." He tucked an errant curl behind his ear. "I'm just..."

She waited, but he said nothing else.

"What is it you want from me?" Her brows knitted, and so did his.

"Believe me, if it was anyone else, I'd be much happier about it."

Now she was getting somewhere. He was exasperated, cornered. Should she be this into that? He could kill her, for all she knew.

"Why?" she challenged, her heart beating fast now. She would not back down. Not now, not ever. "Because I'm the daughter of the woman you blame for your family breaking up?"

His eyes narrowed. "I wouldn't be wrong."

She felt the anger rise inside her like a tide, and squashed it down, keeping it boiling right underneath the surface.

"I'll remind you two families were involved," she hissed. "You're going to stand there and blame my mother, as if your father was an innocent angel. Newsflash, they both made shitty choices."

His eyes bore into hers, and she refused to look away, even as his face flushed. She felt warmth underneath her skin. But when he spoke, his voice was still calm, deep, and clear.

"Don't think I choose to ignore any of that." His hands went back to his pockets. "The truth is, I don't know why it's you."

"Then tell me what brought you to my club." Sophia kept her voice as calm as she could, but she could hear the desperation in it. She couldn't even care about pride at a moment like that. Refusing to look away, she took even breaths until he had to look away.

"We've never met before this." Her voice came out weak, as if something in her didn't believe that for a second. She closed her hands into fists, to keep them from shaking. "Right?"

"I'm not sure that's true, but I can't explain that part either."

Frustrated, she huffed out a breath and finally cut eye contact.

"Fine," she said, stepping away from him. Even though she heard him follow her, Sophia didn't stop, and when she was outside in the cold, she knew that if she wanted to know anything, she was going to have to find it on her own.

9

The night had stretched until, what seemed, the end of times. Sophia couldn't sleep for most of it, and when she actually slept, it wasn't for long. Finally, at four-thirty, she got out of bed and made herself the first of what would be many coffees that day. Inevitably, her eyes went to the pretty amulet Grey had given her. It hung by the front door from a thumbtack.

What could she make of them? When she'd arrived home the previous night, she'd stared at the crystals, the potions, as they lay on her dining table. She didn't want to give in and hang them up, but before she went to bed, she hung them up anyway. A person couldn't be too careful. God, she was being ridiculous.

It was ominous and dark out, heavy clouds rolling, though it was not raining yet. The forecast predicted rain almost all day.

Boxes were strewn about the room, the coffee table holding a pile of empty journals and several photo albums.

A coffee mug balanced on her knee, Sophia stared at the items on the coffee table, where her feet also rested. Her mind was blissfully blank about it, but deep down, Sophia was aware that it wouldn't last long. That she would be thinking about it nonstop until she figured all that shit out. She welcomed the numbness, which would of course not last long, if she knew herself even a little bit. But when her phone screen lit up at five, the emotions came rushing when she saw Jeanette's name on the screen.

"Jeanette?" Her voice cracked from lack of use, or because she wanted to cry, so she cleared her throat.

"Did I wake you?" Jeanette asked, her voice soft, as if she had just woken up.

"No, I've been up for a while. Is everything okay?" The sudden burst of energy rose from her feet, and coursed through her body like an electric current. No one had known her mom the way Jeanette had. They had grown up together, even went to the same college and lived together for a while. If anyone had answers for Sophia, it would be Jeanette.

"I'm not sure, actually," Jeanette said. "I woke up with you on my mind, as you were during my sleeping hours too. Maybe I should be asking that question to you."

Sophia went to answer, but the emotion made her pause. How did she talk about all of this with Jeanette without talking about things she did not want to discuss?

"Sophia?" Jeanette prompted quietly.

Sophia sighed and sank into the chair. "I guess I'm tired today." It wasn't a lie, really.

"Not sleeping well?"

"Not for the last few days, at least." She paused for a moment. "I have some questions I'd like to ask you."

"I will answer your questions," Jeanette said, "but I have questions of my own. What's going on right now?"

The sudden urge to vomit had her doubling over and taking breaths through her mouth. "What do you mean?"

"Sophia Evelyn." Jeanette's voice was gentle but firm. "Don't play games with me."

Their relationship in a nutshell. Jeanette had an uncanny ability to know when Sophia was struggling with something. Sophia, her sister, and Victoria had never been able to do anything to lie to that woman—somehow, she always knew. The thought that there was something mystical about it had occurred to Sophia, but she had always dismissed it, and whenever she'd asked, she'd never gotten a straight answer from Jeanette. Weird how it was the same with Grey.

"I've been stressed," she said. Why was she being coy about it? It wasn't like she didn't want to tell all this mess to someone who potentially understood. Or that wouldn't judge her for it, at least.

Jeanette hummed, long and low.

Shit.

"I promise I'm okay," Sophia added, to try getting ahead of what would come.

"Something about that strikes me as a lie," Jeanette said and Sophia's heart sank. "You won't take days off from work in general, but more so lately."

"I will kill Victoria for her big mouth," Sophia grumbled.

"If you won't take care of yourself, someone has to."

"I took a day off yesterday and I don't plan on going today either," Sophia protested.

Jeanette made an incredulous noise.

"I'm serious," Sophia assured her. "And I do have some things to ask you, if you'd please."

"Go ahead and ask."

"I told you about those dreams I've been having," Sophia said slowly, thinking of how she was going to ask without saying too much.

"You did. But that's not what you want to talk about."

Sophia frowned at her phone, seconds ticking by. Jeanette's voice had shifted slightly, so subtle Sophia might have missed it. But given all she'd seen in the past couple of days, that wasn't something she could ignore.

"No, I guess not," Sophia said, but nothing came from the other end. "Jeanette?"

"Sophia?" Jeanette said and her voice broke up. She was saying something else, but it was so fractured, Sophia caught no words.

"You're breaking up," Sophia said to her, sitting up. How odd.

"Can you hear me?" Jeanette asked.

"I can now." Sophia took the phone off speaker. "Anyway, I found these boxes that used to be my mom's and I wondered if you know anything about what's in them."

Static came through.

"Sophia?" Jeanette said, her voice going in and out as she kept speaking.

"Jeanette?"

Sophia looked at the phone. Full bars.

"Jeanette?" she said. "Can you hear me?"

Nothing. With a churning stomach, Sophia stood up. "I found a bunch of journals and letters, but everything is blank," she said, pacing now.

Then the call dropped.

"Are you kidding me?" She looked at the phone and dialed Jeanette's number again. It went straight to voicemail. She called again, four more times, and failed to connect. Maybe the phone had died.

That just seemed so unlike Jeanette, who, when her phone hit fifty percent, instantly found a charger.

Looking around her house, she was filled with awe at how many notebooks and albums her mom had owned. Which was why it made little sense that they all happened to be blank. Unless her mom was secretly a writer, which would explain it. Julia would certainly know all about that, since she used to like writing before going to school for business.

Sophia stopped moving and everything went dark, then light. Her mind flipped upside down, and she found herself disoriented, as if she had tried to perform a flip on a trampoline and instead fell on her head. When everything righted itself, she was left staring into space for a while, trying to recall what she had been thinking about.

Something about Julia… or Jeanette.

Forgetting the piles of letters and notebooks she'd had every intention of looking through, she went to her room and cleaned the entire thing from top to bottom, pausing briefly to make another coffee, in between loads of laundry and scrubbing the toilet. Next thing she knew, it was noon.

She had gotten sidetracked for almost seven hours, and it both unnerved her and pissed her off. Memories of that morning, talking to Jeanette, seemed so far in the past. Something wasn't right.

Making the decision to look at everything later, she put the stuff back in their boxes and stuck them into the hallway closet. Those journals obviously had nothing to teach, and she was going to have to go back to the person who had the least answers for her and beat them out of him. Grey Constantine was going to hear what she had to say.

For her own sanity.

Minutes later, she undressed and got into a warm shower, her hair in a bonnet to avoid getting it wet. Hair took too long, and though she was due for a wash, she had no time to waste on it. She had a man to go kill.

When she had dressed in jeans and a sweater, she got into her car, and straight on the road without a moment to even think about it. Otherwise, she would back out and she couldn't afford to do that when strange men were attacking her at work, and Grey Constantine could... teleport?

Lord, she thought and chewed her lip. By the time she got to Grey's and parked out front, she was shaking with nerves and anticipation. And it wasn't at all because she was fascinated by him and wanted to see him again. It wasn't because he was cute, and because he looked at her in the eyes when he talked to her. Not at all.

The trek up the ridiculous amount of stairs and incline had her thighs burning, but she didn't slow down.

By the time her fist hit the heavy door, her eyes on the doorbell she could have rung instead, she was no longer nervous. Dull pain radiated on her fist and it brought her back to the present. She felt human, like she was still a part of this world, instead of the weird in-between she had been in where nothing made any sense, and where she was fuzzy around the edges.

He came to the door wearing a simple black t-shirt and a pair of gray sweatpants. That, combined with the tattoo that peaked from his bicep made it difficult to stop herself from panting. A tentacle? She shook her head. His hair was loose and damp around his shoulders, and he was barefoot. Thinking about him in the shower made something flutter in her stomach and she had to swallow twice before she could look him in the eye.

How was this a real person?

He blinked down at her, obviously surprised to see her, if his arched brows were anything to go by.

"I didn't think I'd see you again so soon."

She took a breath to steady herself, though she felt anything but steady. She was shaking, and not just from the cold, as she again had not worn a coat, like an idiot. Her stomach was a knot of nerves, her hands unsteady beside her. She planted her feet.

"I need you to tell me everything. Right now."

∘ ∘ ∘

Grey had been sitting at the piano when he heard her knock, trying to finish a composition for a video game, and unable to come up with anything good to accompany what he already had. He had been running scales over and over, annoying himself, so when her knock came, it was a relief to go answer it.

Now, she Sophia was before him, and he struggled to say anything. Truth was, he wanted to tell her everything, but if she wasn't aware that her mother had most likely been a witch, who was he to let her know? She seemed already be resistant to the idea of magic. And yet, said magic had brought him to her.

As he opened his mouth to answer her, her small hand went up, unsteady between them, to stop him. She looked like a person on the edge, and weary to make it worse when he'd caused it in the first place, he snapped his mouth shut and waited.

"I am not leaving this house without getting answers today, Grey," she warmed him.

The first inklings of annoyance fizzled through him.

"I want to know why you're here," she continued, crossing her arms.

His jaw clenched, and he bit down the curse that danced on the tip of his tongue. "I'll remind you it's my door you knocked on, not the other way around."

"Do not try pulling that shit on me," she snapped, then shivered, her chin chattering. Her skin beaded against the chill, so he took a step aside to let her in. She eyed him wearily, but a gust of frigid wind had her shivering again, and she stepped inside.

Rubbing her hands together for heat as he closed the door, Sophia turned to face him.

"I don't appreciate the cryptic messages," she said. "You got me into whatever the hell you're into, and I want to know everything."

"Did you put up the amulets?" He hoped she did, but wouldn't been surprised if she wished him to go to hell instead.

When she nodded, relief washed over him, which annoyed him.

"I didn't bring the exploding potions," she told him and folded her arms, but quickly let them hang beside her instead, a little awkwardly. "Didn't think I'd need them."

He opened his mouth to respond, but she kept talking.

"Actually, I didn't even think about them when I left my house." She began pacing back and forth, her steps short and quick. Her hand touched her forehead, went into her hair a bit, then wrapped around her own neck, all in rapid succession.

The way she moved fascinated him, and he couldn't tear his eyes away as he watched her fingers wrap around her own neck. A shiver ran up from the base of his spine, and his eyes trailed south to where her sweater molded itself to the curve of her waist. He averted his eyes. Ogling would just piss her off more. Last thing he wanted.

"Why would I think of taking them?" she continued. "I've never once carried exploding potions on me."

She stopped her pacing and faced him, tugged at her earlobe. "I want you to tell me everything, and not in that cryptic way you talk that pisses me off. I need full sentences and context and definitions and explanations."

He ran his hand through his damp hair.

"Okay," he said and walked in front of her, looking back only to see if she had followed, and went straight to the bar. Dark clouds slid across the sky, carried by frigid wind and the threat of rain.

Behind the counter, he stopped while she climbed onto a stool.

"The truth is, I don't know how to talk about all this," he told her. Maybe being honest about his own feelings would help them figure out why she seemed to be the answer to questions he'd had his whole life. Magic sometimes behaved in ways that were unexpected, but always seeking truth.

He knew magic. Loved magic. It allowed him to help others in the best way he could. But this wasn't about him, and if Sophia Candela wanted to know more, he would not be the one to stand in her way.

"How did you find me?" She had pulled her hair to the top of her head, the curls messy and falling all around her face. And her golden skin was gleaming, healthy, and smooth. She didn't have a lick of makeup on this time, and it hit him that every time he had seen her before, she had been wearing some. He wasn't sure which one he liked more. The fresh and gleaming quality of her bare skin, or when she made what looked like actual magic with a brush and some product.

"I cast a spell," he said.

She only stared, her full lips parted slightly, a dusky pink, and silky.

"Okay," she whispered faintly.

Her fingers drummed on the countertop, pinky to thumb.

"Drink?" he offered and she nodded. He heard himself ask if she wanted anything in particular, but he was already putting sugar and bitters into a glass as she shook her head. Cold water next, a quick mix, then spherical ice, and bourbon before he mixed gently with a bar spoon. A twist of orange peel curled on the side of the glass, and he handed it to her. She took it, looked at it blankly for so long, he was sure she had found something like a hair or a fly in it. He peeked into the glass to make sure, but only ice floated at the top.

"Everything okay?"

She looked like she was holding her breath, her cheeks a little puffed up. "This is my favorite drink." Even so, she stared at it for another long moment, as if she couldn't believe it. He wasn't altogether sure why it was weird. It was his favorite drink too.

"Glad to hear that," he drawled as she lifted the glass to her full lips. She continued to look at it, then she tipped it back, and drank the whole thing in one go. He raised his brows. She barely even made a face. Not that she should. It was a delicious drink. The glass clinked when she put it down on the counter.

"More?" he asked when she had wiped her eyes with the heels of her hands. She shook her head. A curl moved around her cheek, and something inside him made him want to reach forward and tuck it behind her ear. He didn't. Instead, he closed his fist over another glass and busied himself with making himself a drink.

"Did you know this was my favorite drink?" She looked up at him, her eyes bright.

"You had it at the club. I assumed it was a good bet, and since it's my personal favorite…"

"Oh, right." She frowned down at the counter. "I don't know anything about you. Are you in the mafia? Is that it? You're into some shady business and you've involved me in it somehow because you hate me."

He frowned, then nearly laughed. He refrained from the latter. She was absolutely, utterly serious. Her eyes were glassy, a little watery, and he followed her every jerky movement as she wrung her hands, crossed her arms, just to uncross them right after. She did that a lot.

"First of all," he said keeping his voice pitched low. "I'm not in the mafia." He took a sip of his drink, but abandoned the glass shortly after. He would not be able to finish it. His stomach was in knots. "Secondly, what would give you the idea that I hate you?"

She stared at him for a few moments, as if mulling over the question.

"I…" She hesitated and looked away.

He looked at his drink again. He knew what she meant.

"That couldn't make me hate you," he said earnestly, and came around the bar. He extended his hand to her, watched every emotion on her brows, until she put her hand in his. There was no bolt of electricity this time, but a humming right beneath the surface ran up and down his arm.

He led her to the stairs, where he led her to his studio. What better way to show her everything than this?

At the top of the stairs, he opened a white door and entered, turning on the lights with a slide of a button. The overhead lights were not the brightest, but it was because he preferred them dim and warm. It was nicer working that way. The space was big, with wooden floors to keep sound pure and undistorted.

He had furniture, but very little, just a couch and a small side table. There were windows, covered with heavy, sound-absorbing drapes to avoid echoes when he was recording in the booth, where a microphone hung from the ceiling. On the side wall, he had consoles, a computer, and several other instruments, including a drum set, an acoustic guitar, a bass, and an electric guitar. He also had a violin, but he wasn't very good at that at all. The keyboard he used to make any other sounds he needed for a recording was still on, and on the side, sat a baby grand piano, which used to belong to his father, and his grandfather before that.

Sophia turned in a circle, admiring the instruments.

"You play all these instruments?"

"Mostly, yes."

She walked over to the piano, played a couple of keys with no rhyme or reason, then turned back to him.

"How does this explain anything?"

He swallowed as a sudden onset of nerves made his stomach flutter uncomfortably. "I am a musician," he explained lamely.

"I gathered that part," she said. "Are you looking to audition for my club?"

That drew a surprise laugh from him. "Only if you need me to," he said.

She bit her lip and something in him unraveled. His face felt suddenly hot as he tore his eyes away from her perfect lips and turned to the piano.

"I compose songs for graphic audiobooks and other things like video games," he said. His heart was pounding. "I also voice characters from time to time."

She gave him a look. "That sounds about right." She came to stand next to the piano, a few paces away from him. She smelled like apricots. "Sounds like a cool job."

"I didn't bring you up here to show off." He sat on the piano bench. "You wanted to know more."

She nodded with a slight flare of her nostrils.

"You asked how I found you."

Another nod, but her eyes were glassy, and he knew in that moment that all he had to do was play.

"Ever since I was a kid, I've researched for a special potion." He ran over his scales, but only because he needed to give his fingers something to do.

"What kind of potion?" She watched his fingers move up and down the piano, and maybe he showed off a little.

"A healing potion." He looked up at her. Her pretty eyes were so clear, like amber, with specks of brown all over. "One that can help a lot of people. But I haven't been able to find a cure in all the years I have tried, so I created a spell to help me find answers." More scales, but her eyes never left his. "That spell led me to you. I know how it sounds..."

"Crazy?"

"Like a lie. Then I watched you sing the other night." A warmth spread through him quickly, and he let it, even though his stomach churned.

Her lips were open, something like a whimper escaping with a breath.

Yes, she was putting it all together now.

"What does my singing have anything to do with your potion?"

He lifted a shoulder. Hell if he knew.

"But you know that what you do when you sing isn't normal," he said and watched her swallow tightly. "Neither is what I do."

She didn't move. She was frozen.

"And what do you do?"

It had started to rain in the moments since they went upstairs, and it belted against the windows.

"When I came to your club, my best friend was ecstatic," he said, remembering Helena's reaction when he'd told her. She'd been trying to take him to that club since it opened, and he'd always found an excuse not to go. Clubs weren't his thing, really.

When he'd walked into Nowhere, though, he'd had to admit that the shows were as amazing as Helena had claimed, and when Sophia had appeared at the top of the stairs like a hell angel, he'd nearly dropped his drink.

"She loves your shows."

Her brows rose smugly.

"Then I saw you sing, and everything changed," he murmured. "When you on stage and you did it. You knew it was coming, and so did I."

His eyes flicked up to hers again, so there was no doubt of what he meant. His fingers rested over the white keys. They itched to play.

"I've never known anyone else who sees it," she whispered.

Same.

Being a witch had taught him that there was no such thing as coincidences, and despite the fact that he hated that she was Silvana Candela's daughter, he had long ago learned to listen to his intuition. And right now, it was trained on her and only her.

"Are you going to play me some music?" Her hand rested on the shiny surface of the piano. She was steady, much calmer than she had been downstairs, so he took it like a good sign.

He reached for the single sheet he had copied from a grimoire he had found in his dad's stuff. It was unfinished, but the melody was lovely. As he played the first notes, the first thing that came to him was the bittersweet cadence of the melody. It had a longing to it that broke his heart a little every time he played it.

After the first run-through, he closed his eyes and played the song again, his fingers steady on the keys, his timing perfect, as he had practiced it so many times before. This was one of the few songs that did it, and he put every ounce of his concentration and emotion, focused on the timing, every legato and staccato. The timing had to be just right, not even one errant note.

He'd created a lot of songs, but none of them were like this. Had never done this. He had never figured out why it was different, what made it so, when so many random songs did too. When the crescendo hit the third time through, the room exploded in warmth, as if the heater had kicked on. The color came soon after, sifting into the air like smoke. It moved, curled, undulated, like the smoke of a recently blown-out candle. It permeated the entire room, everywhere the music echoed. The warmth slid through him and came out of his fingers, warming the keys beneath them, and the keys glowed as if a back light sat underneath them. His own fingers glowed a little.

Sophia was moving now, her mouth open in awe as she turned around and around. The moving colors attached themselves to her, to the breath she expelled through her lips. Light illuminated her, making her skin look brilliant and gleaming. And when the song abruptly ended, after the fifth time he played through it, the colors disappeared and took the warmth with them. The rain sounds came back as if they had been muffled as he played.

She panted, her eyes wide.

His own heart was a runaway train inside his chest, buzzing instead of beating, the sound close to his ears. There was an elation that came when he played this song. As if after it was finished, something inside him was cleansed.

"My mom was a musician." Her eyes were wet, and her words did something to his brain. He remembered feeling something similar whenever he went swimming and flipped upside down to change directions. That moment when there was no sense of direction.

"What did she play?" he heard himself ask her.

"Everything, it seemed," she responded and swallowed. "Like you, I guess."

Her voice was thick.

"She was amazing." She said it almost like a challenge.

It should have been harder, he thought, to hear about Silvana Candela in such innocent terms. But it wasn't. And maybe it was that he liked listening to Sophia's voice, all soft and whisper-quiet.

"Did she study it in school?"

"No. She studied botany."

He wasn't sure what he'd expected, but when she said it, he felt like he couldn't catch his breath. The images in his head became fuzzy, like the edges of a blurry picture.

Sophia pressed the palm of her hand on her forehead, as if checking for fever.

She walked away toward the windows, slowly, her footsteps quiet, noticing she took her shoes off at some point and he hadn't even noticed. Her figure was snug against the fabric of her dark jeans. His blood sang, and he looked away quickly as she turned again. He could die cheerfully, looking at her, but he wasn't in the business of creeping women out.

"Did she sing too?" He just wanted to know, but also needed to quell the tingling around the base of his spine. The lights above her formed a halo around her hair.

"Yes, she did. She enjoyed making music most of all, though. At least as far as I remember."

She walked back to him, placing her hands on top of the piano again. His fingers buzzed with energy atop the keys. He hadn't shown that song to anyone in a very long time. Only Helena, Lucas, and his mother knew about it. Before that, only his father. And now Sophia was in that fold, the only one of those who knew what it was like, who could do the same thing, but with her voice.

"Maybe this will sound weird," she said, "but I feel like this isn't anything new to me."

"Nothing should feel weird at this point."

A nervous little giggle escaped her lips. It made him smile.

"Sometimes it feels like there's a curtain in front of my memories," he told her. When she nodded, he saw how much she could relate.

His eyes were drawn to her full lips, the soft Cupid's bow catching the light.

"I have to ask again because I have to, and just give me a straight answer," she said, her voice still soft, her eyes still on his. "Are you a witch?"

He inclined his head, his hands on his lap now.

"Yes."

She didn't move. She didn't even blink.

"How?"

"I was born this way."

A hysterical laugh bubbled from her, but it didn't last long. Her eyes were wet again.

"What does it mean, then?" she asked. "That I can see the music. Am I one too?" By the end of the sentence, her voice was so low, he barely heard it, as if she was afraid to ask.

"Are you?" he asked her instead. Only she could truly know that. Just because the magic led him to her, didn't mean she was one.

Sometimes the person at the other end of the spell was just a means to an end.

She took in a long breath, then blew it out just as slowly as she took it in. "I don't know. Doubt it though."

A spark of memory came back to him, clearer than all the others.

His father singing, Grey seeing the notes leaving his father's mouth and he sang lovely tunes Grey had never heard before.

"I found books like the one you had downstairs, in my mom's

stuff," she said, and her words snapped him back to the present. It had his heart thumping loudly. "There were several, but they were all blank."

She laced her fingers together, still on top of the piano. Her short nails were a pretty soft pink.

"They look like yours," she continued, "from the bar. Why?"

"No clue, but seems connected. Don't you think?"

"Yeah, I'd say so," she said, and their eyes met once more. Something else passed between them, a heat, a tension, an electric current. He knew she felt it too when she shuddered and her eyes drifted away. "Who else knows about what you do with music?"

"Helena, Lucas, and my mom." No need to keep anything from her at this point. "I mostly make healing potions on demand."

"You make potions for other illnesses, not just the one you have researched all your life?" she asked, coming to sit on the bench, her feet opposite to his, sparking another one of the strange non-memories he was so used to, gone too soon.

"I enjoy making healing potions. It makes me feel useful." That part was true, when the rest of the things he could do, especially ones where music was involved, did nothing but look pretty.

"The colors are impressive."

"And useless."

She frowned. "And you think they should be more than just color?"

"Don't you? Knowing everything you now know, that is." He wanted to believe that there was more to it than that. It made the most sense. There was no way that something so extraordinary like it happened for no reason at all. And if the music was more than just pretty colors sometimes when he played, he wanted to know how it was connected to his research on the void. "It feels like it should be."

He closed the piano's lid and twisted to look at her.

"And this healing potion you're researching," she began, "what is that about?"

"There's an illness, something terrible that's been affecting witches for almost twenty years," he told her. "It causes symptoms that can be dangerous for anyone around them, especially other witches."

Her brows pinched together. "The man who attacked me looked ill."

"He is," Grey said carefully.

She blinked. "So you know who he is now?"

He exhaled. "The man is a fellow witch, Clayton Morgan. He has been sick for a while."

She said nothing, waiting.

"He's an energy worker," he continued. "Well-known in the community, especially here in Seattle, but he has traveled everywhere to offer his services."

"And what does an energy worker do exactly?"

"They can connect with your spirit and with those who have passed to the next life. It is also a form of healing, getting an understanding of who you are, underneath the pressures of human flesh."

She swallowed. "So it's good work."

"It is."

Clayton was a good man, according to the accounts of the people Lucas had met when investigating Sophia's attack. Grey had heard about him through others, mutuals, but he had never met the man in person. It wasn't easy to hear about any witch suffering the fate of this illness, whether or not you knew them.

"I don't know him personally, not well anyway." Grey put his hands in between his knees.

Her face was stricken. "Is it like cancer?"

"Somewhat like it, yes, but with other characteristics that cause witches to behave in ways they otherwise wouldn't."

"Does it affect more than witches?" she asked.

"Not that I know, so far," he answered gravely. "But it isn't outside the realm of possibility for it to spread to non-witches. We call it the void."

"The void," she echoed. "Why?"

"Because it causes witches to lose their minds, their humanity." How could he explain it in a way that wouldn't traumatize her too?

"Then what happens?" she whispered, her tone horrified, just as her face was.

"As the disease progresses, it changes the brain, according to much research. They lose their ability to reason, and they typically exhibit erratic and dangerous behavior."

"And they hunt down other witches for that reason? It doesn't make much sense."

"It's not logical."

"That's horrible." She swallowed dryly.

"That's why I've been trying to find a cure for so long." He had seen friends die, people who did immeasurable good for the world with their magic. He knew what happened when the witches were killed. The world had seen it throughout history, and even in their current timeline, where they were finally getting some of it back, witches working to restore a balance, there were too few witches already without a disease killing them.

"Why don't your potions work?"

He shrugged. "Can't figure that part out. They only help with symptoms so far."

Sophia looked pale in her shock, and her mouth hung open.

"Have you helped Clayton?"

He nodded. "I have, through others, but my potions are not working on him anymore. His illness is too advanced." He didn't add what he would have to do soon if he couldn't find a cure. What would she think then, if she knew that other thing he did? Worse than being in the mafia, he thought.

"So he came after me because he's sick."

"Possibly. Maybe he thought you could help him."

"And I sprayed him with pepper spray instead."

"You didn't know," he told her to reassure her. "Best to be prepared. Besides, when the void is advancing, some witches get dangerous. It's better to be safe, which is why it's important that you always have your protective charms and potions."

She nodded but bit her lip.

"And how does the amulet work?" Reaching into her sweater to pull it out. He was pleased to see she had it, even if she didn't have the potions on her, too.

"When it warms, it alerts me," he said, showing her the bracelet he never took off, with a series of little stones like hers. They were connected to Helena, Lucas, and his mom as well. "Touch it for just long enough and it'll warm the corresponding stone.

Her brows shot up and her eyes widened comically. "So that's how you got there."

He said nothing and watched her. She lifted her head up to the ceiling first, then her shoulders relaxed, as if relieved.

"And this spell you created... how does it work?"

"That's a little more complicated and harder to explain."

"Try me." She had a wicked gleam in her eye.

"It involved a ritual under the full moon and whole lot of waiting." He'd done the ritual to learn more, using a special potion that opened his senses, had Lucas take his blood (which sucked—he hated needles), and dropped it on a map to find the answer to his questions about the cure. He told her this and she blinked long and hard when he was done.

"Sure," she said, pursing her lips.

By the time she left a little later, there was an understanding between the two of them. She had questions, and he could perhaps help answer them. Even if all her questions revolved around her mother.

10

For days, Sophia attempted to call Jeanette back, to no avail. She'd left voicemails, texts, and even sent an email... nothing. She had started to wonder if she had said something to bother Jeanette. Maybe the journals and the dreams were too much and Jeanette just wasn't saying anything. But no, Jeanette had never been the kind of person to pull punches if something bothered her. Sophia would know if she was annoyed.

Two days since she'd last seen Grey, and she also hadn't heard from him. Not that she'd reached out either.

Beside her, Julia kept a brisk pace. They'd spent the afternoon going through their favorite hole-in-the-wall shops around the city. Sophia loved looking through used bookstores and finding little gems, and though she had only found a romance novel she had once seen her mom read, she happily carried the bag by her side, while Julia only had her little brown leather purse across her body.

Through the day, she'd often wished she could tell Julia about Grey and the journals, but knowing her sister, she would not take it well. Julia certainly never wanted to talk about their mom, and if Sophia brought up Will Constantine's son, her sister's head might actually explode. Did Julia even know about magic at all? How could she ask anyway? It wasn't like Julia could give Sophia the help she needed to figure out why the journals were blank.

Julia stuck her hands into her jacket pockets, a pretty white with fluff on the hood. Her straight dark hair was down, sleek on her shoulders, and tucked behind her ears. The two of them were dressed similarly, in dark leggings and comfortable walking boots. Sophia had her hair pulled up atop her head, as her curls would need a wash before they looked shiny and smooth again. She considered straightening it to not have to deal with it for at least a week. Two if she had no qualms about it, which, most of the time, she didn't.

"Are you listening to me?" Julia asked as they took a turn onto a smaller, less-busy road.

"Yes, sorry," Sophia said, "I'm a little distracted."

"Obviously. What is going on with you lately?"

Sophia felt her stomach tighten. "Nothing's going on," she lied and was sure Julia could tell. "I just need to have a chat with Jeanette and she's no answering any of my calls or texts."

Julia raised a brow.

"And two emails," Sophia added to convey how important this really was.

"She's not answering, or she hasn't?" Julia said. "She is a busy woman."

"I know a thing or two about being busy." They stopped at a light, waited for the crossing signal. "It's just weird that she isn't."

"She does tend to answer quickly, I'll give you that," Julia said, "but if she's not picking up, there must be something else going on."

True. Sophia had told herself that already, but hearing it from Julia made her feel a little better. Something about the way Julia sounded like she knew what she was talking about. Julia spoke, Sophia listened. It was as simple as that.

As the light turned, they went to cross, and Julia hooked her arm to Sophia's.

"You've been acting a little odd lately," she said. "Want to tell me what's going on?"

"Why do you think something's going on?"

"Please, I know you better than you know yourself." Her tone didn't allow room for argument. "Now tell me who I need to call to get you out of trouble."

"Why would your mind immediately go there?" Sophia asked her.

"When you're not telling me anything, I have to assume the worst," was her retort. "Honestly, if you killed someone, just tell me now and I will make calls. A lot of them."

Sophia slapped her arm playfully. "It's scary that I believe every word out of your mouth," she said, but as she finished the sentence, the back of her neck prickled.

They reached the sidewalk on the other side, and Sophia quickly glanced back. The usual—people looking harassed while trying to get somewhere.

"Are you looking for someone?" Julia crossed her arms in front of her chest, and Sophia realized they had stopped after reaching the sidewalk.

"Not at all." She tried to smile, but Julia's full lips pressed together, and Sophia was in for it, she knew. She sighed. "I'm okay, I promise."

"I don't believe you." They stood there for a few moments, a cold breeze ruffling their hair. "You forget I practically raised you."

"I could never." Sophia bit her lip. She truly never would. The sacrifices Julia had made, Sophia would never take for granted. Which was why she knew she couldn't keep lying. "I got attacked at the club the other night."

Julia blinked. "Excuse me, what?"

Nerves suddenly rushed through Sophia, making her hands tremble, and she bit her lip, even as Julia's eyes went wide and glassy.

"How? Why? Who were they? I'm going to make some calls." Julia pulled her cellphone out of her coat pocket.

"Julia, put the phone away," Sophia told her in a firm tone of voice and Julia instantly froze. "It's okay. I'm okay. I got help."

She would not tell Julia who the helper was, for sure. She was not going to take it well, not with that deranged look in her eyes. Julia was like a bear, and Sophia didn't even have to see Julia become a mother to know what kind she would be. Absolutely feral.

"Why didn't you tell us right away?" Julia held on to her phone, but didn't dial.

Sophia didn't look behind her again, though she really wanted to. She was paranoid. That was it. This anxious knot of nerves in her stomach meant nothing. Absolutely nothing.

"Because I didn't want to worry anyone, especially since I'm fine," she said and turned to keep walking. Julia followed. "I promise I'm fine."

"Yes, I can see that," Julia said, her tone less than calm. "But what did they want?"

"I'm not sure." It wasn't a lie. She did not know exactly why. Hands trembling, she hung the reusable bag on her shoulder, just for something to do.

They passed a group of business executives in suits, and one man turned to stare at Julia, who ignored him.

"Is this about some sort of illegal activity?" Julia asked in a harsh whisper.

"Julia... no," Sophia sighed. "I immediately regret saying anything."

"If you don't tell me about it, then who would you tell?"

Nope, she wasn't answering that one. It would be a downward spiral quick.

"I'm not doing anything illegal." That she knew. Was magic illegal? They crossed another road, one that would lead to Sophia's neighborhood.

"Okay, you're not doing anything, but whoever attacked you did. You have to call the cops. Did you call the cops?"

Sophia faltered. "I got the help I needed." She would not admit to Julia why she wouldn't call the police on a sick man. "I know you worry, but I am not little anymore, Jules."

Julia was quiet for a while. "It's not something I can turn off, Sophia."

Sophia's heart squeezed, so she took Julia's arm and linked hers through it again.

"I love you," she said, and Julia only smiled a little.

It started to mist, so they picked up the pace, and looked both ways before they crossed another side street. Her body tingled, filled with something like electricity. This was more than simple anxiety.

Sophia picked up the pace, and Julia kept up, probably thinking it was because of the rain.

"We should have driven," Julia grumbled, pulling her hood over her head.

"And then what?" Sophia asked, throwing a look behind them. Nothing, but the tingles in her neck remained. "We'd be stuck in traffic."

"We wouldn't be getting wet," Julia said. "I literally just got my hair done."

"Your aversion to your natural hair is disturbing, to be completely honest with you," Sophia said.

"It's not an aversion," Julia protested. "Have I told you about the week I tried to wear it natural? People in the office looked at me like I killed their mothers."

"You did tell us," Sophia said. "People are dicks."

"People are dicks."

Sophia looked back, and there he was. The same man as the other night at the club. Sophia's heart immediately began to race.

"Is your house protected, by the way?" Julia prattled on.

"You mean like alarms?" Sophia swallowed tightly as she picked up the pace even more.

"Yes, alarms, Sophia." Julia sounded exasperated.

Sophia thought of the crystals she'd hung over every window and door in her house, the amulet she wore even now, and the potions she carried in her jacket pocket, right there next to her phone. Like normal people did.

"Not exactly." She was power walking now, her breath coming in short spurts. "I think I have it under control though."

Julia looked behind them, then turned back sharply.

"Look, I don't care what you think this is, if I'm a paranoid idiot or what, but there's a man following us," she said in a hushed tone as their pace became almost a jog.

"You saw him too?" Sophia practically squealed.

Julia smacked her shoulder. "You knew and didn't care to mention it?"

"I didn't want to freak you out," Sophia snapped. "And you didn't say anything either."

"I've been freaked out the whole time. I noticed him when we left the bookstore."

"That far back?" Sophia yelled, and it robbed her of the little bit of breath she had left. He had followed them the entire time and she hadn't even noticed. Sophia really needed to train herself to be more watchful, especially these days. She reached into her pocket and grabbed the little vial. Grey said to use and shew as about to find out just how well it worked.

Please work, please work.

"Julia, when I say to run, just take off toward the house," Sophia huffed as they kept moving as fast as they could without breaking into a flat-out run.

"What?"

"When I say run, you run to the house, do you understand? Run when I saw run," Sophia repeated as her hand wrapped around Julia's arm like a vice. "I'm right behind you."

Julia swallowed audibly. "Okay, okay," she said, her eyes glassy. "Oh my God."

Sophia looked back one more time, but this time, he was much closer, and he looked horrible. His face was so sallow, her heart squeezed, but she was going to use this potion anyway. Given what Grey had said to her about the illness, the man was dangerous.

A part of her didn't want to do it, but if she didn't, what was going to happen to her? To Julia.

Thoughts of what could happen to her sister, one of her best friends, her protector, made her mind up for her. She squeezed the vial between two fingers, then curled her hand around it.

"Okay, are you ready?" she breathed.

"No," Julia shouted. "Oh my God."

"Run!" Sophia yelled, and they both took off at a run. A shout behind her made her stumble, but she pulled out the bottle, and smashed it on the ground.

The explosion was far bigger than she had imagined, but it was not as noisy as she'd have thought either. What a strange concept, she thought as Julia pulled her forward. Then something grabbed her by the navel. Her head spun, her eyes unable to focus on anything, as if she was spinning on one of those playground whirls. There was a whoosh of wind in her ears, and seconds later, she and Julia fell in a heap inside her living room.

Panting, Sophia got on her knees, the bag's handles somehow wrapped around her neck. She knocked over the little vase on the coffee table as she got up. It shattered with a crash that was much louder than it should have been.

"What the fuck was that?" Julia screeched, her face paling further. Her hair was now in disarray around her like a dark cloud, and stuck to her hood, which was half off her head.

Sophia staved off a wave of nausea, but Julia apparently could not, as she vomited on the black and white rug. Trembling, Sophia reached into her coat for the amulet, allowing it to warm between her fingers. As her phone rang, she grabbed a washcloth from the guest bathroom, wetting it as she answered.

"I need you to come right now." Her voice was equally as shaky. "My sister is with me."

"We'll be there right away," came his deep voice, and he hung up before she could ask who 'we' was.

She went back to Julia, and pressed the towel onto her brow.

"Talk to me," Sophia whispered feverishly, but Julia didn't respond. She closed her eyes, tears running down her face. It was then that Sophia realized she was also crying, breathless sobs wracking her body. It was the shock, she knew. A strange sort of numbness was mixing with the adrenaline now, and she focused on Julia so she didn't freak out any more than she already had.

"What happened?" Julia whispered, her voice ragged, right before she threw up again. Sophia wiped her mouth with the rag.

That rug would never be the same.

"What the hell was that?" Julia moaned. "What was that?"

"I don't know," Sophia said and dry-heaved. She *didn't* know.

When the doorbell rang, Sophia jumped, and Julia screeched before slapping her hands on her mouth.

"Stay here," she said to Julia, handing her the damp cloth, before taking off to open the door. Grey and Lucas stood on the stoop, and Sophia's feet became stuck to the floor. She still had tears running down her face and nausea rolled in her stomach, but she refused to throw up.

"You have to ask us in," Grey said in a very soft voice, as if trying to calm a wild animal. "Invite us inside."

She hesitated. What did it mean, letting them inside her house? Could they just show up whenever after?

No, that's not what Grey had said. She could revoke their invitation at any time and the amulets would keep them out.

"Come in," she said, and they stepped over the threshold slowly. Stepping aside, she briefly wondered what would happen if they tried to enter without being invited.

In the living room, Julia was lying on the floor, off the ruined rug. The cloth was over her eyes, and she was crying softly. Sophia's heart squeezed as she went to her sister.

"Tell me what happened," Grey said, causing Julia to sit up so fast her face blanched—if that was even possible anymore, she was so pale. She eyed Grey, then Lucas, then back again.

"Who are you?" she said far too loudly, then looked at Sophia. "Sophia, what is going on? Am I dreaming? Yes, this was a lucid dream. But no, that makes no sense. Lucid dreaming lets you control what you do, and this is the opposite of being in control." Every word Julia uttered became louder and louder as she spoke.

"Lucas," Grey murmured.

"What's happening?" Sophia's heart raced as she watched Lucas crouch in front of Julia. He took the towel from Julia's tight grip, and she simply looked up at him with her mouth hanging open.

"Hi," Lucas said to Julia with a little smile.

Julia's breathing became faster, but no words left her mouth. She was crying again, and Lucas placed his hand gently on her forehead, and Julia became boneless. Lucas caught her in his arms and rose to his feet. Sophia could only watch him with her mouth wide open, until he said, "She's just asleep. Is there a bed I can take her to?"

Sophia nodded and led them to the bedrooms. Lucas lay Julia down on Sophia's bed and pulled the blue covers over her. She was, inappropriately, glad her room was clean. There was only a little clutter on the side table she used the most, which also had a lamp on it. The room boasted of a couple of windows and white curtains, and a TV on the wall, and not much else, since she tended to put all her messes in the walk-in closet.

"She was panicking," Lucas said, because he could probably see how much Sophia was freaking out.

"I'm panicking, can you put me to sleep?" Sophia said, hysterical laughter bubbling up from somewhere in her stomach.

"I'm going to give her a memory potion," Grey said, and Sophia, startled, almost fell over. Grey caught her, straightening her, his arms protectively around her.

At another time, Sophia would think about how those arms felt around her, all strong and sturdy, but not now.

"You have those?" she screeched. "What kind of memory potion is it? What is she going to forget?"

"The kind that will make her forget this event only," Lucas said as he administered the potion. He muttered under his breath, his hand hovering over Julia's head.

"She won't forget anything else," Grey murmured, and Sophia looked up at him. She was still in his arms, so she stepped away, though she didn't want to. Yes, she needed the comfort, but she would not try getting it from him. She was too aware of how good his arms felt around her. Too good.

"She'll be confused as to how you got to the house, but otherwise, she'll be fine," he added.

The three of them stepped out of the room. They left the door open and went to the living room, where Lucas drank something, and then waved his hand to the mess Julia had made. It disappeared into thin air, along with the broken blue vase, which Sophia had loved.

Her head did a loop, and afraid she was going to pass out, she let herself slide to the floor.

How was this real life?

"Breathe," Grey said, placing his hands on her cheeks, crouching in front of her. "You're going to pass out if you don't take deep breaths."

She did as he asked, and after a couple of moments, felt her head become less light. When he asked her why she used the potion, she told him everything, without sparing details. Then it hit her, and she grabbed on to Grey's forearms as she rose on her knees.

"They saw my sister," she told him frantically. "I need my sisters protected, okay? Both of them. My whole family."

"I'll do everything I can," Grey said, and the quiet strength in his voice reassured her, spread in her like a balm. Why did she trust this person?

"I'm on it," Lucas said from where he was leaning on the wall. He was wearing jeans and a button-down he had rolled up to his elbows. His hair was sleeked back, his beard shiny and trimmed. Then he took a potion and disappeared into thin air with a slight smirk.

Sophia wished she could say she was shocked at that too, but all big emotions had run their course through her and it left her boneless. Maybe she would never feel anything ever again. That would be neat after all this turmoil.

"Nothing will happen to your family," Grey assured her.

She let go of his arms, her stomach so tight, she didn't think she'd ever be able to eat again.

"I will help you as much as I can, but you have to promise me you'll protect my family," she told him. There was nothing she wouldn't do. Even though this was his fault. "That includes Victoria and Thomas, and Jeanette. My employees at the club..." She swallowed as she realized how many people she was responsible for. "Oh God." Her face screwed up and tears ran down her face.

His hand went back to her face, gently. "I'm sorry," he whispered and he looked the part. God, she was so confused.

"Witches infected with the void go after people with magic," he continued, and it took her a moment to understand what he meant. "Their magic becomes weak from the disease and many of them can't do what they once could. So they go after those who have active magic and try to steal it."

Sophia swallowed again. "How do you steal magic?"

"You can't."

The implications of those two words chilled her. They couldn't steal the magic, but they would try anyway, and that probably left innocent people dead. And what did it mean for her? Was she a witch too, then? She shook her head to clear it.

"Julia will wake up soon, so I should be out of here. Stay in the house, do not allow anyone else in, unless you know them well," he told her. "Only those allowed inside by your explicit words will be able to come into the house, and that includes people with magic. As long as you keep the amulets up."

She only sat there, unable to say anything else.

"I'm going to go meet with Lucas now. Will you be alright?"

"Yes," she said, her voice hoarse, and watched him disappear moments later, leaving behind a little ripple of cold air.

She got on her feet, her head spinning, then realized that Lucas took a potion to disappear, but Grey didn't. Now she had to know how that worked.

A while later, Sophia didn't know how long, Julia came out of the bedroom, frowning and stretching deeply.

"When did I fall asleep?" She asked as she removed her coat. "And what are you doing sitting on the floor?"

"Uh..." Sophia looked down at herself, with her coat still on, and still petrified on the floor. "As soon as we got in."

"That does not sound like me," Julia mumbled, frowning and pressing her hands to her head. "And I'm hungry. Didn't we just eat?"

Yeah, but you just puked twice, Sophia thought as she got on her feet and took off her own coat.

"We walked a lot," Sophia said, but Julia's furrowed brow didn't ease. "We can cook something, if you want."

"Should we call Amy?" Julia asked, still sounding a little off, her voice too high.

Sophia almost said no—keeping Amy away seemed like the best idea. Then she remembered that the house was protected. So, she said, "Great idea," as they headed toward the kitchen.

She got busy pulling out ingredients from the refrigerator, as Julia texted Amy.

Ground beef went into a pan, seasoned with Sophia's homemade dry seasoning mix—which she made with all the dry seasonings she typically used, all mixed into a little white container with a sifter for convenience. As that cooked, Julia put pasta into boiling water, and began chopping vegetables beside Sophia.

"Do you want a drink? I could certainly go for one," Sophia said, grateful that she'd been chopping onions and her tears became about that.

"I'd love a drink." Julia sounded happy, in a good mood even, and Sophia wondered what in the world that potion had in it. Could she have some? It certainly couldn't hurt.

Sophia pulled out the drink ingredients, focusing on making things so that her hands stopped trembling. She took out two glasses from a cupboard. She was just glad Julia hadn't noticed.

Bourbon and lemon juice went into a shaker, then simple syrup, ice, and some egg whites. She shook them vigorously, using a cup as a lid.

The clinking of the ice inside the shaker calmed her somewhat. It was as if things were normal and she was just preparing food with her sister on a normal day, where they hadn't been terrorized by strangers with actual magic. Actual fucking magic.

Sophia poured the mixture into a glass, using a little strainer, and dotted bitters on the top, handing it to Julia before she mixed another for herself. As she poured the cocktail into her glass, a warmth went over the house, like a haze, and suddenly, all the anxiety she had felt until that moment left her.

There was a glow to the house, for only a moment, and when it was gone, she felt like she could breathe. Her phone lit up.

GREY: IT'S DONE.

At least she could appreciate that he worked fast. She looked down at her drink, feeling calm from the text alone. Then she picked up the glass and shot the whole thing back, squeezing her eyes shut when the warmth hit her, sighing as it slid down her throat into her stomach, sitting there and churning. It was a while before it settled.

Julia sipped as she watched the stove.

"This is an excellent whiskey sour," Julia said. "It's almost as if you own a bar."

"Right," Sophia said and almost laughed as the doorbell rang, making her jump nearly out of her shoes, which she realized were still on. She slipped them off by the front door, and heart beating fast again, she realized she needed a peephole, or a doorbell camera, or something. The simple way she had lived her life before would not work anymore. Damn Grey.

"Sophia?" came Amy's voice from the other side of the door.

Sophia opened the door to find Amy, sobbing angrily, her face red as a tomato, the collar of her t-shirt tear-stained. Her hair was pulled back into a high ponytail, and she was dressed in a pair of dark flared jeans and a white crop top with a snarky message in bold red letters.

"What happened?" Sophia said, opening the door wider to let her in, remembering that she had to say it out loud. "Come in," she added quickly as Amy's foot came into the threshold. Sophia could swear that she felt the shift in the house, but that was a question she'd ask Grey later.

"Tom is so stupid." Amy blew her nose on a tissue, her purse hanging off her forearm.

"And who's Tom?" Julia asked. Amy was removing her shoes, only to pace back and forth in the small entryway, pulling a cigarette into her mouth without lighting it.

"We literally talked about him a couple of days ago, Julia," Amy snapped, exasperated at having to explain.

"The tennis guy?" Julia asked Sophia, who took the cigarette out of Amy's mouth instead of answering. Julia blinked down at her own shoes, frowning, and Sophia looked away before she gave anything away. There was no simple way to explain to Julia why she had fallen asleep with not just her coat on, but her shoes too.

"He's such an idiot," Amy continued, stalking to the living room, just to continue her pacing. "After six months, he informs me he's been dating other women this entire time because he thought we weren't exclusive." Amy's face scrunched up in disgust. "Can you believe the level of bullshit? He thought I wanted to have an open relationship. Me. Amy Candela Montgomery."

She took out another cigarette and did pull out her lighter this time.

"Oh no, you don't," Sophia said, hurrying forward to pull the cigarette out of Amy's mouth.

Amy huffed. "Would you stop that? I need something to calm me down."

"If I can't get you to stop killing yourself with these, the least you can do is not smoke inside my house. Have a gummy or something."

"I'm out of gummies," Amy wailed, fresh tears sliding down her red face. "Why is this happening to me?"

"God, relax," Sophia muttered and took the lighter from Amy when she offered it. "There's a white container above the fridge. I'll make you a drink, meanwhile."

Amy rummaged in the cupboards as Sophia mixed another drink, throwing the two cigarettes away, as Julia finished making the food.

"Are you sure you had the talk?" Julia asked as they sat to eat at the round table in a breakfast nook. Amy threw her an annoyed look.

"Duh," Amy said, taking a huge gulp of her drink, downing half of it. "He knew I am not the kind of girl to have open relationships—I'd be seeing women too."

"But did you two talk about being exclusive? If not, you're being unfair," Sophia said.

"Sophia, I came here to rage about this guy, not to be called out." Amy sniffed and took a bite of the pasta. Her face slackened into an expression of pure bliss when she tasted it.

"My bad," Sophia chuckled. "What a bastard."

"I know, right?" Amy said and added, "This is amazing."

"Thank you, I'm really learning," Julia said, and Sophia almost wanted to laugh, the drink having taken off the edge of her anxiety.

Later, a few more drinks in, they lay in various states of disarray, having changed into lounge clothes from Sophia's closet, which were big on Julia, but fit Amy well.

It was raining, and the temperature had dropped considerably.

Amy was sitting sideways on the blue armchair, her head hanging back, red hair reaching for the floor. She was a lot calmer. Maybe it was the delicious pasta, or the drink. Or the gummy.

Sophia was lying on the couch, also infinitely more relaxed now that she had food and a couple of drinks in her belly.

"I hope it's okay to stay here tonight," Julia said, perched on the windowsill, wrapped in a fuzzy blue throw. "Harold hates it when I drink, and I really don't want to have to call him to come get me."

"You can call a ride share. We live in the age of too much comfort and convenience," Amy said. "And thank God for that."

"Or, you can both stay here," Sophia said, rolling over, so she was lying on her back. She didn't want to be alone anyway.

"Good," Julia said, still happily looking out the window at the rain. Sophia was glad that Julia remembered nothing. As much as she wished she were the one to remember nothing, at least her sister didn't have to deal with it. And she also wouldn't be asking questions Sophia couldn't answer honestly.

Her phone went off and her heart jumped a little. She picked it up, but the brief excitement—which she would have to decipher later—melted away when she saw the name on the screen. She blinked at it, sure she was seeing things.

ARIC: HOW ARE YOU?

Sophia frowned down at the phone, then rolled her eyes. Aric texting her out of nowhere was not news, and it was not altogether surprising. He did it from time to time, and right after their final breakup, she had stopped inviting him over, which was all these texts were about, anyway. If he thought he was going to reach out just to get into her pants, he was sadly mistaken. That was not a hole she wanted to get into ever again.

She deleted the message.

And much later, when her sisters were climbing into bed, Sophia went to the kitchen to get a bottle of water, and as she walked back in the near dark, her eye floated to the side table, where she had moved the dying money tree. She froze mid-step. How had she missed it? All day, she hadn't looked at it, and there it was. Alive and well, like it had never died at all.

She came closer to it, her heart racing, palms suddenly clammy. When she got closer, she heard its music loud and clear.

"What the fuck?"

11

Four days later, still paranoid as hell, Sophia got to Nowhere with a dull ache behind her eyes making headway to ruin her day. She still hadn't gotten in touch with Jeanette, no matter how many times she'd tried calling. Sophia had resorted to asking Victoria if she had heard from her mother, only to find out that Victoria had, in fact, talked to Jeanette briefly, who had cited being busy at the hospital.

It didn't help her anxiety one bit.

She sat in front of the computer, terribly distracted. She'd had to triple-check everything she did, and had caught several mistakes already, which did not bode well for the rest of the day. Her eyes kept sliding to where the little cactus used to be, finding the empty space sad. But something else stirred in her, a kind of anxiety she had never felt before. It was the kind of feeling that came over you when you were driving down one road, but something led you to another. There was no rhyme or reason for it, but it was there, and with everything that had happened in the past two weeks, she was inclined to pay close attention to her gut. Especially having noticed how the money tree at home was now fine. It made little sense.

There was music and noise, as the dancers and the band practiced for an upcoming performance, and where before the noise had never bothered Sophia, today it was too much. She heard the music reverberate inside her skull, too loud to be anything but uncomfortable.

Sophia stretched her neck. It was tight and achy since she had gotten little sleep in the last few days. She'd always had a little trouble sleeping, but since she and Julia were followed, it had gotten much worse. Her purse on the coatrack behind the door beckoned her. The potions were in there, waiting. Hell if she knew for what.

At least her family and friends were safe. How Grey had done it, she had no idea. She was also a little weary of asking, if she was honest. Insisting on answers had landed her here, hadn't it?

She worked for a while longer, before Victoria entered the office, her phone between her shoulder and her ear, a drink tray in one hand, the other holding her water bottle, keys, and purse.

"I just got to Nowhere and Sophia's here, Mom," Victoria said, blowing Sophia a kiss as she set everything down on her desk. "Hold on."

She offered the phone to Sophia, who took it and put it to her ear as Victoria placed a cup of coffee on the desk.

"Jeanette," she said, her heart suddenly pounding, and her headache forgotten. She half expected for the call to drop.

"Sophia, finally," Jeanette said. She sounded a little out of breath, but relieved. "I've been trying to reach you for days."

"So have I, and your phone ping-pongs between being out of service and going straight to voicemail."

"Hmmmm," Jeanette's pitch was low. "Weird."

"What?"

"Something fishy's going on," Jeanette said. "I have a feeling."

"What kind of feeling?" Sophia asked, and as she did, she knew the answer.

"Something shifted, and I know it sounds crazy to you—"

"Please," Sophia scoffed. "There's nothing crazy about that."

"First, the hospital messed up my schedule and I could barely get a moment to breathe," Jeanette said. "I was forgetting things like never before, and I don't like it."

"What do you think it's about?" Sophia's throat felt hot, like it did when she was getting a cold.

"I don't know. I want to find out, but I don't know where to start."

Sophia thought of Grey. He was a witch, did things Sophia had never seen in her life, and he was related to Will Constantine, someone Jeanette had known. A good friend, if Sophia recalled correctly.

"I really need to see you." Sophia heard the trembling in her own voice.

"Sophie, darling." Jeanette's voice softened, and Sophia had to fight back sudden tears at the term of endearment. "What did you get into?"

Sophia paused, looking into space. How did she explain it all?

"What do you mean?" she said in a near whisper, but she knew that playing these kinds of games with Jeanette never went well. The woman seemed to know everything.

"Sophia," Jeanette warned.

Sophia watched Victoria leave the room with a clipboard, the door now shut.

"I met this guy, and he does things that shouldn't be possible..."

Jeanette said nothing, waiting.

"And I also found Mom's books, her journals, and they're empty and that's not how I remember things. You said you were also having memory troubles. Could it all be related? And I'm having those dreams. I don't even know what to think." It all came out in a rush. She decided not to mention the attack from the other day.

"You need to come see me as soon as possible," Jeanette said, and they agreed on a date and time.

She was hanging up when Victoria walked back into the office.

"She said she will call you back later," Sophia told Victoria and handed her the phone.

"I'm glad you could talk. She's been a little weird."

"I've been a little weird," Sophia muttered.

"You have been." Victoria half-sat on a corner of the desk. "You've been less than responsive in the last few days, and you seem more anxious than normal. What's going on?"

Sophia wanted to tell her, but when she opened her mouth, nothing came out. She couldn't bring Victoria into all of this mess. She wouldn't.

"I've been anxious," she said. It was the truth. Mostly. Maybe there would come a time when Sophia could be honest with her best friend in the world. That moment was not now.

"And now I'm concerned."

Sophia gave her a soft smile.

"There's no need to be," she said. "I've been anxious before, and this won't be that last time."

"More concerned. What's going on? Is it because of the attack?"

"Yeah, actually." Sophia looked at her phone with a sudden urge to text Grey. She put it upside down on the desk. "It just shook me."

Victoria let out a long breath, looking sad. "Of course it did. Anything we can do for you?"

Sophia let her lips curve as Victoria squeezed her hand.

"Nothing at the moment."

Thankfully, Victoria let it go, and together, they headed to the front of the house. Things looked mostly ready, the tables made, centerpieces in place, the stage busy with stretching dancers. They helped with the bar, cutting, prepping for the rush of the evening. It would be busy; they had sold out of tickets for the show.

Sophia washed and cut limes, helped take out the trash, swept and mopped, and then headed back to the office as the back door opened tentatively and a woman stepped through the threshold. She was tall and willowy, with the type of body Sophia had dreamt of having before she accepted that her hips would never get narrower nor her ass smaller. Bright blue eyes and almost white blonde that brushed her shoulders in soft waves, the woman moved forward. She wore black leggings and an oversized sweater that fell off one shoulder.

She looked awfully familiar.

"Can I help you?" Sophia approached her and met her halfway through the hallway.

"Hi, I know this is random," the woman said in a melodic voice. "My name is Helena Bennett and I'm a singer."

"Oh my God, yes," Sophia said as recognition sparked. "I've seen your videos."

Helena beamed. "Thank you for watching. It's nice to meet you." She shifted her weight. "I'm a friend of Grey's. Is it possible to speak in private?"

Sophia felt her smile slip a little. *That* Helena.

"Yes, of course." Sophia gestured toward the office, confused, wanting to know what this was all about, and led Helena there. She closed the door softly and stood against it as Helena stood uncertainly in the center of the small room. "What can I do for you?"

Helena's smile became a little strained. "Actually, Grey sent me."

Another surge of anxiety. At this rate, she was going to have a heart attack before she turned thirty.

"Why?" Sophia asked, trying not to let her nerves show. Not that her heart hadn't done that thing that had nothing to do with nerves, and everything to do with hearing his name. Whether that was because of the magic thing or something else, she didn't know.

"He told me you needed a certain kind of help around here," Helena said with a secret smile.

Sophia would have swallowed, but her throat was too dry. She needed water. Or tequila.

"I'll get to it," Helena said. "I sing, as you know, since you've seen my stuff. Grey asked me to help him in some matters of protection, and I thought what a good idea it would be if I was to audition for you."

Sophia's mouth opened, but no sound came out, so she snapped it shut.

"It would honestly be an honor," Helena continued with a grin. "I love your club."

"Oh my God," Sophia breathed. "You want to sing at my club?"

"Right." Helena widened her eyes briefly, as if trying to communicate a silent message to Sophia. When Sophia looked at her blankly—since she couldn't get her brain to work—Helena blew out a breath through shiny pink lips. "I told Grey he should have talked to you first, but did he listen?"

"Of course not, he's a man."

Helena laughed. "I had a feeling I was going to like you."

Sophia's lips twitched.

"So not his idea for you to sing," Sophia said with a lifted brow. She wondered if Helena could do what Grey did with music. What she did.

"Honey, no, that was all me." Helena waved a hand in dismissal. "He asked me to help him with the protection of your club. He said you asked." When Sophia nodded, she continued, "It is better if I'm here, observing, and putting protections in place, so I thought why not sing and hide in plain sight?"

Sophia considered it for a moment. They had Evan, but Sophia herself was the headliner, and she didn't do that often, due to lack of time for practicing. But the patrons loved when she sang, and they would probably love Helena too. She was a beautiful singer, and it didn't hurt that a lot of people knew who she was.

And the protection thing too, of course.

"What do you say?" Helena asked expectantly.

"I'm reeling, sorry," Sophia said. "I know this can only be a good thing for my club for many reasons."

"I startled you." Helena looked a little chagrined. "I knew I should have insisted with Grey, but that man is nothing if not stubborn as hell."

Sophia took a breath. "Well, I did ask him for the protection."

Maybe it wasn't a terrible idea.

Oh, who was she kidding? Of course it was a good idea.

"I didn't know you were a witch."

Helena lifted her brows. "Yeah, well, I can't be broadcasting that in my music videos."

Hysterical laughter bubbled up Sophia's chest, but she bit it down ruthlessly.

"And can you do what Grey can?"

"No one does the things Grey can." Helena looked so serious, Sophia was taken aback.

"You must be too if he asked you for help."

"What can I say?" Helena's smile was wide and brilliant. Sophia couldn't help but smile too.

"Look, it sounds amazing," Sophia said, "but do you mind if I talk to Grey first?"

Helena seemed to size her up, her head leaned to one side.

"A woman can never be too careful and I respect that," she finally said. "By all means, call him." She pulled out a business card, small and dainty, with gold lettering on a blue background. "Then call me."

Sophia took the card, and Helena turned to walk away. Before she left, she turned back and said, "I know this is all a little crazy, but Grey doesn't act without thinking. Not often, at least—he is still a man."

Sophia snorted. "I think I like you."

One last smile, and Helena walked out the back door. Just then, Victoria walked into the hallway.

"Who was that?"

"That was Helena Bennett," Sophia told Victoria and recounted what Helena had said, minus the magic part.

"Are you kidding?" Victoria asked with her eyes raised high.

"Dead serious."

Victoria looked stunned, her pretty green eyes wide. "Holy shit."

"I know, right?" Sophia bit her tongue about the other half of the visit, but she wouldn't worry about it now.

o o o

THE FOLLOWING MORNING, SOPHIA SAT ON THE ARMCHAIR by the window as she waited for Grey. Her leg bobbed up and down rapidly, and no matter how many times she tried to stop it, it wouldn't. She didn't know the exact moment she'd decided to ask him to come with her, but it seemed like the right idea at the time. Now, she waited and her heart raced, because she also didn't know why she was hesitant to tell Jeanette that Grey was coming with her. Wouldn't she be glad to see Will's son? Jeanette had grown up with Will and Sophia's mom, after all.

And come to think of it, Sophia wondered why Jeanette never spoke of Grey either.

Something fishy indeed.

She stuck her finger between her teeth, chewing on her already super short nail, and imagined Julia frowning at her for it. Grey would arrive soon, but it wasn't soon enough. Her guts felt liquid.

Sophia picked up her phone to check the time for the one-hundredth time, and a text came through. Her anxiety spiked.

"What the hell do you want?" She rolled her eyes at the screen. What he could possibly say to her, she didn't know.

ARIC: HEY

Hey? That was it? Sophia grimaced. Typical of Aric to do the bare minimum and expect anything at all from her.

She hadn't needed to block him before, since he was so good at disappearing when he got what he wanted, but she might have to. There was nothing she wanted less than to do that thing with Aric again. Enough was enough.

She set down the phone as a second message came through.

ARIC: LOOK, I KNOW THINGS DIDN'T END THE
BEST LAST TIME I SAW YOU. I'M SORRY
ABOUT IT.

She frowned. Last she'd heard about him, he was dating a nineteen-year-old and acting like the big man in town. Meanwhile, she had done her best to get over him after four miserable years. When they'd met in college, he was everything she had wanted. Super-hot, smart, and charming as hell. The late night conversations and the incredible sex... But none of that had been enough when he'd cheated on her and then tried to blame it on her.

Bastard.

It had been a year since the last time she saw him, where they'd gotten drunk and spent the night together, for him to disappear right after and claim he remembered nothing.

Now he was apologizing? What parallel universe had she jumped into and when?

SOPHIA: ARIC, WHAT DO YOU WANT?

ARIC: FINALLY, A RESPONSE.

She rolled her eyes. Typical.

ARIC: I'M SORRY ABOUT THAT.

ARIC: I'M JUST SO HAPPY TO HEAR BACK
FROM YOU.

SOPHIA: WHAT DO YOU NEED, ARIC?

ARIC: I REALLY JUST WANTED TO TALK TO YOU.
CAN WE MEET? COFFEE?

She was ready to type 'hell no' when his next message came.

ARIC: WE CAN GO TO THAT PLACE YOU LOVE
SO MUCH IN MIDTOWN.

Did he mean Sutton Place? Where she went every Sunday to be with her sisters?

Fuck. No.

She decided to not respond, as she made a mistake engaging in the first place.

The doorbell went off, and she breathed in relief as she hurried over and opened the door to find Grey standing there, dressed in his typical black, though his jacket was a cool forest green that did something to his skin tone that had her doing a double take.

He was smiling a little, that little dimple twinkling on his cheek. She wanted to put her pinky finger to it.

"Thanks for picking me up," she said, walking outside and locking the door before she did something she'd regret.

"No need for both of us to drive." He gestured for her to walk ahead of him, and she took the steps down to the driveway. His car was nice and sleek, a matte black, electric—which wasn't shocking, given the city they lived in.

He opened the door for her and she stepped in, settling in the leather seats as he rounded the front of the car, running his hand through his hair. When he was inside the car, she noticed he had changed his nose ring for a tiny golden hoop.

"How often do you change it?" she asked him as he turned the car on. It didn't make a noise, and she noticed the screen on the dashboard with a map of the city. They pulled away from the curb and he looked at her quizzically.

"How often do I change what?"

She pointed at her own nose, wondering if she was brave enough to get one someday.

He reached up and touched the hoop with the tip of his finger.

"Whenever the mood strikes," he said.

Her brows shot up.

"Oh, as simple as that."

"Yeah," he grinned and she found herself staring.

Her phone dinged.

> VICTORIA: WHY IS ARIC TEXTING ME, SOPHIA
> EVELYN CANDELA MONTGOMERY?

"Oh, God," she groaned.

"Something wrong?" Grey asked, instantly concerned, and her heart squeezed a little.

Something was wrong with her alright.

"Nothing I can't put an end to quickly," she told him, before focusing back on her phone.

> SOPHIA: HE TEXTED ME OUT OF THE BLUE THE
> OTHER NIGHT. I DID NOT RESPOND, AND YOU
> KNOW HOW HE IS.
>
> SOPHIA: STRIKE THAT. I SLIPPED AND RESPONDED
> TODAY, BUT I QUICKLY STOPPED. PROMISE.
>
> VICTORIA: SWEET JESUS... WHAT DO YOU
> WANT ME TO SAY TO HIM?
>
> SOPHIA: I SHOULDN'T HAVE ENGAGED TODAY.
>
> VICTORIA: OBVIOUSLY.

Sophia was typing a profuse apology when Victoria's next message came through.

> VICTORIA: IT HAS TO BE GOOD TO GET HIM TO
> STOP.
>
> SOPHIA: YOU DON'T HAVE TO ENGAGE, VIC.
>
> VICTORIA: DUH.

Sophia sighed heavily.

"Handled?" Grey asked, his eyes on her instead of on the road, since apparently his car essentially drove itself.

"I guess so." If she knew Victoria, the woman would have it handled quickly.

"Efficient." He looked at the road, then back at her for a quiet moment, where his brown eyes flicked down her body, then back to her face. "Nice."

She felt the heat suffuse her face and neck and decided it was best if she looked out the window instead. Was he flirting with her, or was she imagining things? What was wrong with her? She would have to get a hold of herself because it was a two-hour drive, including getting on the ferry, which was wildly romantic in a rom-com kind of way. Even with the topic of conversation they were having with Jeanette.

Was she into this man? What was wrong with her?

She braved a peek at him. He was focused on the road again, his teeth digging into his bottom lip distractedly. A breath left her in a whoosh, and she focused on the shifting landscape instead, her hand flat against the back of her neck.

Yep. Definitely into him.

Damn it...

"Anything else you'd like to know?" He glanced at her again, a sly look crossing his face.

"Nothing. Why?"

"Because you were staring and all." There definitely was a smirk gracing his lips.

"I was not staring," she responded, indignant, and watched the small smile grow until she was smiling too. "Jerk."

"Why?" he laughed.

"For bringing it up."

Her anxiety dissipated, allowing her to take deeper breaths. It was so easy being around him, he was so calm.

When they were on the Ferry, they got out of the car and headed upstairs to the deck. She buried herself into her jacket, which was lined with faux fur on the inside. The wind was bitterly cold against the exposed skin of her face and neck, even though the sun was shining for the first time in days.

Grey went to the very front of the deck, watching the city drift further and further away. She stood by him, her hands in her pockets, as he leaned on the green railing. His hair was on his face, but he didn't move to fix it. It would have driven her insane, so she was glad she had pulled hers into a ponytail.

"How do you do that?" She was unable to keep herself from smiling.

When he turned to look at her, there was a question in his brown eyes. He had expressive eyes, surrounded by thick, dark eyelashes she would have killed to have.

"How are you so calm?" she clarified.

"I'm not always calm." He twisted to face her, one forearm still on the railing. She mimicked him.

"You seem so relaxed and unbothered," she said. "Even when there's been agitation, like the other day with my sister."

"It's best to stay calm and clear-headed in high-stress situations."

"Do you ever feel anxious?"

His lips pressed together, but not in an unpleasant sort of way, and looked out at the cityscape.

"I do," he said. "I've just learned coping mechanisms."

"Isn't that nice?" She deadpanned. "Can you teach me coping mechanisms?"

Their eyes met again. She found herself not being able to look away from the velvety depths of his eyes. Something about them pulled at her.

"Any time." His dimple flashed, and she finally looked away, so he didn't accuse her of ogling him, which would be easy to do without even trying. Because of that, she changed the subject.

"I haven't thanked you for sending Helena to the club."

"You're welcome," he said.

She nodded, picking at the cuticle of her thumb inside the pocket.

"I do wish you had told me she was coming," she added. "I was caught like a deer in headlights."

"I apologize."

Her eyes narrowed. "That simple, huh."

He shrugged one shoulder. Little else was said for the rest of the ferry ride. When they were about to dock, they headed down to the car and exited slowly, behind a long row of other cars, and soon, they were on a winding road. There were walls of pine trees on either side of them, dark and tall. It gave her a sense of protection somehow.

Jeanette's house was as charming as they got. It sat in a cul-de-sac, the little porch in the front housing two rocking chairs that looked ancient. The other two in the set were in Victoria's house. She had a lot of plants, all dried now from the cold, but in the summer, her yard was incredibly lush and colorful.

Sophia trudged the little walkway with her bag slung on her shoulder, Grey by her side, his hand briefly reaching for the small of her back. It sent shivers up and down her spine, and her skin beaded underneath her coat. When they stepped onto the porch, the door opened, and Jeanette appeared, dressed in a pair of black leggings and a colorful poncho with geometric patterns at the bottom. She kept her braided hair tied away from her face with a red band.

She smiled widely at Sophia, but as she opened her arms, her bright green eyes focused on Grey, and her smile slipped, leaving her looking slightly ashen. Her arms fell to her side, and her mouth was slightly ajar.

"Will," she murmured, but shook her head soon after. A glassy quality entered her eyes.

Jeannette leaned forward and kissed her on the forehead, but her eyes were on Grey.

"Bless you, darling," she breathed, then smiled at her. Her green eyes were sparkling with the mist of tears. Sophia clung to her a little, and she ached for her mom. She wished to have this all the time. Sophia closed the distance and hugged her. The familiar scent that was so purely Jeanette was so overwhelming, she almost wept.

A breath shivered out of her as she turned to Grey, who stood awkwardly to the side.

"Jeanette, this is Grey," she said, watching Jeanette closely. There was no expression now.

"Hi, it's a pleasure to meet you," Grey said, offering his hand to Jeanette. She shook it.

"Come on in," she said, her voice an octave lower than normal.

They followed her to the kitchen and stood just inside as Jeanette busied herself with a kettle. Sophia and Grey shared a bewildered look.

"Sit," Jeanette said and pointed toward the kitchen table, an old, heavy thing with many lines spread over the top. It was just off the kitchen, in a little dining nook by a pair of small windows. The kitchen was clean, heavy on the clutter. Stuff that was familiar to Sophia, though she had no idea what they were. Jars of dried things, and others with liquids in them. Dried flowers hanging off the window by the sink, and a broom by the door.

"I will make tea," Jeanette announced, opening a dark blue cabinet and reaching for a jar of dried leaves. She busied herself at the stove, while Sophia watched her.

Beside her, Grey cleared his throat softly. He was watching Jeanette move, his lips slightly opened. Of course he had noticed the odd behavior. One did not have to be familiar with Jeanette to see the jerky movements and the way Jeanette was avoiding looking at the two of them.

"How's everything, Jeanette?" Sophia asked her, and Jeanette turned to her with a forced smile.

"Almost done," she said in a sing-song tone instead of answering Sophia's question, and went back to steeping leaves into clear mugs. A few moments later, steaming mugs in her hands, she joined them at the table. This time, Jeanette was staring at Grey as if she couldn't believe her eyes.

"I guess you know who I am," Grey said quietly. Jeanette let out a breath so long, Sophia thought Jeanette might have been holding it for a while.

"Of course, I know you," she said, her voice still deep. "You look just like your father."

Grey's cheeks reddened. Sophia just stared from one to the other, trying not to let her mouth gape.

"Except for the eyes," Jeanette continued. "Will had these eyes that were neither brown nor green. Something in between that was magical."

Sophia frowned tightly. She had never heard Jeanette speak of her mother's lover that way, with a yearning in her voice. Sophia fought down a sudden wave of nausea as the contents in her stomach swirled hotly.

Whatever was happening, she didn't like it.

"You look so familiar to me," Grey said quietly, his deep voice a rumble. "We haven't met, right?"

The way he said that... It was the way Sophia thought of him.

Like no, but also yes.

"Jeanette." Sophia's head was spinning. "Tell me what's going on."

Grey and Jeanette turned to her and stared as if they'd just noticed she was there.

"I don't get any of this," Grey said and stood, the chair teetering before he put his hands on the back and set the legs firmly on the floor. He was more agitated than Sophia had ever seen him. "I feel as if I should know more. As if I should remember more. How am I connected to you? Who are you? Why am I here?"

Jeanette's frown deepened. "Believe me, I'm just as confused as you."

Sophia couldn't breathe. Her chest rose and fell rapidly as she watched Grey freeze.

"Answer something for me," he whispered, as if afraid to ask.

Jeanette waited, still on her chair, as Sophia pressed her hands to her stomach.

"How do I know you?" he asked. "Because I obviously do."

Jeanette's eyes went glassy.

"I..." She shook her head, and her eyes cleared again.

Sophia could hardly breathe.

"That's because I knew you as a child," Jeanette finally said. "You've been in this house before."

Sophia had the sudden urge to laugh but Jeanette was perfectly serious.

"But that's not possible," Sophia said a little too loudly. The other two's attention snapped to her. "I think I would remember that. *I* was here all the time."

Jeanette stared up at Grey, who looked rather pale.

"And so was he. You were inseparable." The moment the words left her mouth, Jeanette shook her head, and the haze around her cleared.

"How is that possible?" Sophia felt hysterical, and worse when Jeanette smiled at her, a little dazedly.

"How is what possible, darling?"

Sophia and Grey looked at each other. It was like her stomach lost its bottom.

"Jeanette are you okay?" Sophia reached for Jeanette's arm. The skin was soft under her fingers.

"I don't know," she said. "I feel queasy. What were we talking about?"

"We were talking about Grey," Sophia said.

Jeanette blinked, obviously confused.

"Oh," Grey breathed, bending over the chair. "Oh, I know what's going on."

Sophia looked up at his pale face.

"A spell."

Jeanette's eyes lit up. "A spell? What spell do you mean, boy?"

"You tell me," Grey bit out.

"How can she tell you anything?" Sophia snapped, tired of not understanding anything. "She obviously doesn't know."

Jeanette held up a hand.

"Hmmmm," she hummed. "You say there's a spell on me?"

"Us," Grey said. "It's pretty obvious to me."

"It makes us forget..." Jeanette said, and anger came into her eyes like lightning. "I am going to kill Silvana."

Already dead, Sophia wanted to remind her, but couldn't say it. She wanted to laugh and cry all at once.

"Your mother was a talented witch, and she could do things you could never imagine." Jeanette said to Sophia. "How could I not notice it before?"

"Depends on the parameters of the spell," Grey said. "If it was vague, maybe that's why it slips away."

Jeanette nodded with a wild look in her green eyes. "I grew up with your father," she told him, "and Silvana. We were friends all our lives."

Grey opened his mouth, but Jeanette held up a hand and he snapped it shut.

The silence was like a void, as if any sound made after it would be swallowed. Sophia's body was boneless, and even if she had wanted to move, she probably wouldn't be able to.

"I don't understand," Grey mumbled.

"How are you two together?" Jeanette asked to neither in particular, but she didn't wait for them to respond. "Never mind that. She should have known this wasn't going to work for long."

"Please explain to me. I don't understand any of this." Sophia wanted to stand, but her legs were jelly.

"Things haven't felt quite right since your mom died, and I thought it was because I'd just lost my two closest friends. And then that happened the other day when I tried calling you so many times and got nowhere. I couldn't figure it out. Every time I think about magic it happens."

Sophia couldn't have said anything. Words no longer existed at that moment. They wouldn't make sense.

"Will would have never done this kind of spell," she continued as if she were speaking to an empty room. "This has Silvana written all over it."

It hit Sophia right then, what that meant. Her memories of her mom doing special things... it was real.

"She was a witch," Sophia whispered. Jeanette nodded, eyes wide. "And you too?"

"Gift of sight," Jeanette said. "Nothing active, really, unless I take potions."

"So Silvana was a witch," Grey said, "and so was my dad, according to his notebooks. And you're a witch like I'm a witch."

"Are you now, Greyson?" Jeanette's attention was back on Grey. His name in her mouth sounded so right. A sound Sophia had heard before, something that was as familiar to her as the hair on her head.

"My dad was the only person to call me that," Grey murmured.

"And now you know for sure," Jeanette told him before she took a deep breath.

An understanding passed between the two of them, and Sophia shivered at the intensity of their gaze on each other.

"Why would my mom do this?" Sophia said and her voice didn't sound like her own. She wanted to understand because things were making less and less sense as they unfolded.

"She must have had her reasons." Jeanette's voice was soft, but her eyes narrowed. "Your mom was a powerful witch. She could do things I have never seen anyone else do."

Sophia held her breath, enraptured. Only when her lungs were screaming did she let it out.

"Are memory charms like this not common then?" she asked.

Grey shook his head. "No. They don't last very long. At most, a few weeks, and usually for smaller things and a single subject."

Sophia thought of Julia. She would remember sooner or later. Then what?

Grey looked at her, his eyes focusing on her as if he was seeing her for the very first time. And she couldn't look away from the stories swirling in his eyes, as if they were a vortex she could lose herself into.

Sophia felt the tears warm her eyes, countless feelings rushing through her veins. No wonder she'd questioned her own sanity.

A spell. One that made her forget.

What?

"What gave her such power?" Sophia asked, her voice raw, as if she had been screaming.

Jeanette opened her mouth to speak, but suddenly, she shook her head once, twice.

"I'm sorry, darling, what were we talking about?"

Sophia was glad she was sitting because everything became black for a split moment, and she was hot. Sweat ran down her back. Breathing was difficult. This could not be happening.

Grey was sitting very still, as if he was afraid to move.

They had entered an alternate universe.

"Nothing important." Sophia didn't know why she lied, but it felt like the right thing to say.

Jeanette only smiled softly. "You know, your memory is just not the same as you get older."

"Tell me about it," Grey said.

As they were getting ready to go, a few short minutes later, Sophia realized they were still wearing their shoes and coats. At the door, Sophia stopped, as Grey stepped out onto the porch.

"Jeanette, do you remember Mom writing in journals?"

"Oh yes, all the time. There wasn't a thought she didn't record. I wish I had them all."

Confirmation. She wasn't crazy.

And if her mom was a witch, maybe she did something to the journals to make them difficult to read. Or impossible in this case. Because how did you read something you couldn't see?

12

They drove in complete silence, but for the piano music coming through the speakers. They both stared out the windshield, where the wipers worked against the falling rain. After a while, she looked at him, annoyed that he seemed so calm when her mind was racing. She couldn't have had a clear thought in that moment, even if she tried really hard. She was no longer dizzy and on the verge of fainting anymore, so at least she had that going for her.

They got on the ferry but sat together inside the car instead of getting out for the duration of the ride over the water.

He looked at her, finally, a line between his brows.

"That explains a lot," he said, his voice deeper than normal, if that was even possible. His long fingers rested on his lap, stark against the black of his jeans. He rubbed his index finger over a spot by his knee, over and over, the way she did when she was feeling anxious and needed grounding.

"I still don't remember anything."

"Me neither." He paused, worried his bottom lip between his teeth. "But somehow, I can make sense of all this a little more."

She deadpanned. "How the hell are you taking all that and making sense of it at all?"

"The familiarity seems more natural now," Grey said.

She leaned her head against the headrest, still facing him. She felt like she was made of goo.

"How can a spell be this powerful?"

"I have no clue."

Sophia wanted to cry, but thankfully, they didn't speak again until they were in front of her house.

"I think we should look at the journals," she said into the deafening silence.

"You said they're empty."

"Yes, but if there is a memory spell, then maybe there is something in the journals too," she said. She was convinced that was the way to go, at least for the moment. "Maybe she put a spell on them to make them seem empty."

"That's a definite possibility."

"Alright, so your place or mine?" she asked, and watched him blink a few times.

"You want to look into them right now?"

"You have anything else going on?"

He frowned, as if thinking about it.

"No." He pulled into the driveway instead of staying on the street. "I vote my house, since I have all the magic potions, and all."

Sophia led Grey up to the house, where they grabbed some of the boxes and brought them into the garage to the back of her car. She followed him to his house and parked in the driveway, at his instruction. Her anxiety had escalated, and by the time they took the boxes upstairs, she was in a mild state of panic.

Her phone rang as she took off her shoes by the garage door, which led straight into the kitchen.

Seeing Aric's name on the screen, she declined it. He wouldn't leave a voicemail. It wasn't his style.

And thank God for that, she thought.

They settled on the living room floor after Sophia and Grey pushed the loveseat and armchair out of the way. Grey stepped away for a moment, coming back with his arms filled with books, and he lay them on the floor along with hers. All the books looked similar. Even the journals. Some were notebooks, others were bound in leather, and the big tomes were all a soft brown leather. Exactly like her mom's.

"So the magic led you to me because we knew each other from before," she said because she needed to vocalize it to make sense of it.

"From a past life, you could say." His lips twitched slightly.

"Indeed."

It seemed like so much time had passed since he had come to the club that fateful night, and she didn't know if it was because she now knew they had grown up together for a part of their lives, or if it was because he had found his way into her life so thoroughly. At another time, she'd have been counting the red flags, but so far, none. He was running his hands through his hair again. A bit of a nervous gesture, she noted.

Honestly, she didn't know how to feel about knowing some of his tells already.

Maybe she was watching him too closely.

They sat on the floor, both rendered immobile by the enormity of the job they had to do. Going through blank books. Who would have thought?

Either they were on the right track, or were they losing their minds.

A little of both, perhaps.

Sophia dug into the last box, pulled out a bunch of envelopes wrapped together with a piece of brown twine. There were several other bundles that looked the same.

"Where do we start?" he said out loud, but she suspected he was saying it for his own benefit.

"Beats the hell out of me." But she blew out a nervous breath. She'd only opened one letter, blank, which should have been suspicious enough. She could be really dense sometimes.

She set the envelopes on the floor in front of her crossed legs, putting each bundle in neat piles.

"I guess the envelopes are the best way to go." He picked up a bundle. When he pulled at the twine, her heart jumped, and her stomach fluttered.

"Is it weird that this is making me anxious?" She couldn't tear her eyes away from the envelopes in his hand.

"Not at all. It's weird as hell."

Their eyes met for a brief moment, but her nerves didn't let her linger there, though she wanted to.

Then he moved suddenly, and her eager eyes went back to him with a question.

"I think I have something that can help." He got up without another word and returned with a small clear vial with a red liquid inside. Her mouth hung open when he put back his head and put a single drop of the potion into his mouth. His face scrunched up. It was so cute, she wanted to laugh. Like a little kid taking a medicine he didn't want.

She briefly wondered if he made a face when he shot tequila, too. Or if he ever shot tequila. Maybe she would have to find out. It was her favorite party trick, not making a face when she took a shot, or when she chased it with a lime.

"Watch this." He rubbed his hands together as if to warm them. "Ordinariorum coetus aliter," he said, his voice clear and firm, and Sophia sat back in awe.

Something came out of his hands, like a smoke with shimmering crystals inside it, and the stacks of envelopes rose in the air. It was like reading her favorite childhood story with the wizards for the very first time. The awe, the sense of wonder. But in real life, which was bizarre. She pressed her hand over her thundering heart as neat stacks of envelopes now waited for them to read. Nothing should have surprised her anymore, but then she remembered that this was all new to her, anyway.

The envelopes shuffled like playing cards in the air, and when they were done, they sorted into neat piles.

Everything sorted, they sat and got to work. Sophia opened a letter, carefully avoiding ripping the envelopes. Somehow, it felt like she'd be seriously transgressing if she broke even one little corner. There was a silence in the house, as if the walls knew what they were doing.

She didn't think she'd ever written a letter by hand, which she would have to remedy. There was something special about having a physical piece of paper and read the words someone took the time to write out for you. She unfolded the letter and found herself staring at the yellowing sheet of paper. At first, her mind couldn't comprehend what she was looking at.

"This is new," she mumbled. The lined sheet was full of strange little symbols and numbers instead of letters. They were neat and every symbol was carefully written and uniform.

She showed Grey, who was also staring at the sheet in his hand. He showed it to her. It was the same.

"It couldn't be that easy." She didn't miss the sarcasm in his tone. He ran his hand over his face. Her eye drew to his forearm, and she forced herself to look away. Maybe Victoria was right—it had been way too long. How could a forearm turn her on otherwise?

"We need to make a key," she said a little too loudly because she had to distract herself from ogling him like a creep. He got them a notepad and a couple of pens and sat so close she could smell that scent of his. She wondered what it was. A cologne, or soap, or maybe just the laundry detergent he used, but something about it made her feel warm and fuzzy. Like wrapping yourself inside a blanket right after it came out of the dryer.

She breathed it in, trying to not feel too daunted by the task in front of them.

He scribbled carefully on the white paper pad. Of course, his handwriting was pretty, too. It was neat and even. The kind of handwriting she saw fleeting across her social media from time to time when people showed their impressive bullet journal spreads. She couldn't say hers was anything like that. It was legible, and that was enough for her, even if it looked like she mixed several fonts in one document.

"This looks like it could be my mom's name," she pointed to the top of one letter.

"Or my dad's if they used his full name."

"Good point."

They worked on it for a while, and hours later, they had a sheet of symbols and their corresponding letter. Of course, they still didn't know if that was correct or not. It was tedious and frustrating work, especially when she grabbed another sheet, and began translating one of the letters, and realized some of the symbols were wrong.

She sighed and laid down on her back, her arms stretched wide. She had taken off her sweater and put it on the arm of the chair, where it sat like a gray cloud.

"This sucks."

He said nothing, and she lifted her head to look at him. He was frowning down at the papers.

"Any ideas?"

He looked at her, but she was pretty sure he wasn't actually seeing her. "Maybe."

She snapped her fingers in front of his face. "Talk to me, maybe I can help." She doubted it, but she would try.

"This will take ages if we keep at it this way," he said.

"Yeah, no shit. If only there was a way to—"

His eyes opened wide, his back going straight.

"What?" Her heart jumped.

"I might be able to make this process simpler."

With a grin on his face, he stood, the dimple flashing. She felt the effects of that smile down to her toes. God, he was sexy.

She sat up quickly, her head screaming as she did so. "Are we doing magic?"

She would have hated the eagerness in her voice, but she was too excited to care.

His eyes twinkled. "Yes, I'm doing magic." His emphasis was clear. She glared at him and got a smirk back as he stood and moved toward the kitchen.

"What are you doing this time?" She followed him, refusing to let her eyes wander down his body. What would her sisters say if Sophia admitted to them that she was attracted to Grey Constantine, of all people? Sophia couldn't imagine that would go well at all.

"Let me show you something very cool," his deep voice rumbled. She found him grabbing a large wooden cutting board and a chef's knife, and he had placed a huge black cauldron on the stove. How he moved that fast, she didn't know. Maybe the cauldron had always been on the stove and she just missed it before.

"So this is what modern witches do." She leaned on the counter and crossed her arms as she watched him work.

"What did you expect it would be like?" He moved into the pantry and brought out several dried things in his hands, along with jars of other ingredients she couldn't have placed if she wanted to.

Back at the cutting board, he chopped a dark green herb so fine it was close to a powder when he was finished.

"Honestly, no idea."

He snorted. "Fair."

That made her feel a little better. "Can I help you?"

"Yes." He pointed at the door that led to the pantry. "Find me a jar labeled moon water."

"I've heard of moon water," she said, spirits lifting because she wasn't completely ignorant. She headed to the wall and her gaze went to the bottom shelves, where he had bigger jars with silvery lids. Some had dark liquids, others looked thick and dark, a little gross. She found the moon water easily. The jar was glass, covered with a metal lid, and at the bottom, a pearlescent stone rolled around. It was white, pure, and ethereal, with flashes of blue and green as it moved.

Back in the kitchen, though she wanted to spend a few hours (or days) in that pantry, she handed him the jar.

He took off the lid and dropped a little of the water into the cauldron. The flame was still off.

"There is another potion in there, labeled 'seeing'," he said.

She found the tiniest vial she had ever seen, thin and fragile-looking, smooth, and brought it to him.

He opened it.

"This is a potion you use when you need to see more than your eyes allow you to," he said. "It's not very strong, just a boost." He emptied the contents into the cauldron. A faint line of mist floated up into the air and she looked into the cauldron, crossing her fingers that it didn't explode on her face. It smelled like dirt.

Kind of underwhelming.

She turned when he took a step toward her, towering over her. Her heart stuttered as he reached forward and turned a knob on the stove, close to her hip. So close she could feel his warmth on her own skin. She didn't move, even when his arm brushed hers.

"Now we let it simmer for a while," he whispered, then stepped back.

What a bastard, she thought with a thrill that started in her stomach and spread to the rest of her. She crossed her arms again as the cauldron behind her hissed. She stepped to the side. It wouldn't do to have her hair burned off because she was too busy staring at Grey and that dimple, and the nose ring, and the man-bun. Who knew she'd be into that?

"How did you learn to do all this?" She gestured to the cauldron and herbs.

"My dad." His expression suddenly shuttered. He picked up a wooden spoon and stirred slowly. "It was his favorite thing, making magic. He taught me a lot of things, and I also did some traveling with my mom, and I learned from others who were much better at it than I was. And am."

She regretted asking. Knowing that Will Constantine had been a witch was as unsettling as finding out her mom was one too. If only Sophia and Grey didn't have to deal with the fallout of their choices.

"I think you're good at it," she said, though she was aware she didn't know what she was talking about. He lifted a brow to show that he thought the same, and she almost laughed.

"I wonder if my mom taught me too." She'd always known her mom was different, still had *that* memory. "My dad never said anything about it."

"Maybe he lost all his memories too."

"That, or he's avoiding talking about her, which is a whole thing."

She hadn't considered her father not having all his memories, but the more she thought about it, the more it made sense. If only her mom's spell would have taken away the memory of her running away with another man.

"My dad had the power of telekinesis, moving things with his mind. It was the coolest thing anyone had ever seen, though he rarely used it. He said it drained his energy, which is typical of magic."

She raised her brows. "It is?"

He nodded as the mixture in the cauldron lit up faintly now, and she looked inside to find it swirling like the night's sky, with a million stars within it. It didn't smell like anything anymore, which she had also not expected. In her mind, potions would always smell terrible.

"This potion is my invention," he said quietly. "I created it because I'd get frustrated with puzzles when I was kid, and I made it to decipher them more quickly."

She smiled at the image of him as a little boy, scrawny, nose scattered with freckles, playing with magic in the kitchen where his parents cooked him dinner.

"That sounds like cheating to me."

His grin transformed his face.

"I call it being resourceful."

"Whatever you have to tell yourself." But she smiled too. "So, you invented this potion. What else is there?"

"If you thought I was cool before, just hold on." He had a small smirk, like a self-satisfied male getting attention from a woman. She almost rolled her eyes—not a him, but the whole situation, because she felt like a dumb teenager.

The mixture was bubbling, so he reached down and turned off the burner. Quickly, he turned and picked up the cutting board with his pulverized herbs and dropped them into the cauldron. Then he turned and grabbed her by the arm, and she found herself engulfed in his arms as the potion exploded behind them. She jumped, and a gasp escaped her when it happened. Her heart was beating wildly as he let go of her and went back to the potion. She thought maybe he let go a little too soon, and knew that he didn't have to hold her. He could have just told her it was coming... Sneaky.

"I should have warned you first." He was funneling the potion into a dark brown bottle, as if unaware of the effect he'd had on her. Her heart was shuddering inside her chest, and she resented the fact that he seemed perfectly unfazed. The potion was no longer glowing blue, but was now an indistinct shade of brown.

"It's okay." She swallowed hotly.

"And now, we use this to put the puzzle together," he said when he finished bottling. "I don't know if it will work as well as I imagine, but it doesn't hurt to try." He gave her a few small, porcelain bowls, which she carried, curious.

They went back to the living room and set everything on the floor. He picked up one of the keys they had made, took a picture of it with his phone. When she raised her brow at him, he said, "You'll see."

In one of the little bowls, he put the key, and then a few drops of the potion he'd just made. The paper dissolved with a cloud of blue smoke. It left behind a small amount of blue liquid that glowed slightly. Grey picked up the bowl and dumped the liquid on one letter. Sophia held back a gasp. She was barely breathing. Nothing happened for a moment, but then, as she watched, some of the symbols disappeared into the paper, as if they were being sucked into it by a force unseen. The symbols they had attempted to decipher were replaced by letters.

"Wow." She could feel the energy in the room shifting and swirling. She was shifting and swirling.

He pointed at the letter. The name William had appeared at the top.

"I can't believe that worked," she said.

He smirked and lifted a brow. "You doubted my genius. Should I be offended?"

"You can if you want to waste your time."

His smile was less cocky this time, and they went back to work on the key. It took them a while of writing, copying, infusing the potion with the key. Finally, as night fell, they had a full key that would be the correct one, and they did one last infusion. When he put in a few drops on another letter, it revealed neat letters on the page that read perfectly.

"Yes," he muttered under his breath, in triumph. When he grinned and bit the corner of his lip, something stirred low in her belly. She needed to go home. This would not bode well for her if she stayed around him for extended periods of time.

The first letters were from when the trio was only nine or ten, according to the date at the top of the page. They wrote to each other like people texted these days. Sending the same sheet to each other and passing it around, filling pages upon pages of carefully written text on lined paper.

Sophia had been nervous, going into those letters. She loved her mom, the wonderful memories she still had, but Sophia also never forgot how when her mom died, she had been running off with another man. But reading about annoying adults and school trips, crushes, and special memories, Sophia couldn't help but smile sadly. Her mom, in particular, wrote a lot about home and how her dad was a miserable person, always angry, always shouting. It seemed to be a theme, and Sophia felt a pang for that kind of upbringing she would never be able to understand. Sophia knew little about that life, as she had been too young to ask those questions before her mom died. And now, there it was, right in front of her.

She snapped out of it when Grey spoken after a while.

"Listen to this," he said. "From my dad. Dear Silvana and Jeanette, when will I see you next? My dad says there's a solstice, and I heard him say we were coming to Silvana's house for the celebration. Is that true? Have you heard anything?"

"What's the response?"

"Neither of the girls knew." He looked over at the other side of the page. "They change subjects after that."

"How were they sending these to each other?" Sophia wondered, noticing that the first bunch of letters did not have stamps on the envelopes. There were no addresses or anything else either.

"No idea," Grey murmured and went back to reading.

It was close to two in the morning, as the wind howled past the windows, when Sophia started seeing double. With a letter in her hands, she lay on the floor, yawning hard and long. All the words blurred together, and before she knew it, she nodded off. Maybe it had only been moments, or maybe she'd been out for hours, but suddenly, she felt weightless.

She didn't open her eyes, only half-awake as her arms snaked around a warm neck, her head on a hard shoulder. She liked the way he smelled, and how he drew soft, warm blankets over her before she fell in deeper.

13

Silvana hung upside down from the lowest branch of the large maple tree in the fields behind her house. She had thought about it and worn pants instead of her preferred dresses, which was good, since her best friend, Will, was in one of the higher branches of the same tree, picking out the little seed pods and dropping them to the ground. They floated down like tiny helicopters, and to Silvana's ear, they made the best sound. It sounded like trumpets, but it wasn't too loud and obnoxious. The music was soft and fuzzy around the edges. It sounded like a hug would.

It was the middle of summer, unusually warm, and Silvana longed to climb higher on the tree. She didn't have the guts to, though. Heights were a little scary to her. And besides, her dad didn't like her climbing trees. Said it was for boys. At least from the lower branches, she could get down quicker if she happened to see her dad before he saw her. Her mom didn't care. Silvana just didn't understand why her dad did.

"Look!" Will said from above and she looked up to watch him shower her in seed pods. They twirled around her, got caught in her hanging hair, which her mom convinced her to straighten, so they could see how long it was. So far, it reached halfway down her back, but her mom said it was because Silvana was a really small nine-year-old.

Will did the thing with his hands, where he made them look like the waves in the ocean, and the little helicopters floated back up toward him. He let his hands fall, and they fluttered down toward her again.

"That's so cool." She grinned, and he grinned down at her. He was missing one of his canines. His hair was dark and straight, falling over his forehead, where he had mud smeared from when they were running in the stretch of forest between their houses earlier.

Will was rarely clean. He preferred rolling around in the mud more than anything else in the world, but Silvana thought he had a very nice voice. If only he'd sing more. His eyes were a pretty shade of hazel, somewhere between green and brown. They looked kind of like how hibiscus flowers sounded when they were happy. He could also draw, and that made Silvana jealous because she wanted to know how to draw.

"You should come up higher and sit with me," he said, shifting so his legs were both coming off the same side of the thick branch. He was wearing jeans and a blue t-shirt, the collar distended where he pulled at it when he was distracted.

"I think I'll stay here," she told him, throwing a look toward the house to make sure her dad wasn't watching her swing upside down like an overgrown bat.

It was a small house, yellow with white shutters, and a small porch in the back where her mom kept her plants. The lands surrounding it were the best part of it, in Silvana's opinion, because there was so much space for her to run with her friends. The grass was spotty, overgrown in some spots, but her mom also had a garden with fruits and vegetables, which was cool. Silvana enjoyed being around the plants, and she spent a lot of her time helping in the garden. Her parents sold a lot of vegetables and fruits in a local market, usually blackberries, which were overgrown and taking over a small ravine on the side. Her mom also made remedies in tiny bottles she gave to people when they came knocking on their door. It was all very serious, and Silvana wasn't sure that if she asked questions, her mom would even answer.

For a long time, when Silvana was younger, she'd wondered if her mom was a doctor. She made medicines, after all. But later, her mother would confide to Silvana that she was more of a healer, and Silvana accepted that, though she didn't know what the difference was.

The window that looked over the garden remained empty, so Silvana sighed with relief that her dad wasn't standing there watching her.

"But wouldn't the tree want you to climb higher?" Will asked. She looked up at him again.

"Why would it want me to climb higher?"

"I don't know, you're the one who hears them singing," he said and went back to picking pods and dropping them. "Trees are made for climbing."

"Maybe you're made for climbing them instead," she said, but he wasn't listening to her anymore. She pulled herself up, her little arms burning, and sat on the branch instead, and watched Will for a while, envious that he could be so high up and that his parents wouldn't care. The tree did like having him up so high. She could tell because of how the music sounded when Will was climbing it. It changed and became a little faster, more cheerful. It seemed to come through the bark, but only when she paid close attention to it, when she pressed her palm to the branch and relaxed.

Only Will and their other best friend, Jeanette, believed Silvana when she talked about hearing the music of the plants. Not that she told anyone about it, lest people think there was something wrong with her head.

And maybe there was, but she loved the music. The tree had its own, just like every other plant she had ever come across. She could tell when a plant was about to die because the music became softer, a little sweeter, but also a little bitter.

But when a plant was happy and well-cared for, the music did something to Silvana. It made her want to dance with her arms up in the air, to go out in the rain and soak in water like it was her last day breathing.

She supposed most people would think that was weird. Her mom always said that Silvana was a strange child, even as a baby. That she'd been serious and pensive, like an old lady in a tiny body.

Silvana knew she was weird, but she couldn't help it, and part of her didn't care, either.

She had often tried to play the music of the plants on her piano and her violin, but she couldn't make it work. Sometimes the songs sounded like tribal drums, and sometimes like the strings of a guitar, but whenever she tried to play the same melodies, it didn't work. It frustrated her because if there was something she was really good at it was playing instruments. She understood music in ways she understood little else.

Her name echoed in the distance, and Silvana lifted her head to see Jeanette run toward them from the direction of the house. She pulled herself into a sitting position as Jeanette ran closer, her dark brown skin glistening with sweat. She was wearing a yellow dress, her curly hair wild in the wind and sporting an equally yellow bow nestled into the hair at the top of her head.

"Jeanette's coming," she called up to Will, who started climbing down right away and came to sit by her on her branch.

Her best friends were the closest thing to siblings she had, and she had often dreamed of having sisters. It would have been nice, but her mom said she'd die if she had another kid, so Silvana was okay with it. She considered Will and Jeanette her brother and her sister, and they were the best ones someone could have, anyway, so she never felt like she was missing out on anything.

"Do you think something happened?" Will's voice was worried. He'd been worried about his dad, who had a sick heart, and was always waiting for the bad news. Silvana touched his arm with hers, but briefly, so he didn't feel like she pitied him.

Jeanette reached the tree, bending over, her hands on her knees, heaving.

"You have to come inside," she said between gulps of breath.

"Why?" Will and Silvana asked in unison, and Silvana grinned and punched his arm.

"Jinx!" She yelled and laughed when he scowled at her. Silvana always won jinxes. She could tell when they were coming. She didn't know how, and neither did her friends, which boded well for her when she got all the treats.

They both jumped off the branch, and together, the three of them started heading back.

"What did they say?" Will asked, trying to sound like he was relaxed, but both Jeanette and Silvana knew better.

"Oh, we're just ready for the lesson," Jeanette said. Her voice was even, and looking into her face would not betray that Jeanette felt bad that Will had to worry about his dad.

"Lessons are my favorite," Will said, his shoulders releasing some tension.

Silvana smiled. There was nothing in the world she loved more than solstices, when her mom would teach a small group of people how to make special brews. It was like a cooking class, except much cooler. Tonight, they were going to make a potion Silvana loved above all other potions—the knowing potion. It tasted disgusting, but it helped her see and hear things better.

When they made the potion, Silvana often imagined what it would be like to run in a field of plants of all kinds. Maybe next time her mom left some of the potion lying around, she'd sneak some and go into the woods behind her house. Imagining it had her eyes going dreamy.

"I just really hate the way it smells." Will stuck out his tongue and wrinkled his nose.

"It's not that bad," Silvana said, excited.

She took off in a run, Jeanette and Will trailing behind her. The heat was uncomfortable to all of them, but there was something nice about it too. Living in Washington meant that it rained a lot, and where Silvana's mom, Evelyn, loved the rain and thought it was magical—Silvana agreed —her dad, Ruben, hated the rain and constantly talked about how much he missed the Caribbean.

The three raced to the door, bursting through it. Silvana came face to face with her father and froze. He was short and a bit on the thin side. He had on a yellow t-shirt that contrasted with his brown skin and his hair, which was tightly coiled and cropped. His mustache was hard and black too, framing his unfriendly face. His dark eyes were like voids, where all laughter and happiness went to die. They reminded Silvana of viper eyes, how they always looked angry somehow, without even trying.

He said nothing to her, simply walked out the door. He hated the celebrations, and Silvana thought it would help him be happier to participate, but she didn't dare tell him that. Her dad wasn't always mean, but it seemed like he was angry most of the time these days. The door slammed behind him.

Silvana would never admit to her friends how embarrassing it was to her that her father acted the way he did. He was like one of those dumb kids at school who tripped other kids just to laugh about it.

Silvana shook her head a little as Will and Jeanette took off their shoes by the door. She didn't want to care what her father thought or did, so she focused on why her mom said it was important to celebrate the solstice.

"We stay connected with our roots, nuestras raíces, when we celebrate these things, mamacita," she often said as they worked together in the kitchen, making remedies and such things.

Silvana was more than eager to connect with her roots if they were making the special tea potion, as she liked to call it. Thought calling it a tea was not right either.

To Silvana, it was more like a shot of sludge that tasted of way too many things at once. So many flavors that should not coexist, but somehow worked. Silvana loved being able to hear the plants, the ground, all the things that were alive around her. She wanted to hear it more, learn its lovely patterns, then make music like it, so others could hear what she heard all the time.

She didn't really know what other people got from the tea, but she didn't really care.

They headed into the small kitchen, with the bright blue cabinets and white trimming. There was a single window right by the sink, which was clean. On the window sill, there was a tiny succulent Silvana had been tending to.

The black cauldron sat on the old gas stove, ready for ingredients, and everyone stood around, close so they could see everything that went into the potion.

Jeanette's parents, Jean and George, stood side by side, chatting quietly, while Will's mom, Meredith, a tall blonde, sat silently at the kitchen table. Will's dad, Jack, who looked exactly like Will, was by Jean and George, listening in to their conversation. Silvana loved Jack, he was funny and loved music, but she didn't like Meredith. The woman always had a pinched look on her face that intimidated Silvana for some reason.

Evelyn, her mom, instructed her to wash her hands, as well as Will and Jeanette, and the three of them did so together at the small sink. She had all the ingredients for the potion on the counter. Herbs, and barks, and other things Silvana had no idea what they were. There were containers with liquids too, and a knife, a cutting board, and a wooden spoon.

"Good afternoon, friends, and happy solstice," her mom said with a smile. Silvana, giddy, watched. Her mom was curvy, with wide hips and a soft waist and narrow shoulders. Her hair was curly and short, though she always kept it tied up. Silvana wished her mom would leave it down because it was beautiful. She had brown eyes, but hers were kind, unlike her father's.

Her mom was wearing Silvana's favorite dress. It was long and loose, a pretty off-white color, with lace and long sleeves that made Silvana feel like her mom was a good witch. She *looked* like a good witch. The lightness of the dress only accentuated the lovely velvet of her mom's brown skin.

"I'm so glad you all came to learn how to make this wonderful potion."

"Thank you for having us, Evelyn," Jean said, getting nods from everyone but the three kids and Will's mom, who looked like she wanted to be anywhere but in that kitchen.

"Get your pens and paper. There is not a lot of time for repetition, as we have to work fast with this particular brew."

Everyone shuffled around, finding their pens and notepads.

"The best part of this summer solstice is that it's a full moon tonight, which makes it an ideal time for potion-making," Mom said. "Especially this potion."

Her mom started rattling off the ingredients as people took notes. Silvana made mental notes, as she'd forgotten her notebook upstairs and didn't want to leave and miss anything. Will was enraptured with everything her mom said, but he loved making potions, so that wasn't surprising to Silvana.

She helped bring stuff to the counter when her mom asked, and Will helped chop some herbs, as Jeanette simply watched.

Silvana and her friends would later write about the potion, the way it made them feel to help out, and they wrote spells, in hopes of one day being able to use them. So far, none of them worked, but Silvana was learning slowly and asking tons of questions. Her mom was patient, but Silvana knew there were things she wasn't saying.

Later that night, Silvana wrote in the big grimoire she had made with Will and Jeanette. They had saved their allowance for what seemed like months to find the materials they wanted. Now, the big, leather-bound book was shared between the three of them. Everything they thought of when it came to magic went in it.

She wrote down everything she'd seen her mom do, humming along to the sweet music of the tiny cactus she kept in her room. She had a smile on her face when she went to bed that night.

14

From his seat in front of his computer, Grey watched gray clouds slide across the sky like dark bruises. His brows were tight as he looked out into the still darkness that preceded morning, his headphones resting on his neck. He'd tried to write a melody but failed, his mind too busy replaying the previous day to concentrate on anything else.

He had been up much earlier than he would have wanted to, but sleep had eluded him. For most of the night, his mind raced when he thought of Jeanette, the way her mind felt so lost sometimes. A spell.

How could there be such a spell? And then there were the letters. He'd always known that his dad was close to Silvana when they were younger, and reconnected later as adults. Grey, of course, didn't have all the information, only what his mom knew. He'd avoided everything that had to do with the way his dad died. Except when he'd found out she'd had three daughters at the time of her death, which happened one drunken night with a severe lack of self-control.

Until a couple of weeks ago, he'd thought he was the only one who could make music visible. Then Sophia showed up after the spell, and he knew that things were so much more complicated than he'd anticipated.

Knowing Silvana was a witch was both like finding a treasure and grabbing a rattlesnake instead of a rope. It made the heart beat faster and harder. Same as reading about the trio talk about making special potions in their letters, which was so similar to the potion he often made when he needed a boost.

Could it be the same thing? He had, after all, gotten the recipe from one of his dad's books. It was a simple recipe, and the potion didn't do more than allow the user to see and hear slightly more than normal, but the way Silvana wrote about theirs told Grey there was a lot more to it. Hopefully they'd find a recipe, and he could compare it to the one he had.

With another sigh, he exited the mixing software and removed the headphones from his neck. He stretched his arms above his head, a couple of his joints popping, when something made him swivel the chair to face the door. Sophia stood by the open door, and a warmth spread inside him. She was just as pretty in the morning as she was any other time, with her hair disheveled around her like a dark halo. Sexy.

He leaned back in his chair as she stood, maybe a little awkwardly, by the door.

The previous night, taking her into his arms as the potion exploded, had revealed a couple of things for him. One, he desperately wanted to remember her when they were kids. And two—and this realization had come when he'd lifted her in his arms to take her to the guest bed—he really enjoyed having her around.

"I didn't know if I should interrupt you," she said, walked into the office more, as he avoided looking at the shape of her, in the same clothes she'd changed to when they got back from Jeanette's. Her leggings molded themselves to her body, the white shirt buttoned only halfway, rumpled from sleep.

He forced his eyes to stay on her face.

"You can interrupt me anytime." Came out more suggestive than he intended.

Her brows shot up.

"How did you sleep?" He struggled not to smile.

"Great." She tucked her messy hair behind her ear. "Thank you for letting me stay here."

"Any time." He echoed, and he meant that too.

"And for carrying me to bed," she added, her lips quirking. "You could have made me walk."

"And miss out on carrying you?" He stood and approached her. "Fat chance."

A smile played around that mouth that made his thoughts go to every naughty corner of his mind.

"You got a potion for energy?" Her tone was lighter now.

"Coffee," he said, and her lips twitched.

"Witches drink coffee?" she asked in mock surprise, her eyes comically wide. "How mundane."

"Modern witches or whatever."

They headed toward the kitchen, and once there, he made the coffee, opting for the French press. Once she had her mug filled almost to the brim, they went back to the living room and the neatly arranged letters.

She was lying on her stomach, about to pick up a letter, when she stopped.

"Is there such a thing as a cloaking spell?" she asked, eyeing the books.

"I mean, I have never used one, but I assume there's something like it."

She pursed her lips and pressed her hands to the sides of her face.

"This is so frustrating." She looked up at him. "And I know we haven't been looking into it for long, but it sucks. What happened to writing in diaries and leaving them around for your kids to read your embarrassing stories?"

"Unless what's in them shouldn't be read by just anyone."

She rolled her eyes playfully.

"Can you just agree with me?"

He almost laughed, but schooled his face, though his lips trembled.

"Sorry. Yes, you're completely right, Sophia."

She was fighting back a smile. "Smooth."

"That's me, smoothest guy on the block."

"If you have to say it, it's not true."

"We can't all be cool like you."

Her eyes narrowed, but she said nothing else, though he wished she would. He wanted to know how her mind worked, and he liked the way she teased him.

"Do you have anything that can uncloak the journals?"

"Provided they have anything on them, you mean," he said.

"Fair enough."

"I don't know that I have anything," he said, thinking of the full moon and the crazy number of potions he had to make before the next delivery was due. One more wouldn't be a big deal, if he could figure out what he needed to make it work.

"This sucks," she grumbled. "Why isn't there an app for this?"

He chuckled.

"Potions usually work."

"I trust you've had a lot of experience?"

"With hidden texts? Loads. A real-life Indiana Jones."

She laughed.

"And you what? Play music for your enemies?"

He gave her a surprised look. "Ouch."

She laughed harder, and it was the best thing he'd heard in a while. She laughed with abandon, throwing back her head, and it made him what to laugh too. Her teeth were straight and white, the line of her neck smooth, golden, and soft. He imagined what it would feel like under his fingers, his lips. His teeth.

"So, what next?" she asked and snapped him out of his reverie.

He blinked far too slowly, like an idiot caught with his hand inside a jar of honey.

"What?"

"Are you alright?" She sat up, fully facing him.

"I'm fine." Just fantasizing about biting your neck, that's all. He flexed his jaw so he didn't do something embarrassing.

"You know," she said, "I believe what you said to Jeanette yesterday."

"About what?"

"There are holes in my memories and some of them seem..." She tried to find an adequate word. "They seem off."

"I can relate." What a stupid situation. "We'll have to talk to

Jeanette again at some point, but for now, this is what we got." He pointed at the letters.

For the next few hours, they read, often out loud, when they found something interesting. They only stopped to cook food together, a simple meal of chicken, rice, and vegetables, then went right back to reading.

Grey found it charming, the way his dad, Silvana, and Jeanette kept a chain of letters going, talking to one another as if they were siblings. His father had been an only child, and Grey realized he'd never asked Sophia about her mom or Jeanette. He asked, and looking up from the letter she'd been reading, she confirmed both Silvana and Jeanette were only children as well.

About an hour later, Sophia gasped and sat up. She read, "The fighting is getting out of control. My mom keeps pretending that everything's okay, but it's not okay. My dad yells all the time. I wonder if he loves me at all. My mom cries a lot and I don't want to hear her cry anymore. I wish the potion would help me figure out how to make it better. S."

"What potion was that?"

Sophia shrugged. "I don't know. Maybe the one from solstice?"

It made sense, but he knew better than to make conjectures at this point.

"It sounds like something out of a fever dream," he told her. She snorted.

"You mean like a beautiful man showing up at my club and then proving he's a witch who does actual magic?" Her brows arched. "That kind of fever dream?"

He raised his brows, his heart taking a roll throughout his entire chest cavity. "You think I'm beautiful?"

She rolled her eyes comically, but her cheeks bloomed soft pink.

"That's what you got from what I said?"

"I stopped listening after that."

"Of course you did." A laugh shimmered out of her. It was contagious, and he bit his lip to keep his laugh from coming out. She was, quite possibly, the sexiest woman he had ever laid eyes on. Her shirt had ridden up over her gently curved stomach, exposing a tiny strip of that smooth, golden skin.

He slid closer, still sitting on the floor, just wanting to be closer to her, though he didn't get into her space too much. Mostly because he didn't want to freak her out.

"Oh, listen to this," she said, as she had already moved on to the next letter. "Dear Will and Jeanette, I think I got it figured out, finally. I was playing music and my mom had some tea left, which I took." She glanced up at him. "I'm guessing that's the same potion that keeps coming up." When he shrugged, she continued. "She might be mad I did it by myself, but what is it going to do that it hasn't before?" She paused, taking a breath. "Listen to the tape I put in this envelope. It's the best I've gotten and you will see why. I think I may have made magic with the music. Love, S."

He took the letter from her, reading it over again, his heart suddenly pounding so hard he couldn't hear over the thundering of it. He read it once, then three more times after that. It was the first time he had heard anyone else say something like it, other than himself in the shroud of night as he played music that was incomprehensible to the ears and the eyes.

That was what Silvana talked about. How many times had he thought that he was making magic, just to dismiss it because no one had ever heard of such a thing? And then he'd cast the spell that had led him to Sophia, to finding her when she was singing and doing the same with her voice. Acid rose in his esophagus, making his eyes water.

"There's a tape with this music somewhere," Sophia said distantly. His head moved of its own accord to stare at her.

How much did Silvana Candela have to do with his special music? She had been a brilliant musician—he looked her up and found articles from before he was even born. Silvana had played piano beautifully.

"Jeanette would have mentioned a tape," Sophia said. "If she knew about the music thing, she would have said something." She ran her hands over her hair. "Right?"

He stood, an idea sparking.

"Come on," he said, taking her hand and pulling her toward the kitchen. He pulled on his shoes, which were sitting by the garage door, and Sophia did the same.

"Where are we going?" she asked when she was done slipping on her shoes.

"My mom's."

She stepped back quickly, an alarmed look entering her face. "Are you insane?"

"Why?"

"Do you remember what our parents did? I highly doubt your mom will be too keen on meeting the daughter of the woman who came between her and her husband."

"She probably won't be there." His mom volunteered at a local shelter most afternoons, so he was sure she would, in fact, not be there.

"Probably," she mumbled, looking down at her feet.

"I promise it'll be fine." His mom would never make Sophia feel uncomfortable, and she would not blame Sophia for the sins of her mother.

"What do I do?" There was a note of panic in her voice that nearly made him laugh, if he didn't think she'd smack him for it.

"Just hold on to me."

She squinted up at him, suspicious, and he did laugh then. "I can port without needing potions, unlike other witches," he told her. "But if you'd rather take a porting potion instead, I'm happy to give you one."

"As if I'd know how to use it anyway."

"Right, you'd probably end up in Timbuktu, or the middle of the south pole."

Her eyes widened. "Is that a thing that happens?"

"Magic is a great and terrible thing." It was the truth, but he would be damned if he wasn't trying to freak her out just so she'd hold on a little tighter. "It won't be as traumatic this time," he added, and her lip quirked. She was just too cute.

She stepped closer. "This is just an excuse to have me wrapped around you," she teased.

"I can't say the thought didn't occur to me." He got a whiff of her scent, that smell that was so personal to her—a mix of warm sweetness and soap, and he breathed more deeply. "Don't let go until we land there, when your feet are firmly on the ground."

She stepped closer until her hand was touching his side. The skin there warmed, and he had to clear his throat again. But having her so close he could feel the warmth of her body would make him clear his throat so much his vocal cords would disappear altogether.

"Last time I did this, you gave my sister a memory potion," she said, grimacing.

"You're with me this time," he said, at the risk of sounding cocky. It was the truth. He was good at what he did.

She still looked a little skeptical, but her hand fisted on his shirt. He put his hand on her back, visualized his mother's house, and ported.

There was a rushing in his ears, like being caught outside during a windstorm, and in a few moments, they appeared in his mother's garden. It was misting slightly, and he shivered. His mom was nowhere to be seen.

He looked down at Sophia, who looked pale and frazzled when she let go of the ironclad hold she'd had on his shirt. The absence was pointed.

"Where are we?" she asked, looking around the garden. The raised beds were old—Grey had helped his mom build them when he was a teenager, and had needed to start planting his own herbs. On the far side of the large piece of land, there was a blackberry bush that was getting out of control, so he knew his mom would soon request he come help her trim them. Not his favorite pastime, but he enjoyed spending time with her, so he'd do it gladly.

"A few hours outside the city," he told Sophia. He took her hand automatically and led her toward the back door, which sat on a wooden deck, and his mom had updated recently. The house was a faint yellow color with white trimming, as it had been when Grey was growing up. He knocked before he opened the door, which led straight into the small kitchen, also updated to be more modern.

Sophia cleared her throat twice, then pulled her hand away and smoothed her hair. It was a nervous gesture, he now knew. And when she was concentrating, she bit into the nail of her thumb, and she enjoyed reading out loud to herself, softly sounding out words.

"You okay?" he asked and turned to her before he opened the door to the kitchen.

"Fine, I just think it's a little early to introduce me to your mom, but okay."

He laughed.

"We won't be here long. And she's not here, besides."

"All I'm saying is buy a girl a drink first."

"Are you asking me to take you on a date?" He leaned his head to the side, and for a moment, wished she would say hell yes, so he could stop pretending she didn't do things to him.

"You wish."

He didn't know what to do with his hands as he stood in front of her, so he stuck them in his sweatpants' pockets. She quickly glanced down at his hands, but said nothing.

"Maybe I do," he said and had the pleasure of seeing Sophia's eyes widen slightly. She had an expressive face. He could almost see every thought that crossed it.

"We'll see how this goes," she said with a smirk.

He felt his mouth stretch, but he turned from her before it became a full-on grin. He was going to take her on a date. Soon.

He opened the door and entered the kitchen. It was tidy, with little clutter on the white marble countertops. The kitchen opened into a dining area, small, holding a round wooden table and four chairs. His mom had obviously been buying new furniture.

"Mom?" Grey called as he led Sophia down a hallway that led to the entryway, living room, and a set of stairs that led toward the bedrooms on the second floor. There was another set of stairs, tucked on the other side of the house, which led to the room over the garage. His dad kept his recording stuff up there, but his notebooks went to Grey's room for storage when his mom found a leak in the garage.

The sitting room was small and cozy, with an old school wood stove in the corner. Soft light was streaming through the windows, casting the place in a glow that brought back many memories of his childhood. He had always loved this house. There was a nice, calming aura about it.

When no response came, after he called for his mom once again, he took the stairs, Sophia trailing behind, quietly. The stairs were dark and creaked as he went up, but Grey could still see the photos on the wall.

Sophia stopped twice and laughed when she saw pictures of him during his awkward stage. He'd been gangly and awkwardly tall when he was a teen, with terrible skin, which thankfully, had cleared out when he went to college.

"A skincare routine and longer hair do wonders for a man," he said.

"I'll say." She tittered as they reached the top of the stairs, and stopped in front of a large photo of him and his parents. He must have been six or seven in the photo, and he sat between his parents on a couch. They were all smiling, him with a gap in his teeth, as he had lost both his front teeth almost at once. Sophia's expression was shuttered, then her phone rang, making her jump a little. She looked down at it and groaned.

"Do you need to take that?" he asked her, curious at her reaction.

She declined the call by pushing on the side button. "Nope."

"I'm going to guess that's complicated." He was prying and he wasn't ashamed of it.

"It isn't complicated at all. Entitled ex is entitled."

"Ah, yes. One of those."

She peered up at him.

"You have any of those?"

"Exes? A couple," he said. There were few, and none of them had stayed in his life after, except for Helena.

Sophia didn't press for more, which was fine with him. Nothing to revisit there. But he was a hypocrite. He wanted to pry into hers.

"Your room," she said, stopped at his door. There was a little plaque with his name on it screwed to the door. The room beyond was small, almost perfectly square. The twin bed was still there, pressed against the wall, dressed in a floral-patterned quilt his mom had most likely made.

"Cute," she said, smiling at the bookshelf in the corner.

"Maybe he has an emergency," he mumbled.

"Who has an emergency?"

He pointed at her phone, which was still in her hand and she raised a brow.

"I highly doubt that's about anything urgent," she said and glided right in, looking around. The video game posters he'd had for years as a teen were still there.

"Maybe he misses you," he said. Just to get a reaction because he was an asshole sometimes.

"He can, but that means nothing to me."

"You sure about that?"

She rose back to her feet and placed her hands on her curved hips. He bit back a smirk. She might slap him.

"Really?" she said. "We're doing this?"

"Doing what? It's just a question."

"Sure it is."

He walked toward her, coming up close. She seemed to hold her breath as he reached past her waist to take hold of the doorknob to the closet. His heart thumped as she took a shuddering breath. It sounded the way his stomach felt when he was this close to her. What was this pull between them? It was obviously there, probably stemming from whatever past they had shared. Or maybe it was as simple as him being outrageously attracted to her. How could he not when the tiny gold flecks in her eyes sparkled when they caught the light?

"Just through here," he murmured, his eyes sliding down to her mouth deliberately, and froze there. Her Cupid's bow was a soft line, just a slight dip that beckoned him.

Sophia stepped away, breaking the spell, and he opened the door.

"Where do you want to start?" she asked, her eyes now focused on the bins that were stacked inside the closet, though she shivered a little.

"I guess we just pull these out and look through them." He pulled a bin out and set it on the floor as Sophia reached for another.

They dug into the bins. "So, your dad used to make music as well."

"Yes, he did. Mostly, he liked to sing, but he played the piano."

"Interesting how both him and my mom did that," she said as she pulled out a series of music books.

"And me and you now."

"Right." She nodded slowly. "I almost wish your mom was here."

That made him pause. "Oh, now you want to meet my mom?"

"She might remember things we can't."

"Right." He pressed his lips together to keep from smiling like a dumbass. "Or you just want to meet my mom."

She deadpanned. "Yes. Truly. Can hardly wait."

He chuckled.

"Unless," she added, more serious, "the spell got to her too."

He thought about the times he had talked to his mom about magic, and her lack of desire to hear anything about it. He'd always wondered if she knew more than she let on.

"Maybe," he said but didn't offer anything else. He would have to talk to his mom again another time. Gauge her reactions and answers.

"Maybe?"

"Magic has never fascinated her much," he said. "Who do you know that wouldn't freak out if something incredible happened in front of their eyes? I'm a witch, and she's never really asked questions about what I do." Not that he would ever want to tell her what he did regularly. He shuddered at the thought. All she knew, so far, was that he made potions, like when he was little.

"Like Julia."

"Precisely."

Sophia seemed to think about it. "I'm curious, but you can't make her talk if she doesn't want to."

"Oh, there are ways I can make her talk, but they're less than ethical."

"What do you mean?" Sophia's eyes snapped up to his. "A potion?"

"There's always a potion." He'd never used it, and didn't make them to sell either. It felt... wrong. Sophia continued pulling out books, notepads, and loose, empty sheet music. Annoyance ran through him when his first thought was that they were most likely bewitched to look blank. Not everything would be, and he needed to remind himself of that, so he didn't lose his mind with frustration.

He picked up a few notebooks from the box he was looking into, then dropped them when he checked they were all blank.

They looked through other bins, mostly in silence. There were stacks of other letters, and she started putting them into an empty bin to come home with them.

No tapes, though.

After a long time of searching through the bins and boxes, he sat on the floor, resting his head back against the bed.

"No tapes," Sophia said from beside him. She was leaning her head on her drawn-up knees.

Grey let his head fall sideways so he could look at her profile. Her eyes were closed.

"I'm tired of looking for things that aren't there," she whispered. "Why did they have any need to hide things to this extent?" She straightened her legs and leaned her head on the bed.

"There's a reason for everything," he said and got an annoyed roll of the eyes.

"You just have all the answers."

"I don't, otherwise we wouldn't have to do this." He rested his elbow on his knee. "The less we find, the more convinced I am that there's something there."

"I don't know," she mumbled, and closed her eyes.

He realized then how much her life had changed in such a short amount of time. One day, she was singing in her club, and the next, she had to confront the fact that magic was real, that her mother had been a witch. He thought he should feel a lot guiltier about being the one to bring it to her, but in the end, she had been having experiences with her singing already. He'd just nudged her to the rest. At least he could tell himself that to be able to sleep at night.

She let her head fall sideways and her eyes opened. Grey couldn't look away as their eyes met, and longing pooled low in his belly. She reached forward and touched the bridge of his nose with a soft fingertip.

"There should be freckles here," she breathed and her voice was so soft, it made him tingle all over.

"I had them when I was little."

The unnerving feeling of déjà vu overtook him. Sitting this close to her, her scent surrounding him like a blanket. It made him want to lean forward and press his lips to hers, to let his tongue trace that soft Cupid's bow...

"I feel like I remember you." Her voice went even lower. "Like I've seen you in my dreams."

"Me too."

"But then I wake up and I forget." Her hands were between her knees now. "I'm sick of forgetting."

He leaned forward a little, tentative, his heart rate increasing when she didn't move away. Her eyes flickered to his mouth, then her lips parted. There was nothing else but the cloud of her scent and the loud beating of his own heart as he moved forward, as if in slow motion. He was so close he could feel her shuddering, warm breaths, and just as he was in the homestretch, her phone went off. They jerked away from each other, like two kids caught doing something they shouldn't, and she picked up her phone with a shaky breath.

"Work," she said and set it down when she was finished sending a string of texts.

His blood sang in his veins, and wondered if it was the same for her. She certainly looked put-together and unbothered.

"Well, there isn't much here left to look at," he said, thinking they could go up to the room above the garage, though there shouldn't be anything left up there. He would have to speak to his mom about it and get some ideas. He stood, suddenly antsy, and offered his hand to Sophia to help her up. She took it, but she let go quickly when she was on her feet.

They left shortly after. When they ported, Sophia didn't hand on to him like she had before, since he had the bin. He missed the feel of her body against his.

15

The forest was a symphony for Silvana and her friends, as they wrote in a large tome with a smooth, brown leather cover. It was a spell they had devised the last time they took the knowing potion. The three, together, had successfully enchanted the grimoire to add pages as they needed it, and in the two years since they'd started writing their spells in the book, it had gotten big and heavy.

At only twelve-years-old, the trio knew magic in a way that few magical adults did. Even more than parents who wanted to pass on the legacy of magic to them. Only Will's dad, Sophia's mom, and Jeanette's parents knew the kinds of things the three could do, or what they could be capable of with more practice. They were always careful not to do special, magical things around people who wouldn't understand. Even at that age, they knew it could be bad, even though magic was so good.

Jeanette had discovered an affinity for energy work. She could read energy so well, and listened to her intuition so closely, she avoided most trouble. And now that they knew how good their friend was at knowing things no one should know, Silvana and Will hung on to her every word. It wasn't always accurate—human behavior would always shift how things happened—but Jeanette was rarely wrong.

Will and his telekinesis had served him well—especially when she didn't want to get up after he was comfortable in bed. His way with words, and how easily spells came to him, was his favorite thing, though. Writing spells was a lot like writing songs. There was a special rhythm to every line, and in his mind, Will always heard music when he was writing spells. He had also discovered he was especially good at making potions. Like cooking a meal—creating a symphony from simple herbs.

Then there was Silvana. She had a special brand of magic, where she made music that could do things they had only seen in movies. She understood them, when they sang to her, and in return, they allowed her their magic. When she replicated their sounds, things happened, and she wasn't sure if it was just her or if there were others like her.

The three of them were going to change the world. Silvana knew it like she knew her own name. There was a reason she heard music from plants, and there was a reason she had such a talent with instruments. Though, for the moment, their spells were simple charms to get rid of a pimple, or heal a bone a little sooner than it would take otherwise.

What they were going to do with said magic, she still didn't know, but that would come with time. Maybe a cure for something, but she would have to know the curative power of plants much better before she could do that. Her mom could definitely help with that. She was an excellent Curandera.

Silvana sat with the book on her lap, revisiting the spells they'd written. Will and Jeanette foraged for a specific ingredient to make more of the potion, so they could continue with the spells. They knew they should not be foraging on their own, let alone be making a potion without supervision, but they knew what they were doing, even if their parents didn't get it. Silvana had watched her mom make that potion so often she could make it in her sleep. And Will was great at potions anyway.

Finding the right ingredients was the key problem, as some of them were difficult to come across. She also knew about the intentions needed when making it under the full moon. The intention counted a lot, which was why Silvana knew that she could make this potion herself. Will understood how some things could not be mixed and how others were fine as long as you did it in the right order. He paid attention. But Silvana did too, and no one knew her intention better than herself.

Maybe by getting good at magic, Silvana could convince her mom to leave her dad. They fought all the time, a big and frequent topic of conversation with the trio.

Silvana's father continued to be mean for no reason, saying things that Silvana knew were hurtful and wrong, even in her limited understanding of adult affairs. He said them to Silvana, and he also said them to her mom, and Silvana could take it, but she hated seeing her mom cry because of it. People often forgot that she heard things differently than everyone else, and they often spoke around her as if she didn't get it. But she did. And she remembered well, too.

Whenever Silvana thought about making a spell to make her mom leave her dad, she felt guilt—not that she thought she could really do that anyway, but a girl could try. Divorces were sad, as Will liked to remind her, but Jeanette would then propose that maybe divorce wasn't that bad if people were miserable together anyway. Silvana agreed, but she didn't say it out loud, because it was all so much more complicated than that, as her own mother liked to remind her.

She would never understand what the point of staying together was if you were going to fight all the time. Peace was a far better option that remained underrated because people insisted on needing a partner at all costs.

Will reappeared from behind the trees and came to sit by Silvana as Jeanette stayed in the trees, still looking, being careful not to step on any plants that could help them make potions. She was getting good at identifying the good ones from the ones that wouldn't help. Or would poison them.

"I couldn't find the spores," Will said, and Silvana closed the book with a shrug.

"They're difficult to find. My mom always complains about it," she reminded him.

"We have to find out where is best to look," he said. "If Jeanette and I can't hear the music, we can't help you. You can't do it alone."

"You two need to learn to listen," she said. She had been hounding them about it for months, but they claimed it was too hard for them without the potion. Silvana didn't understand how it could be hard when the plants were so loud.

Will grimaced. "It's easy for you to say, since you were born with it. Jeannette and I have to figure it out from scratch."

"Who said I was born with it?" She frowned at him.

"You've always been able to hear."

Silvana rolled her eyes. "We will have to figure something out about the ingredients." She looked into her best friend's eyes.

"Don't worry. There is never need to worry." If only she could believe that herself.

"Sometimes we have to worry." Will hung his head. His dad had already died. He'd thought maybe there would have been a way to help him with magic, but he had been too young. He was a witch. He should be able to do anything—especially save his dad from dying. Somehow, his twelve-year-old brain convinced him he would become a doctor someday, and he'd use his magic to help. He'd be a true witch doctor.

"Sometimes things will happen anyway," said Jeanette as she came out of the trees. In her hands, she held several herbs and one brightly colored mushroom. It was a vibrant blue, with a big cap. "I know this isn't the one we need, but look how pretty."

Silvana reached for it, bringing it close to her ear. She heard the drums first, then something like running water, and something else, like strings. The music was soft, but rousing, grandiose in a way that Silvana couldn't explain. It made her feel like the music was inside her and she longed to have her guitar with her, to try replicating the complex patterns she heard.

"Does it sound nice?" Jeanette asked, like Will, wishing she could hear as easily as Silvana did.

"It's fading," Silvana said. "They fade so fast once they're picked."

"What does it sound like?" Will inquired. Both he and Jeanette now sat in front of Silvana, their legs crossed, eager to understand.

"Like drums," Silvana said, and brought the mushroom to her ear. "And water, and strings. But not like violins. It sounds more like a guitar. It makes the melody, and it follows the rhythm of the water."

It made little sense to her two friends, who longed to understand, but still found it a little strange. This wasn't like the other kinds of magic they knew so far.

Distracted, Silvana opened the book one more time, grabbed her pen, and began drawing a staff.

16

Sophia decided it was best to go home after returning from Grey's mother's house. That near-kiss had rattled her. If the phone hadn't gone off, Grey would have kissed her, or she would have kissed him first. She certainly wanted to.

What was it about him? It was familiar and foreign, and felt so right, and somehow so wrong, all at the same time. Seeing pictures of him when he was a kid, with his mom and dad. Seeing his dad... it was a lot. Will Constantine had been handsome in a sweet sort of way. Grey looked a lot like him, except with darker hair and eyes, but the resemblance was uncanny. There was a softness to their gazes, like they were staring straight into you somehow, and it made her buzz from the inside out.

Sophia had never gone out of her way to see what the man her mom had fallen for looked like. It had never been an impulse for her, or her sisters, that she knew. Not that they'd ever talked about it. But seeing his face smiling at the camera, sitting next to his wife and child, as if he wasn't cheating with a woman who also had a family, had been jarring at best. She had felt herself dissociate almost instantly, finding it easier to think about the freckles smattered across young Grey's nose, than think about the rest of it more than she had to. It had made Will human in a way she hadn't allowed herself to think of.

o o o

THE FOLLOWING MORNING, SHE HEADED TO THE CLUB. SHE had missed enough work, and Victoria, being the best business partner and friend ever, had not asked for any help. And yes, she wanted to do more digging with Grey, but she couldn't neglect her relationships for it.

When she got to Nowhere, there was music coming from the front of the house as the band practiced for the next show. She briefly wondered if Helena was singing for the next show. She'd been so preoccupied with the letters she didn't know what was going on in her own business.

She found Victoria in front of the computer, a frown on her face. She looked tired, with bags under her eyes, which was alarming when she was always so put-together. Sophia faltered, her hand up in the air as she went to hang her purse on the coatrack, a feeling coming over her. The air felt heavy.

"What's going on?" Sophia asked.

Victoria looked up, her frown smoothing briefly.

"Hey." Victoria tried to smile, but it was nothing more than a grimace. The music stopped and someone said something unintelligible into the mic. "Helena will headline our next show."

"That's great," Sophia said, but Victoria's bottom lip trembled a little. "Something happened. What happened?" She eyed her friend critically. Victoria's hair was pulled up tightly, instead of being in one of the pretty pineapple buns she was so good at. Bags under the eyes, an oversized sweater that had a stain of what seemed to be coffee on the front. Something was definitely off.

Victoria blew out a breath, abandoning the mouse, which she had been gripping tightly.

"Thomas and I got into a stupid fight last night," she said. "He was gone before I woke up, so we didn't talk about it and it's driving me crazy."

Sophia's heart gave a lurch. "What do you mean? That's so unlike Thomas."

"I know, which is why I'm worried now." Victoria rested her elbows on the desk and put her face in her hands. "We've never fought and not made up right after."

Sophia took a seat across from Victoria. It was true. They had mild arguments and then had sex right after. Arguing was like foreplay for those two. "What was the argument about?"

"He complained that I've been at the club too much."

Sophia felt an instant stab of guilt. Victoria had been forced to pick up her slack, and if her friend's relationship suffered because of it, it was all on Sophia.

"I know what you're doing and it's not your fault, Sophia," Victoria said. "I haven't been here excessively. We have another manager and she's been working really hard because she needs the hours. It's not like I never go home."

Nice words, but Sophia still felt awful.

"Well, maybe he just misses you," she said, perhaps to make herself feel a little better. Didn't work.

"Enough for it to become an argument, though?" Victoria shook her head. "I think he's stressed at work, too. Tech companies demand a lot from people."

Maybe. Sophia reached over the desk and took Victoria's hand. "You two are what romance books are written about. You'll figure this out."

And they would because Sophia had helped Thomas shop for a ring a few months ago. He was just waiting for the right moment to propose. He was nothing if not a planner, and as he and Victoria had been planning a vacation for a while, Sophia assumed he was waiting for that. There was no way they would go from blissfully happy to being done over work. Sophia shook her head. She was blowing this out of proportion. Typical. She always thought of the worst thing that could happen before being rational.

"I hope so," Victoria said. "What about you? What have you been up to?"

"Nothing important." She immediately regretted the lie, but she didn't elaborate either.

"I just need a change of subject. I have to get out of this funk."

That Sophia could do. "Aric called me twice."

Victoria deadpanned. "Are you shitting me? He texted me from an unknown number after I blocked him. I told him to have some dignity, and he called me a bitch."

"Classy." Sophia rolled her eyes. "I'm sorry you had to do that for me."

"Aric doesn't scare me and neither do his sick burns hurt my feelings."

Sophia groaned. "So original and hilarious."

That got a mild smile from Victoria. "And how is tall and gorgeous?"

"Still ridiculously tall and even more gorgeous," Sophia responded, her mind back in his childhood bedroom. "He almost kissed me."

Victoria's eyes widened. "Almost?"

Sophia told her what happened, minus the letters and the fact that they were at his mother's house. She wasn't ready to talk about that yet. Or the magic part.

"Are you kidding me?" Victoria had a small grin that seemed genuine enough.

"Not even a little," Sophia said. "The worst part is that I wouldn't have minded one bit."

"Why is that the worst part?"

"He's Grey Constantine."

Victoria waited in silence, as if Sophia needed to add more to that.

"He's the son of Will Constantine?"

"And?"

"Vic, you know the history." Sophia stood, restless. She wasn't wrong for feeling conflicted about all this. This was the son of her mother's lover. How much more complicated could it get?

"Who cares about the past, Sophia? You're not your mom, and he's not his dad."

"Can you imagine how my sisters and dad would react?" Sophia said anyway. She couldn't imagine the reaction would be pleasant in the least. Thinking of it made her shiver.

"Good thing this isn't about them at all."

"But it is about them," Sophia said. "And besides, it was a non-kiss. My phone went off with a message from Hayley, and he jumped back so fast, you'd think I burned him."

"And I'm guessing you didn't do the same?" Victoria raised a skeptical brow.

Sophia rolled her eyes, and Victoria finally laughed. "You're a child," she said. "I can't not be wary about this whole thing."

"You know it's not just about that."

Sophia took a shaky breath. Of course not. She was wary of all relationships, period. It wasn't like she had much positive representation of what a good one looked like. She'd never had illusions that her parents' marriage was perfect, since her mom cheated on her dad, so there was that.

"I say don't close yourself off before you even know what it's about with him," Victoria said softly. "Unless he's a dick."

"He's not." On the contrary. Grey was a perfect gentleman. What a weird, parallel universe this was.

Moments later, and thankfully finished with the conversation, Sophia and Victoria went out to the floor, where they were greeted by the band and Helena. Another thing to remind her of Grey; his best friend working in her club. Delightful. As if she needed incentives.

"You sound amazing," she said to Helena and the band. They all beamed and called out their thanks. Helena looked happy, her hair pulled back in a messy bun, and a light sweater over leggings.

"She's a delight," Victoria said when Helena started talking to the band.

"Is she, now?"

"Oh yeah. Everyone loves her. Personable, pretty, and talented."

"I do like her singing." Sophia turned to watch Helena speak to one of the band members as she pointed at a speaker. "Did you know she's close to Grey?"

Victoria paused and raised her brows, but Sophia didn't see it, still focused on Helena, who was gesturing with delicate hands. Those hands could do magic. She wondered what kind.

"Interesting."

"Yeah."

"And why does it bother you?"

Sophia blinked at Victoria.

"Why would that bother me?"

Victoria shrugged. "I don't know. You tell me."

It dawned on Sophia what Victoria was asking, and she sat with it for a moment. Was she jealous?

She searched inside herself for an answer and realized that she wasn't. It was a different, curious feeling. More like not wanting to step on anyone's toes.

She told as much to Victoria.

"You'd tell me if you were jealous," Victoria said. Her voice lilted at the end, so it sounded like a question.

"You'd be the first to know," Sophia assured her.

"You nearly kissed the guy."

"Well, it didn't happen," Sophia said as the back door opened and shut loudly. Sophia turned, as did the band members. Someone whistled as Sophia's heart took a dive straight to her feet when her eyes found Aric walking into the club.

"I have tried calling, and you won't answer," Aric said, standing by the door with his hands in the pockets of his fur-lined, brown leather jacket.

She stalked toward him, anger immediately replacing whatever else she had been feeling.

"What the hell are you doing here?" she snapped as she came up to face him. She reached for the door and pushed him through it as soon as she had it open.

"Sophia, listen to me," he said, trying to touch her, but she side-stepped him. His dark hair was short and slicked back, in his usual way. His blue eyes were so blue and sparkly, it could make anyone think he was an angel just because he looked like one. He had clear, smooth skin, with a straight nose, and lips that were made for sinful things.

"I don't have to hear a word you have to say, Aric."

"I just wanted to see you," he said, and had the decency to look sheepish, as if he'd just realized that he was there uninvited. "I called—"

"So you thought you could just come here and I'd be ecstatic?" Sophia tried to calm down her erratic heart, but her hands were shaking.

"I wouldn't have come if you'd answered my calls." He sounded so perfectly reasonable she wanted to slap him just to wipe that dumb, hopeful expression off his handsome face.

"When someone won't take your calls or answer your texts, your first instinct shouldn't be to come into their place of work." Sophia was aware she was speaking too loudly, but she did not care. She just wanted Aric gone.

"Please, I just wanted to talk to you," he pleaded and looked… sincere?

Sophia shook her head because she must be either dreaming or had gone insane.

He'd dressed differently than normal, in casual jeans and a t-shirt that molded itself to his incredibly fit body.

"You have to leave." She tried to calm down her breathing, resisting the urge to reach for the amulet Grey gave her. This wasn't an emergency, though she felt like bolting.

"I just wanted to make sure you're alright," he said. "I really worried when you wouldn't answer."

She had to close her eyes and gather the strength to resist punching him. It was that thing he did where he repeated himself over and over to try and gain sympathy or get someone to finally agree with him. It was infuriating.

"You don't need to concern yourself with my wellbeing."

"But I do." He stepped forward, and she stepped back automatically, but his hand found her shoulder, and she looked at it, then up at him, frozen in place.

"Sophia, I want to start again," he said, leaning forward as she leaned back. She hit the wall behind her, and panic clenched her stomach tightly. "I fucked up; I know I did. I was a terrible partner, but I need you to believe me when I say I have changed."

She said nothing, just looked into his blue eyes, paralyzed, her breath stuck in her throat.

"I want to spend my life with you. Cook together, travel. Everything you always wanted and I failed to give you, Soph."

"Get your hands off her, or so help me God," Victoria growled from the door. Sophia hadn't even heard her come closer.

Aric stepped back, instantly furious. "Stay out of it, Victoria," he snapped, his cheeks turning red.

Sophia stepped away from him. "Don't talk to her like that. You are in our place of business, uninvited and thoroughly unwelcome."

His nostrils flared with anger, his blush spreading to his neck.

"I'll call you later," he said and left Sophia and Victoria staring after him long after the door closed behind him.

She turned to Victoria, her limbs trembling.

"You okay?" Victoria asked, taking Sophia by the shoulders and pulling her in for a hug. Sophia trembled and clung to Victoria.

Aric had never entirely respected boundaries, but it had never been like that before. Not the incessant texts and calls and showing up at her club unannounced. Every one of her senses lit up. Truth be told, she wanted to cry, but she'd be damned if she would give him another tear.

She pushed away from Victoria, so she didn't give into the urge.

"I'm okay," she said because she would be, not necessarily because she was.

"Has he shown up like that before today?"

Sophia shook her head, meeting Victoria's worried gaze.

"You have to call the cops," Victoria said when they headed back to the office. Helena appeared through the door that led to the main floor.

"Did something happen just now?" she asked, her gaze focused on the back door.

"Uh," Sophia stammered. Did she say something?

"Sophia's ex was just here," Victoria said before Sophia could deny anything happened.

"And I'm going to assume this man is not welcome here," Helena said, then put her hand to her mouth. "Or woman. I'm sorry, I shouldn't assume. I didn't see who came in."

"Man, though barely," Victoria said. "And no, he's not welcome here. If you ever see him, let us know immediately."

"Will do," Helena said and sent a significant look at Sophia, who just shook her head slightly. She'd tell Victoria, but not yet. Not until they knew more.

"On another note..." Victoria voiced and Sophia knew what she would say before the words left her mouth and she could only bury her face in her hands in pure mortification.

"Can I ask if you're in a relationship with anyone?"

Helena blinked at Victoria, obviously surprised at the sudden change in subject.

"You can ask," she said softly with a twinkle in her crystalline eyes. "The question is why I should answer."

"You don't have to," Victoria said in a tone that said that she actually wanted to know, and Sophia did not miss the look that passed between her and Helena.

Helena smiled a little, looking from Victoria to a mortified Sophia.

"I'm not in a relationship at the moment," she answered, paused, looking at Sophia. "I can talk to him."

"You can?" Victoria said sounding delighted, all thoughts of Aric gone, while Sophia said, at the same time, "No, thank you."

Sophia slapped Victoria's arm.

"I'm just trying to help," Victoria said between gritted teeth, slapping her back.

"I do not need your help." Another slap.

Sophia looked at Helena.

"I'm so sorry. Victoria is sleep deprived, and doesn't know what she's talking about."

"Seems to me like she knows exactly what she's saying." Helena's smile was wide now. Like she was enjoying it all very much. Sophia groaned.

"Just forget it," Sophia pleaded with Helena, who only nodded a little, her smile still in place. Sophia turned to Victoria.

"And you, go home and talk to your amazing partner."

Victoria made a face. "Fine."

Later, when Hayley arrived for her shift, Sophia went home, always watchful. Now, she wasn't only watching for strangers going after her, but Aric, and she was still quivering from his visit to the club.

She was getting out of the shower, fully intending to dry her hair straight, to avoid having to deal with frizzy curls. Wrapped in a fluffy, warm robe, she began sectioning her hair and clipping it. But then, her phone rang, and the doorbell went off several times in a row.

She swore and headed toward the door.

"Sophia!" Came a voice from outside.

She opened the door without thinking, and stood just inside, her hand still on the knob. It was miserably cold outside, dark, and wet. Aric stood on the stoop, his hands on the doorframe. He was wearing the same clothes as earlier.

"I thought I asked you to leave me alone," she snapped, not bothering to keep the sharpness from her voice.

"You know I left because of that bitch, Victoria," he said, his face a mask of anger.

"You don't get to call her that," she snapped. Never had she felt more ready for violence than at that moment. He pushed her buttons like no one else could. Maybe it was all the years of she spent with him, taking responsibility for his bullshit.

"When I asked you to leave the club, it wasn't an invitation to come to my home."

He stepped a little closer. "I just want to talk to you without your nosy friend getting into our business."

So he sought her out when she was alone. Seemed right on brand for Aric. He sighed, and that's when the smell of alcohol hit her. His red eyes betrayed his inebriation.

"There is no business between you and me. You made sure of that the last time you cheated on me," she told him. "And please tell me you didn't drive drunk."

"I wouldn't do that, and you know that," he said, as if it was the most obvious thing in the world. But she didn't know that. Not really.

"I want you to leave." She hated that her voice sounded so breathless.

"Or what?" He took a step forward, and she took one back automatically, her body instantly shivering with the look in his eye. "I was just trying to talk to you and you wouldn't answer me."

She thought about arguing, but she'd said all she had to say.

"You need to leave."

He ran his hands through his hair, his expression shifting to one of desperation.

"Sophia, please." One more tiny step.

Sophia reached for her amulet, her first instinct to call to Grey, but she had left it on the counter in the bathroom before her shower. Aric did not move forward anymore, and she wondered if it was the protections keeping him back, or self- restraint. She was going to assume it was the former, as Aric had never been one to do anything for other people's sake.

"I just want to chat about everything that happened between us. Maybe we can fix things. I miss you and I feel horrible about how everything went down." His words were rushed, like he knew she would stop listening or would interrupt him to get him to leave.

Two emotions warred inside her. The first, horror. Her body was on high alert, her heart beating so fast it was a buzzing in her chest. The second, pure anger. His words raised wave after wave of it. Anger won. She gripped the door handle so hard her fingers hurt.

"You have some nerve coming here after all this time," she ground out. She could feel her face becoming hot. "We were together for four years. Do you think I forgot everything you put me through?"

"I just kissed a girl at a bar once when I was drunk," he recited, his voice tight, like he had when she'd originally found out and had confronted him about it. "It wasn't a big deal then, and it isn't a big deal now."

"It was always a big deal to me, but you manipulated your way into me forgiving you, convincing me I was being unreasonable," she said hotly. "I was not being unreasonable. You know how many times I went out with my friends or my sisters, got drunk, and cheated on you with a random guy? That's right, zero times!"

He took a deep breath, his wide, muscular chest expanding. Then he let it out, and it was like all the fight left him.

"Do you remember how long it took you to not only kiss someone else after I took you back, but to sleep with them? Four months. Do you remember that?" She hated recalling all that stuff. It wasn't productive, it wasn't good for her, but if he was going to stand there and demand she speak to him, then he'd hear what she had been wanting to say and never did. It was called closure.

"That can't be right," he gulped. "That timeline doesn't sound right."

"Keep telling yourself that." She rolled her eyes. "You not only cheated, but when I found out about it, via the woman you slept with, who didn't even know you were engaged, what did you do? Do you remember?"

He shook his head, his nostrils flaring wildly, like a bull. She had never seen him so upset. He couldn't even deny what he'd done. How many times in his life had Aric ever been confronted with his mistakes?

"You tried to blame me for it," she reminded him, gripping the doorknob tighter to keep her hand from shaking. "You tried to manipulate me into thinking I was to blame for your actions. And when I woke up and dumped your ass, you told all our mutual friends what a bad girlfriend I was, spending so much time at my new bar, meeting men every night. Remember that?"

"I know I did all those things and I regret every single one of them," he said, his voice deflating. His shoulders even sagged, and she stood there staring at him, waiting for another head to sprout next to the giant one he already had. "I want to change. I don't know why I'm like this."

"You have shown up at my club, then my home unannounced, and I need you to understand that I will not put up with any of it. You come here or my place of business one more time, and I will call the cops."

That or she'd sick Grey on him. What would the witch do in the face of such dumb-assery?

"Have I really messed everything so much that you won't even listen to me?" Aric's chin trembled, his eyes glittering with tears.

Sophia didn't know if he was playing a part or it was sincere, but either way, shivers ran up and down her spine. She pulled the lapels of the robe even tighter around her.

"Leave," she said, quietly this time, and closed the door with a resounding click. A shivering breath came out of her in a rush and her eyes filled. She locked the door, bolted it, just in case. Her hands were shaking so much, she had to talk to herself under her breath, telling herself that she was perfectly safe. She checked all the amulets Grey had given her, to make sure that they were all in place, and when she looked out the window at the street, she finally sighed in relief when she saw Aric get into a rideshare. At least he wasn't going to drive drunk.

In her bathroom again, hands on the cold counter, looking at her pale face in the mirror, her phone buzzed next to her.

ARIC: I HOPE YOU KNOW I LOVED YOU THEN
AND I LOVE YOU NOW.

Sophia believed he believed that somewhat, but she didn't for a moment. She deleted the message and finally blocked him. She should have blocked him when he'd first called her, and maybe she could have avoided all this.

A second message made her gasp, her heart sinking as her fingers tapped the screen, and she dialed Victoria.

"What do you mean you broke up?" Sophia demanded and heard Victoria take a sobbing breath on the other side of the line.

"I really need you. Can I come over?"

Sophia pressed her hand to her chest, and her heart instantly shriveled.

"Of course."

Victoria hung up without saying goodbye, and assuming her friend would be there soon, Sophia pulled on some sweatpants and a tank top, foregoing the sweater. It was cold, but she was sweating.

She opened a text thread she had with her sisters and typed a quick message.

SOPHIA: YOU NEED TO COME OVER.
EMERGENCY SESSION. IN NEED OF GIRL TIME.
URGENT. BRING WINE.

She sent it, thought of it, and added:

SOPHIA: MAKE THAT TEQUILA. LOTS OF IT.

AMY: I'M THERE. NOT FEELING THE BEST
THOUGH, SO IF ANYONE GETS SICK, NOT
ON ME.

JULIA: AMY, IF YOU GET ME SICK, I WILL KILL
YOU. BE THERE IN FORTY.

AMY: IT'S CALLED PREEMPTIVE CAUTION,
JULIA.

Amy added a Gif of someone rolling their eyes, but Sophia closed the thread and opened a different text box.

SOPHIA: ARE YOU OKAY?

Thomas's text bubble appeared and disappeared four times before Sophia put the phone down on the counter and busied herself with drying her hair. She worked quickly, sectioning her hair and using a big round brush on it.

Her phone dinged.

THOMAS: NO, I'M NOT OKAY.

SOPHIA: WHAT HAPPENED? THIS CAME SO OUT
OF NOWHERE.

THOMAS: I DON'T GET IT EITHER.

THOMAS: I'M NOT REALLY READY TO TALK.

Sophia's heart cracked for him. Knowing him, he would want to be alone for a while before seeking his support system, which comprised his two brothers and two best friends from high school. She wished she could go to him, but Victoria needed her now. She swallowed a peculiar lump in her throat.

SOPHIA: I UNDERSTAND. I LOVE YOU. PLEASE
CHECK IN AND LET ME KNOW HOW YOU ARE.

THOMAS: LOVE YOU TOO.

When she was finished with her hair, she pulled it up to keep it away from her face and went to the kitchen to put together a charcuterie board. If they were going to drink, and they probably would—a lot— they would also need food. She was jittery, full of questions. It was like they were suddenly living in a parallel dimension. Aric, Victoria and Thomas, Grey... Magic. What else could be there? Oh yes, the magical disease too. She put the board on the table as she heard the key at the door and her nerves immediately spiked.

"Soph?" Victoria called from the other side of the door and Sophia sighed in relief. The spikes in adrenaline left her utterly exhausted. She opened the door to find Victoria heaving a green duffle bag. Her eyes were red and swollen.

"Oh, Vic," Sophia said and reached for Victoria.

"Can I stay here for a while?"

"Honey, of course," Sophia said, her heart going out to her best friend. "Come on in," she said for the spell, and pulled Victoria inside and grabbed the bag.

"Thanks," Victoria said and her pretty face scrunch up and she sobbed into her hands. Sophia went to her, taking her into her arms and holding her while she cried.

"What happened?"

"It's all over," Victoria sobbed as they sat on the couch. "I went home to talk to him and this afternoon everything exploded out of nowhere. I don't even know why. He was so upset and then I got upset and I just don't even know where all of that came from. We never fight like this; we always talk things through."

"Everything was going so well," Sophia said, thinking of the ring. "How could this happen?"

As Sophia spoke the words, something clawed at her, but it was gone quickly, like one of those fleeting memories she had so often these days.

Victoria shrugged and blew her nose on a tissue she had crumpled in her fist. "I thought we were about to take the next step. I was sure he was going to propose. How dumb is that?"

The crack in Sophia's heart widened. It wasn't dumb at all, and Sophia would take that knowledge to her grave.

"Has he said if anything is bothering him?"

"Nothing. Life was okay one moment, and the next, we annoyed each other for breathing."

"I'm so sorry," Sophia said, and hugged her again. She didn't know what she could say.

For the next little while, as Julia and Amy made their way to meet them, Sophia listened to Victoria rant, cry, then calmly proclaim that she was fine before bursting into tears again.

When Amy and Julia arrived, Victoria was lying on the couch, eating a bowl of lettuce with no dressing or any other ingredients. She had insisted it would be way better to have something that didn't taste good because she didn't want it ruined by being so depressed.

"What's the emergency?" Julia demanded, walking in the door after Sophia was explicit in inviting both of them inside. They'd been there since Grey placed the charms, but one could never be too careful.

Julia had a silk sleeping mask on her head, and was dressed in her pajamas, also silk. The fact that she had driven there in her pajamas was sign enough to Sophia that she was concerned. Amy was also in her red and black flannel pajamas, long sleeves and long pants, and had four reusable bags hanging from her arms.

"Who cares what it is? I brought your tequila, which ew, and also wine, whiskey, and vodka." Amy grinned, lifting the bags. She was breathing a little hard from carrying the heavy bags. "So what's the party for?"

Sophia widened her eyes and pointed to the living room with her head.

"Vic is here." Sophia spoke through her teeth, low enough that Victoria wouldn't hear. "She and Thomas broke up."

Twin gasps from Amy and Julia and Sophia suddenly had all the bags as the two went to Victoria on the couch and bombarded her with hugs and questions. Sophia put everything in the kitchen. She poured them each a glass from the bottle of merlot Amy had picked out.

"What the hell happened?" Julia asked as she and Amy looked down at the bowl of dry lettuce with twin grimaces. "You two are the most stable couple I've ever known. You are made for each other. Twin souls."

"I know, but suddenly, we were fighting for no reason. Until today, we fought so hard and said such hurtful things to each other and I walked out. I told him I don't want to see him again, which is a lie. I want to see him again." Victoria's voice broke and tears started running down her face. "I want to see him. I want to be with him right now."

"But what are the fights about?" said Amy.

"Nothing. That's the frustrating part. He seems so stressed but he won't talk to me about it."

Sophia brought all the glasses to the living room, balancing them precariously between her fingers.

"I'm so sorry," Julia said, squeezing Victoria's hand. "Breakups are the worst. But also, let me take this sad bowl of leaves off your hands and make you some proper food."

"I made a board. It's on the counter," Sophia said when Julia went to the kitchen to drop off the bowl of lettuce.

A while later, having gone through every possibility of what could have happened, the four of them sat together, Julia perched on the windowsill, her favorite spot. She looked pensive, Sophia thought, but didn't ask.

They'd drank the bottle of wine, and they were now sipping on whiskey, after each shot of tequila, though Amy had groaned and moaned about it the entire time and eaten an entire lime on her own. Dramatic.

"I have missed you all so much," Victoria said from the couch, blissfully drunk. She hadn't moved at all, but at least she wasn't crying anymore.

"We can't go so long without hanging out," Amy said, laying on the floor, on her stomach. She was painting Sophia's toenails after digging in a bathroom drawer and finding a little box filled with nail polishes. Amy had chosen the brightest red in the pile.

"I wish we all lived closer," Julia said, looking out the window. Sophia could see her reflection in the glass, and she looked somber. Pensive.

The wind howled outside as clouds rolled across the dark sky, and for a moment, Sophia could only think of the potion Lucas had given Julia. Something about it didn't sit right with her, but she knew Julia was safer not knowing what happened that day.

It was then that Sophia saw it. The sadness in Julia's eyes was so clear, but she hid it well. She never spoke about her feelings, though, so asking wouldn't yield anything they could work on. Sophia never took for granted just how much pressure Julia had put on herself from a young age, being caretaker, taking the role of mother for Sophia and Amy, and even Victoria at times.

As they sat in silence, looking out the windows into the sparkling lights of the city, rain started falling again, which Sophia loved for so many reasons. There was music playing now, soft, tinkling, and pleasant to the ear, and Sophia's eyes went to the money tree.

In that moment, she thought maybe she had drunk more than she thought, because as she watched the plant, the leaves seemed to move all on their own, bouncing happily to its own music. When Sophia blinked, she could swear there were sparkles around it. Her heartbeat increased and Sophia wanted nothing more than to crawl closer to the plant and press her ear against the pot.

"Harold wants to have babies." Julia's voice sounded faraway, and her words snapped Sophia out of her quiet reverie. Their eyes met on the window's reflection, but Julia quickly looked away.

"You don't sound so thrilled." Amy cleaned a smear on the side of Sophia's big toe.

Julia drank the rest of her whiskey, then grabbed a cup of water she'd placed on the windowsill by her feet, her eyes leaving Sophia. "I'm not."

"I thought you wanted to have kids," Victoria said.

"I do." Julia slipped off the windowsill to sit on the floor, crossing her legs under her, watching Amy work on another coat of nail polish. "I did. I don't know. This is so confusing. A part of me wants to have babies, but the other half wants things to stay as they are. Kids complicate everything."

Sophia wanted to ask what it was specifically that kids complicated for Julia and Harold.

"I want to have kids," Amy said. "The problem is finding a man who deserves me enough for me to allow him to impregnate me."

Sophia, who had been taking a drink, snorted and liquor shot out of her nose. Her eyes instantly watered, and she coughed. Julia handed her a glass of water, which Sophia took and drank from. It didn't help at all. Her nostrils stung like hell and tears streamed down her cheeks. Amy smacked her leg playfully.

"You ruined your big toe," Amy grumbled and moved to find some cotton. "I guess I don't have to have a man to get pregnant. And I don't know if I can date men every again."

"God, what's it like to have that kind of self-esteem?" Sophia said when she was done coughing and wiping her eyes. She blew out her nose.

"Well, first, you stop giving a shit what anyone thinks," Amy explained as she used acetone to remove the ruined polish. "Then, you give yourself the love you claim to want to give to some romantic interest."

Everyone looked at Amy, who shrugged one shoulder and painted the now-clean toe.

"It's true. Try it sometime."

"Meanwhile, you find someone who's everything you want, and then you end up hating each other for no apparent reason." Victoria sighed heavily.

"Or you spend years with someone waiting for them to love you and they never truly do," Sophia said, thinking of Aric, anger and panic shooting through her. With a trembling hand, she took another sip of her whiskey.

She thought about telling them about the whole fiasco with Aric, but decided against it right away. Tonight was not about that.

"Or you marry someone and realize he's maybe not the best?" Julia lay down on the floor, her cup beside her.

"What do you mean?" Amy had never liked Harold, but Julia had also never confirmed what everyone in her life suspected of Harold. That he was a prick, namely. Julia was anything if not loyal.

"Everything is perfect all the time," Julia said, her eyes closed. Sophia knew she did that when she was about to cry and Julia had a very hard time showing emotion. "The house is perfect, everything in place. He thinks he's perfect too, but that's only because I stay quiet about all the dumb shit he spews and does."

"What do you mean?" Sophia echoed Amy, frowning.

"He wants kids, but he is so controlling. How am I going to bring children into this family if they can never make a mess? If they can never be kids?" Julia opened her eyes and met Sophia's. There was anguish there, so much emotion, Sophia felt it as if it were hers. Right in her solar plexus. "He wants everything done his way, whenever he wants it, right then, no questions asked."

"I guess then the bigger question is," Victoria said, "do you want to stay with someone like that, kids or not? You deserve to have your voice heard."

Julia did not respond, her eyes closed again, but her erratic breathing told Sophia she was listening. Sophia stood up.

"Alright, we need to drink some water," she said and headed toward the kitchen. She filled a filter pitcher with water from the tap and brought it back to the living room, filling empty wine glasses and trying not to think how Harold sounded so much like their father. Sophia loved her dad, but he was controlling and stubborn, and growing up had its moments of wondering if everyone else's parents were like that or not.

A pang of guilt made her want to hide. Her father was a good man, if old-fashioned and backwards in some ways.

"Are you safe?" Sophia asked Julia.

"I think so." Julia sat up and drank her water, and said nothing else, so Sophia didn't pry any longer.

After a while, Amy declared she had an appointment in the morning for which she had to get up early, so they all went to bed. Victoria next to her, Sophia thought of the letters, and the continued work she had to do with Grey. The illness he was trying to find a cure for, and the things she was learning about magic.

She felt utterly useless in all this and wondered if there was something she was missing. Maybe she would have to repay a visit to her dad at some point. He had to know more about the whole thing. There was no way he had been living with a witch under his roof and knew nothing about it. He would at least know about the friendship between her mother, Jeanette, and Will.

Unless the spell also affected his memories, which was a true and devastating possibility.

She thought about the moment she shared with Grey, when they'd gotten so close to kissing, and as she fell asleep, she failed to plug in her phone and missed a waiting text from him. And when she dreamed, it was about a small cactus in a blue pot and a money tree.

17

Silvana was in the treehouse behind Will's house. She wrote music as she waited for her friends to show up for their daily meeting, but her heart wasn't in it. The grimoire sat open in front of her. It had gotten huge, now hundreds of pages filled with music and spells. She didn't mind the weight of it, and neither did Jeanette and Will, but it was about time they started another.

They had been working on the spells for a while, though they still hadn't learned how to make the tea correctly. It was always too wimpy and didn't have the desired effects. Silvana had convinced herself that she could figure it out all on her own, but after hundreds of ruined batches, even someone as stubborn as she could admit that she needed help. She'd asked her mom, but she always said Silvana would know when the time was right. It was frustrating, to say the least. Silvana suspected her mom knew what she and her friends were up to, but she never said anything about it, and Silvana wouldn't be the one to offer any other knowledge.

Even when her mom wouldn't tell her how to make it, Silvana paid close attention every time her mom made the potion, and she snuck small amounts of it when she could. The knowing potion had become an obsession for her and her friends. It was the reason they could all hear more, and hear more they needed if they were going to change the world. This would not work if Silvana was the only one who could hear all the time.

She couldn't do this by herself.

But meanwhile, she had discovered patterns in plant music. It wasn't the same as other pieces of music, even the most celebrated, beautiful concertos and symphonies. They were so much more intricate than that, and Silvana spent all her time trying to become a better musician, so she could play them. She had a habit of taking notes on the patterns, which was why the grimoire was so big now, because now she could make music appear to her as if solid in the air when she played. The day she first did it, she'd thought she was dreaming. The colors had appeared so suddenly, and now she could do it all the time. It was her favorite thing in the world.

The issue was that seeing the music, the colors and the swirls and the beautiful patterns did nothing but look pretty and impressive. She wanted more from it. She wanted for it to do things no other magic could do. And if there was a time when she needed a magical miracle, it was then. Her mom was sick. Breast cancer, aggressive, detected early enough that she had done treatments, despite how expensive they were, and how much stress they brought.

But Silvana thought she knew exactly what would happen. Things would get better, the chemo would work, but something was going to go wrong in the end. She just knew it. She didn't have to have Jeanette's gift of foresight to know it. The thought made her bones ache, even when she didn't yet understand it fully. Will and Jeanette told her often that she needed to keep a more positive outlook, and Silvana wanted to. She really wanted to. And couldn't.

Will crawled into the treehouse after a while, with Jeanette trailing right behind. The three had begun to shed that awkward stage between childhood and adulthood, though Jeanette had acne that she resented with her whole heart. Even the spells they had created for acne didn't work for long, and Jeanette said that she was weary of using any spell that altered the course of nature in such ways. Though, she also thought that when life was already hard, skin problems should not be a thing on top of it.

"How is everything?" Jeanette asked as she sat in her favorite corner of the cramped treehouse. They had painted it together one day, to Will's mother's chagrin, and every wall was a different color. Jeanette had sewn a pouf that she sat on every time they were there, while Silvana and Will preferred to sit on the wooden floor.

"Fine," Silvana said, but she didn't want to talk. She wanted to make a charm that would ensure that her mom would be okay. That after the chemo, things would go back to normal. Even her father's lack of anger and complaining was disturbing.

"Did you figure something out?" Will asked, and Silvana shook her head, though she continued to write on the grimoire. She had notes memorized, things she wanted on paper to avoid ever forgetting. In reality, Silvana wanted to cry, but she wouldn't allow herself to. Crying wouldn't fix anything.

"Stop doing that." Will's voice was soft but firm. His voice had deepened in the last couple of years, and it made Silvana see him differently than she ever had before. He kept it low as he spoke, but Jeanette had ears that could hear far and well, and she had it on her two best friends as she looked out the small window to the ground.

"Stop doing what?" Silvana asked, being obtuse on purpose.

"That thing you do."

She looked up then, and there was a sadness so deep in her dark eyes that Will's heart became a tight fist inside his chest. He wanted nothing more than to take it all away. The energy of his entire spirit went to her, and she accepted it almost gladly.

Jeanette instantly sensed the shift in the treehouse's energy, and scooted closer to Silvana.

"Talk to us," Will said, and Silvana didn't know what it was about him that made her want to talk. It wasn't magical in nature, but it was magic, the way she felt safe with him. His eyes almost seemed to glow softly in the twilight.

She opened her mouth once, twice, and nothing came out. Her friends waited, patiently sitting by her in silence.

"I wish I could make it go away." The lump in her throat made it painful to speak without bursting out crying. Her throat felt as if it could surely explode from the pressure. "I wish I could make a potion that could make it all disappear. Like the one we made for instant trav-el." A handy potion they used to send each other letters without needing to get together, to communicate instantly. So far, it was too weak to help any of them actually travel. "I want to save my mom."

Silvana was panting when she was finished, and her two friends simply sat with her in complete silence. Jeanette gripped her hand and leaned her head on Silvana's shoulder, while Will took the other. Silvana clung to both of them as if they were her lifeline. And maybe they were.

"I know," Jeanette whispered as she let out the tears her friend would not.

She knew too much. Her visions weren't always correct, but this one was. She knew it deep in her bones. Her own parents had divorced, happier now than they ever were before, and Jeanette knew the privilege that afforded her to have parents who loved her and respected each other. Silvana had never had that, and now her mom was ill, and Jeanette knew what would happen. Evelyn would die, and there was nothing they could do. Even with magic on their side.

She met Will's eyes over Silvana's head. He knew because he'd asked, and Jeanette had needed the support to carry the weight of the vision. She both loved and resented this power that allowed her to see so much and hide something so monumental from her best friend in the world. She looked away, back at the floor.

If Silvana noticed them sharing looks, she'd wonder. Neither she nor Will would ever tell Silvana what they knew; they couldn't bear bringing more sadness to her than they had to. They would stick together, and they would go through it together, as they had when Will's dad had died almost four years before.

Will cleared his throat, still hanging on to Silvana's small hand. Musician's hands, the fingers long and narrow, delicate. He could hold her hand forever, the soft skin warm under his larger hand, though he would not allow himself to feel anything other than a deep, friendly love for her.

"We will perfect the potion." His voice was confident. He had worked hard and long at figuring it out, and he was so close. He could feel it. "I will get every ingredient, and I'll keep trying. Maybe you could try your mom again?"

Silvana nodded, though she was skeptical she'd get anywhere with her mom.

"We will work it all out." Jeanette wiped her face of her tears.

The three agreed; Silvana would pry. Now having something to think about, they looked through the scribbled musical notes Silvana had been working on. In a tiny keyboard she kept with her at all times, Silvana played a few bars of music. It was the only bit she had been able to play perfectly. The timing had to be just right. When the colors exploded, emotion filled her entire body, as if it wandered through every vein, every corner of her being. The bright colors swirled and moved like tiny snowflakes of pure light.

Happy for a moment, she played the tune over and over again as the three relished in the beauty. That was until Will said he had to go. He had a date with Brooke Charles from school, a pretty blonde with blue eyes that made Silvana have strong, unwelcome thoughts and feelings. Silvana's reaction, a twitch of her tightening jaw, was lost on Will, but definitely not on Jeanette.

18

Julia gasped awake, and the moment she did, Sophia shot up in bed, her back straight as a rod, a chill running down her back. She glanced at Victoria, who was still fast asleep. Her friend didn't move when Sophia slipped out of bed and went out into the hallway just as Julia came out of the guest room, her short hair in disarray.

"What happened?" Sophia's heart raced.

Julia's eyes were glassy as she regarded Sophia. "I had a dream," she said, voice trembling. "We were out in the city, and a group of people started following us, and you did something to get us to the house..." Julia's voice drifted off.

Sophia's heart stuttered.

"You did magic." Julia whispered and looked at Sophia again. In the dark, Julia's eyes glittered with unshed tears. "Then we got here and a man..." She trailed off again, and didn't seem to realize it. But then her eyes narrowed, and she said, "What happened?"

When Sophia didn't respond, Julia made a face and grabbed her by the elbow, pulling her to the living room. It had stopped raining, but there were still ominous clouds sliding across the sky like a blanket. A promise of more rain.

Sophia swallowed a wave of guilt. "I can explain."

Julia let her go abruptly in the middle of the dark room.

"It wasn't a dream."

Sophia shook her head. "It wasn't a dream."

She tried to swallow a knot in her throat, unsuccessfully. She realized how much she needed to talk to someone about it all. "I know what you're thinking right now, but I promise I only let Grey do it because I wanted you to be safe."

"Grey?" Julia's brows came together, but it wasn't in confusion, and Sophia knew in that moment that Julia knew exactly who Grey was, and she had to take a step back.

"Julia." Sophia's voice was soft, though she was suddenly chilled. "Tell me what you know."

"Why are you talking to Grey Constantine?" Julia's voice was devoid of emotion now.

"How do you know it's Grey Constantine?"

Julia just waited, face impassive, and Sophia pressed her lips together.

Damn it.

She opened her mouth to speak, but found no words there. How much did she say? God, she really wanted to talk to Grey. He'd gotten her in this mess, and now she had to gauge what to say to her sister without putting her in danger. Knowing Julia, she would move heaven and earth to find the people who'd tried to hurt them, and Sophia wasn't sure her sister would understand the danger they'd be in.

"Say anything." Julia's tone was one of pure impatience, and she tapped her foot accordingly. Sophia suppressed a stab of annoyance.

"Stop treating me like a kid," she snapped, not bothering to keep the anger out of her voice.

"I wouldn't be if you'd answer me. How the hell do you know Grey Constantine?"

Sophia crossed her arms, mirroring Julia, who let her arms drop instantly, which only annoyed Sophia more.

"How do *you* know Grey?" Sophia asked.

Julia looked away. Her stubbornness made Sophia want to throttle her.

"Oh, so now you don't want to talk?"

"I'm sorry, but you're the one who has a lot to answer to here, Sophia Evelyn."

"Don't you middle-name me. You know I hate that."

"Then tell me why you're in contact with the son of the man responsible for our mother's death."

It was Sophia's turn to bite her tongue. Her first instinct was to defend Grey, and that was definitely something she'd have to look at later. Much later.

"How do you think I know of him?" Julia said, a little too loudly. "I have researched the Constantine family since I learned about online searches."

"Why in the world would you do something like that?" Not that it surprised her. It was just like Julia to do something like this. And she would also never admit that she was obsessed with their mother's case, nineteen years later.

At least in that Sophia could relate.

"Why do you think?" Julia yelled, and Sophia shushed her and grabbed her by the arm. "What are you doing?"

"Amy and Victoria are sleeping," Sophia whispered harshly, "do you want to wake them up and explain all of this?" She gestured wildly into the darkness.

"Fine!" Julia threw her arms up and stomped to the front door. Sophia joined her on the stoop, making sure to look both ways to make sure they were alone, and thumbing the amulet around her neck.

It was cold as hell, but she was annoyed enough that she barely cared.

"You want to know everything? Fine, let's talk."

Julia lifted a brow and gave Sophia one of those looks she was so good at. The kind of look that got people to do whatever she wanted out of sheer fear.

"Go ahead, then. Tell me why you're suddenly chummy with Will Constantine's son."

Sophia started to tell her she wasn't chummy with Grey, but stopped. Wasn't she, though? She'd rather walk on hot coals than say anything to Julia about all that.

Instead, she told Julia what happened that day in the city, the potion, Grey and Lucas showing up when she alerted them. Julia listened silently, but her nostrils flared from time to time, and her mouth opened as if she wanted to interrupt and changed her mind every time. Her face betrayed nothing more.

"Why is my memory of that day coming back then?" Julia's voice was shaky.

"Grey said it wasn't a perfect potion."

Julia stopped mid-step. "What is he? A wizard?"

Sophia's throat was dry. "Close. A witch."

Julia let out a rush of air and paled in the dim yellow street lighting. "That didn't come through in the reports about him."

Sophia looked at her. "Why did you investigate him and his mom?"

"I investigated Will Constantine's entire lineage."

"Sweet Lord," Sophia whispered and let down her hair, as the bun was bothering her suddenly.

"Don't you judge me," Julia said, and when Sophia looked at her again, she was pale and shaky. "I needed to know more about the man who took our mom from us."

Her heart shriveled. "Julia, he didn't kill her."

"Didn't he? Her death never added up to me."

"So now you're a detective?"

"And now Will Constantine's son is in your life," Julia continued like Sophia hadn't spoken. "How and why?"

"Well, apparently he has always been in our lives," Sophia said and Julia stared. "We went to see Jeanette and she confirmed it."

"How could Jeanette confirm a lie?" Julia's face was turning red now.

Sophia's stomach heated. "How can you say that?"

"Don't you think I'd remember if Grey Constantine had been in our lives back then?"

"God, you're exhausting!" Sophia ran her hands over her hair. She was trembling from head to toe, because she knew Julia was only suspicious because she didn't understand.

"I wouldn't be if you fucking told me what the hell you're into." Julia gripped the cold railing on the stoop.

Sophia squeezed her eyes shut. "Grey came into the club about a month ago and left me a card. I sang that night and something happened that I don't know how to explain."

Julia waited silently. There was a tension to the set of her sister's shoulders, but Sophia allowed herself to relax.

"Sometimes, when I sing, I can see the music, Jules." Sophia couldn't look at Julia, so she focused on the wet road instead. "I don't know why it happens, and I can't even explain with words how it feels, but it's the truth."

She looked at Julia then and found her sister staring at her with an inscrutable expression.

"I hear music in my plants too." At that statement, Julia's nostrils twitched, and Sophia knew in that moment that Julia also knew. "Please tell me what you're thinking."

"Mom always talked about that." Julia's voice trembled. "She said that listening to the plants could lead you to answers you didn't even know you were looking for."

"I don't remember that."

Julia said nothing, so Sophia continued.

"I've never met anyone else who can do what I do, not that I've asked. Grey showed up that night and he could clearly see what I saw." Sophia wasn't afraid of looking into Julia's eyes now, a strength growing in her. This was the truth and she would speak it. "And when we went to see Jeanette, she told him that our mom and his dad had grown up together, which I already knew, but Grey had no idea."

"How could he not know that?" Julia, looking restless, pulled closed the lapels of her robe.

Sophia shrugged. "Jeanette thinks there's a spell on all of us."

"A spell." Julia raised a skeptical brow. "One that takes his knowledge of something but not ours?"

"I don't know how it works, Julia. I'm not a witch."

"Aren't you?" Julia put down her mug with a clink. "You're telling me you can sing and make music visible, and that you can hear plants singing to you, and in the same breath claim you're not a witch?"

Had she thought about it? Yes. Did she want to be a witch? To be determined.

"And Grey Constantine drugged me to make me forget about the other day."

"He didn't drug you." She heard the defensiveness in her own voice and cleared her throat, but Julia noticed. "I called him when it happened and he came to help us. The potion was meant to help you calm down. You were panicking and I was so scared."

Julia was still, but finally, she nodded as a faint tinkling of music reached Sophia's ears.

"There's an illness that he's been trying to cure for years," Sophia told her. "He asked for my help, and I said yes."

"And you don't think it's odd that he has a connection to you in this way?" Julia ran her hands through her hair. "Sophia, think."

"He did a spell, and it led him to me. The fact that we're connected explains why he showed up when he did."

They were silent for a while.

"I've been dreaming about mom a lot," Sophia said, both hands on the cold railing now. "So many strange dreams that I can't understand, even when I try to. And then there are the journals."

Julia blinked. "What journals?"

"Mom's. I asked you about them the other day."

Julia nodded.

"I found them and I explicitly remember mom writing into them. She always had a journal with her." Sophia thumbed the little amulet between her breasts, under her shirt. "They're all empty, Jules. It doesn't make sense."

"Empty? No, that doesn't seem right."

Sophia almost sighed in relief, having gotten a confirmation she hadn't known she needed.

"I still don't remember Grey being around when we were kids," Julia said.

"Do you remember Will?"

Julia's expression darkened, but she shook her head.

"I don't remember him at all," Sophia told her. "All I know is the story of mom running away with him. There are holes in my memories."

"Product of the spell Jeanette thinks is at play?"

Sophia shrugged.

"I thought I'd see you again soon."

The voice was unexpected and unfamiliar, and both Julia and Sophia jumped and turned toward the bottom of the stairs. A man stood below them, looking up to where they were standing on the stoop. Julia stepped forward in front of Sophia, who instantly reached for the amulet, allowing it to warm and vibrate.

"I just want to talk," he said, his voice breathy.

Clayton didn't look good. Even worse than he did when he'd attacked Sophia outside the club. His skin was gray and sunken. He looked like a walking cadaver.

"You need to leave," Sophia said to him as she reached for the doorknob behind her, heart pounding.

It all happened very quickly. Sophia opened the door, but before she could pull Julia inside, Grey appeared in the middle of the road, from thin air, and Julia gasped and fell backward into the entryway.

Clayton jumped forward, higher and faster than any human should be able to move, and he was on the stoop right in front of Sophia. She raised her arms defensively in front of her, just as Clayton reached forward with nails that were too long and too dirty. His breath was rancid as he grabbed her by the neck, squeezing so tightly she was sure he would smash her windpipe. His nails dug into her skin and Sophia struggled against him.

Julia screamed and hit him, but Clayton pushed her aside so hard, Julia hit the side of the house with a sickening thud and fell to the ground sobbing. Grey was there the next moment, and from behind him appeared Helena and Lucas. Grey ripped Clayton from her and Sophia took in a ragged breath and fell, only to be caught by Helena before she hit the ground. Julia was back on her feet, crying and holding on to Sophia's arm.

Helena, dressed in silk pajamas, with loose hair and bright eyes, led them to the door.

"Stay inside," she said as a scream, something unnatural and terrifying, came from Clayton. Every hair on Sophia's body rose, but she went inside with Julia, though she left the door open, unable to look away.

Helena went back to assist Grey. Julia had a hand pressed to her mouth, and Sophia was frozen to the spot. Grey dodged Clayton's kicking legs as Helena opened up a small bottle of a swirling white potion and tipped it into Clayton's mouth while Lucas held him from behind. Clayton became instantly boneless.

Lucas, dressed in sweatpants and a t-shirt, threw a look up toward Sophia and Julia before he vanished into thin air, and Julia made a sound in her throat that was a lot like a stunted scream. Grey said something to Helena, and she also disappeared.

Grey came up to the door. "Are you okay?" he asked both of them, but he trained his eyes on Sophia's throat, which was throbbing. She lifted a hand to it and felt the welts from Clayton's fingernails.

"That's all you have to say?" Julia had tears streaming down her face. She was red as a fire truck.

Grey stepped into the house and closed the door behind him. The three of them stood in the entryway's darkness, a little light from the kitchen illuminating them enough that Sophia could see the grim expression on his face.

At least Amy and Victoria hadn't woken with that whole thing. Slept like the dead those two, thank God.

"We need a first aid kit." Julia's voice sounded strained, and she disappeared through the archway, as Grey took out a potion from his pocket. They stood in the kitchen as he wiped some of the potion on her wounds. His hands were shaking as he did so. He looked upset, which was both sad and flattering.

What the hell was she thinking? She'd almost been murdered.

Priorities.

"Thank you for coming," she said and winced when he touched a particularly sensitive scratch.

"I'm glad you called." His dark eyes stared into hers, and he was so close she could smell him. His scent drove her crazy. "Are you alright?"

She took a trembling breath. "I think so. Is Clayton going to be okay?"

Grey grimaced, and the importance of finding a cure hit her like a brick. Not that she hadn't considered it important before, but more so now that she had seen the condition Clayton was in. His mouth had been almost completely black, and the stench. She shivered.

"You're cold," he murmured, frowning. He was only wearing a t-shirt and sweats. His hair was mussed from sleep, his eyes still a little swollen. His gentle fingers lingered on her neck, then slid toward her hair, taking a lock between his fingers. She swallowed hard.

"I've never seen it straight."

"I see you've already put something on her," Julia said, slapping the kit on the counter before she came closer. Grey didn't move, only looked down at Julia with a cocked brow.

"It'll heal her faster."

Julia stared him down, so steady it made Sophia cringe.

"I don't remember you," Julia said.

Grey threw Sophia an inquiring look.

"The potion wore off. I had to tell her everything."

He nodded and turned back to Julia.

"I have to ask you not to talk about anything you've seen or heard tonight with anyone," he told her.

Julia bristled and her mouth was a white line of anger.

Sophia tried to catch Julia's eye, but failed when Julia continued to stare at Grey as if they were the same height. She had a special way of doing that, and many a man had scurried away like a rat when at the other end of it. The reason she was an excellent businesswoman.

"Why did you get close to my sister?"

"She said she told you, so not sure why I have to repeat myself." Grey's voice was soft, but there was an edge to it Sophia had never heard before. Julia was getting on his nerves.

Join the club, Grey, she thought.

"You mean to tell me you're not here trying to get something from us?"

Sophia could see Grey measuring his breath. It was the most agitated she'd seen him, so far.

"I'm not here to talk about my dad, or hear *you* talk about him," he said with finality. "I did a spell, and it led me to Sophia. Period."

Julia blinked, surprised by his tone. She nursed her hand, which had a nasty scratch on the back of it.

"I have a potion that can help with that." Grey pointed to the wound, but Julia narrowed her eyes and cradled her hand tightly against her chest.

"Something else that will take away my memories?"

Sophia sighed. God, she was exhausted.

"Julia, it's like any medicine. It just works faster. Take it so you can stop freaking out," Sophia said, losing her patience.

"I'm not freaking out," Julia snapped, indignant. "I just don't like my head messed with."

"I apologize for that." Grey took out a little brown vial and showed it to her. "This is a healing potion, not a memory one."

Julia eyed the potion suspiciously, then looked up at Grey again. When he offered the vial, she took it, holding it gingerly between two fingers.

"Were you this calm last time?" she asked Sophia.

"Not at all," Grey said, and Sophia rolled her eyes at him.

"Traitor," she mumbled at him. "Just take it. It'll help."

"I'm only taking it because my sister is vouching for you," Julia said, and drank the potion as if it was a challenge she was unwilling to back down from.

The wound almost disappeared entirely, and Julia watched her skin go back to her normal color. Only a pink line remained.

"That should go away in a few hours," Grey said.

Julia stuck her tongue to her cheek. "Thanks," she mumbled, and added, "I still don't trust you."

"I don't need you to."

Julia turned around and left through the archway, and Sophia sighed in relief. She wanted to sag all the way to the floor.

"Does it feel better?" Grey asked, touching the scratches on her neck lightly. A shiver ran down her body, a remnant of the outside cold, and something else.

"Yeah," she said around a bundle of nerves in her throat. All that was forgotten when he reached for her and pulled her close to his body. She put her arms around his lean middle, pressing her nose to his chest, that clean scent all she could manage to focus on. "Thank you for coming."

"I'm glad you did."

She looked up, found him already looking at her, his eyes half-lidded and dark. The light was dim enough that shadows flitted across his face, so she could only see one side.

Fuck it, she thought, and reached for his face, bringing it close to hers, stopping only for a moment to allow him to pull back if this was not what he wanted. But he didn't pull back. Instead, he closed the rest of the distance between them, and his warm lips brushed her softly. They were gone so quickly, she stepped back from him, her heart pounding.

"I'm sorry, I—"

A hand caught her wrist, and she was back in his arms as his mouth took hers. It wasn't tentative or soft—possessive and hot and it made her tingle all over. His hands gripped her waist as her arms went around his neck, standing on the tips of her toes. His teeth scraped her bottom lip, then soothed the sting with his tongue.

She let her hands roam into hair, which he had half-bound. It was soft underneath her fingers, as was his skin. His hands gripped her, roamed up and down her back, as if he couldn't get enough of her in his hands, and just as he reached for the plump flesh of her backside, his phone went off.

He didn't let her go right away, but his phone insisted loudly, vibrating in his pocket. With a sigh, he pressed his forehead against hers and reached for the phone.

"I'm sorry," he said. Before he pulled away from her, he gave her one last small kiss. Just a long press of the lips that made her feel warmth and fuzzy tingles inside her chest.

As he answered his phone, Sophia could only stand there watching him. Her heart was still racing, her stomach in knots, but it all went away when she noticed his expression. His mouth tightened as he listened to whoever was on the other line—she suspected it was Lucas or Helena—and the line between his brows was so pronounced she wanted to smooth it with her finger.

"I need to go." His voice was deeper than before, if that was even possible, and she nodded. "I don't want to."

"I know," she said and touched his cheek softly. Before he left, they kissed gently, like it was a habit. "Will you be okay?"

"Yeah. I'll call you later."

He felt faraway, like he wasn't even in there anymore, and curiosity —and worry, if she was perfectly honest—rose in her like the waves of a stormy sea. She nodded, then stood back and watched him port.

° ° °

Grey had wanted to tell her about the letter, but it would have to wait. She would see the text at some point anyway, and they would freak out together.

When his amulet had vibrated, he'd woken in a panic, and seeing Clayton with his hands around her neck nearly gave him a heart attack.

It made his blood curdle, even as it had just been singing in his veins when he kissed her. He wanted to stay with her, continue what they started with that kiss, even now as he ported to his house to get the potions he needed to do the job. The elation left his body the moment he was inside the pantry, facing the wall of potions.

Clayton deserved the dignity, despite what had just happened.

He put the potions into a pouch and strapped it to his side, just as his phone dinged with Lucas's location. His heart dropped and his hands trembled.

When he ported, moments later, he found himself in a mountainous area. There was snow on the ground and on the evergreen trees, as the sky started turning purple with dawn. Lucas met him at the door, his warm eyes worried, mouth set in a grimace.

It was quiet inside. The furniture looked shiny, made of blonde wood and covered in green plaid. There were, in common cabin fashion, pieces of art of animals and sweeping hillsides, as well as heads of animals mounted onto the tall walls.

He headed back toward the private quarters, his feet silent on the wooden floors. It was much warmer inside, a small wood stove radiating warmth.

He found Clayton sitting up on a bed. His hands were on his lap, palms pressed together, like he was about to pray.

A woman came up to Grey, her red face blotchy and angry. Her dark hair was short, to her shoulders, and pin-straight. She was tiny, probably just shy of five feet. Clayton's wife. He didn't know her well, but Clayton was crazy about her, and very protective.

"You are not welcome here, Grey Constantine," she spat.

"Cecilia." Clayton's voice stopped her from moving forward and she sat on a corner of the bed and sobbed into her hands. Clayton looked up at Grey. His eyes were completely red, irises that had once been blue were almost black, the pupils dilated to the max. His skin was gray and wrinkled more than it should be, since Clayton was not an old man, by any means. He was, at most, forty-five years old. He looked like he was eighty. The stench from his mouth was overwhelming and filled the room.

"Grey," Clayton said. "I have committed the worst sin."

Lucas took up a corner of the room, crossing his arms, always watchful. Grey wondered where Helena had gone. She was supposed to have followed Lucas and help him with Clayton. But he didn't have time to focus on Helena. She would do as she needed to, and he would talk to her later.

"Do you want to talk about it?" Grey asked the older man, keeping the bout of resentment down. He had gone after Sophia again. Who knew how long he'd been sitting there waiting for her to venture outside?

Clayton pressed his lips together, as if speaking of it was difficult.

"I didn't mean to go after her," Clayton said, his tone too soft. Regret etched his lined face, and Grey's simmering anger died down. "I can't do magic anymore and I wanted hers. Or theirs. I can't even tell anymore."

Theirs.

Grey's eyes flickered to Lucas, whose brow twitched. They would need to investigate, though the possibility of one of Sophia's sisters having magic didn't shock him. He'd just never thought about it.

"These things happen, Clay," his wife sobbed. "You didn't kill anyone. Please, we have to find something that can help." She looked up at Grey, her face a mask of pure pain that sent stabs down Grey's body. "Please."

Grey swallowed a lump, his eyes hot.

"Cecilia, he's tried," Clayton said to her, taking her hand gently. "If there were a cure, I'm sure we'd know. I have tried everything everyone's brought to me; nothing has helped and you know this."

Cecilia didn't take her eyes off Clayton as she cried.

"I would never want to hurt someone." Clayton closed his eyes. "I wouldn't forgive myself. It would be all over for me anyway, if I did something against another witch, or any human, for that matter."

"Stop," she cried, and her body shook with the force of her sobs. "You won't hurt anyone. I will stay with you all day and all night."

Clayton looked up at Grey, and the look in his eye showed he was ready. Grey gestured toward Lucas, who nodded almost imperceptibly and moved forward.

"Cecilia, I think it's best if you step outside with me," Lucas said, but Cecilia turned to him with an expression of pure outrage.

"No," she snarled. "I will not move from here."

"Ceci, please," Clayton whispered, sounding tired. "I have to do this. Let me die with dignity."

"No," she wailed and threw herself on the bed. "I will go with you. Please, Clay. I will go with you. I will go with you. Please."

Clayton shut his eyes briefly, putting his hands at her hair, then nodded at Lucas, who picked up Cecilia. She spat and screamed, tried to kick Lucas, then scratch him, unsuccessfully.

Grey heard her screaming all the way, but after only a few moments, her screams subsided, and they could hear her crying softly. If there was something Lucas was good at was helping people see things they refused to look at. Cecilia was in excellent hands.

"Are you sure?" Grey asked quietly. He was half-hoping Clayton would say he wanted to wait, but that was self-serving, and it wasn't safe anymore.

Clayton sighed. "I have little time left and we both know it."

Grey set down the bag with the potions on the side table. Clayton looked at them with a slight grimace.

"I've heard they don't taste pleasant," Clayton muttered.

"Been talking to people who have taken it?" Grey asked, his brows lifted. Clayton laughed, and his face transformed. For those moments of laughter, he was his old self, even when his pupils were still enlarged.

"Your service will never go unrecognized," Grey said softly. Clayton grimaced. "I'll make sure of it."

Clayton's brows drew together. "I had Sophia Candela followed in the city."

Grey knew, or at least he'd had an inkling it had always been about Clayton.

"Why her?" Grey asked.

"It's not like this has any rhyme or reason," Clayton said. "But there is something about Sophia Candela... It stirred something inside me, and I can't explain."

A thirst for power that one couldn't control. But why Sophia? Why now? She had never been attacked before this.

"Your power attracted me, you know." Clayton looked out the window into the lightening sky. "It's not everyone who has your talent for potions. I sense the power in you, but something is missing. And Sophia..."

Grey swallowed and waited, frozen.

"She's powerful. I can't explain it. I've never felt energy like hers."

Grey's skin prickled at the words. Had he noticed something different in Sophia? He had, but he had chalked it up to how familiar she felt. Could Clayton be onto something he hadn't realized? Could other sick witches come after her now? A definite possibility.

"Please make sure Cecilia is okay," Clayton pleaded, his hands beginning to tremble. "Promise me."

"Cecilia will be fine," Grey promised. He would make sure she was. "Would you like to speak to her? Before..."

Clayton nodded.

Grey stood outside the room as Cecilia went in and talked to Clayton. There was crying, begging, cursing, screaming, and finally, quiet sobbing.

Lucas put his hand on Grey's shoulder, saying nothing, always a man of few words. How long had they been doing this together? It seemed like forever. When Grey had met Lucas while in college, they had instantly recognized magic in one another, and their friendship had been steadfast since. Lucas was the only person other than Helena who knew what he did. How it affected him, and how much he wanted to find a cure so he never had to do it again.

"Thanks for coming so quickly earlier," Grey said.

"I'm just glad we got there in time." Lucas scratched his beard, which was less put-together than Grey had ever seen it. "What do you think about Clayton's comment earlier?"

"That he might have gone after Julia Montgomery, as well as Sophia?" Grey met his friend's dark gaze.

"Not shocking. Witch blood can run in the family."

"Why didn't I sense it?" Grey turned to his friend. "Why didn't you?"

"We weren't around them for long, and she was having a panic attack, so I didn't think of it."

"Then let's keep an eye." Grey reached for the doorknob. "Ready?"

"Never," Lucas said, and followed.

Cecilia lied on the bed next to Clayton. She clung to his side, her eyes shut tight.

Grey took out the potions, arranged them on the side table.

"Are you sure you want to watch this?" Grey asked Cecilia. She nodded, still not looking at him.

"I'm not going anywhere," she said, the tears flowing freely out of her pretty green eyes, focused on her husband, still clinging to his side.

He administered the potions as he always did, and Clayton took each one, making a face when the taste hit him. When he'd taken all the potions, Grey stepped back.

"Farewell, Clayton. May the arms of the mother welcome you home."

Clayton was calm as he looked at Cecilia, a smile in his eyes. His skin was clear again. Gone were all the lines and the gray hue his skin had taken at the end of his illness.

Grey's heart broke a little every time he had to do this, but today it was different. It was harder to walk away. But he and Lucas left before Clayton faded away.

❀ ❀ ❀

GREY WASN'T SURE HOW LONG HE AND LUCAS SAT OUTSIDE on the porch after getting back from Clayton's. He suspected Lucas didn't want to be alone either, but his friend was a man of few words about his own feelings. Clayton had been an important figure in the magical community, having done work similar to Lucas's before he got sick.

They were silent for a long time, watching the calm water in the distance, mirrored by the gray clouds above it.

"That really sucked," Lucas murmured, never taking his eyes off the water. Grey looked at his profile, and found Lucas frowning tightly. As a therapist, he had been just as quiet, choosing to listen more than he spoke about possible solutions to his clients. As an energy worker now, having abandoned his traditional practice for a more magical approach to mental and emotional healing, that part had remained the same.

"Yeah."

They still didn't move. Grey had thought about getting a blanket, it was certainly cold, but didn't have the motivation. He folded his legs underneath him to keep his bare feet warm and took a deep breath of crisp air. Lucas was bundled in his jacket.

Grey's eyes were dry, but the sadness throbbed in him, his thoughts on Clayton, Cecilia, the young girl from other day, whose name he still didn't even know. He had always thought that not asking for names would make it easier. That the lack of connection would make it hurt less.

"You're full of shit," Lucas mumbled. "It'll always hurt the same."

"Stop doing that."

"Doing what?"

"Using your powers on me." Not new, but just as annoying the hundredth time it happened. It wasn't that Lucas could read his thoughts, but he was an excellent energy worker, and that seemed to be the secret. His unorthodox ways of helping people certainly benefited from it.

"I did no such thing." Lucas continued to look straight ahead.

"Now who's full of shit?"

Lucas shrugged. "It doesn't help to intellectualize it."

"That's what I keep saying." Helena appeared suddenly and

plopped herself between them. Both Grey and Lucas hadn't seen her since earlier, when she'd showed up to help with Clayton. She was dressed casually now, in dark jeans, a fluffy sweater, and boots. The hollows of her cheeks were more pronounced than ever. He could see right through the light layer of makeup.

"What are you two doing out here? It's freezing."

"Brooding," Lucas said.

"Maybe you're brooding," Grey grumbled.

Helena sighed in exasperation.

"You two are idiots."

The scent of faraway rain reached them simultaneously, that very particular smell of wet earth floating through the air.

"You two need to stop punishing yourselves," Helena added after an extended silence.

"You must have the situation confused," Lucas said. "I'm not the one punishing himself."

"Shut up. We both know that's a lie." Grey opened his arm for Helena when she leaned against him. Her warmth against his side was comforting, so he leaned his cheek on top of her head to give her the same. She had always been there for him, but she was getting sicker, and after helping Clayton pass on, the urgency in his gut only got bigger.

"I only stayed because I was worried about you." Lucas leaned forward and looked at them both.

"You keep telling yourself that." Helena smirked.

The heaviness didn't leave completely, but it alleviated. Helena's presence always brought a lightness that he craved to be around when things got to be too much to bear. Like her calm had the power to quiet his world when it got chaotic.

"How's singing at the club?" Lucas asked her.

"I was actually just there," Helena said. "Things are under control."

"Never doubted you for a moment." Lucas raised a brow. "That dumbass, on the other hand…"

Grey smacked his arm playfully, then squeezed Helena's shoulder. "Thank you."

"I've enjoyed myself too."

"I thought you would," Lucas said. "That place is great."

Grey, surprised, found himself staring at Lucas.

"You've been to Nowhere?"

"Of course. Their Latin Nights are fantastic," Lucas replied. "Just wish they had it more often."

Lucas loved dancing, so that made sense. Grey just wished he'd known Lucas frequented Nowhere.

"I wish I could Latin dance," Helena said. "I can sing, but dancing is not my strong suit."

"I'll teach you, if you want." Lucas patted her knee. "If you have the energy."

Her shoulders sagged a little. "I do get tired more easily these days."

If she was admitting to that, then it was worse than he had thought. Helena had a habit of downplaying things so he didn't worry.

Lucas met Grey's eyes over her head, briefly.

"I'll have more potions for you soon," Grey said. His entire body was tight with anxiety.

"I know that." She squeezed his side before she leaned back on the couch. "Meanwhile, I really like Sophia."

"Yeah?" Grey thought about that kiss, how much he wanted to repeat it.

"I'd work there even without having to protect the place. I can see why you like her." Helena's voice softened, in a tone she adopted when she wanted to know something but wouldn't flat out ask. He raised a brow at her profile, saw that she had a small smirk.

"Just admit it and we can get the conversation out of the way." Lucas smirked.

"I don't know what you want me to say."

Helena and Lucas laughed.

"Please," Lucas said, "you're so full of it. Out with it."

Thoughts of Clayton blissfully out of his mind, he allowed himself a small smile.

"Is it the thing with your dad and her mom? Because that's getting old," Helena said.

Lucas nodded in agreement.

"Who said I'm thinking about that at all?"

"It's as if he thinks we're dumb," Lucas said to Helena, as if Grey wasn't even there.

"We've also seen her," Helena added, her eyes half-lidded. "You'd have to be dead not to see what she brings to the table."

Grey rolled his eyes at them both.

"Just let me know if you're not going for it, so I can, buddy." Lucas's voice trembled with barely controlled glee, though Grey knew Lucas would definitely hit on Sophia if he knew he could.

"Same," Helena said, and snorted laughing when Grey pushed her against Lucas.

"Alright, that's enough." But Grey wanted to laugh, and at the same time throttle them both.

"You think I'm joking," Helena mumbled.

"Actually, I know you're not, but back the fuck off."

Helena dissolved into giggles and snorts, and Grey and Lucas joined her.

"You sure you can focus on the research or do we have to step in?" Lucas asked.

Grey's stomach dropped. What did he say? That his dad had been in love with Sophia's mom when they were teens? That they were no closer to answers than they had been when it all started? The existence of that letter hung in his mind.

"I can manage," he said and a gust of frigid wind made him shiver.

Helena stood up, pulling her coat closer to her body, and she faced Grey and Lucas.

"I have stuff to do, but you two should maybe go inside now."

"Yes, Mom," Lucas smirked and she threw him a narrowed-eye look.

"Watch your mouth, Lucas, I know what you're thinking." She pointed at Grey. "He's not the only idiot punishing himself here."

"Grieving isn't punishment," Lucas said mildly as he stood up too and went to stand by Helena. "There was nothing else we could have done for Clayton. He could have easily killed Sophia or her viper of a sister."

Helena frowned up at him. "Julia? She's actually nice."

Lucas made a face like he didn't believe her.

"I have to take off now, but call me if something else comes up," Lucas said.

"Feeling ready to be alone?" Grey teased, and Lucas smirked.

"No, I have a client this afternoon."

"What kind of work are you doing with them?" Helena asked.

"Regular old energy work, this time. They think they have energy stuck on their hip and that's why it hurts."

"Is that why?" Grey asked.

"Hell if I know."

Helena laughed, and her eyes widened a little as she looked over toward the front stoop. Grey followed her gaze, and his heart took a dive into his stomach when he saw Sophia standing by the door. Her wide eyes went from Lucas to Helena to Grey. Her cheeks and nose were pink from the cold. There was a rip on the knee of her blue and white striped sweatpants, and the hoodie looked like it had once been black. Her hair was becoming wavy with the humidity and hung to her waist.

"Hello," she said, a little awkwardly, as she approached them. Grey stood abruptly, nervous.

"We were just leaving," Helena grinned and took Lucas's arm again. Lucas only nodded at Sophia with a half-smile, and he and Helena ported with a potion.

"That was subtle." Her brows were arched and laughter danced in her eyes.

"They're nothing if not tactful." His fingers itched to tough her hair, or to wrap around her neck and pull her forward for a kiss.

"You said we had to talk, so I thought I'd come do that. Then there was that text you sent."

Right. This was about the letter. Nothing else.

"It was in my dad's stuff, from my mom's house."

She put a hand to her chest.

"At least my dad seemed to think he was in love," he continued when she didn't say anything.

"Did my mom respond?" She sounded the way he'd felt when he found the letter—breathless.

"Not that I saw, but I also didn't keep reading."

She nodded slowly. "Would you show me?"

In the kitchen, he made coffee while she read the letter. When she was finished, she put it down and flattened her hands on the counter.

"I don't even know what to say."

"Join the club."

She unzipped her hoodie and pulled it off, revealing a white shirt with a big black NO printed on the front.

"Well, my mom kissed him while literally sitting in a tree," she said, and he smiled a little at the image. "I think that probably means she felt the same." The last part came out as a question.

"Have you never kissed someone without being in love with them?" he asked, throwing her a sidelong glance, gauging her reaction. Her lids dropped, and a faint blush tinted her cheeks. At least now they were both thinking about that morning.

"I'm not answering that, but I am disappointed in your lack of self-control, reading without me."

"I didn't mean to."

Her eyes narrowed playfully. "Excuses," she said, but then leaned her head sideways, and her face smoothed. "Something happened."

His stomach took another dive, and the scent of the coffee suddenly felt cloying.

"What makes you think that?"

Her brows pinched, but she shook her head.

"I'm sorry," she mumbled. "I do that a lot."

"What?"

"Assume I know things."

There was a tingle deep in his chest. Could it be, he wondered, scrutinizing her. Her palm had told him she had a strong sense of intuition. Maybe Lucas could sense more.

He rested his forearms on the counter and held her eyes.

"And what are you assuming right now?"

"I'm not sure. Maybe I sense a sadness," she said, but quickly burst out laughing. "What the hell am I talking about?"

Grey still didn't move, and he certainly wasn't laughing. Her laughter stopped abruptly.

"Don't be so quick to dismiss your intuition."

Her throat worked as she swallowed.

"Something did happen then," she said.

He straightened, his skin suddenly itchy and stretched too tightly on his muscles. Maybe if he didn't face her when he said it, she wouldn't think less of him, he thought as he turned away and took out two mugs from a cabinet. Putting them down on the counter, he turned back to her.

"Your opinion of me might change."

"And what's my opinion of you, exactly?"

"Dashing, charming. I think I also remember you saying something about beautiful."

She snorted. "Please do not let any of that go to your head."

"Too late."

She cocked a brow, waiting, and he sighed. His avoidance games would work on her as much as they did on Helena and Lucas, which was not at all.

"Clayton..." His breath faltered.

"What happened?" Her voice was unsteady, as if she sensed it before he even said the words out loud.

"He's dead." He pressed his lips together, before he could say something that would send her running for the hills.

"From the void?"

He shook his head, then nodded. He wished he could disappear, so he didn't have to tell her.

"It was a part of it," he said.

Her eyes went comically wide. "Did you kill him?"

His hesitation had her blanching.

"It's not what you think," he said hastily. He met her startled gaze. "He requested help from me to pass on."

She blinked. "What do you mean?"

"Clayton's illness was too advanced," he explained. "As you know, witches react violently to the void."

She touched her neck, as if just remembering what had happened only hours ago. Had it only been hours? God, it felt like a month.

"There would be no coming back from where he was. Not without a cure."

He saw the moment she realized, finally, the kinds of things he had to do. She pressed her hands to her chest, like something in there hurt. Tears shone in her eyes as she rounded the counter to come closer.

"Have you had to do this before?" she whispered.

He could only nod.

"How does it work?" she asked, catching him by surprise.

"Well, usually someone sends a signal of distress," he explained. "There are potions for it, but more often than not, Lucas hears about it first. I made these potions that help with symptoms, but in high doses..."

He couldn't put it into words.

"I've tried for so long to find a cure, I never imagined I'd be administering potions that kill witches instead."

A trembling breath passed her lips as she reached for him, her arms circling his middle. With her face pressed against his chest, his arms came around her, pulling her in tightly. As warmth filled him, he understood that he didn't care what happened with his dad and her mom, he wanted her this close.

"I'm so sorry," she whispered, and let go far too quickly. The loss of her warmth was immediate. "I didn't realize how much you've had to sacrifice."

"I'm not the one sacrificing, the witches dying are. Their families are. I just happen to be good at making potions."

"There's something else," she observed. "What is it?"

He took a deep, grounding breath. "Helena has the void."

Sophia gasped softly, her breath shuddering out of her. "Oh no."

"She's managing." He cringed at his own words. "For now."

"I get so many things now," she said. He looked quizzically at her. "Helena's devotion to you." She had a little smile on her lips. "She thinks the world of you, and you obviously think the same of her."

"You've seen us interact maybe twice," he reminded her because it was the truth.

"You're the one who said I'm perceptive," she said. "But it's obvious. You love her."

"I do." Nothing but the truth. "I will be damned if I let this illness take her." And he'd be damned if he was the one to have to help her... He shook his head. He wouldn't give that a thought.

She reached up and touched his jaw with soft fingertips.

"We'll find the cure," she said and sounded so much more confident than he had ever felt. He nodded, but his heart still raced. He hated the anxiety, how it made his body feel, and how it prevented him from thinking straight.

"We need to get back to work," she said and headed for the living room. He followed her. "I keep thinking that my mom's obsession with music is definitely connected to our abilities with music."

He nodded slowly. "Yes, I thought that part was obvious."

She raised a brow. "And you never mentioned it. Why?"

"Because I thought it was obvious."

She deadpanned. "Yes, to you, the actual witch in this scenario."

"I don't know about that." He thought of what Clayton had said.

"You mean because Clayton came after me."

"And your sister," he clarified and watched as it dawned on her. "Julia?"

"Maybe. It's not outside the realm of possibility."

She sat frozen. "But I haven't manifested any powers."

"Are you sure about that?"

She raised her head to throw him a surprised look. Her hazel eyes were glassy.

"I mean," he said, "have you ever done anything you couldn't explain?"

She was silent for a long time. So much that he thought she wasn't going to answer. He wondered if she realized how tense her shoulders were. They were practically up to her ears, and he could swear he could hear her teeth grinding.

"I'm not sure." She shook her head.

"You can tell me."

She shook her head as if to clear it. "I don't think so." She walked away and paced twice before she stopped and stared into space. Her phone went off, but she didn't even look at it.

"Want to get that?" he asked.

"It's probably Aric," she grimaced.

"Do you need me to help with that?"

Her eyes glinted. "How?"

"I'd call in a favor with the police, for starters."

Her mouth twitched. "I thought you were going to say magic."

He grinned. "I can do that too, but it goes against my moral code."

"And where can I find a copy of this moral code?"

He chuckled. "I don't do things that take away people's free will, for the most part."

"Fair enough," she sighed. "If Aric shows up at my place again, I'll call the cops myself."

"Good plan."

"He's never respected boundaries, exactly, but this is not like him."

His jaw clenched. "How so?"

"The last time I rejected his advances, he finally disappeared and I didn't hear from him for a while, months. But now he's back and being... off."

He felt his brows draw together. "Did something happen?"

She sat on the couch, slumped against the back.

"He came to my house the other day and was drunk out of his mind. I told him to leave, but he seemed desperate. Almost sincere, which believe me when I tell you is new to me."

"And when did his behavior change?" He had an inkling, the beginnings of an idea. An inkling, really.

"I can't say for sure. It's all really annoying." She scowled. "I don't want to talk about Aric."

Same.

"Besides, I have other worries."

"Like..."

"Nosy, aren't you?"

He grinned. "Only way to know things."

She rolled her eyes. "Well, if you must know, Victoria and her boyfriend broke up, and it's been weird. I thought he was going to propose, so the breakup doesn't make sense."

There it was again, that feeling. He went with his gut and asked the first question that popped into his mind. "Why did they break up?"

Sophia shrugged. "No idea, to be honest. They're the perfect couple."

There it was. He grabbed on to the feeling.

"You have a look on your face," she said, narrowing her eyes at him.

"Have you ever made things happen by just saying it?" He gestured with his hands, wiggled his fingers.

A dawning came over her features. "There was this thing that happened with my plants," she said. "But I thought it was nothing."

"Sophia, Clayton came after you in his delirium, because he sensed great power in you, and possibly your sister." He watched as the meaning of his words sunk in. The color left her cheeks, and she was breathing through her mouth.

"I know it sounds weird," she said, and when he raised his brows at her, she rolled her eyes again. "Okay, maybe it doesn't sound weird to you, but it does to me. Last night, I was with my sisters and Victoria, when I saw this plant that had died." Her eyes became unfocused, swimming in a memory that felt beyond him. He watched her, enraptured. "I might have under-watered it, or over-watered; I can never tell which plants need what. My mom was the plant expert. But there is this second plant at work, which was perfectly alive one minute, and dead the next. Do you know what I mean?"

He stared. "I really don't." If this was magic-related, it was like no magic he'd seen before.

"I woke up one morning to find the money tree at home was dying. Its music was faint, almost entirely gone. But I felt so guilty. I can't seem to keep plants alive. Then I went to work, and the cactus was dead, which was crazy because the cactus was fine just a day before."

"And last night you noticed the money tree is alive again."

She nodded slowly, opening her eyes even wider. "See what I mean now?"

"Almost." He had never heard of anything like that. Or had he? He couldn't remember. He drummed his fingers on his knee. "Maybe we can find out."

She perked up. "How?"

He went to the pantry and came back with two little brown vials, both labeled. "Remember this potion?"

"Not even a little."

He gave one to her. "When I played music for you, I took this potion to help me access the music I wanted to play for you."

"Okay…"

"What if you take it to find out if there's something to your suspicions?"

Her face went blank. "And how do you propose I do that?"

Another idea came quickly, and he went back to the pantry, picked up a blue vial this time, and came back to the living room, where he picked up two of his smallest potted plants. He placed them in front of her, took out the cork from the vial, and dropped the potion into the soil of one of the plants. It shriveled instantly. The leaves paled and dried out.

"Just put one drop on the tip of your tongue. Any more than that and it might not work like you'd expect."

"I don't even know what to expect in the first place."

"This is an enhancing potion," he told her. "It clears your head and helps you focus. I use it when I need to do something… magical that's difficult to do."

She didn't ask, holding up the bottle, looking at the liquid moving within, slowly, like molasses.

"How do you even begin to make something like this?" she asked.

"Practice, like a chef," he told her.

"Can you cook as well as you make potions?"

"You want me to cook for you?" His heart did a thing.

"Maybe." A sly little smile played around those full lips of hers.

"Let me know when you're hungry, then," he said, and her cheeks bloomed with color.

"First this, though," she said, handing him the potion bottle, her eyes focused on him. He took the bottle, unscrewing the dropper and picking up some of the potion within by squeezing the rubbery top.

"Be clear in what you want it to do for you," he said, knowing what kinds of things could happen if you didn't. Like simply get high and want to go run outside naked in the rain or lie around doing nothing for an entire day. The potion would enhance the intention going into it tenfold. He'd learned that the hard way.

He held the dropper in front of her, but instead of taking it, she stepped closer until their faces were close; until he could smell that scent of hers, like peonies and fresh rain. She opened her lips, and he froze, unable to take his eyes off the shine on the pink skin. His neck was hot as he squeezed the drop of potion on her tongue, but he laughed when she made a disgusted face as the taste of the potion registered.

"It gets better," he said, putting the lid back on the bottle.

"When?" She dry-heaved once, then her expression changed as he knew it would. It relaxed and she blinked.

"Right about now?" he said with a smile, and when she swayed, he took her by the elbows to steady her. "It's a bit of a shock, but you'll feel steadier in a minute or two."

"If you say so," she muttered, but after a minute, her entire expression changed. She looked around the room in wonder, her eyes wide.

The room was dimmer than normal, but he liked it, especially when working with this potion. Not that he intended to take it, but something about dark spaces was comforting to him.

"Are you okay?" he asked her when she briefly closed her eyes.

"A little dizzy, but otherwise okay." She looked up at him. "Your eyes are the prettiest shade of brown."

He could feel the blush creeping up from his neck to his face.

"Thank you," he mumbled.

She laughed. "How can anyone be this good-looking and this adorable all at once?"

He led her to the couch, and she plopped down on it. "Wait here."

He sailed toward the kitchen and brought back a glass of cold water. He found her lying on her stomach, in front of the two plants, her intense gaze on them.

One was a lovely green dieffenbachia, the green so dark and shiny, and the white veining in the leaves contrasting and making it almost glow. The wilted plant was an asparagus fern. Leaning closer to it, she placed her ear close to the plants, as if trying to hear something.

Grey could only watch, trying not to tense up, forcing himself to unclench his jaw. He wondered if one drop had been too much for her, as she sat with her hands in her chin now, observing the plants. As her eyes unfocused, he came to crouch next to the couch, and placed his hand on the middle of her back.

She started.

"Focus," he said softly, meeting her gaze. "Just do what you remember from before."

She nodded, sitting up, her attention back on the plants. She was so intent that he could almost hear the wheels turning in her head.

It was a while before she moved or said anything, and he stood, transfixed. Something was happening. He didn't know what, but it was. There was an energy about her, surrounding her. It came out of her in droves, shimmering in the air like heat reflecting off pavement. She leaned forward, toward the dying fern, and her finger caressed one of the little drying branches.

"I'm so sorry," she whispered to it. Sophia eyed the healthy plant, then her attention went back to the fern. "I wish for you to live."

The words hadn't left her lips when things began to change. Together, Grey and Sophia watched in real time, as if watching a time-lapse video, how the fern came back to life, perking up, now flushed with a soft green color throughout its leaves. Sophia put her ear to it, as if listening. At the exact same time, the other plant lost all color and wilted.

Grey's mouth hung wide open. Had he not just seen it happen, he would think she was imagining things, or lying.

Sophia panted and grabbed on to his sleeve. There was a buzzing just beneath the surface of his skin, moving there like electricity, and he realized it came from her. Her fingers had a current. He could feel it all the way down his arm, down his leg, even.

"What did I just do?" she whispered, her wide eyes focused on him.

"Magic," he said. Magic that looked different from what he had ever known.

The corners of her mouth turned down. Her pupils were huge as he took her chin in his hand, and forced her to look at him.

Those lips beckoned him, parted and soft, and warmth spread throughout his body.

"You're amazing," he told her, and elation lanced through him as she moved a little closer, her knees on either side of him. Her eyes almost glowed in the forced dimness of the room. He was a furnace. There could have been a fire and he wouldn't notice it. When she came down on his lap, his hands instantly found the curve of her hips. She slid even closer, so close her lips were only a whisper from his, and he knew if their lips touched, it would be an apocalypse. The world would shatter and come back together, and he didn't care how dramatic that sounded.

"You're only saying that because you really want to kiss me right now," she whispered, her plump bottom lip grazing against his slightly. Her face was above his, and the surrounding haze enveloped both of them like an aura.

"And if I do?" he asked her before he met her glowing eyes once more.

"Kiss me."

He leaned forward and gently sunk his teeth into her bottom lip before he licked it. She sucked in a breath, her eyes going wide, her hands fisted on his shirt. Chills ran up and down his spine when her hands slid down his arms, slowly tracing his skin, and wrapped themselves around his neck.

He heard himself gasp, with both pleasure and surprise, and he moved forward just a little, allowed her the time to back off if she wanted to. She didn't. Instead, she closed the final distance between them.

Her lips were soft, warm, and sweet, just as they'd been that morning.

Her hands left his neck when he pushed forward and deepened the kiss, and buried into his hair. His heart hammered inside his chest, his own hands gripping her thighs. Teeth scraped against his lips, and his head spun as the heat spread throughout his entire body. The scent of her was all around him, like a cloud, and in that moment, he realized he couldn't recall a time where she wasn't in his life.

The moment he had the thought, another image came, and he gasped as he pulled back, panting. Images slid by one by one, quickly. A swing, a late summer afternoon, countless plants, green grass. The sun was setting, and he sat on the swing opposite her, but they were small. Her little hands were dimpled, wrapped around the chain of the swing. She was darker, as if she'd spent a lot of time outside, and his eyes closed when she pressed a kiss on his lips, wet and sweet.

He was breathing heavily as the image left him, and his heart jumped off a cliff when he saw Lucas appear right in front of them.

"Jesus," he gasped, gripping her hips tightly.

"Sorry," Lucas said from the archway, and Sophia stuck her face into his neck. "I didn't think you'd be..."

Sophia moaned miserably, the sound vibrating against his skin.

"I thought you left," Grey said with clenched teeth.

Lucas fought back one of those stupid signature smirks of his, but the mirth danced in his amber eyes.

"I just came back for some potions."

"Does it look like we have your potions here?" Grey could swear his teeth would disintegrate. Lucas chuckled softly and disappeared toward the kitchen.

"Oh my God," Sophia muttered against his neck and that, too, sent chills down his body. How long had it been since he'd been with a woman? Too long.

Or maybe Sophia was just that alluring.

Both. He'd go with both.

Lucas came back, holding up the potions he'd put into a pouch. They clinked as he showed them.

"Thank you. I will leave you to it." He disappeared, his laughter echoing long after his body had ported.

"I would kill him if you asked me to," Grey grumbled. She snorted with laughter and looked up, the bridge of her nose a little pink.

"None of that," she whispered, her eyes hooded with desire. "Maybe it's for the best that he interrupted."

"How was that for the best?"

She raised a brow.

"Are we going to ignore what just happened here?" She pointed at the plants, and his heart thumped. She had intoxicated him. If she asked him his name, he wasn't sure he could tell her what it was.

"Have you ever done it before?"

"Consciously? No." She shook her head. "But I was a Disney-obsessed child and made a lot of wishes upon a star."

"I don't think that's how it works."

"And how would you know?" She pulled away from his lap. He wanted to stop her but didn't. With a lot of regret. Her eyes widened again, and she gasped. "Oh my God, I have to know what I've done.

One time, I wished for my mom to not be dead, and now I'm horribly glad it didn't come to fruition. What have I done?" He took her face in his hands.

"It's going to be okay."

"No, it's not. I..."

She stopped. Her mouth dropped open.

"What?" he asked, alarmed.

"The spell is on us," she said, breathless. "It's preventing you and me from knowing something important. It makes so much sense."

"But Jeanette lost her memories too. It seems much more complicated than that."

She was quiet for a moment.

"Can a spell backfire?" she asked.

"Yes."

"And what can make it backfire?"

"A badly made potion, a spell that's too vague or simple and doesn't cover loopholes."

She was frowning, and he thought about telling her of the images that came into his mind when they were kissing, but thought it best to wait. There would be time for that. Now, they had to find out more about that spell.

19

Silvana poised her blue pen over the page, but froze before any words came. It was warm, thankfully, but it was getting dark, and her father would wonder where she was. For the first time in a long time, she didn't care. She wanted to be out of that house, where her angry father thought he was emperor supreme, and Silvana wasn't allowed to even breathe without him freaking out. Her diary was almost full, hundreds of pages inked with her life.

> *Diary, I still don't feel like calling you "dear" as if you're a sentient being. It's weird. I'm in the treehouse, but it's getting uncomfortable hanging out in here. It's too small now, but I can't give it up.*
>
> *My mom taught me that when I feel troubled, I should write. She said writing was cathartic, and of course she was right. It's just too bad she isn't here to see me do it.*

Another pause and Silvana wiped away the tears that had run down her cheeks.

There are too many thoughts in my mind, and I have a hard time remembering everything I need to write, whether that is to remember them, or to get them out of my head.

I wish there was a spell that would make it so I didn't have to do this by hand. It would be neat, I think. Maybe that will have to be my next project. Does it defeat the purpose of journaling?

Whatever the method, I hate my dad.

That's not true. I don't hate him, but I resent him. I need him right now and all he can do is get drunk and pass out in front of the television every night. I know he's hurting. I can hear him crying sometimes, but he hides, and he's always angry with me, as if I did something. As if it's my fault that my mom is dead. I lost her too.

I can't even write in you without fear of him going through my stuff and finding out what I'm saying, so everything is in code. Or I wonder if there's a spell, or a potion that can make my writings invisible to anyone other than me. I wish I knew another language, one that he doesn't know, but I don't have time to dedicate to another language. Not when I'm trying to get good at magic. I want to become a doctor, and I want to use magic to heal people. I want to eradicate cancer.

Silvana wrote fast—so fast, she was convinced the pages would catch on fire, but she didn't care.

My mom died a week ago today. It feels like a hundred years have passed. She promised she was going to be okay, and I believed her. But she died anyway. She went into remission, and only three months later, it was back.

Jeanette knew my mom was going to die, and she said nothing. I'm so mad at her. She hid this from me. When I was happy that the cancer was gone, Jeanette knew all along that it wouldn't last, and I didn't even get a chance to prepare for it.

More tears fell, even onto the paper, but she didn't stop writing.

Both Jeanette and Will knew. They knew. I feel like never seeing them again, but needing them at all hours of the day because they're all I have left. My body feels like it will split in two from this pain that doesn't go away, even when I sleep.

What use is having magical powers if I couldn't save my own mother? When I can't use it to save others. I hate cancer. I hate that people we love die. I hate that Will's dad died. I hate that my best friends didn't say anything. I hate them.

And you know what they said? That they wanted to protect my feelings. What a load of bullshit. They just don't know how to have hard conversations. That's all this is about. It had nothing to do with me.

She stopped writing then. Of course, it had nothing to do with her, because nothing did. When Will's dad had died, Silvana felt like she'd lost a parent herself. Maybe it was the same for Will and Jeanette. But she still felt the waves of anger coursing through her. She shook with it. She wanted to rip the world into pieces.

Her mom had always taught her that every emotion was valid, so Silvana would bask in her anger for as long as she needed to.

Screw Jeanette for not telling her. Screw Will for also not saying anything, and for dating someone and forgetting that he had two best friends, one of which really needed him.

Even as the thought came, she knew it was unfair. When Silvana felt like her world was falling apart, they held her together.

The world made little sense now that her mom wasn't there. Now that her body was six feet under. Now that her eyes no longer saw. Now that Silvana missed her like she had lost a limb.

Silvana pulled out the little bottle she'd been carrying around and tipped the contents into her mouth. She was used to the foul taste now, and it barely registered. In the past week, since her mom died, Silvana hadn't been able to hear plants singing at all. It scared her to think of a world without the music she was so accustomed to hearing everywhere she went, so she depended on the potion to help her. Thankfully, her mom had shared the recipe with her.

The tree's song started dim, and slowly became louder, until Silvana closed her eyes. It sang slowly, sounded like a flute, and the song was somber, but sweet. Soothing, as if it knew how much she needed it.

She put down the journal, her hand smarting from writing for so long and so fast, as Will crawled through the little door at the top of the ladder that rested against the trunk.

Normally, Silvana would have been happy to see him, but he was coming back from a date with Brooke Charles, a girl who his mother liked and thought was perfect. Silvana had noticed the way Will's mom looked at her, as if she was faulty somehow. As if she wasn't as interesting and funny and pretty.

And she was all those things. She had nice skin that was always a deep shade of gold, and eyes that looked like the earth, and hair that curled darkly down her back.

"I didn't know you'd be here," he said as he sat by her. He smelled good, like he had put on cologne for his date. She wanted to push him out the little door and watch him fall to the ground below.

"Neither did I," she said, hoping he'd just go and leave her to bask in her misery.

"I know why you're talking to me like this. I don't like it, but I get it." Will sat by her. He knew her heart was hurting, that she was close to falling apart, and he wanted to be there for her if she would allow him to be.

He knew what it was like to lose a parent, and that he knew perfectly well how to give her the support she needed. It made her angrier that he did. That she couldn't blame him for going on a date with another girl. Dates, plural. He talked about them from time to time, told her and Jeanette how they'd gone to the carnival and he had won Brooke a pink stuffed penguin.

A pink penguin sounded supremely stupid to Silvana, but she didn't say it, lest he think she was jealous. She wasn't jealous. She needed her friend, and he was busy with someone else. That was all.

Silvana was aware, as was Will, and even Jeanette, who didn't look up from her books long enough to notice anything, how Brooke Charles looked at Will from across the halls at school. And Silvana saw how Will smiled at Brooke, and all she wanted was to smack the grin off his face.

"I don't know what you're talking about," she said. "I thought you were on a date."

She instantly hated herself for mentioning it.

"We broke up."

Silvana refused to let her surprise show, but felt her brows twitch. The tree continued to sing.

"Why?" she asked, convinced her voice sounded neutral.

"Nothing important." He was a terrible liar. Mostly because he had a tell, and he was not even aware that he did. Will always looked down when he lied. He didn't do it often, but Silvana was observant enough that she remembered every instance when he had. One of those times had been when he told her that her mom would be okay.

Silvana wanted to know more, but knowing she'd always ended up with her feelings hurt, she chose to shut her mouth. It was better not to pry. It would be another complication, and God knew she didn't need any more of those.

"I'm sorry." She didn't mean it, and she didn't feel bad as she picked up her notebook. "I'm going home."

She headed down the ladder before he could say anything, but he caught up with her as she went into the trees. Her jeans were loose, too loose for her liking, but her dad hated her wearing form-fitting clothing and wouldn't let her get anything that could show her figure. It pissed her off. She could work if the problem was money, but he also wouldn't let her do that.

"Hey, hold on," he said, running to catch up with her. He was so tall now she had to look up. "Where are you going?"

"Can you just leave me alone, William?" she rounded on him, her voice harsh, and he stopped.

"What did I do?"

"Just go back to the tree house and let me get home. Okay?"

"Can you at least tell me what's wrong?" He stuck his hands in his pockets, his hair plastering to his head with the fine rain. "Maybe I can help."

"You can't help," she snapped because she felt like crying. "At all. Go back. Goodbye."

She kept walking, leaving him there, but when she turned back, it was to see him walking away from her, his head bowed, hands still in his pockets. He was lean and his body had started to fill out from his swimming.

Her heart fell, and guilt eating at her, she turned back and followed him. She took her time because shame and pride warred inside her. Thankfully, he climbed up to the treehouse instead of going home.

Silvana stopped at the bottom of the ladder, to gather up courage to talk to her friend. He'd told her he'd broken up with his girlfriend, and she'd snapped at him instead. She was the worst.

Will was on the far side of the small space when she made it up, leaning against the wood, his elbows on his knees. His brows shot up in surprise when he saw her, but his eyes looked sad.

She crawled toward him. Her hair, which her dad also wouldn't let her cut for some stupid reason, was frizzy from the rain and fell around her, laying partly on the floor of the treehouse as she sat cross-legged in front of him. He mirrored her and crossed his long legs too. His hair, straight and dark, fell on brows that were also straight.

"I'm sorry," she said and meant it this time. She couldn't look him in the eye, so she fidgeted with a corner of her notebook.

"It's okay." His voice was nothing more than a murmur, and she did look into his eyes then.

"It's not okay." She set her diary on the floor next to her, the pen stuck in the metal spiral. "It's not your fault. None of it. It's a hard day today, that's all." The music of the tree enveloped her as if in a warm hug. She could hear a French horn in there somewhere, and it tugged at her heartstrings.

"It's only been a week. It takes time."

She sniffled. "I really miss her."

"I know. Me too."

That broke her heart even more and she had to fight back the tears.

"Do you want to talk about it?" he asked.

She closed her eyes and took a steadying breath. "It feels like it'll never get better. I know you'll say it does, and I know it does. But a part of me doesn't want it to get better."

"Because if it does, it feels like a betrayal."

She felt her face screw up, and she nodded.

He moved a little closer, his knees now touching hers. She'd never had a hard time expressing how she felt. Her mom always encouraged talking through feelings, but it wasn't the same now that she was gone.

"I don't want to forget her." Her throat was tight and painful.

"How could you, though?" He kept his voice low. "There's no way to forget someone like your mom."

"How did you do it?"

His mouth pressed into a grim line, and he shrugged.

"One day, you wake up a little bit stronger, and it seems lighter."

She peered toward him and found him looking outside.

"I know you wanted to use magic to help her," he said. "I'm sorry we couldn't figure out how."

All the anger she had felt drained out of her, and left her trembling. Crawling next to him, she leaned her head on his shoulder. In a gesture that was as familiar as it was heartbreaking, he put his arm around her. She leaned into his warmth, closed her eyes to stop herself from crying, and took in his scent. He smelled woodsy and a little like the pool he was in almost daily.

"I'm sorry," he whispered.

"I'm sorry about Brooke," she said, lifting her head to look into his face. He was so beautiful, with his kind eyes that were equal parts ethereal and grounded, as if he lived in a different plane of existence than everything else.

"It's okay." He squeezed her shoulder. "We weren't a good match, anyway."

She sniffed, looking out the sole little window into the tree. It had stopped singing. The effects of the potion had gone.

"Why not? She's pretty and popular." And white, but she wouldn't say that out loud, so people thought she wanted to make everything about race, like she'd been told in the past. She was young, but she wasn't stupid, and it was obvious that Will's mom didn't like her for that reason. It was a look on the woman's face, one that Silvana had seen often from others. Hard to run from that when you're a darker skin Latina.

"Yeah, well, she's not..." He pressed his lips together, as if unwilling to finish the sentence.

"She's not what?" she insisted, now curious, but Will's face was determined and his jaw was tight. She didn't push. Will would talk when he was ready and not a minute before.

She relaxed against his shoulder again.

"Thanks for listening," she said. "I know it's been difficult to be around me lately."

"There's no place I'd rather be."

She believed him.

"Silvana," he whispered, and when she looked up at him, his face was very close. She should have moved away. Should have turned her head when he came even closer. It wasn't wise, but when her best friend in the world leaned forward and kissed her, she kissed him back.

20

Sophia was lying on the couch, one leg hanging off the side, when her eyes started to unfocus. The letter she had been reading slipped from her fingers and floated to the floor. A long sigh floated from her. She was sick of reading. Knowing her mom's thoughts as a young girl was special, but there were no answers still, and Grey was running out of time. They were running out of time.

Grey was on his stomach on the floor, cradling his chin in his hand as his eyes flew over a letter. His confession had rattled her, but not more than what she saw in his face when he spoke about it. He hid it well, and it broke her heart a little. How much had he done it that he was so good at hiding how it made him feel? And he believed he was going to lose his best friend too. She couldn't imagine.

No, she could. If it were Victoria's life on the line, or one of her sisters'. She'd already lost Roselyn.

Sophia shook her head as her stomach tightened with anxiety. She would have never known that Helena was ill—she was always so put together and cheerful, as dependable as a human being could be. Sophia didn't know what she did to protect the club, but so far so good. And the patrons loved her. Those who knew her from her online presence, and those who had never heard of her before. She regretted that she hadn't seen Helena perform more, since she'd been so busy, and the urgency to spend more time with her only grew.

Sophia sipped on the water Grey had put by her side a while back. She tried not to get mushy about it, but it was hard not to when he was thoughtful and sweet, as well as ridiculously good-looking with his hair pulled back to the back of his head, and his sleeves rolled up to his elbows.

The bare minimum, she told herself. It was the bare minimum to expect a man to be nice or think about getting her water when he went to the kitchen without her having to ask. Still, it made her like him even more than she already did. There was something about his quiet disposition that made her feel utterly comfortable around him. She'd always felt that way, she realized.

He sat up, his elbow over his knee, as he read something on a letter with a small frown. He had a pen in his other hand, as he had been taking notes, which she had been meaning to ask about, but she hadn't wanted to interrupt him.

There was a little bit of music, a twinkling sound coming from the plants in the room. The one she had experimented with was still on the coffee table, and Sophia glanced toward it, a prick of anxiety going through her at the memory of what she had done. It felt so far away, but so vivid in her mind. She had performed actual magic, and if she was completely honest, she had no clue how to feel about it.

She stood and stretched, her arms high above her head, hands clasped. Her butt was sore, as were her back and legs. She was so used to being on her feet all day, that sitting around for hours on end wasn't what she'd consider ideal. Her t-shirt rode up her abdomen and she caught Grey's soft blush and a hasty refocus on the paper in front of him.

So cute, she thought, with a sudden urge to tease him that surprised her. Still, she slipped her fingers over her skin and pulled at the hem of the shirt, watched his blush deepen. He was no longer averting his eyes, and neither was she.

He opened his mouth, as if to say something, but her phone dinged, shattering the moment. She groaned when she noticed the unknown number. She opened it.

> UNKNOWN: I KNOW YOU BLOCKED ME, BUT I
> STILL WOULD LIKE TO TALK TO YOU.

She closed her eyes and breathed deeply, to calm the instant jitter of nerves that made her stomach queasy and her head spin. She considered not responding as her finger hovered over the delete button, but instead, she typed a message back.

> SOPHIA: I REALLY WISH YOU'D STOP DOING
> THIS.

And as soon as she sent it, something became unsettled within her.

> UNKNOWN: I CAN'T UNTIL YOU TALK TO ME.

> SOPHIA: I'VE BEEN CLEAR ENOUGH, ARIC.
> PLEASE STOP.

> UNKNOWN: I JUST WANT YOU TO SAY YOU
> FORGIVE ME.

> UNKNOWN: I KNOW YOU DON'T BELIEVE ME,
> BUT I DO LOVE YOU, SOPHIA. I JUST WISH I
> HAD FIGURED IT OUT SOONER.

She looked at the texts, then turned off the screen. A sour taste lingered in her mouth. She couldn't put her finger on why it made her stomach roll uncomfortably, why she felt like throwing up and at the same time had a knot so far into her throat, she couldn't even speak if she'd wanted to.

"Everything okay?" he asked as he put the pen behind his ear.

"Aric again," she told him with a roll of the eyes. He didn't pry for more, and she was glad.

Aric was the last thing she wanted to discuss with him, but a nagging feeling stayed with her as she went back to reading for something better to do.

After another hour of reading, Grey sat up suddenly.

"What?" She abandoned the letter she was about to start.

Grey's eyes scanned the letter and turned it over.

"It's a recipe."

"What's a recipe?"

She sat next to him on the floor, instantly aware of his scent. Had anyone ever smelled that good?

"I noticed a pattern a while back, in the way they wrote to each other as they started getting older. They were being more and more clever about how they said things."

"Cleverer than writing in code?"

He shrugged and showed her the notepad he'd be taking notes on.

"They left code words on some of the letters. Words that didn't go with the rest, out of context."

A list of words was written in his neat handwriting, but none of it, save a few common ingredients, made any sense to Sophia.

"Spores, blue cap, death cloud, green oregano, cat eye." She grimaced at the last one. "Is this serious?"

He laughed. "Not literally cat eye. It's probably a potion that might look like a cat's eye in the vial."

"Or it could be a real cat eye."

"You never know." He was still smiling. "But the point is that some of these ingredients are familiar."

"How so?"

"I make a similar potion. I found a recipe for it in my dad's stuff, and I called it the knowing potion before we ever started reading these letters. It's like what the trio talks about in their letters, though it doesn't do what they talk about either."

"Well, how do we find out more?"

"It looks labor intensive," he said, looking at his notepad. "It has a lot of ingredients."

"What are they?" He handed her the notepad, and she read, "Molasses, monkshood, moon water..." The last ingredient gave her a disgusted pause. "Is this for real? They want us to put blood into a thing we will ingest?"

His face scrunched up. "That's gross, but there must be a good reason."

"And could the reason possibly be?"

"To make it more potent." Grey snapped a picture of the notepad and typed a message with quick fingers.

"Who's that for?"

"Lucas," he said, still looking at the paper. "He'll help me find ingredients."

"How hard will it be?"

"It may not be easy, but Lucas has contacts."

Grey looked at his phone when it vibrated in his hand.

"He's on it." He eyed the piles of letters they still hadn't gotten to. "The instructions have to be somewhere."

"And according to what I've read, the way it's made matters."

"There are also the tapes..."

Right. She'd forgotten about the tapes. They were obviously connected to the special potion, but Sophia couldn't fathom how. She remained sitting as Grey stood up and paced slowly, deep in thought. She jumped to her feet and stood in front of him, forcing him to stop. His arm muscles jumped when she held him in place.

"We've been reading for hours. This is good news," she said, gesturing to the letters, though she wasn't sure that was even true. "We need to rest."

His cheeks puffed as he blew out a breath.

"Let me say that again," she said, "*I* need the rest or *I* will lose my shit."

He laughed. "You're right." He took her hand. "How about I cook you that dinner you've been begging me for?"

Her mouth opened in mock outrage. "The day I beg a man for anything, you'll have seen everything," she said, but let him lead her to the kitchen.

He instructed her to sit down, even after she offered to help. She took a barstool and sat at the counter as she watched him work. But not before he went to the bar just off the kitchen and made her an Old Fashioned, which she sipped with her stomach fluttering every few seconds. She could easily get used to this. A man cooking her food and making her drinks... She'd take it.

He moved easily around the kitchen, chopped vegetables, as water boiled on a stainless-steel pot behind him.

"Tell me you have no food allergies," he said as he crushed garlic with the flat of his chef's knife.

"Not a thing," she said. "Well, milk, but only a little."

"Cheese okay?"

"Cheese is always okay."

He smiled softly, tipping a handful of pasta into the boiling water. It was way too much pasta, but she wasn't about to tell him that. He was far too cute to stress him out about it.

Her phone dinged.

VICTORIA: ARE YOU COMING HOME?

Unlikely. She typed it, then erased it, then typed it again before she sent it, a secret smile playing around her mouth. Her eyes went back to Grey, as he industriously chopped a few fresh herbs and set them aside. Heat pooled low in her belly as she watched him work, stirring pasta, grating cheese, pulling out other ingredients as he hummed under his breath.

She wasn't going home. No way in hell.

VICTORIA: WAIT, WHY?

VICTORIA: ARE YOU WITH GREY?

VICTORIA: OMG, PLEASE TELL ME YOU'RE
FINALLY MAKING A MOVE.

Sophia laughed under her breath, as every message showed up before she could even form a thought on how to answer.

SOPHIA: YES, I'M WITH GREY. I WILL HAVE TO
CATCH YOU UP LATER.

Her phone dinged a few more times.

Victoria sent a gif of an actor rubbing his hands together, and Sophia laughed under her breath.

VICTORIA: I CAN'T WAIT.

She set the phone aside, trying to avoid getting sucked into the texts. She would much rather watch Grey cook for her. It was better than her favorite funny sitcom.

"I'm going to guess that's not your ex."

She rested her chin on her hands. "Reading my mind?"

"You don't smile when it's him," he said, and something fuzzy spilled in her stomach, warming her whole body. "You do when it's Victoria or one of your sisters."

She bit her lip. She was so not going home tonight.

"It's not Aric," she said, and her voice was a little breathless.

"Good," he said quietly, holding her gaze with an intensity that sent shivers running up and down her spine. She was the first to look away, nerves dancing along every inch of her.

That intensity of his showed up when she least expected it, since he was typically so gentle and quiet, and it unsettled her as much as it thrilled her. How different would her life had been if they'd grown up together? Would they have been doing this all along? Or maybe they would have been such fast friends, nothing would happen between them. She didn't like that possibility, so she set it aside. She wanted things to happen with him. Everything; she wanted everything.

Her mouth watered, so she downed the rest of her drink and nearly choked.

"I'm impressed," she said, a few minutes later, when she had swallowed the first bite of pasta, which confirmed that he was, in fact, good with his hands in many capacities. How thrilling.

"Feel free to tip, if you're so inclined." He was smiling softly, a little mischievously, she noted. They ate in comfortable silence, and polished almost an entire loaf of garlic bread between the two of them, but when he went to clean up afterward, she wagged her finger at him.

"No, sir," she told him, taking the plate off his hands. "Cooks don't clean on my watch."

Still, when she started washing dishes, he picked up a towel and dried and put things away, his body brushing against hers from time to time.

He was doing it on purpose, because every time he came close, she visibly shivered. In the ten minutes it took to leave the counters gleaming, she went from feeling a little feverish, to swearing she was going to spontaneously combust. Her sweatpants were entirely too tight now.

"Your turn to sit," she said and pointed at the small bar right off the kitchen. She had to keep her hands occupied or she would embarrass herself. He sat as she rounded the bar and watched her, which made her even more nervous. She turned away from him to take a shaking breath.

With a small smile, pretending she was at the club during a busy night, she turned back and grabbed two glasses, turning them right side up on the counter with a clink. His brown eyes followed her every move, just the way she wanted it, even as it twisted her insides into a knot.

Pulling a few ingredients out, she mixed bourbon and lemon juice into the silver shaker. Ice went in next, and she shook it, then poured into a glass. She garnished with an orange slice and a cherry.

"Simple and classic," she said as she began mixing one for herself. "It helps that you have great bourbon."

"Life is too short to drink bad alcohol."

She saluted him with the shaker in agreement.

"Very good," he said after a sip.

"Feel free to tip," she echoed him and was rewarded with a brilliant grin, which transformed his face. He looked younger, boyish almost, even with his rugged good looks and that nose stud that worked a little too well to get her hot and bothered.

Her stomach shivering, hands a little shaky, she drank deeply until there was almost nothing left in her cup. Eyes watering, she gently put down the glass. Both his brows lifted high on his forehead.

There was a flutter in her stomach, little butterflies tittering as the warmth of the cocktail spread throughout her body.

"What's on your mind?" He stood and her eyes followed, up and up —God, he was so tall—focused on that face of his.

She bit her lip, waiting impatiently for the moment when the drink hit the rest of her senses. She looked down at his glass. Damn working at a bar. Her tolerance was high.

"You should drink that," she said.

"Why's that?"

"So you can be at my level."

He leaned his head a little, but picked up his glass and drained it, all the while watching her. He handed her the glass, and their fingers brushed. Like the first time they'd met, a jolt passed between them.

"Am I at your level?" His brow was still arched. The little blue stud glinted in the overhead light.

It was dark out now, and wind howled past the house.

"I don't know," she said, shrugging as she washed and dried the glasses, willing her shoulders to relax. "Are you?"

"You trying to get me drunk or something?"

"Oh, I wouldn't dream of that." Drunk people couldn't consent, and she desperately needed him to. Her tongue was a little bit numb. Pleasantly so.

"You're fidgety," he said. "What's going on?"

"I don't know what you're talking about." But she was fidgety, she knew. She was always fidgety when she got nervous. She could never play it cool like Julia, and she had never been able to flirt like Amy or Victoria.

"Sure," he murmured, narrowed his eyes. It was a look of pure amusement, and suddenly, they were playing a game, and she relaxed further, even when his hands came to rest on the bar, on either side of her. Trapped between his body and the counter, her heart raced.

"I've been wondering." His voice was a murmur, so deep and rounded at the edges, like the smoothest chocolate. She could listen to his voice all day long. He could read her a dictionary and she'd be drooling in a minute flat.

"What do you wonder?" Her voice was weak, but she didn't give into the urge of clearing her throat again.

"How it was before with us," he crooned. "Our childhood, when we were friends, growing up together. I don't remember it, but the moment I saw you in your club, I knew."

She could say nothing, her heart doing a thing she could never explain with words. A tumbling and rolling, a pressure that went all the way down to the bottoms of her feet.

"Yeah," she whispered and swallowed.

"I knew I had known you in another life." The wind continued to howl violently outside.

She only nodded because she understood completely.

"There was always something else..." His eyes sought hers. "I just didn't know it was you I'd always missed."

His words stunned her further into silence. Her heart beat in the rhythm of tribal drums and heat ran up her body, from the bottoms of her feet to the top of her head. Of their own volition, her hands lifted to his chest, and she fisted his shirt as she rose on her toes and kissed him.

He did not hesitate as his lips opened against hers, his tongue warm. He tasted of oranges and spice, better than the cocktail. His hands were at her hair, pulling her head back to allow him better access to her lips. On the tips of her toes, she reached for his face, as his hands went to her waist and he lifted her onto the counter, her knees on either side of his hips. He pulled her to the edge, pressed himself against her, his finger roaming somewhere inside the hem of her t-shirt.

She pulled back to look up at him. His eyes were, if possible, darker, heavy-lidded with desire. His lips were open, glistening, and bright pink.

Her hands roamed down the hard planes of his chest, toward the shirt's bottom edge, grazing soft skin underneath.

He cupped her chin, lifting her face to his.

"Do you want me?" Her fingers gripped the edges of his shirt as she waited for what was maybe a second or two, but felt like hours.

"Hell yes," he said softly, the low timbre of his voice doing something obscene to her insides right before she melted against his kiss. This time, his lips were demanding, hard and soft all at once. Teeth biting and teasing, tongue darting out to soothe.

She wasn't sure at what point her shirt disappeared, and she further lost consciousness when his mouth found the swell of her breast. She threw back her head, allowing full access to her body. She was hot and wet and ready for him. Desperate.

His fingers were expertly reaching for her skin, touching her like he would one of his precious musical instruments. The reach of his hands into the waistband of her pants registered only slightly. She lifted her hips when he pulled them down, and there she was, naked on his counter, while he still wore all his clothes.

Lips roamed from her face to her neck, lower to pause at her peaked nipples, and then lower still until she was leaning back on her elbows, her knees now hooked onto his shoulders. His tongue was magic, made her see color even without music playing anywhere, and in a moment of pure bliss, she forgot herself and let her head drop. The smack of her skull on the counter registered only slightly as she shivered with her orgasm, which was quickly followed by a shriek of laughter and a snort. He lifted his head, eyes bleary, lips wet from her.

"Oh my God." His voice was both alarmed and shaking with underlying laughter. "Are you okay?"

Another snort and a tremble of her leg on his shoulder, and she nodded, tears running down her face. She sat up, and her laughter stopped when he picked her up like she weighed nothing, and kissed her again.

"Too many clothes," she muttered into his mouth, but he didn't stop kissing her or moving. A door opened, and he stumbled forward and suddenly her back was on a soft bedspread. And when he pulled his shirt over his head, straddling her, she gasped and stared. Sitting up, she ran her fingers over the colorful tattoo, an octopus that wrapped itself around his chest and over his shoulder.

"Just when I thought you couldn't get any hotter, you have a secret tattoo," she murmured, drew another laugh from him.

"Wait 'til you see the moons on my spine," he murmured before he kissed her again. Fuck the tattoos, she wanted more of him.

Another deep kiss, and his pants disappeared, and he only left her for a brief moment to find protection.

She pushed him onto his back when he returned, and took him into her mouth, showing him she could make him feel just as good as he made her feel. It was music to her sensitive ears, hearing him breathing her name, then growl when he got impatient as her mouth tortured him close to orgasm. He pulled away, sliding out of her lips with a loud pop, and a giggle escaped when he threw her down on the bed. Straddling her, his eyes never left hers as he slid on the condom, and warmth gushed out of her in anticipation.

The only sound now was the rain pelting against the window, and when he finally slipped inside her, they sighed at the same time. It was as if he'd always belonged there, as if they should have been doing this all along. Falling rain was the perfect soundtrack for it as they moved together, their eyes locked on each other. His skin was flushed, the bridge of his nose pink where long ago freckles had been when they'd shared a sweet kiss on a late summer afternoon. The memory didn't shock her.

Sophia realized it hadn't been that long since she found him again, when he had come into her life so suddenly. But it felt like he had always been there, hidden behind the curtain of her memory, just out of reach.

He had become her friend, her teacher, and she wanted more of him in her life. His intensity, which was shy and charming all at the same time. His voice and what it did to her. His magic.

She moved her hips in time with his, their skin damp, sliding together as if in dance. Then everything built to the point of no return and her back bowed off the bed as he picked up the pace and intensity. She reached for his lean hips, her nails digging into his skin as her vision left her. Everything turned white, her head became light, her toes curled, and a squeal of delight escaped her throat. He drank her sound as he followed her quickly after.

After heart rates and breathing had calmed down, they lay side by side, facing each other. He'd pulled a blanket over them when they had returned from doing the unfortunate task of after-sex cleanup, which had consisted of more laughter, soft kisses by the bathroom sink, and a warm, damp rag he had found for her.

Snuggled into the crook of his arm, she slept.

o o o

SOPHIA WOKE UP TO THE SOUND OF MUSIC. IT WAS something soft and lilting and curious. She slipped from under the cozy blankets and dug into one of his drawers for something to wear. She found a plain t-shirt and pulled it on. It barely covered her ass, but she padded down the hallway toward the main room anyway, following the music. The house was chilly, and outside, the morning was foggy and moody.

Then, his voice joined the melody, the notes softer than she would have ever expected. It was like he was two people with two different voices, his range was so insane. The melody carried toward her, the vibration of his vocal cords piercing through her. Her heart tucked and rolled, and she stopped right before she entered the kitchen to watch him.

Grey was tending to a pan on the stove, then moved to add bread slices into the toaster. He didn't have a shirt on, and she discovered the phases of the moon running down his spine in simple black ink. She never thought she'd want a tattoo, but in that moment, she wanted nothing more.

He moved effortlessly, carefully, and she smiled like an idiot as she watched him. When he turned to pick up a plate from the counter, he saw her, and he smiled, his dimple flashing. So hot.

"Good morning," he said, rounding the counter to come to her. He kissed her softly, then grabbed her hand and led her to the island, where she sat.

She looked at the spread. Poached eggs, bacon—which it impressed her that he'd cooked that while shirtless—a perfect avocado, toast, and orange juice.

She sat, smiling, as he served her.

"It smells amazing. I'm starved."

"Good sex will do that," he said, kissing her lightly before taking a bite of toast.

"Pretty proud of yourself, aren't you?" But she smiled slyly at him anyway because he should be proud of himself. The man knew his way around a woman's body.

"Very much so." He bit his lip and looked at hers, making her face hot.

"Who would have thought?" she said and ran her knife over an egg, which she had placed on top of the toast, along with the avocado. It oozed bright orange onto the other food on her plate.

"What?" he asked, observing her.

"That you were this cocky."

He laughed. "I wouldn't say cocky."

"And I'd disagree." He pinched her side gently, and she squealed when it tickled. "But you get to be."

"Oh yeah?" He was smiling like an idiot, and reached forward and pulled her in for a kiss, this one a little deeper, a little harder.

After they finished eating, ignoring all the reading they still had to do, they sat outside on the porch, snuggled together on the outdoor couch. She was on his lap, and he had wrapped a big fuzzy blanket over them. His naked chest against her skin was warm, though, so she burrowed herself into him, curling her legs off the side of the couch. His fingers were drawing little patterns on the skin of her thigh as her head rested against his shoulder.

"I could stay here forever," he whispered, pensive as he looked out at the sea.

"Me too." She buried her face in his neck, taking in a long breath impregnated with his scent. He smelled like the rain itself, clean and fresh and crisp. She rejected an alternate universe where she didn't get to be with him like this. Where being in his arms wouldn't feel like coming home after a long day.

Her heart sighed, and fingers trembling, she sat up and looked at him, into those brown eyes that were like the earth itself, and she kissed him deeply. Emotion welled behind her eyes, and an achiness settled heavily in her chest, around her heart.

No, it wasn't possible to stay in that moment forever. Something would change. She could feel it coming. But right then, in that moment of quiet and rain, the ocean, and the cold breeze, she straddled his hips, pulling the shirt up to hover somewhere around her waist. His hands became urgent against her thighs, sliding to other places that needed his attention. A murmur to make sure it was okay, and his arms tightened around her as they moved together, forgetting everything and everyone outside of their bubble.

21

They spent the entire day in bed, and talked, told each other stories of growing up. He told her how much magic meant to him, and she told him how much she wanted to learn. Making love between deep conversations, before they cooked food together, only to end up christening his kitchen too.

Later in the afternoon, as they lay in bed, wrapped in a blanket, they finally touched on the letters and the recipe. Sophia had tried calling Jeanette about it but couldn't get through. As she waited for a callback, she worried Jeanette didn't get the call, or something was preventing them from talking again, like before.

"It might be time to go see my mom about the tapes," Grey said, blankets sliding down his gloriously naked body.

She knew he was right, but the possibility of meeting his mom made her anxious. How would the woman react to meeting Sophia? Could they pretend she was someone else?

"There's nothing to worry about." His fingers tipped her chin so their eyes could meet.

"Do you read minds now?"

"Not at all, thank God." He kissed her lightly. "The tapes seem to be important, as they mention them often."

"Do you think there's music in them?"

He shrugged, looking uncertain.

"It would make sense, right?"

She slid out of bed and pulled on her pants. He followed, dressing in a pair of black sweats and a matching long-sleeve shirt.

"We should go now," she said, suddenly anxious. "Do you think your mom will care?"

"I can call her and ask, if that makes you feel better, but she won't."

She had no idea what was worse. Calling her to give her a heads-up, or just showing up unannounced.

As if reading her mind, he took a hold of her and hugged her.

"It might be best to talk to her," he said. "She might know things we don't."

"I know."

"She enjoys playing racquetball at the local gym in the evenings, so we might have to do it another time."

"I'm impressed and jealous of her stamina."

He smirked. "Your stamina seems just fine to me."

She rolled her eyes playfully and slapped his arm.

"Is this what I should expect from now on? Innuendos?"

"Exclusively." He pulled her in for a kiss. "It'll be fine."

She tried to take a deep breath, but she felt like she couldn't breathe.

"If you say so."

"Ready?"

"Not at all." But she held on to him anyway.

They appeared at the back, like last time. He knocked, and getting no answer, twisted the knob to find his mother in the kitchen with a pair of headphone in her ears as she danced around putting away dishes.

She was tall and willowy, with short hair that was more white than blonde, and her eyes were blue as the sky. She beamed up at Grey when he went to hug her, but her smile slipped when she saw Sophia, and instead looked curious.

"Sophia, this is my mom, Margaret Constantine," he said, his cheeks a little pink.

"Maggie's fine. Welcome, Sophia."

"Thank you." She could only stand there, awkwardly, trying not to wring her hands together. There was a thin layer of sweat on her. It was one thing letting herself act on her attraction to Grey, but being in front of his mother was something else entirely. It upped the ante in more ways than one.

She swallowed. There it was. The guilt that she carried around with her as if the mistakes of her mother were hers.

Grey came to her side and took her hand gently, as if he knew every thought running through her mind. And maybe he did to some extent. Maggie didn't react. Her eyes simply flickered to where their hands were joined and looked up at her son. Maybe she also liked to play poker. She would kill at it.

"To what do I owe the pleasure of this visit?" Maggie asked.

"I've been looking over dad's stuff and there's a mention of tapes. Any idea if I can find them here?"

Maggie raised her thin brows slightly. "If they're anywhere, it would be in your room, in those boxes."

"I already looked there."

Maggie leaned her head in question, but she didn't ask. "Anything else might be above the garage, though I cleaned it a long time ago. I don't remember seeing any tapes."

"Do you mind if we look?"

Maggie shrugged. "Be my guest. I'll make you two some coffee." To Sophia, she smiled gently, and said, "Welcome."

Sophia gave her a tight smile, and Grey led her outside to a door on the far side of the house. He pushed it open and let her in first, and she found herself inside the garage, where a single SUV was parked. There was a workbench on one end of the space, and behind it on the wall, gardening tools were neatly organized on the wall.

At the far end was another door. It was painted black and looked like a hole in the wall. Grey had to pull it hard to make it open, and it reminded Sophia of the attic door in her dad's house. It smelled similarly, too. Like old potions and books. Grey flipped a switch, but nothing happened.

"This lightbulb has been out for a long time," he murmured. His voice was almost a shock to her senses at this point. As if she had forgotten he was there next to her.

She followed him up the stairs, which were awkward, the steps uneven and narrow. It opened to a small space, roughly half the size of the garage below it. The walls were dark blue with white trimming. Grey went to the center of the room and turned on the light by pulling a small chain on the side of the lightbulb, which hung straight from the ceiling.

There was a simple desk in the corner, with one small box on top of it. Otherwise, the room was empty. The wooden floor had a thin layer of dust. Grey's exhale was long, as if frustrated.

"I guess it's just this," she said, approaching the desk. Sophia felt the trepidation course through her as her phone started vibrating in her pocket. She ignored it, focused on the box, ordering her fingers to stop shaking as Grey opened one.

He pulled out a bunch of white envelopes with the same symbols as the letters they'd found in her mom's stuff. There were a few dozen, and at the bottom of the box, there were tiny vials, like the ones she remembered seeing in her mom's attic. All had labels still attached, and there was a single potion with a tiny bit of a bright golden liquid in it. It almost looked like perfume.

She swallowed the vomit that rose to her throat. Her body was shaking uncontrollably, as if they were outside in the cold—though the coolness in the attic wasn't much better.

"I feel sick," she moaned, her eyes darting around the room to find somewhere to sit, but finding nothing. Her head was so light, she was sure she would pass out. Grey moved the box off the desk and lifted her to sit on the cold, hard surface.

He pressed his hand to her forehead.

"What do you feel?"

"Like I'm going to barf," she said, dry heaved, and put her hand on her mouth.

"What can I do?" he asked. "Do you want to go back home?"

Home to his home?

No, she wanted to go to her home. To her best friend and her sister, where things felt familiar, but she knew she would not abandon Grey now. They had to find those tapes.

"No." She looked up at him. He was looking down at her with

concern, so she touched his jaw, where a five o'clock shadow made him look like a sexy pirate when combined with his finger-combed hair. "We need to do this."

"Only if you're up to it."

She pulled him forward for a brief kiss.

"I want to," she said. "I don't know why looking through this is making me feel this way."

His lips flattened into a grim line.

"Maybe because there are no tapes and we had our hopes up." He leaned his forehead on hers. "I know I did."

She nodded, but it was more than that. It was because this space had belonged to Will, and being in it made him human. Made his loss painful in a way she hadn't expected.

A rustling at the stairs got their attention. Maggie stood there with two mugs, looking at them with an inscrutable expression. Sophia wanted to shrink, like a kid caught doing something she wasn't supposed to.

"I didn't know how you took it, Sophia, so I made it as Grey likes it. I hope that's okay." There was a tightness around her eyes and mouth, and Sophia swallowed as she took the mug, which had a design of the Seattle skyline.

"That's perfect, thank you," Sophia mumbled, the heat suffusing her neck and face.

Maggie crossed her arms.

"You haven't brought a girl home in a while." She narrowed her eyes at her son.

Grey placed the mug by Sophia, and his fingers brushed her hip lightly, as if to comfort her.

"That's a good thing since I'm a grown man."

His lips twitched when Maggie's eyes rolled.

"See what I've dealt with his entire life?" Maggie said to Sophia, who almost laughed, if she hadn't felt so awkward.

"Anyway, did you find what you were looking for?"

"No tapes," Grey said. "And you're sure this was all that was left?"

"As far as I know." Maggie let her arms drop to her side.

Sophia felt a pang, but she couldn't tell what it was. She jumped to her feet.

Grey blew out a frustrated breath.

"I wish we could stay and visit, but we have work to do," he told his mom.

"What kind of work?"

"The kind you don't like talking about."

Maggie's mouth tightened again, but she added nothing else.

"What do the tapes look like?" she asked.

"We don't know, but there is another place we can check out," Sophia said and looked at Grey, who looked back inquiringly. "My mom's..." She pressed her lips together, shocked at her own stupidity.

"Oh, you stop that," Maggie said, and Sophia almost passed out right then. Beside her, Grey stiffened, and Maggie rolled her eyes once again. "You really thought you'd bring Silvana Candela's daughter here and I wouldn't be able to tell?"

Sophia's mouth dropped open. She could barely breathe.

"You look just like her," Maggie added and there wasn't any venom in her voice that Sophia could detect. "And those two were into some weird stuff with their friend—I can't remember her name now—"

"Jeanette," Sophia and Grey said in unison, and he took her hand and gripped it tightly. She could feel the energy coming from him, something nervous and shivery.

Maggie nodded. "Right. I liked Jeanette, though she was really busy back then." Maggie's gaze turned faraway, as if memories were rushing her, but after a moment, she shook her head, and her eyes glazed over. She smiled softly, a little wistfully. "Well, did you find the tapes?"

Sophia fought hard to not react, but she couldn't help but look up at Grey, whose eyes had widened.

"No, we didn't." Grey's voice was soft and denoted his own confusion. "But there might be another place we can check."

Maggie smiled as if they hadn't just discussed the most painful chapter of all their lives. "Well, make sure to come visit me soon. You too, Sophia."

She turned and walked away, leaving Grey and Sophia standing there in shock.

"If that's not proof enough of what the spell can do, I don't know what is," she said, and he nodded.

"We better go."

"Yes, but first, let's stop at my house for a change of clothes. Or at least clean underwear." She led them back outside.

"We can do that. Or you could just spend all your time with me naked."

She tried to roll her eyes, but smiled instead because how could she act annoyed at him?

Maggie was nowhere to be seen as they rounded the house. They went to his house first, and dropped off the box before going to hers, appearing in the garage. Her car was at his house, so the garage was dark and empty and she opened the door, which led to the entryway.

"Hello?" It was quiet and dark, but Sophia heard the rustling of movement in the living room.

"Sophia?" Victoria called from the other room, and a light turned on. Both Victoria and Julia appeared over the threshold. Julia looked like hell, her hair in disarray, and her eyes almost swollen shut. Victoria looked more put-together, even as she had dark circles under her eyes.

"What happened?" Sophia said, instantly alarmed.

"I left Harold," Julia said, her voice shaking, but her stance tall and proud. There was so much grief in her eyes, Sophia's heart shriveled for her. She took Julia into her arms.

"What happened?" she repeated.

"He just pushed and pushed until I couldn't take it anymore," Julia said, but her eyes found Grey. "Hi."

"Hello, Julia."

The tension was palpable between the two, and Sophia held her breath.

"Your voice will never not be startling," Julia said. "Not in a bad way or anything." Sophia released the breath.

"I get that a lot." Grey shifted his weight.

"Do you want to talk about Harold?" Sophia asked her sister.

Julia grimaced. "God, no. I'm sick of talking about men, honestly. No offense, Grey."

"None taken. Men really can be the worst."

All three women turned to him, and Grey stood like a deer in head-lights to their scrutiny. Victoria grinned.

"So, you two have been together this whole time?" Victoria looked like the Cheshire cat, and Sophia gritted her teeth as she gripped Victoria's shoulder and led her toward the bedroom. She threw Grey an apologetic look, only to find him fighting back a grin of his own, which only annoyed her more.

"Sit and wait." Yes, she sounded snappy, but didn't care.

In her bedroom, Sophia closed the door once Julia was inside.

"Spill it," Julia said, plopping herself onto Sophia's bed.

Sophia ignored her, going into the closet, her face hot. She busied herself finding a duffle.

"She's not saying anything because she totally boned him," Victoria said from the room.

"Oh my God," Sophia moaned as she opened her black overnight bag. "Why did I come here?"

Victoria and Julia came into the closet.

"Obviously, there's something to tell, or you wouldn't be acting so weird," Julia said, leaning against the wall as if she didn't have a care in the world. If Sophia hadn't known her sister was going through things, she would have believed it. Except for the swollen eyes and blotchy face. Had Julia also lost weight? Already small-framed in a way Sophia had always envied, Julia looked gaunt and pale.

"I think the one who needs to do some talking is you," Sophia said and Julia made a face.

"There's nothing to say." To distract herself, Julia pulled open one of the built-in drawers Sophia had installed when she'd renovated the house a few years back. "I left him because I couldn't stand him. I was sitting with him at dinner and he was rude to the server, and it bothered me. He had been rude before and I'd ignored it, but I just couldn't anymore. And besides, if his mere presence makes me want to throttle him, how can I even think of having kids with him?" Julia shivered.

"It's a good point," Victoria said, always the perfectly supportive friend, and Julia gave her a small, sad smile.

Sophia approached her sister. "I'm so sorry." And she was... For Julia. Harold could suck it.

"I'll survive," Julia said with a shrug. "Your turn."

Victoria and Julia looked at her and waited.

"What do you want to know?" she sighed.

"Did you sleep with him? Was it good? I need to call Amy." Julia started pulling out her phone.

"Stop." Sophia held up her hands.

"I'm sorry, it's just been so long," Victoria said with sympathy. "I was so worried about your health."

A surprised laugh sputtered from Sophia. "I haven't even told you if I slept with him or not."

"Please. A sexually satisfied woman has a look about her." Victoria made a gesture with her hands, her finger making circles in front of Sophia's face. "And you slept over there."

Julia nodded at Victoria's words, and Sophia heaved another long sigh.

"We did."

Victoria squealed into her hands.

"And it was good."

"Just good?" Julia raised a cynical brow.

"It's so creepy how excited you get about me having sex," Sophia said. "Also, a little insulting."

"And..." Julia waited expectantly.

"And what?" Sophia demanded, pausing as she pulled out clean underwear from a drawer.

"Details," Victoria said, as if it was perfectly obvious. "How was it?"

Sophia rolled her eyes and considered saying nothing, but her heart jumped anyway, and a smile played at her lips. She couldn't contain it, the way he made her feel.

"Oh my God, she is so smitten," Julia said.

Sophia started to shake her head but grinned instead, her gut effervescing.

"I am," she admitted. Julia's expression went from shocked to slightly concerned. "I know what you'll say, Jules, but just be excited for me. He's... wonderful."

Julia ran her hand over her face. "I guess I can't fault you for falling for the guy. He is gorgeous."

"He really is." Sophia turned to finish packing. "And eager to please."

Julia positively melted into the wall. "God, that sucks," she whined. "I hate dating so much and I'm going to have to do it again."

"Tell me about it," Victoria said miserably.

"Wait, what happened with Thomas?"

"Nothing," Victoria said. "We talked, and it didn't go too terribly." Sophia started.

"That's good news! What did he say?"

"Well, he asked me to come to the house to talk about what we should do about our situation," Victoria began as Sophia folded clothes into the duffle. "He admitted to feeling insecure about us and our future, which was the worst to hear."

Sophia frowned. "That doesn't sound like Thomas at all." That made absolutely no sense. How could Thomas be insecure about his future with Victoria and be planning to propose at the same time? Sophia supposed those two things could live in the same person at once, but it wasn't computing.

Sophia felt a shiver go down her spine.

"That's what I said," Julia said.

"He told me he doesn't know how it happened; it just did." Victoria put her head down for a moment, deflated. "And all I wanted was to love him and have him love me back. Spend our lives cooking and traveling. Have babies."

Sophia tripped over her own feet at the words.

"And that's not lost yet," Julia said, rubbing Victoria's arm gently. "Thomas loves you."

"I know." Victoria shook her head sadly. "And I love him, but we have to either figure all this out or move on."

Sophia zipped the bag and looked at her sister and her best friend. A pang of guilt went through her, thinking of going to spend time with Grey when her girls needed her.

"I see that face, and no, you should still go with Grey," Julia said. Sophia should've expected it. Julia would never let anyone take care of her.

"How do you do that?"

"Honey, we know you." Victoria crossed her arms. "Go with Grey. We're going to be fine. We'll invite Amy over, have us a delightful pity party."

"Are you sure? I can stay with you." She meant it.

"And do what?" Julia asked, not a little sarcastically. "Watch us lament about our stupid men when you could be climbing all over that one?"

It surprised a laugh out of Sophia.

"You're the worst," Sophia said, wiping her eyes. There was a lot to do, truly. One of those things was definitely more sex, but also the tapes. He had taken her to his father's private space, and now she was going to take him to her mom's. What a pair they made.

She hugged them both and made them promise they'd call her if they needed her, and met Grey in the living room, where he was sitting like she asked him to. He took her bag and flung it over his shoulder, earning approving looks from Victoria and Julia.

Much later, when they were going through the letters found in Will's office, Grey stared at an envelope with wide eyes and a slightly ajar mouth. It was sealed, and his name was on the front in neat cursive.

"What is it?" Sophia asked, chilled at his expression.

"It's my dad's handwriting." He stuck his finger under the flap and tore the yellowing envelope open.

"Dear Grey," he began, then stopped to take a shaky breath. "If you're reading this letter, then that means I'm gone, for which I am deeply sorry. I always dreamed of growing old and teaching you everything I know about magic. But we have done so much already, and you're such a talented witch, I'm not worried about you, son."

Sophia's mouth was hanging wide open as Grey continued.

"There was so much Silvana, Jeanette, and I wanted to do with magic, and we worked so hard to make it happen. Silvana doesn't want me to tell you this, but I feel like I have to, anyway. There is a special potion, shared between the three of us, and it needs blood to work. Silvana's blood, and a full moon. The ingredients must go into the cauldron in order, and you must use the tapes. Silvana has them. It's important to infuse the potion."

Grey looked at Sophia, then back at the sheet of paper. He turned it around, finding the key there.

"This could have been useful weeks ago," he murmured.

"A drop of blood from my dead mom," Sophia said, her heart shivering inside her. She closed her eyes as Grey got to his feet again. His phone was on her his ear.

"We need the ingredients by the full moon." He listened. "We're running out of time. Do you have leads?"

Sophia walked away, the jitter of nerves making her knees quake. If they couldn't make the potion in four days, they would have to wait another month. Who knew what could happen in a month?

She thought of Helena.

What the hell could Sophia do? Could she wish to find the ingredients? What would happen if she did?

And the tapes. How did they play into any of this?

"Oh God," she murmured to herself, breathless, as her jitters turned into a frantic pacing along the kitchen. She couldn't wish it, could she?

No, of course not. She didn't know what that power could do. She had killed a plant wishing for another to live, so there was an exchange of energy happening.

She became light headed as realization dawned on her.

Victoria's words from earlier...

Understanding coursed through her, and she stopped, staring into space.

He admitted he was feeling insecure.

The bottom of her stomach fell out when the words came back to her. It wasn't Victoria saying the words, though. It was Aric.

I want to spend my life with you. Cook together, travel. Everything you always wanted, and I failed to give you, Soph.

Aric's sudden insistence, Thomas's change of mind...

"Oh God," she said and pressed her hand to her mouth as she ran to the sink, where she dry-heaved for so long, her throat was on fire by the end, when she finally vomited all the contents in her stomach.

"Sophia?"

Grey was right behind her, looking alarmed. He turned on the faucet and held back her hair.

"What happened?"

She rinsed her mouth, her nose wrinkling with distaste as she blew her nose into a paper towel Grey handed her.

"I'm sorry," she moaned miserably, but his look remained concerned as opposed to disgusted, and her heart melted a little.

"What happened?" he asked again as she fought back an onslaught of tears.

"I caused Victoria's breakup with Thomas." She pressed the heels of her hands to her burning eyes. Her eyes watered with more nausea, but she held it down. "I think I wished to have their relationship. Of course I wished that, they're adorable and I wanted nothing more with Aric."

"You wished to have a healthy, loving relationship with your ex?" His lips pressed into a grim line, color rising in his cheeks.

Was he jealous?

She shook her head. There was no time for that now.

"Not on purpose," she assured him. "I want nothing to do with Aric."

There was no world, no time when she would ever want to be with Aric again. The parallels between Aric's behavior and the suddenness of the breakup. The insistence and the tears... and her ability to cause something like it.

How many times had she done this in the past without even knowing?

But the plants she had to truly wish, and she meant it when she wished it. She would not mean a wish in which Aric was back in her life in that capacity.

Through another wave of nausea, she pulled up Jeanette's contact information on her phone and dialed the number. Jeanette answered right away.

"Sophia, are you alright?" she said as soon as she picked up. She had a knack for knowing when Sophia didn't need a greeting. What were those abilities called? Was it just intuition, or was there a more powerful name for it? What else did Sophia ignore?

"The potion you took with my mom," Sophia said without preamble. "Do you remember it? When you were kids."

Silence.

"Please, Jeanette." Sophia could hear the underlying desperation in her voice. "I need to know."

"It was a thing we did when we were very young. Your grandmother Evelyn was always the hostess, and it was an incredible time of magic and beauty."

Sophia's eyes filled, thinking of her mom as a little girl, making magic. She hadn't missed her mom in so long, but the loss hit her like a bag of bricks had been dumped on her head. Her mom would have had all the answers, would have been able to tell them what they needed to know to fix this mess she had created.

"What else do you remember, Jeanette?" Sophia asked, another idea forming in her head.

"The most I remember was when we were kids, but those memories are also spotty. What's on your mind?"

"The spell that was placed on us has everything to do with magic. Think about it," she said, but she was looking at Grey, because this had everything to do with him too. "I forgot I'm a witch." She pressed her lips together. It was the first time she'd said it out loud. That's what she was. There was no use being in denial about it any longer. She was a witch.

"Do you remember where to find the ingredients for the potion?" she asked, but Jeanette was silent again. "I know you guys made it as you grew up. I saw it in some letters you sent to each other. We need your help."

"You have our letters?" Jeanette's voice was full of wonder. "I thought those got lost after we lost Silvana."

Sophia swallowed tightly.

"We used to forage for what we needed," Jeanette continued. "And sometimes we'd steal the ingredients from your grandma."

Sophia wanted to stop and imagine it, but she was far too anxious to let her mind wander. A grandmother she had never met.

"There's a full moon soon, and as I understand it, we need the full moon to make it successfully."

"Honey, I don't know what you're talking about," Jeanette said and Sophia wanted to scream.

"And the blood..." she said.

"Blood? For what?" Jeanette's voice was surprised.

"We found a letter from Will that claims I need a drop of blood from my mom."

Silence again, then the call dropped. Sophia dialed the number seven times before she gave up. It went to voicemail every time. It was either that the phone had died, Jeanette had turned it off, or the spell was back at work.

Grey approached her and placed his hands on her shoulders. She leaned back against him, desperate for his support.

Had Jeanette always known Sophia was a witch?

Grey turned her to face him when her mind started swimming with questions and too many possibilities to put a name to them.

"You need a break," he said.

"We need to find a cure."

"I know, but you also need a break." He pressed a kiss to her forehead. "Let me take you to bed. You need to sleep."

"I can't sleep. I can't possibly after all this." She looked up at him. "Grey. What do I do?"

He left toward the pantry and came back with a vial.

"We take this," he murmured. "We both need a clear head for what comes next."

Her ear on his chest, she nodded, and went with him when he led her to bed.

22

Things changed after the kiss, as Silvana knew they would. She'd avoided Will as much as possible after. Nothing good could ever come out of that, anyway. She desperately wanted for things to be as they were before, but she'd ruined it by letting him kiss her. By kissing him back.

Will and Silvana didn't tell Jeanette about it, but they didn't have to. Jeanette noticed the awkwardness, and she had also pulled a card that told her some things were about to change drastically. She didn't know exactly why, but Jeanette was good at learning to see the signs as they came, not just rely on a single vision. It was what would make her a good doctor later in life. Always keep an open mind, and willingness to learn and change her mind.

The letters had continued, and they used a handy potion Will had concocted to send them to each other instantly. It was a marvel. No waiting included. All the letter needed was a single drop of the clear potion, and it would disappear from one place and appear in the other. They usually went in order so that everyone had a say.

One night, as Silvana attempted to write a melody from the little cactus she kept on her bedside, she got a single letter from Will, addressed only to her.

Fingers trembling, she opened it. The note was brief.

Dear Silvana,
Will you talk to me about what happened? I can't stand this distance between us. If I had known it would change things so much, I would have never done it. But you need to know that kissing you has been the highlight of my life. I love you.

She didn't write back, and wasn't surprised when he wrote another note, in a new piece of paper.

Sil, would you talk to me, please?

She wrote back then, on the same paper.

I don't know what use it is to talk about it. It can't happen again. Romance will only complicate our friendship. It already has. I couldn't bear to lose you.

His response after that was that she could never lose him, but she didn't write again. Will could be really stubborn if he set his mind to it, but so was she. No one could ignore something as successfully as she could. Even though her heart soared when she thought about him wanting her. It made her want to pack a bag and run away with him, but since they were minors, that would never happen. Where the hell would they go? What would they do? Plus, he hadn't even made another move. Not that hanging out with Jeanette gave them the opportunity for it.

Still, they met at the tree house often. Sometimes to take the tea, sometimes to make music, but most times to throw each other furtive looks when they thought the other wasn't looking. Jeanette simply pretended not to see anything, and she would until one of them said something to her directly. It was easier that way.

One afternoon, Silvana was just finishing writing out musical notes into a grimoire when it hit her. She gasped as she looked at the music, then the array of potions she and her friends had created. Finally, the idea struck, and she couldn't believe that she hadn't thought of it before.

"What?" Jeanette asked from across the room. They were in Jeanette's bedroom, as it was the friendliest place for the three of them to meet, since Will's mom hated Silvana, and Silvana's dad hated Will. The room was small and cluttered, which was a lot like Jeanette's personality. Colorful, warm, and a little chaotic. Will sat up in bed, where he was laying back with his guitar on his lap.

"It's always been about the music." Silvana left the grimoire open on the floor and paced as she thought about it, letting the idea form fully in her head. "I always knew there was something about the music, but I couldn't figure out what it was. I thought they sang to let me know when they were happy."

"And that's not it," Will said with a cocked brow.

"It's so much more than that, William. So much more than that." Silvana grinned, looking into space. "I knew the music was important, but it didn't hit me until now."

"Okay, but what is it?" Jeanette, impatient, stood in front of Silvana, who was slightly taller, and took her by the shoulders. Silvana trailed off often enough that her friends had learned to snap her out of it. "What is it about the music?"

"The potions aren't more potent because we need to infuse them with the music."

Will and Jeanette blinked at her for a moment.

"Don't you see it?" Silvana held on to Jeanette's wrists. "The music has always been important, but I didn't know how because all it did before was make pretty lights with it. It's the music that makes the difference. We have to make the potions with the music."

"How do you make a potion with music?" Jeanette asked earnestly. "That doesn't make any sense."

"Wait." Will set his guitar aside. "It does make sense. We have to replicate the music from the plant exactly and play the music as we use the plant for the potion."

"But that's crazy," Jeanette said. "We use a lot of plants for potions.

It would be insanely loud and chaotic. And how do we know it would infuse the potion the right way?"

"It could work." Will swung his legs off the bed. "We just have to try it."

Jeanette looked skeptical, but soon, she nodded, and Silvana knew they would try as much as they could to make it work. This was important work. She was going to see it through. No one should lose a parent, or a child, to cancer. It was unfair and painful, and she needed to do what she could to make it work.

Shortly after, when they left, Will insisted on walking Silvana home. She swallowed nervously. Not just because he was with her, but because her dad hated him so much. He was convinced Silvana was going to do something to ruin her future—like get pregnant or something like that. His words. He was ridiculous.

"You didn't write back," Will said, his voice only a murmur. They were close to the house, but they stayed in the trees a little longer than was necessary. The truth was, Silvana didn't want to go home. She wanted to be away from her father as much as she could. Life had become unbearable with a father who didn't understand his daughter, and a daughter that needed to be understood and cared for.

"I don't know if I have anything to say." She couldn't meet his eye. Both were aware that she was avoiding the subject, but Will's patience was running out. And he had a lot of patience for a sixteen-year-old person. Silvana wouldn't even look at him in school. They had once had lunch together and now Silvana disappeared during lunch and left him and Jeanette wondering where she had gone and what she was doing.

"I think that's bullshit." The fleeting bout of anger had him snapping his mouth shut. He didn't swear often, as his now highly religious mother did not like it, but every time he did, it caught Silvana by surprise.

She didn't look at him. She was being awkward, and hated that she was, but she didn't know how else to be.

"I don't think your mom would appreciate you swearing," she said.

"She isn't here." He stopped her by gripping her arm. "Come on, Sil."

She tipped up her chin, so she finally met his gaze. It was a mistake, because the moment she looked into his pretty eyes, she wanted to kiss him or cry or both. She hated it. She hated that he was hurting, but she couldn't let this go further.

"I know what you're thinking," he said, sadness in his voice.

"Do you?"

"I do. I know you too well." His shoulders sagged. "It's okay if you don't like me that way. I just want you to know I love you no matter what."

It was so simple, so sincere, and her chin wobbled. With the grimoire stuck between them, she pulled him in for a one-armed hug. His scent, his familiarity, the way he loved her, lodged a lump in her throat.

Silvana had known him all her life, and she had always known that he was different to her than all the other people in it. But even she had to admit that loving him the way she did could only result in them being separated in the future. They were young, inexperienced, and their lives complicated. It was bound to happen, and she couldn't bear the thought of losing him, too.

"It's not that," she heard herself say, even though she knew it wasn't the smartest thing. If it killed her, she would be honest with him this one time. "I love you. So much."

He pulled away to look at her, and his eyes were misty.

"I just can't even imagine what it would be like if we do this and then I lose you. You are one of the most important people in my life. I love you too much to mess this up."

"And who says we will mess it up?"

Experience, she thought, but didn't say it. Seeing the way her father had treated her mom, how he treated her... It couldn't be anything but that, could it? But when Will pressed his forehead against hers, she closed her eyes, and everything else disappeared. It was just the two of them, and her mind was calm for the first time in forever. So when he kissed her, she tipped her head and accepted it, and she knew Will was it for her until the day she died.

23

The anxiety returned early the following morning and escalated when Sophia was on her way to her father's house with Grey. Every dream she'd had was about Victoria and Thomas, Aric, and Julia, and her mom and Will. Everyone yelled at her to figure things out, as if she had all the answers.

Her father was busy, as always, and he'd been traveling, but he sounded excited to see her. Not that she'd told him about bringing Grey. It seemed wholly unnecessary. Or maybe she was a coward.

They'd decided to drive, mostly because she needed the time to settle down her stomach, and she sat next to Grey, his hand resting on her knee. He was quiet, probably because she was. The music coming through the speakers was low. As they drove down the long driveway that led up to the house, trepidation climbed and climbed, until she felt like she was floating, and not pleasantly.

She ventured a look at Grey. He was a quiet man, but never to this extent. Something was off.

"What's on your mind?" she asked as she linked her fingers with his.

He gripped her hand. "I'm not sure." He kept his eyes on the road, but a frown marred his features. He'd kept his hair loose, just as she had, and they both wore jeans and sweaters. When he finally looked at her, there was worry in his eyes. It made her stomach drop. He parked in the driveway and the car, always silent, created a cocoon. She touched his face, which now sported a two-day scruff she found sexy as hell, and with confidence she did not feel, she said, "Everything's going to work out."

He leaned into her hand, and his eyes closed.

"I guess it's strange coming here."

"Just as meeting your mom was for me." That and the strange way Maggie had acted toward the end, forgetting everything they were talking about. Then Jeanette... If she thought about it long enough, she might cry, so instead, she reached for the door handle, and they unfolded themselves from the car and out into the chilly air. Surrounded by pine trees, it was clear they were headed toward the holidays, though it felt anything but to Sophia. Grey held her hand as they walked up toward the porch and kissed her lightly before she opened the door.

Something sparked in his eyes when they entered. He paused when they passed the stairs, looked up toward the top floor of the house.

"Do you remember anything?" she whispered. The energy that emanated from him felt different, like a weight in her gut. Her skin felt chilled, despite the warmth of the house.

"Not quite." He looked down at her. "But if I had any doubts that I knew you before we met at your club, they'd be gone now."

"You remember this house?"

"It's not really a memory, but a feeling." He frowned lightly, taking a few steps toward the sunroom, looking out one of the big windows there. "It's like the longest sense of déjà vu."

She could relate.

Sophia took his hand, laced her fingers with his.

"I remember that swing." He pointed at it as it swung in a gentle breeze, then looked down at her. "I kissed you on that swing."

Her heart stuttered, rolled, and righted itself, leaving her breathless.

"I know," she whispered.

"You do?" He looked at her expectantly.

She nodded hoping they remembered everything at some point. There was nothing she wanted more.

"Sophia?"

Her father's voice startled them apart. For a moment, she'd forgotten they weren't alone in the house, and she glanced up at Grey before taking his hand and leading him toward the study. He looked a little green.

They found her father sitting at his desk. He was on the phone, instructing someone about some business deal, but his eyes darted between Sophia and Grey. The modern-looking office would always feel off, tacked on, but her dad fit in it well. There was a tightness around her father's eyes, even as he smiled and motioned them to come forward.

"Deal with it. I have to go, Sophia's here." He hung up before he ever got a response, and his smile widened. Her heart softened a little, though the chill under her skin remained. Her father had a blue button-up tucked into a pair of gray slacks. He got on his feet and opened his arms for her. "Look at you, my beautiful girl."

She hugged him tightly, relishing in the way he smelled. Pine, his favorite scent. He'd worn it since she remembered, and it was comforting to her.

"How was your trip?" she asked as he zeroed in on Grey, who stood back by the door with watchful eyes.

"Oh, you know," her father said, "work, work, work." He smiled at Grey and offered a hand, which Grey took. "Conrad Montgomery."

"Dad, this is Grey," Sophia said. "He's my... friend."

She swallowed when she said the word. It sounded inadequate, but he wasn't her boyfriend. He was also more, they just hadn't discussed it. Her father obviously noticed because his brows shot up, but she ignored him.

"It's nice to meet you, Grey. Please have a seat." He gestured toward the small sofa he kept in the office, where he could be found reading from time to time.

"I'm alright, thank you," Grey said, and sounded oddly formal.

"By all means," her dad said. "How are you, doll? How's the club?"

"The club's doing great, but that's not why I'm here."

"Okay, let's hear it."

"I need to ask you something about Mom," she said, and took a breath of courage. He was never too keen to talk about her. She imagined it was because it was difficult for him. And as far as she knew, he didn't do magic, or she would have noticed. Right?

"Okay," her dad said cautiously.

"What do you remember about what she did?"

His frown was deep, as if he was confused.

"Did with what?" Conrad's gaze flickered to Grey.

"Her music, for example," Sophia said, hoping that it would spark something. "Did she record her music somewhere?"

"I don't think so," her father said. "She loved her plants, and she adored music. I've always told you girls what a lovely musician your mother was. Multi-talented, and so proficient at all of it."

Something in her stomach pulled at her, but she ignored it. She knew her mom was a talented musician because she remembered it well. It was one of the few things she remembered distinctly.

Her father looked at Grey, then back at Sophia, and there was something in his eyes that she hadn't seen. Sophia wasn't sure she had ever seen her father sad. Angry, stressed, joyful, yes. Sad—never. She didn't know what to do with that.

"But why the question?" her father asked.

Sophia thought about how she could answer. There wasn't a lot she could say that her father would understand of what she and Grey were doing. She could certainly never tell her father that she was a witch.

"I guess I was just curious," she said and pasted a smile on her face, even though the last thing she felt like doing was smiling. Her father smiled too, all traces of the sadness now gone.

"And you're dating this young man," he said cheerfully, but the smile strained. "What did you say your name was?"

Sophia's heart jumped.

"Grey," said Grey simply, and when her father would have asked for his last name, Sophia went to Grey's side.

"Dad, do you mind if I go up to the attic? I left something there the other day when I was here." She pulled Grey out of the office, her entire body shivering with nerves. She would never recover from the cortisol levels.

"Yeah, but—" His phone rang insistently, and he picked up, back in business mode in a flash.

"Oh my God," Sophia huffed as they hurried up the stairs toward the attic.

"My heart is beating so fast it might jump out of my chest."

They stopped at the top of the stairs, by the attic door. She wanted to burst out laughing, and he looked like he was holding one back too, as his lips were trembling. It was at that moment when she felt it. A wave of warmth went through her, and settled low in her belly, and emotion rising to her eyes, she reached for his face again, her fingers lightly grazing his jaw. She saw it in his eyes too, the unspoken words between them, hovering there like music.

Soft, light, brilliant.

"Sophia..."

She raised herself onto the tips of her toes and grazed his lips with hers.

"I know," she whispered.

"I know it hasn't been long."

"Only all our lives." Just because the memories were buried didn't mean it was any less true.

He kissed her, his hands on her face, and nothing could take away the feeling of safety she felt around him.

"Did you find what you need, Sophia?" her father's voice came from downstairs.

With regret, she stepped back, and without taking her eyes from Grey's, she called back, "Not yet."

There was no response from her father, but the moment broken, Sophia opened the door. It stuck, but not as it had before. She remembered the last time she came here, how it was so stuck she'd spoken to it. Had she used her magic then, too? The familiar anxiety returned, but she had to push it away. She couldn't think about the things she may or may not have done right now. She had to focus.

o o o

GREY WASN'T FOND OF THE WAY CONRAD MONTGOMERY had looked at him. It had raised warning bells in his head, but he couldn't altogether understand them. Maybe it was that Conrad

Montgomery obviously recognized him—Grey looked just like his dad.

Or maybe Conrad tried to remember, and the spell was working on him too. Grey couldn't be sure, but he felt uneasy. Sophia was jerky and anxious. He hated seeing her like that, pale, out of sorts, but there was nothing he could do to help her, save give her a calming potion, which she wouldn't take.

The moment they'd just shared outside the attic had left him feeling soft and warm, in spite of everything else. He may not remember her entirely, but who she was to him now, even after so short a time, was everything. She was everything.

He didn't think he'd actually felt like this before—a connection so deep it took his breath away.

"My mom spent all her time up here," she said as she moved around the room, taking careful steps, retreating, taking them again, as if listening for something. "When she wasn't up here, she was with us. My oldest sister was ill, childhood cancer."

"I'm so sorry." He'd heard about her oldest sister, but Sophia didn't speak about her much.

"Now I'm thinking my mom was trying to cure her." Sophia threw him a questioning look. "It makes sense, right?"

"It does. I would too."

She nodded. "And the letters speak of her desire to cure cancer after her mom died of it. It makes sense." She repeated it over and over, as if she was trying to convince herself. "Why would she hide this cure if she wanted to do such good?"

"I don't know."

"That's the mystery." Her voice trembled. "My parents met when my mom was in college. She was like nineteen, and my dad was almost thirty."

Grey said nothing and wondered what the timeline looked like, how Silvana and his dad could have been so in love one moment, for her to marry someone else so soon after. But time moved differently when you were young.

"She was playing music at a benefit for the university," Sophia continued in the same soft tone as before. As if she was speaking mostly to herself. "She was so talented, that even though she wasn't a music student, they invited her to play. My dad says he was so mesmerized by her talent that he knew he would marry her that day. And he's always loved her so much that he never remarried. He barely dates."

So many questions that he wanted to ask, but refrained, because she was in a trance.

"And I've had dreams of Will in this house. Right here in this attic." She took a step forward, toward the edges of the room, under a window, and it groaned under her weight. She froze, took a step back, then forward again. It groaned. "It just doesn't match my memories of my mom."

"What doesn't?"

She looked over at him, her eyes faraway.

"She was so loving and soft."

He got it then, even in her silence. Silvana's character didn't match the woman who ran away with her lover and left her children behind. But Grey knew humans were complicated. That they made choices that went against everything their loved ones knew about them, and that didn't mean they were terrible people. Human, plain and simple.

She crouched, apparently done talking, and her fingers pried at a floorboard. He went forward then and crouched next to her to help her lift it. He held on to the floorboard as she whispered something under her breath as she cleared cobwebs from the hole they uncovered. In it, there were two wooden boxes, both smaller than shoeboxes. His heart hammered somewhere around his ears as Sophia pulled them out. She slid one lid to the side, and it opened without issues. Inside, they found more paper, yellowed with age, all neatly stacked, flat.

"Sheet music," Grey whispered. He couldn't even feel his heart anymore. It was beating so hard and fast, his entire body trembled with anxiety and excitement.

Sophia slid open the other lid, and a breath whooshed out of her, as if she had been holding it. Neatly arranged on their sides, the spines marked with the loveliest handwriting Grey had ever seen, were the tapes.

"And there they are."

Their eyes met after her whispered words, and hers had tears swimming in them.

"I have to help Lucas find the ingredients," Grey told her. He knew they had no time to waste. They had to get to work, or they'd miss the full moon and would have to wait even longer than he already had. He couldn't bear the thought.

"Can I help?"

His first instinct was to say no. Clayton had come after her, and though she hadn't been attacked since Clayton died, it didn't mean someone else couldn't come after her next.

"Please, I have to feel useful."

"I worry someone will come after you again, Sophia."

"I understand the need to protect me," she said, her voice firm, "but I'm a grown woman. And how is foraging with you any more dangerous than not going with you?"

His brows drew together.

"Sound logic."

"Stating the obvious." She let out a tired breath. "But I also need to go to the club at some point. I need to talk to Victoria."

"Would you rather I come with you?"

She smiled a little.

"No, I have to deal with this one on my own." She looked everything but prepared for it to him.

"But what if you didn't cause it?" They had no proof that she wished for it to happen, even with her ex's bizarre behavior. People were stupid sometimes, especially entitled men.

"I know there's a possibility," she said, "but I can't take chances. I have to talk to them."

"Do what you feel is the right thing," he told her soothingly, holding her hand. "But they might resent you, and it will only hurt you and them even more."

She bit her lip uncertainly. "I know."

"Then wait until we make the potion. I have a feeling all the answers we're seeking are there."

She took a deep breath, then let it out, and nodded. "Okay. I'll wait."

His phone went off and he picked up immediately, just as Sophia's began ringing urgently.

"Lucas, talk to me," he said.

On the other side of the line, Lucas said, "I have all the ingredients."

Grey didn't have time to rejoice at his friend's words, because when he looked at Sophia, he found her deathly pale, her phone at her ear.

"What happened?" He hung up on Lucas before he even knew what he was doing.

Sophia looked at him with glassy eyes.

"It's Julia."

24

Grey sped through the city like a madman, running red lights, knowing that if he got pulled over, he would not stop. He would use magic if necessary. Beside him, Sophia sat frozen, silent. There were no tears, no freak-outs, just a terrible, heavy silence. There was nothing he could do about it, and he didn't know how to deal with that. But this wasn't about him.

Her father had taken off the moment Sophia told him Julia was in the hospital, without another word.

When they got to the hospital, at the emergency entrance, she opened the door before the car had even stopped. She paused before she got out.

"Please come with me." The tremor in her voice pulled at him.

"Of course." He wouldn't dream of leaving her to deal with this alone. He didn't have siblings, but he had friends that felt like they were, so he could empathize. Or maybe he deluded himself into thinking he did.

She rushed into the hospital as he parked in the first available space. He found her waiting for the elevator when he rushed inside. Their hands entwined as they waited together. She gripped his hand so tightly, his joints protested, but he didn't move. He doubted she was aware.

They stepped out once they reached the fifth floor and Sophia stopped. Her breathing was shallow as she stared at the long hallway.

The nurses' station was bustling with activity, but they could have been alone. Everything was sterile in that way only hospitals were. The walls were an off-white color, the doors a nondescript blonde wood.

Sophia took shivering breaths, and tears were rolling down her face silently. Her hand was like a vice around his, so he stood in front of her.

"Look at me," he whispered. She did. The panic in her eyes cracked his heart. "Focus on my voice."

She was shaking from head to toe, her nose bright red, hair in disarray. Whatever was going through her mind didn't have to be spoken out loud. He knew. He just knew. This was about Julia, but it was so much more than that.

"I'm here for whatever you need," he told her softly. She nodded, but he wasn't sure she understood what he was saying. Her eyes were glassy, and she had gone so pale, he was sure she was going to pass out. Her neck curved forward, and a sob tore out of her, and the sound widened the crack that was already in his heart. It was a stunted sort of sound, like she didn't want to let it out, but it came free regardless.

"Do you want me to take you somewhere else before you go in there?"

She shook her head, but her feet didn't move. She let go of his hand, and she gripped his sweater and buried her face in his chest. He hugged her then, softly wrapping his arms around her.

"Keep breathing." In that moment, he knew he would do anything to help her sister. There were no stones he wouldn't turn, no potion he wouldn't make. He wasn't sure how long they stood by the elevators, but was thankful that they didn't open again, so she could be still as long as she needed. When her breathing calmed, she straightened her spine and looked up at him.

"It's going to be okay," he said. "I promise."

She nodded.

"Are you ready to go see her?"

"Yeah," she said and let go of her death grip on his sweater. Her hands were trembling as he took her by the hand again and led her toward Julia's room.

He knocked twice before he pushed open the door and stood aside. Sophia went in before him, and when he entered, it was to find Julia on the bed, asleep. Amy and Victoria were by her side, their faces as pale as Sophia's. They jumped up when they saw her and enveloped her in a group hug as they sobbed. Conrad was not there.

Grey stood by the door. He felt like an intruder, but there was no way in hell he would leave Sophia to deal with this alone. Julia was deathly pale, her lips a little blue, and something inside him wriggled unpleasantly. Her hair was in disarray. She looked like she'd aged ten years since he saw her last night.

"What happened?" Sophia asked them when they'd stopped crying.

"She just collapsed," Amy responded, her voice thick.

Victoria rubbed Amy's shoulder. "She said she wasn't feeling well last night after you left. We had a couple of drinks, and she went to bed saying it was because she's so stressed."

"And this morning, she was making breakfast, and she seemed so happy, but she didn't look so good." Amy started crying again. "And she came out of the kitchen and she just collapsed."

Grey stuck his hand into his sweater pockets to keep them from shaking as Conrad finally rushed into the room. He started snapping and making demands. A nurse came into the room, and he kept going, talking about suing if no one told him what happened to Julia, which was ridiculous.

"Dad, no one knows what's going on with her," Amy said calmly, though she looked angry. Her face, once pale, was now as red as her hair. "They're doing everything they can."

"Sir, I assure you we're running all the tests we can at the moment." The nurse spoke calmly, as if she was used to this kind of treatment. Grey wasn't altogether surprised. Nurses put up with a lot, unfortunately.

"Run every test you know, spare no expense," Conrad's angry voice caught, and for the first time in a very long time, Grey wanted to punch someone. Anger churned inside him like a vat of hot lava.

He didn't like Conrad Montgomery. At all. He ordered himself to be calm, to think about it logically. Conrad Montgomery was Sophia's father, and Grey loved Sophia, so he was going to have to put up with the man somehow. Still, that off feeling didn't leave him, even as he tried to see Conrad as a worried father.

Victoria also stood aside, threw a furtive look toward Grey, and rolled her eyes lightly. So, this happened a lot, he imagined.

Another nurse came into the room just minutes later, carrying a blue tray with her with many tubes and paraphernalia. She announced she needed Julia's blood to send in for the testing requested— demanded, corrected Grey silently—and got to work. He watched from the door; the warmth started somewhere in his thighs and spread upward. The nurse used the port already in Julia's arm for the IV, and the moment the blood flowed into the tube, Grey had to turn away. He became lightheaded, nausea rolling, and before he embarrassed himself, he walked out of the room.

∘ ∘ ∘

Sophia had been watching the nurse, but the moment Grey turned around, pale as death, she felt her heart stutter. She followed him and found him outside the door, pressed against the wall.

"Are you alright?" she asked him, touching his face. She found it clammy and cold. Otherwise, he seemed okay.

"I'm fine." He sounded a little breathless, but he wouldn't look her in the eye and Sophia, unable to believe what was going on right in front of her eyes, crossed her arms.

"Grey..."

He threw her a sideway glance, color rising from his neck to his cheeks.

"Are you..."

"I don't really like blood," he said in a rush, and blushed to the roots of his hair.

In another moment, when her sister wasn't in a hospital bed, she would have laughed, but she couldn't make herself do so. She touched his face again, smiling wanly.

"It's okay," she said and felt her throat tighten, so she stood beside him, her hands pressed behind her, on the wall. "You had to have one flaw."

"I have a lot of those." He bowed his head. "But the better question is, are you?"

"Okay?" Her brows twitched. "No, I'm not."

She wanted to tell him how freaked out she felt. How she had panicked the moment Victoria had called her about Julia. How every time she thought about it, all she could see was Roselyn dying so young, and how she couldn't lose another loved one. But she couldn't say it, so she didn't force herself. If she let those floodgates open, she wouldn't be able to close them.

The rush of memories was too much. The doctor's visits, being in the children's ward between school and extracurricular activities, and the worry on her mom's face. Then going back to the hospitals when her mom had died, heavy with grief, only to lose Roselyn so shortly after.

She hated hospitals and never wanted to step into one again. Now Julia was in one of those rooms, possibly fighting for her life—looking lost to them already, even as Sophia refused to admit it. There would be no way to know for sure. Not until the results of the blood tests came back, but Sophia already knew.

"She has bruises on her," she told Grey. "Her arms and neck, and I'd assume everywhere else on her body."

She looked up at his face and found him looking down at her with his brows furrowed. Her heart dropped. She had been waiting for him to tell her it wasn't the void. That there was nothing to worry about, that Julia was probably just really stressed out, and had caught some virus.

"Why did she react like this?" Sophia asked, more to the halls than him. "Helena doesn't look like this, and Clayton..." Oh God. Would Grey one day have to help Julia die like he had so many others?

"It's different for everyone. Helena has stints when she's sicker, and has been hospitalized in the past."

Sophia fought the waves of grief rushing through her.

"I won't let my sister die," Sophia whispered, not to him, not to herself, into the universe. To whoever was listening. She would do anything to save Julia's life.

"She won't die."

Sophia met Grey's gaze again, found him staring fiercely at her. She believed him instantly. She trusted him so implicitly, all he had to do was breathe in her direction and she would do anything he asked. Maybe she'd gone crazy, letting herself fall in love so quickly with this man that consumed so much of her. It was as if the moment they had found each other again, time had resumed, when it had paused for so long.

For so long, she had wanted a relationship like that. Where she could trust that he would hold her up when she needed it, and where things felt easy. Where it made sense. She held on to the way it made her feel, warm and sweet, like slipping into bed right after pulling blankets out of the dryer.

"What are we going to do?"

"We're going to make a knowing potion," he told her, and she felt her eyes widen when the meaning sank.

"He got the ingredients?"

"We do."

She let out a breath. Her body trembled, as if she had been holding her breath for far too long. Two more nights and they'd have answers. They'd figure it out.

They were going to save Julia and Helena.

25

The day arrived in a haze of anxiety. Sophia had hardly slept between staying at the hospital with Julia and preparing for the potion. The letters had revealed how to make the potion, so that it worked the way they needed it to. Thank her mother and her notes in the margins of the music they'd found in the boxes from the floorboard.

She'd carefully written the music for every ingredient they'd use, and the notes on the margins explained exactly how to play it and with which instruments. The tapes were old and barely had any sound left, but Grey had matched the songs to their respective plant, with Sophia's help, and had decided to re-record the songs again to make sure they were clean and sharp for the potion.

Some were instruments Grey already played, like the piano, guitar, and percussion. The saxophone, which apparently made its appearance often with plant music, was all Lucas's, as he had played it all throughout high school. The violin and other string instruments, Grey hired out from friends in the music business. It was lucky he did what he did. Or maybe destiny. Now the tracks were neatly arranged on Grey's program in his computer, which made things so much easier.

Right now, Grey walked around the house with a metal bowl

hanging from a chain. He had put a little cake of coal in it, and a bundle of herbs of unfamiliar scents to Sophia. The house was smoky but smelled nice, if a little strong. Lucas did the same, muttering under his breath just as Grey was. Sophia did not know what they were saying, but she didn't have the mental capacity to ask and receive a complicated answer. Or a simple one. Her brain no longer worked.

Next to her sat Jeanette, with her eyes closed and her legs crossed underneath her as if she was doing yoga. The journals all lay in piles around her. Sophia had finally gotten in touch with her, but because it was about Julia. She knew that if she had called Jeanette with another intention in mind, she wouldn't have gotten through.

Damn that spell.

But now Jeanette was here, and Sophia felt more hopeful.

Sophia knew she looked calm, though she was anything but. She wondered if Grey was as calm as he looked. Jeanette fidgeted a bit, but otherwise looked calm. Sophia noticed a lot more these days, it seemed. She now knew that she had always heard music for a specific reason, that she saw it the way she did because magic ran through her veins. A gift inherited from her mom, and her grandmother, and all the ancestors that came before them, from so many different parts of the world. A heritage she had never been all the way familiar with because of how she grew up. Deep inside, she had always yearned for that part of herself, and finally, she felt connected to it, through magic. Through the rituals, even if she couldn't speak the language.

"You're thinking loudly, darling." Jeanette opened her eyes.

"Look who's talking," Sophia shot back, but in jest. The anxiety she had felt had leaked from her body as she breathed.

Jeanette's brows rose high on her forehead.

"You know, you're more like Silvana than you think."

For the first time since her mom died, Sophia saw the compliment in that. She realized that she'd held on to an underlying anger when it came to her mom. Every time someone had told Sophia she looked like her mom she'd wanted to strip the name Candela from her life, even as she kept it as her primary name for reasons she couldn't explain. But she understood now that her mom's mistakes didn't define her. And neither did they define Sophia.

Mistakes didn't make a person bad, just as good deeds didn't make someone good.

"Tell me about her."

Jeanette smiled sadly.

"You know, Silvana was a grouchy kid. Her dad wasn't the nicest to her mom or to her, and Silvana wanted so badly to use her magic to make her mom leave him. Then Evelyn got sick and they couldn't go anywhere." Jeanette looked into space, shadows of the past passing over her smooth, dark skin. Her green eyes were lost in that place that Sophia didn't know. "But she was a good friend. The sister I never had."

Sophia knew—the letters had described a love so deep between Jeanette and Silvana and Will—but knowing it didn't stop tears from swimming into her eyes.

"I just wish I remembered more," Jeanette said.

"I know," Sophia murmured, taking Jeanette's hand. Her two favorite people in the world, her brother and sister in every sense of the word, were gone, and she couldn't even remember what happened to them other than an accident that didn't fit the story anymore, somehow.

Jeanette looked out the window as she stretched her legs out in front of her. It had been raining on and off all day, the clouds ominous, as if they were telling a story of how the day had gone.

"Are you feeling okay?" Sophia asked because she knew Jeanette's energy dropped every time she tried to remember. She had been living like that for so long, and Sophia had been oblivious to it. Why in the world would her mom cast a spell like this?

"I'm fine. Just looking forward to all this being over."

"Have you heard from your doctor friend?" Jeanette had promised to keep in touch with Julia's doctors.

"Nothing yet." Jeanette looked straight into Sophia's eyes, hers fierce. "Nothing's going to happen to Julia."

Sophia nodded and looked away. She was sick of crying, but it seemed like tears were the only thing she had left, and they wanted to be seen.

"Will this work with all this rain?" Sophia asked, but only to change the subject.

"The moon is still there, even when we can't see it."

"There's something profound about that." She thought about Julia. Amy was with her now, though they had taken turns watching their sister. Julia had been Sophia's rock for so long, Sophia couldn't even think of her being so helpless now. Not that Sophia hadn't been able to tell before, but even their father relied on Julia so much that he was falling apart now that she was stuck in a hospital bed, as if in a deep sleep. It was a lot to think about the responsibility that had been placed on Julia's shoulders at such a young age.

Sophia shook the thoughts away. Things would change. She would see to it.

"You know, I could swear your mom had stuff written in these journals," Jeanette said, rifling through a blank notebook. "She always had a notebook on her and she made notes constantly about everything. It was infuriating. She even had a charm on some of them, where they wrote things that happened without her having to pick up a pen. We communicated with each other that way for a while, when we were adults having to deal with adulting and unable to see each other as often."

Sophia's sternum tightened. "What did you write?"

"About everything. When we were kids, it was about whatever was happening in our lives. When Will lost his dad to a heart condition, and when Silvana lost her mom to cancer. When my parents divorced."

"That sounds so incredible." And so sad at the same time.

Jeanette smiled sadly. "It was very special."

"What did Mom have to write about that she charmed her journals to write themselves?"

"She loved keeping records. It was like a hobby for her. She said she never knew when she would need information, and she was absent-minded. She forgot things constantly because she was thinking of everything at all times."

"So she created a spell to write those things down automatically?"

Jeanette chuckled, as if it just hit her how incredible it sounded. "She did. It was amazing, the things she could do with magic. She was so clever, even when we were kids." Jeanette spoke of Sophia's mom with awe.

"And what about Will?"

"Will was the potions guy. He could make a potion like no one else, and he was the one to figure out the order he needed to add ingredients for maximum effect. He foraged for days, looking for the right ingredients, the right stage to use them."

Sophia thought about Grey and his talent with potions. "Sounds like he was really smart."

"That he was."

"And music came into it as you guys figured things out together?" Sophia knew how they would make the potion that night, but she wanted to hear from one of the people to come up with the method. She wanted to know exactly the thought process.

"Silvana always heard music everywhere she went. She told us as little kids. We took the knowing potion when doing rituals in our coven, and Silvana only wanted to hear how it amplified the music. Evelyn was our teacher, a talented witch herself, but even she didn't know the kinds of things Silvana could do." Jeanette's eyes were lost again. "Silvana said she was going to change the world. She wanted to learn more about plants, to use them to make strides in modern medicine."

"So I get it from her," Sophia said. "I've heard the music too, but I ignored it all my life. It was more of an annoyance at the back of my mind until I could see music when I sang. I thought there was something wrong with me." Not to mention that strange magic she could do by simply wishing things out loud.

Jeanette's knowing smile returned. "Definitely your mother's daughter."

"And how did she use the music for her spells?"

Jeanette's face went blank, and she blinked several times, as if waking up from a long nap. "I'm sorry, darling. What did you say?"

Sophia tried not to let it defeat her. She knew she was pushing it when she asked the question. "Nothing," she said gently.

Grey and Lucas appeared in the sitting room, finished with the cleansing of the house. They smelled strongly of herbs and tobacco, and something woody she couldn't place.

Grey was in his signature sweats, but unlike the sea of black clothing he owned, these were a very light gray. His t-shirt was white, and he had a hooded sweatshirt on top, unzipped. Lucas was in his usual garb: gray slacks, a white button-down, and suspenders. Sophia wondered if he ever wore sweats or comfortable stuff, or if he slept in his formalwear, like a vampire. Then she remembered he'd worn sweats the night of Clayton's attack.

Lucas's eyes twinkled when she caught his eye, and she had a powerful sensation of being x-rayed.

What was Lucas's deal, exactly? Grey had said energy work, but what did that mean?

"I think we're ready to begin," Grey said from the archway to the sitting room. Sophia stood, restless, and so did Jeanette, whose eyes had cleared somewhat. She was back.

"It's exciting, isn't it?" Jeanette wrung her hands together. "I haven't been a part of a ritual since..." She frowned. "I can't remember how long."

"I appreciate your presence, Jeanette," Grey said. "But know that once we take it, memories may come rushing back and it could be uncomfortable."

Jeanette's nostrils flared when she sighed. "I'm ready, if it helps Julia."

When twilight came, as Grey had been checking to make sure they started on time, they huddled together in the kitchen. Every appliance was in the pantry, to give them all the space they could need.

Jeanette and Lucas would mostly supervise and make sure Grey and Sophia were safe after they ingested the potion, though Jeanette insisted they would be fine.

It's the intention that matters, Sophie darling.

Her mom's words came back to her now, as if she was in the room with them. Sophia wanted to believe that was the case. That somehow her mom was present for this, willing them to remember, to find a way to help Helena, Julia, and everyone else that was sick.

And if intention was everything it took, Sophia put her hopes out in the ether, into the unseen stars, the full moon, the universe itself. God, if they were listening.

Please, please, please.

The mantra repeated over and over in her head. Pleading to whoever listened that her sister would be okay, that Helena would survive her illness, that Sophia could help fix the mess she'd made of Victoria's relationship to Thomas.

Grey began making potions. All were simple, and he played plant music to strengthen them, to make them as potent as he possibly could. Some were simpler, an extract of the ingredient, but each of them responded in a way that made Sophia stare in awe. As the house became dark, only candles to illuminate them, the music soared around them in swirling colors. They were more brilliant than she had ever seen them before, and as the plants dissolved into the cauldron, the music soared higher and higher, in a vortex of light and color, before it disappeared into the cauldron as well. The potions glowed so brightly they hurt the eyes, even in their vials, as Grey bottled them carefully.

The fact that these were melodies her mom had written down, that she had taken the time to write out in this way, was special to Sophia like nothing else had ever been.

Finally, when he'd finished all the extracts—it took upwards of an hour—Grey ran his hand over his sweaty forehead and pulled back his hair before he started on the big potion.

Carefully, Sophia, Lucas, and Jeanette read the instructions to him as needed, though Sophia was sure that Grey knew exactly what to do and when. He had been poring over the notes left by her mom and his dad for the past forty-eight hours straight.

His movements were sure, as if he had made this potion before a thousand times. And maybe he had. He had told her he'd made a similar one before. A boost.

Grey stirred as the instructions showed. The music played around them, every instrument all at once, like a forest symphony. Musical swirls became bigger, brighter; the fractals took up the entire house. Sophia felt hugged by its infinite warmth, where words weren't necessary, because the music did all the talking. Musical notes soared, brightened as they reached the climax. Every note from every plant melted together when none of it should even work. The house, which had been dark before, was alight with color now, and tears filled her eyes and spilled down her cheeks.

When she looked at Jeanette and Lucas, their eyes were also swimming with emotion.

"Now the blood," Jeanette whispered as she read from the instruction, and Sophia stepped toward Grey. The vial in her pocket was warm from when Jeanette had drawn her blood earlier. There was no need to do something like cutting herself in front of Grey. She didn't need him to pass out on her at a time like this.

She opened the vial and tipped it into the cauldron, and when she did, all the music swirled around them faster and faster and became a tornado of light and wind. Her hair whipped around her, up into the air, and Sophia could swear it smelled like a forest. Then, the vortex rushed into the cauldron, and when it was in, the entire house exploded with light that blinded them all for a few moments.

Panting, Sophia opened her eyes to find a lovely golden potion inside the cauldron. It looked serene, like the waters of a lake in winter. Her heart galloped.

Beside her, Grey's breaths were ragged too, and they looked at each other for what seemed like an eternity.

Sophia swallowed bile.

It had to work.

"I've made many potions in my time, but nothing like this." Grey wiped more sweat off his face.

He served the potion in teacups, which was almost comical to Sophia, and they went to the living room where the journals awaited them. They sipped the potion as they sat on the ground. It was hot as lava, but the bit they took changed things instantaneously.

The potion managed to be bitter and sweet at the same time, but Sophia didn't even care about the taste. She drank faster, used to drinking her coffee far too hot for human consumption, and finished well before Grey did.

She could see the air between them.

Jeanette and Lucas disappeared. It was just her and Grey in that space between the tangible and a world that lived just beyond their reach. There was a luminescence to the air. It breathed.

Her head was light as the music from Grey's house plants stirred around her like a symphony. There was color everywhere, like the color from Grey's music, from her music, but far more intense, the colors more brilliant, the swirls more fluid.

When she looked at Grey, his eyes were like vortexes, filled with black holes and galaxies. She couldn't look away.

There was a lightness to her body, as if she were floating in one of those pods of sensory deprivation, but less terrifying. Everything around her felt distorted in the most interesting way. She could still see the walls of the house, but she could also see through them, and when Lucas touched her arm, she felt the warmth of his fingers on her flesh, but deeper, right below the surface, like his skin was hot water in a bathtub.

Lucas led her to the sofa, where she sat and closed her eyes for a moment. As she did, her body felt lighter still, as if she levitated, reaching for the sky.

Even the rain tapping against the house made music, and it wasn't percussion like she would have imagined. It was like a harp instead, complex and sweet. The plants responded to it with their own music, some providing melody, some rhythm. And someone sang. She opened her eyes, realized it was her singing along with words she did not understand.

Grey grinned at her, and she saw his heart beating. It was bright pink, right under his skin, and it was big, and pure.

"Do you hear it?" she whispered, but even that whisper was far too loud for her own ears.

"Yes." His voice came from far away.

There were tribal drums, a sweet percussion, and then... violins?

Her eyes filled with tears, thinking of the music her mother used to make when she was little. From a guitar, from a violin, and from a piano. She heard all of it as if her mom was in the room with them. Maybe upstairs in Grey's studio.

And she knew that every time she had heard music coming from her plants, it was this that she heard.

She hummed along, her vocal cords coming together like the wings of a butterfly, and when her voice harmonized with the music, her mind raced. Every memory she had ever lost smacked into her like high tide during a storm. It crashed into her so hard she fell back into the cushions of the sofa.

She didn't feel her beating heart; she just knew it was there. Her entire body buzzed with memories.

Grey was there, since they were babies, barely able to walk. She remembered seeing him for the first time, when he was born, though she was a baby herself. A rush of emotion, something hot and cold rushed through her body, filling her, and she shivered, nausea rolling in her stomach.

Her hands trembled, and suddenly, she sat on a swing. Little Grey, his cute little nose smattered with freckles, sat opposite to her on the same wooden seat of the swing. The surrounding plants chattered as they climbed up the sides of the swing, into the white frame her mother had insisted they have. It looked more magical that way, and her mom, of course, was right. She was always right. Her mom knew everything. She was the smartest person in the entire world. The plants were good company.

"I want to tell you all my secrets," Little Grey whispered to her.

"I will keep every single one of them," she told him. "I love you, Grey."

His brown eyes looked into hers, and she leaned forward and pressed a sweet kiss against his lips. It was wet but warm, and she loved it. It made her stomach flutter with butterflies and her heart thumped, and she knew, even then, that she would love him until the day she died. Sophia also knew things, and the things she knew were real. Or they became real later.

In the present, Sophia shook her head, her heart certainly making itself known now, with its erratic beating. She opened her eyes, panting. She wasn't sure if she had gone back there to her childhood yard, or if she had stayed in Grey's living room all along. Grey touched her hand, and she looked at him.

"I remember now," he murmured and slid to the floor, to sit in front of the journals and grimoires. She sat next to him just as her mother's voice came to her.

"Sophie, darling," she said and Sophia yearned with everything within her, to see her face one more time. To feel arms around her, smell that soft scent of roses and greenery again. She knew the tears were running down her cheeks before she felt their warmth. "Everything is intention, my darling."

Tears streamed down Sophia's face, and she held her hands over the journals. They trembled there, but nothing happened. Still, she did not move, letting herself cry for the mother she had lost far too young.

She now knew what she had to do.

It started in the soles of her feet. A current in her toes spread upward to her ankles, to her shins, to her knees, as if filling every inch of her. It went up her entire body, warm and cold and making her shiver violently with its power, every hair on her arms rising as if to watch. Her hands lit up with golden light.

"Show me," she commanded to the pages, and the first grimoire opened violently. The lid smacked against the floor, adding to the music. Pages flipped open, as if caught in a wind. And as every page fluttered open, the words, images, and musical notes appeared.

26

It took them months to figure out how to infuse the potions. Mostly because of their limited ability to play musical instruments. Jeanette had little talent for instruments, according to her, and Silvana already played piano and violin. Will played guitar well, but the plants also needed other instruments, and none of them had access to such things. They had succeeded in a potion to port from one place to another instantly. Of course, there already were potions like it, but the infusion with the plant's music made it so that they only needed a single drop to travel.

It hadn't been easy, but it had worked, and now the trio knew there was a lot they could do with plant music magic.

Jeanette, who continued to look into her cards, had found that there were other ways to tell the future. All those ways were not steadfast, or altogether accurate, but mostly, she had a good idea of what was going on. She enjoyed looking into things and waiting to see how everything panned out in the end. Sometimes it was spot-on, but sometimes bits and pieces, and something about it helped Jeanette see things from different perspectives. She loved her magical abilities, as simple as they seemed.

Will, on the other hand, had been busy with swimming, going from meet to meet with his mom, who seemed more than eager to keep him from Silvana and Jeanette. Not that it worked well at all. Will found ways to be with them, to create music, and to stare at Silvana when she wasn't looking.

Jeanette said she preferred listening to the music and helping when she could, but her brand of magic would forever be to take peeks at the future and hope for the best.

Magic didn't solve everything, she always said, and Silvana wanted to agree, but she also wanted to be idealistic. There had to be a way to make things better, and magic could be that.

It never escaped Jeanette that Will took Silvana's side on a lot of those things. It would have bothered her, but she knew it had nothing to do with her, and everything to do with the fact that Will was in love with Silvana, and Silvana with Will. They could deny it all day, but they could never convince her otherwise.

It would be sweet to watch, if it didn't make Jeanette feel left out of the group. She didn't want to feel that way, but she couldn't help it. She also didn't want them to get together only to break up and ruin what they had. And every time Jeanette tried to peek into Silvana and Will's future, none of it made any sense.

On the night of All Hallows' Eve, they got together under a gigantic full moon, and they had the knowing potion. They sat in a circle inside Will's room. The tree house had become too crowded now that they were getting older, and since Will's mom was at work, it was safe to be there together. They could never meet at Silvana's unless her dad was passed out drunk.

Will had a few plants in his room, though most of them were fake.

Silvana heard the music clearly as the potion worked, one of them a lovely harp. He also had a terrarium in a corner, with a salamander, and all the plants he had in them also sang happily in the humidity. It sounded like the music her mom used to listen to before she died. Lively and happy, with drums and horns, and strings, and keys all at the same time.

It made her yearn for a place she had never known, the place of her ancestors. One day, she would visit the small Caribbean Island, and she would honor her mother and their ancestors so they would be proud.

Will opened the lone window to let in crisp air, which the three of them welcomed, as the knowing potion made them sweat like crazy. The moonlight seeped into the room, bright silver, but warm at the same time, a contrast to the cool air.

Silvana's fingers itched to play the keyboard sitting by the wall in Will's room. She wanted to play what she heard, see what it could do with a potion. She wanted to know more, do more, see more. But she sat with her eyes closed instead. The plants spoke, and she wanted to listen.

But then Will played.

Silvana's eyes flew open when he picked at the first string. His long fingers flew over the board. He knew the frets expertly, knew which strings would do what. She enjoyed playing guitar too, but she was better at playing the piano.

"I hear violins." Silvana looked around the room. She wanted to know which plant sounded like that. It molded itself to the melody Will played. It was harmonizing, as if it responded to his music. Silvana grinned because it felt like they were at a concert.

"I think it's the fern hanging by the window." Jeanette's eyes remained closed as she spoke.

Silvana looked at her best friend, how Jeanette's dark skin gleamed healthily in the dim room. Jeanette swayed, her lips curved in a soft smile. She was the happiest person Silvana knew; always positive, looking on the bright side of things. And with wisdom in her eyes Silvana had only seen in much older people. Jeanette wanted to be a doctor, and what a wonderful one she'd make.

Silvana couldn't help but smile, too. Then she looked at Will and found him staring at her as he played. His eyes were very far away, soft, and a little sad as his fingers picked out the notes.

Silvana couldn't look away from him, even when his eyes closed, as if he felt the music deep inside his soul.

In that moment, she wanted to kiss him, but of course, that would never be a good idea. And besides, Jeanette sat right there by the two of them, and Silvana wouldn't put Jeanette in an uncomfortable situation.

"Oh my God," Jeanette snapped. Her green eyes opened and

focused on Silvana first, then Will, who had stopped playing abruptly, his last note still ringing inside the guitar. "I'm going to step outside, be in nature, touch some grass. You two figure this out."

"What do you mean?" Will frowned as Jeanette got on her feet, swaying for an instant, before she put her hands at her rounded hips. She was gorgeous, her limbs long and lithe. Her hair was in two long braids with curls escaping around her face.

"You know what I mean, William," she said, but her voice had softened considerably. "You two have a thing going on, and I know it." She eyed them both as they stared at her openmouthed. "Yes, even though you haven't told me about it, because you're as transparent as a jellyfish." She turned to walk away, but turned back at the door. "Ouch, by the way. Not like I wouldn't have understood."

Silvana looked down at her lap, a stab of guilt going through her.

"It's time to stop pretending like nothing's going on." Jeanette opened the door. "I will go for a walk. You two either end this now, so we can get back to normal, or get it out of your systems so we can start a new normal."

Jeanette walked out of the room and shut the door softly. They heard her steps all the way down the stairs and out the front door.

Silvana still wouldn't look at Will, who was definitely looking at her, his hand around the neck of his guitar.

"Well?" he murmured. Where Silvana wanted to go after Jeanette to make sure she wasn't mad, Will wanted to explore the part where they *got it out of their systems*. Of course he did.

"Well, what?" Silvana snapped as she stood.

She used to the potion enough that she did not struggle as she walked to the door.

"Wait, Sil," Will called, but Silvana was already opening the door. In a moment of frustration, as Silvana had every intention of going after Jeanette, Will lifted his hand and willed the door closed.

The rounded knob slipped out of Silvana's hand, and the door slammed shut. She turned around, stunned.

"William," she gasped. He had never used his magic in that way. In fact, he rarely used his telekinesis because it drained his energy too much. But he did not look like his energy suffered at all as he stood and went up to her. Her mouth hung open.

He was so tall now that she had to look up into his face, which was a little pale as he stalked toward her. His shoulders had broadened with his swimming, though he was still not a big guy by any means. His eyes were soft when he came closer, and Silvana pressed her back against the door. Her hair was loose behind her, trapped between her body and the door. She had straightened it, since her dad had insisted it looked more put-together than her natural curls.

She didn't know what was wrong with her curls, but she did as he asked, if only to avoid an argument.

"Will…" She couldn't get any other words out. He crowded her, and she would be lying if she said she hated it.

"You heard Jeanette." He stood in front of her but did not make a move to touch her. His hands fisted and released at his sides several times. He would never touch her unless she wanted him to, and she loved him all the more for that.

"I'm still scared," she said, and sounded breathless. That day in the trees had been amazing. She had loved every moment of that kiss, but they hadn't kissed since then and that was months ago. She looked up to find his eyes on her.

"Listen to me," he said. "There is nothing to be scared about. I love you and you love me. I'm not going to stop loving you. Even if we don't do this."

Every fiber of her being wanted to believe him when he said that. So when her hand rose to touch his soft hair, she didn't stop it.

They would be eighteen soon, her just after him. They were still young, still trying to figure things out, but everything they felt for each other was as real as any other feeling they'd ever had.

The surrounding music gave them a lovely soundtrack for the moment, like a cassette that didn't need to be rewound, punctuating every emotion going through the two of them. Will placed his hand next to her head on the door, and her heart leaped in excitement.

There was a question in his eye, and she nodded, so he finally kissed her.

When she went home later, Silvana couldn't stop smiling, but as soon as she entered the house, her joy slipped away. Her father sat at the kitchen table, one of her journals in front of him.

"I knew it." His voice was angry, guttural.

That was the moment Silvana knew she would make another spell. This time, it was not to know things, but to hide them.

27

They had to get creative about how they met these days. After Silvana's father found her journals, she pretended to throw them all away, and instead made up a spell with music magic, and hid everything in her journals. The only way to see anything in them would be to take the knowing potion.

They still saw each other, but now they had to sneak around. School was a good bet, but they had little time to meet before, between, or after classes. Sometimes, when they met at Jeanette's house, their friend would walk off for a while to give them some privacy. Silvana's father had spoken to Jeanette's mom, but Jean didn't care to listen to Ruben Candela, a man she could hardly stand.

One evening, close to Christmas, Silvana entered the church behind her father, her head down. Her hair, straight at the insistence of her father once again, hung down her back like a curtain of dark silk. She wore a green dress, pale against her tanned skin, the little sleeves resting right at the bend of her shoulders. The black leggings kept her warm, as well as the coat she took off as they entered the warm church. Her sleeves looked like they would slide down and bare more of her skin. She liked how precariously they sat there, enough that when she moved, they slid a little more. God forbid someone saw her shoulders. She almost rolled her eyes but refrained.

Her rebellion was more subtle that way. Baring her shoulders just enough, meeting with her boyfriend in secret every night. And, of course, there was being a witch and all that.

Her father mostly ignored that part, as he thought it was just games, but little did he know. Silvana didn't know how he could pretend magic wasn't a thing when her mom had so obviously been a witch, too, but she'd take it.

Her father truly thought he had won. That she no longer saw Will, unless it was at school, which he couldn't control. It wasn't like he could keep her from going to school. That, and Will had come by many a time to see her when her father went to bed, porting straight into her room, and leaving when the first rays of sun appeared over the mountains.

Her shoes were flat and simple, a little old, and her steps felt cushioned, light as she walked closer and closer to the gigantic cross on the tall wall at the front of the room. The tall windows were pointed arches, with incredible designs in painted glass. Scenes from the bible, things that Silvana didn't believe had happened, but still found interesting.

As she walked past a nearly empty pew, a hand brushed against her skin for nothing more than a split moment. She didn't look at Will, didn't dare make it known that she was even aware that he was there, sitting with his mother, who wore a little veil over her head for reasons that were lost on both Will and Silvana.

She sat next to her father toward the front of the church as a priest sang on the side of the altar, where hundreds of candles sat, some burning, some not, at the feet of the mother of Christ.

A few more people staggered in, but the church wasn't full by any means. It was a little Christmastime tradition to have mass, and her father loved going to show how pious he was. Though he never so much as looked toward a church for the rest of the year. He'd insisted Silvana go to see a priest to confess her sins, which she'd pretended to do. Instead of speaking to the stranger about sins her father was sure she'd committed, she'd sat in silence for thirty minutes and listened to the priest reciting his prayers instead.

He had prayed for her soul. Nice of him, but unnecessary. While

Silvana understood the reaches of religion, what people got out of it, she would never get how telling some man about her decisions would do anything for her in the afterlife.

The echo of the singer's voice was soft and well rounded. It made Silvana think about silk and chocolate, so much she even smelled it around her. She closed her eyes, her hands pressed together on her lap, and she let the music wash over her. The only thing that made coming to church worth it was the singing, which seeped into her skin and found places in her soul that needed the magic of the melody to heal. It made her want to sing, though she didn't know the words. The acoustics made her wish there were plants in there so she could hear them sing, too.

Silvana could almost feel the piercing of Will's gaze on the back of her neck, and a shiver ran down her spine. Her father, next to her, sunk to his knees, his mouth moving, his fingers busy with the shiny black beads of his rosary.

Ah, yes. Because being an ass could be cured by banal repetition.

She looked at his balding head. What was left of his hair was mostly white now, and she almost felt sympathy for him. Could she blame him for being a terrible father, when his own had abandoned him as a child? Could she hold everything over his head without acknowledging that patterns were passed down and couldn't help but continue to be repeated?

She had tried to see him with compassionate eyes, but if life had taught her anything, it was that the ripples of heartbreak remained long after the person who caused them apologized.

Not that he'd apologized ever.

Silvana stood and exited the pew. Her steps were soft as she headed toward the front of the room. The area around the altar was warm, and she approached the statue of the mother. Silvana realized she felt something like sympathy for the woman. She was depicted with lovely peachy skin, dark hair, and a veil over her head. But it was the sadness in her eyes that always caught Silvana right in the gut. Maybe she was sad because God had impregnated her without her consent. Or perhaps because she was depicted with white skin when that made no sense in a historical context.

Silvana picked up a candle, long and thin, almost translucent in its whiteness, and brought the wick to one of the already-lit candles. The flames took the soft material, and Silvana had to wonder if anyone who worked in that church knew what white candles symbolized to witches.

Still, as it was a Monday evening, and the moon was a lovely crescent in the sky, Silvana placed the candle inside a little hole in the stand, and whispered,

"For protection and peace, harmony and a calm mind."

And the calm washed over her immediately, as she had expected. She breathed in the warm air of the church and thought of her mom, who had always taught her that the magic they could do with candles could surpass barriers with its sweet energy. She wondered if the religious people of the town knew that they practiced magic when they lit candles to their saints. That was what prayers were, anyway. It was always about the intention behind them and how it came back to the person uttering the spell.

I hope you're happy, Mommy, she thought, feeling the familiar pang. She swallowed, reaching into the tie around her waist, and picked out the small piece of paper. She placed it under her candle before she turned away and walked back just as Will raised his head and his eyes bore into hers. A thrill went through her, but she didn't look at him longer than needed. There were always watchful eyes, and his mother was a freaking hawk.

As she took her seat, a shaky breath left her, and her heart thumped loudly in her ears.

Will didn't move toward the candles right away—they had to be smart about their little games. So he let others do what she had done first, and finally, he did. A thrill went through her, knowing they were doing this in front of everyone. Including his hateful mother and her ignorant father.

They were only waiting to turn eighteen and it would be over then. She would never again have to put up with her father's control, and they could love each other and be together without his mother's shadow over them.

She would never have to deal with her father getting angry over stupid small things and using his hands on her because it was the only way he knew how to deal with his anger.

Oh, how many times had Silvana fantasized of turning him into a potted plant, or a crawling critter. But no. Magic had repercussions, especially negative magic. Not that she'd tried doing those things.

She watched as Will found her note. Her heart raced, but as her father stirred next to her, she put down her head and pretended to pray.

Much later that night, after church had left Ruben Candela feeling softer than normal, a little less intense, they went home and she made dinner, which pleased him. He poured himself a drink, then another, and another after that as he watched whatever came across the screen in the living room. By the time her bedtime came, the bottle was empty, and he was drooling in his chair.

In her room, she changed into her warm pajamas, pulled back her hair to keep it out of her way, and locked her door with a special potion Will had concocted. It made it so no one on the outside could enter without express permission from her, and they could also not hear a thing going on inside.

She played on her little keyboard as she waited for Will to show up. When he did, he was also wearing his pajamas, which were a pair of plaid blue pants and a t-shirt. He bit his lip and grinned widely as she left the keyboard and jumped him. Her legs went around his middle, and she hugged him with his entire body as she looked forward to a future where they could be together without hiding.

He held her just as tightly, and when he tipped his head to look at her, she leaned down and kissed him.

They laughed like maniacs as they moved toward the bed, as they removed each other's clothes, and lay together underneath the sheets.

After, they faced each other under the covers, relished the warmth of each other's bodies.

"You're amazing." His voice was soft, a mere whisper.

She bit her lip and grinned. "You're only saying that because you love me."

"I'm saying that because it's true." His face was serious. "You are everything, Sil."

Her eyes misted, and she reached for his face, her fingers at his jaw.

"I love you."

"And I'll love you until the day I die," he whispered right before they fell asleep.

Waking up was chaotic. They overslept, since she forgot to set the alarm, and bleary eyed, his hair sticking up in crazy angles, he rushed to get dressed. A small kiss, and he ported, knowing he would be in so much trouble if his mom happened to try getting into his room.

Later, when Silvana went to school, Ruben walked into her room and searched. For what, he didn't know, but there had to be something. He didn't believe for a moment that his slut of a daughter wasn't going behind his back. When he saw the boxers under her bed, he knew.

28

A week later, Silvana still winced whenever she moved. Her back was almost raw with deep welts from her father's belt. She hadn't seen Will or Jeanette since school had ended for the winter break.

Ruben had nursed her back to health, glad that she was not in school anymore, afraid he had gone too far this time. He hadn't been able to control his rage when he found that boy's underwear, which he had obviously left behind to taught Ruben. To show how he had defiled his only daughter. Right under his nose, in his own house. Rage swirled through him at the thought of it.

Ruben had done what he'd needed to do, and borrowed a coworker's car to do the job. He didn't mean to hurt Will Constantine seriously, just scare him, but he hadn't calculated it right. He'd been too angry.

Then, he had taken a belt to his sinful daughter and left her bed-ridden for two straight days, with fevers and chills, and a bleeding back.

"Show me your back," he said now.

Silvana wanted to cuss him out. She wanted to scream at him for what he did to her, but the look in his eye scared her. He was unhinged.

Humiliated, she turned and showed him her naked back. She held the blankets up to cover the rest of her body. He rubbed something on her back. It stung horribly, and she was trembling by the time he finished. But she didn't make a peep, and when she turned to him, she had schooled her features ruthlessly.

She knew he enjoyed when she reacted to his abuse, and she wouldn't give him the satisfaction. He wouldn't hold power over her for long.

Ruben's eyes were keen and seeing nothing on her face, his anger grew. It was supposed to hurt, to keep her from ruining her life.

"All men want is an easy, stupid girl to use and then discard," Ruben said to Silvana, unaware of the cruelty of his words, how they would mold the way she saw the world. He believed every syllable.

Anger lanced through her, though her father didn't care, and never had she wanted to hex someone more.

"Maybe you do, but Will is nothing like you," she spat, then lay down and faced away from him. The door slammed closed as he left. There was a crack in her heart. She had tried sending Will letters, but they wouldn't go out, even with the use of potions. Silvana had also tried writing to Jeanette, but she'd gotten no response, either. Her life was falling apart, and the two people she loved most had disappeared.

The tears came then, and she thought of her mom. None of this would have ever happened had she been alive. Silvana missed her so much, and she hated her dad with every muscle in her body.

She didn't know if Jeanette would get it this time, but she pulled out a notebook from her tiny bedside table and wrote her friend a letter. That her letters to Will wouldn't even disappear with the potion could only mean one thing. She didn't have permission to write to him wherever he was.

Her father brought her food, but she didn't eat it. She'd be damned if she let him feel like he was being a good father for doing the bare minimum. Sluggish and in pain, she packed some clothes, all her journals—they were her most important possessions—and the grimoires she'd shared with Will and Jeanette. That night, when her father passed out in front of the TV, as usual, she took a drop of her porting potion, held on to the bags she'd packed, and disappeared. She reappeared straight in the living room of Jeanette's house. She breathed in relief that she could still port into the house. That she was welcome.

"Jeanette?" she called out, her voice shaky. "Jean?"

Silvana hadn't even considered that they might not be home, and tears fell down her face. She stood in the middle of the living room with her bag at her feet, hands on her face, sobbing softly. Never had she felt so hopeless and so alone, and she fell to her knees among the things she'd packed and cried. Her back smarted, so hot and painful it only made her tears come faster.

She just wanted her mom. She wanted to run away, go back to the Caribbean, and disappear forever.

"Sil?"

Silvana's head snapped up. Jeanette was by the stairs, her eyes wide in surprise. Silvana's face screwed up as she beheld her friend, who rushed toward her and hugged her. But Silvana's back spasmed, and she gasped in pain.

"What happened?" Jeanette asked urgently as her mom, came downstairs.

Silvana told them what her father did. Jean swore, then promised she would take care of Ruben Candela if it was the last thing she did, but Silvana asked her not to. She would hate for Jean to have to deal with the consequences of retaliating. Even against someone as hateful as her father.

"I've tried calling your house and Ruben kept saying you were not home," Jeanette told her later when she and her mother had taken care of the wounds at Silvana's back. The ointment smelled like something Silvana's mom would have made, and it comforted her as much as it helped with the pain.

"Why didn't you write? You have potion left, don't you?"

"I do, but the letters wouldn't even disappear."

Silvana pushed down the anger that surfaced. It bubbled inside her like lava.

"What about Will?" Jeanette asked, and Silvana's stomach dropped.

"I was hoping you'd heard from him."

Jeanette shook her head. The look on her face was one of concern when Silvana told her everything that had happened with him.

"I can't go back to that house, Jeanette."

"And you won't have to," Jean said as she stood by the door with a pillow and blankets for Silvana. "I will hide you if I have to. I won't let him hurt you again."

"You could get into trouble. I'm a minor still."

"And what are you going to do? Leave to be on your own who-knows-where?" Jeanette said. "Mom, we need a spell or something."

"Working on it. I should have done this a long time ago." Jean's face was a mask of fury.

Jean left them alone, and Silvana and Jeanette lay on the bed together, on their sides, facing each other.

"Will and I planned on running away together." Silvana measured Jeanette's reaction. "But you knew that."

"Of course I knew. I know you better than anyone else."

She regretted keeping Jeanette in the dark about her relationship with Will.

"I'm sorry we didn't tell you. I'm sorry I kept this from you. You're my best friend, and I shouldn't have hidden it." Silvana had tears in her eyes, fear in her heart that her friend would turn away from her. That the only person she had left would be too angry with her.

But Jeanette did not judge her friends for keeping things a secret, when she herself knew the excitement of being with someone you loved. She put her hand on Silvana's shoulder.

"You don't need to be sorry," she said. As Silvana sighed in relief, Jeanette smiled. "I totally understand. I knew the moment you two started seeing each other differently. It was only a matter of time."

"But now Will won't get our letters. I don't know what to do."

"I'll go to his house tomorrow," Jeanette said.

Silvana nodded, grateful to her friend, and finally, she slept.

The following morning, Jeanette headed to the Constantine house and found it empty. There was a sign outside that said it was for sale, and the dread that settled inside her was dark, ominous. She tried searching for a clue, something that could spark a vision, but nothing came.

Several hundred miles away, Will lied in a hospital bed, comatose. He had survived the attempt on his life, but only barely. He had seven broken bones and was recovering from internal bleeding that had nearly taken his life.

He was sleeping, bandaged, miserable, and his worried mother never left his side.

29

For an entire year, and beyond that, Silvana attempted, on and off, to reach Will. But it was to no avail, because her letters never went anywhere.

At first, her heartbreak was at the forefront of everything. Hiding from her father until she turned eighteen, then moving away when he couldn't control her anymore. Thank God for Jean and Jeanette. Silvana couldn't have made it without them.

And as the months passed, she'd gotten it through her head Will simply was out of their lives now. Silvana didn't know what had made it better, or if it was that she'd actually learned to heal and move on.

Now, she sat in a concert hall at her college, where she had moved with Jeanette, and played the piano swiftly for a large audience.

The music flowed through Silvana like a river, sent the magic surging through her veins, and her fingers flew over the keys as a smile came to her lips. It was a delicate melody, complicated but not busy. The music hit the keys before she even pressed them, as if her body knew what the sound was like at a molecular level, and her heart surged as the music echoed through the auditorium.

Everyone disappeared. Only the music remained in its lovely swirling colors. Every person in there, hundreds of them, simply became part of the music to her, and she was alone in that room until the moment she finished, when the very last note echoed. She stood from the bench, her black dress brushing her knees. Applause exploded, and she bowed with a smile, then turned and walked off the stage.

Her professor, a lanky man in his sixties, grinned at her, his glasses perched low on his long nose.

"You did wonderfully, Silvana." He shook her hand with a firm grip.

"Thank you, Dr. Carney." She felt the heat suffuse her face, but she was proud of herself for showing people the piece. One of her own.

"Beautiful."

She turned toward the voice as Dr. Carney left to talk to other faculty. Her eyes landed on a man who was far too good-looking to be a real person. He looked like the kind of man who knew he was cute and used it to his advantage.

He flashed her a smile, his teeth impossibly straight and white. His hair was light, golden, but he had a tan, as if he'd recently spent time outside. She couldn't look away from his sharp blue eyes.

"Thank you," Silvana said, and took his hand when he offered it.

"Conrad Montgomery," he said, that dazzling smile still on.

"Silvana Candela." She shook his hand firmly. His skin was softer than hers.

"What was the piece? I'm not sure I know it."

"You wouldn't," she said, and he raised his brows in surprise. "It's my original composition."

But that was a lie. She just couldn't tell him it was plant music she'd plagiarized from the botany department.

How would he react to something like that?

He looked as shocked as he sounded when he spoke next. "That's impressive. Are you a music student, then?"

"I'm not." She felt a little odd as she said it, but didn't know why. "I'm a botany student."

His brow twitched. "What an odd combination of things."

She felt her brows want to contract, so she schooled her features and tone to show nothing. Of course he would think that. He didn't know the kinds of things she could do with a group of plants, a couple of instruments, and a special potion.

"Not as odd as you'd think," she said, and he gave her a dazzling smile.

Oh, he knew he was cute, and she was wary of a man who knew his charm. Still, something about him drew her in.

"Tell me more," he said, picking up a glass when a waiter went by.

"About what?"

"Your music," he said, as if it was obvious. "Why are you not studying it?"

She thought about it for a moment.

"Because I love plants." She didn't have to tell him she wanted to be among the plants because she studied their music with a passion she reserved only for it. "But what do you do? Are you a student here?"

He laughed in a way that set her teeth on edge.

"I'm not a current student, no," he said.

He didn't look much older than she was, but what did she know?

"I just like these events," he added.

"You go to a lot of these?"

He made a movement with his head that was a mix between a nod and a shake.

"It's my pleasure to support my alma mater."

Ah, yes. One of those wealthy donors who got to have their name on a building if they gave enough money.

"Thank you for the support," she said, smiling politely, suddenly needing to be away from this handsome stranger. Thankfully, at that moment, she spotted Jeanette coming in through the door. "I see my friend, so I should go. Nice meeting you."

He took her hand when she extended hers and squeezed it firmly. His gaze held hers for longer than she expected, as well as her hand. She tugged it away, her eyes unable to look into his for any longer.

Awkward.

Her knees trembled as she walked away toward Jeanette, who wore a backpack that looked ready to burst at the seams. Her bright green eyes looked around the room quickly, and when they found Silvana, she smiled.

"I missed your performance. I'm sorry," she said, leaning in for a quick hug.

"It's fine. Nothing you haven't already heard a billion times."

"How did it go?"

"It went well." Silvana looked back to find the handsome stranger still looking at her and she looked away quickly, still unnerved. "No one seemed to notice the colors, so I guess there are no witches like us around here."

"There are no witches like us anywhere." Jeanette pulled out a paper from her bag.

"Good point."

"Check this out." It was literature on the breast cancer that had killed Silvana's mother. "I saw this and thought I should bring it by. Maybe there's something in there we can use for that potion we worked on so long ago."

Silvana suppressed the urge to sigh. It shouldn't hurt so much still, but it did.

"Do you really think we're going to find a cure for breast cancer?"

"You never know." Jeanette gave her the paper, and she took it. It wouldn't hurt to read about it.

As the night ended, Jeanette and Silvana said goodbye to the people they had been speaking to, some professors, some students, when Conrad Montgomery made his move. She was at the exit, right behind Jeanette, when he approached, a white card in his hand.

"Silvana?"

She turned and so did Jeanette, instantly curious about the handsome stranger, who her friend had failed to mention.

"It was a pleasure to meet you," he said. "Forgive me if I'm overstepping, but I would love to take you out sometime."

Jeanette just stood there, looking between the two of them.

Silvana took the white card he offered her, and he grinned before he walked away. A car waited for him, and he got into it without looking back. He was elegant in his long coat and his shiny car, and his... driver.

Who had a driver?

Silvana and Jeanette stared after him, one more concerned than the other, but unable to put her finger on why.

° ° °

A week later, Silvana met Conrad for a date at a fancy place in the city. She sat across from him, feeling inadequately dressed, which she hated. Her dress was new, but it was simple, and compared to her surroundings, she felt cheap. The place was lit moodily, and every chair was red velvet and more comfortable than her bed. The utensils were gold, which she had certainly never seen before, and when she looked at the menu, she swallowed uncomfortably at the fact that there were no prices.

"Thank you for coming out with me," Conrad said with a small smile. He had a glass of whiskey before him.

"Thank you for inviting me," she said. Her eyes focused on the vase in the center of the table. It was clear and held a single red rose in water. Its music was so faint, it made Silvana's heart hurt.

"Tell me about you," he said softly. His eyes were so pale, icy. She couldn't help but think of Will's eyes. How warm they were, how she could see everything he was thinking reflected on them.

"What do you want to know?" She gave him a small smile as she pushed down the pang that went through her when she thought of Will.

"Why botany and not music?"

She felt her lips press together. This again. She didn't know this man well-enough for him to discuss her career with her as if he cared.

Or maybe she needed to relax. That was certainly an overreaction to a genuine question.

"I thought I answered that question already," she said anyway, but kept the small smile to remove the bite.

"You love plants?" he said, squinting a little. He took a drink from his glass. She didn't like having alcohol around her. It reminded her too much of her father.

"I do love plants. They're fascinating."

He smiled again, as if he knew something she didn't, and it irked her. She got the sense that he liked the fact that he was older than she was, that he had more experience than she did. While she had just turned nineteen, he had told her he was thirty. It seemed like an ocean existed between them, as far as experience.

Maybe a part of her liked that too.

They ordered and talked about his business, which was in retail, apparently. His family owned a huge amount of retail shops around the country and were thinking of expanding overseas. If she had felt intimidated by him before, she was more so now that she knew the type of power he had. Old money. The kind that didn't need prices in menus or tags.

At the end of the night, when he drove her home in his fancy car, he thanked her again for coming out with him and that he wished she would go out with him again.

"I would like that," she said genuinely because she'd enjoyed his company. He had an easy humor and a gentle disposition. He was kind to the server and other waitstaff, which she appreciated.

"When can you?" He turned to her on the seat, his eyes shining expectantly. "See me, I mean."

"It will be a busy couple of weeks at school and work, with registrations for next semester, but I should be a little freer after that."

"Unlucky me," he said, putting his hands on his chest. "I wish I could see you sooner."

"I know, but work is work," she said, giving him a soft smile, mostly because he was so cute and she felt flattered. Also a little guilty.

He grimaced slightly. "You should be able to just go to school and focus on your studies."

A pang of annoyance, but she smiled. It had become compulsive to hide how she felt these days. "Most of us don't have that option."

He seemed genuinely surprised, which surprised her. How could he not know not everyone was born in a golden cradle?

A week later, his reactions made a lot more sense when a supervisor at the registration office handed her an envelope. Inside, she found a letter and a statement. It detailed that she had been awarded a retroactive full-ride scholarship. She knew right away that it was Conrad, and she hurried home to Jeanette and showed her the statement. Jeanette responded by showing her an identical one.

"Who does that?" Jeanette said, then opened her mouth as if she was going to say more.

Silvana picked up the phone. It was black against the stark white walls of the dorms. She dialed his number, and he answered after the third ring.

"Conrad Montgomery."

"Conrad, you shouldn't have done this." Her hand was trembling on the receiver.

"I don't know what you're talking about." But there was a smile in his voice.

"Don't do that." Her fingers tightened on the phone. She heard him sigh.

"Silvana, I have been given so much," he began, mumbling, as if he was a little embarrassed. "I wanted to do something for someone and when you told me about having to work so hard, I couldn't sleep."

Her heart squeezed, even as her brain knew that people worked every day. There was nothing wrong with working hard.

"And Jeanette, too?" she said.

"Please don't be mad," he said, sounding sheepish. She wished she could see his face. No one had done something that nice for her in her life. She hadn't known him that long; this seemed so over the top.

"I'm not mad," she sighed into the phone. "Of course, I'm not mad. Thank you. It's amazing, but it's so much, Conrad."

"Just let me do this for you, Silvana," he pleaded. "Even if we don't go on another date, ever again, I just want to do this. Just to help. Go part time at work and dedicate more time to school. Pretend you got a full ride scholarship instead. You would for your musical talent alone."

"A scholarship's exactly what I got," she mumbled, mortified. She didn't know what to do with her other hand, so she wrapped the cord on her finger. "Thank you. This is so generous and sweet of you."

A moment of silence. Then, he said, "You're welcome. I hope to see you soon now that you work part time."

She could almost hear his smile through the line, and she laughed under her breath.

They didn't talk for a few days after that, and when they did, she agreed to a date, mostly because she felt grateful. Well, half. He *was* really cute, and she liked the way he looked at her, like she was the only person in the room. It was as if no one else existed when they were together, and he never interrupted her when she spoke. He was so normal, so unlike her father, and she craved normalcy. She wanted it so badly.

When they started seeing each other often, she didn't mind. Jeanette was supportive in the way best friends were supportive. Conrad was a dream to date. He was charming, a gentleman. He opened doors for her, and held her hand while they walked, and when he kissed her, he put his hand on her waist, another on her face.

And he didn't push her, which was the best part of it all, so when he showed up with a bottle of luxury perfume, she took it and cherished it, even though the scent wasn't her. She didn't tell him she didn't actually like perfume, and she spritzed it on when she was going to see him because she knew how happy it made him. Within eight months, Conrad had proposed, and Silvana said yes.

30

Less than three months after her wedding, Silvana got pregnant with her first daughter. She knew it was a girl the moment she knew she was pregnant, and she would call her Roselyn. Her sweet, gentle baby girl.

Jeanette was there for her as she went through morning sickness, for which Conrad had little stomach and patience. Quickly after their wedding, Silvana realized that her new husband was not the kind to spend much time at home. He worked a lot, and he enjoyed being at work, so Silvana only saw him in the evenings, and on weekends when they went to the country club, where he loved to show her off.

Sometimes Silvana felt like a prized horse, but Conrad was sweet, and he was mostly kind.

She tried to convince herself that she was imagining things. That she was this way because of what happened with Will, but it never sat well with her.

It was like Conrad had two faces. One was the charming man she had met on campus, with that dazzling smile, words of encouragement, praising, good-natured. At home, he was all those things, but with an edge Silvana hadn't seen before, and it left a film in her tongue, as if she had tasted something foul.

She continued her work with music, noting that it helped with her morning sickness. She spent her days working on the healing potion, since she now had plenty of time for it. Conrad had insisted she stop going to school while she was pregnant, since she was so sick, and when she'd had a hard time keeping water down, she'd agreed.

Silvana and Jeanette worked on the potion together, which seemed wrong when Will wasn't around, but it was that, or not doing it. Silvana would rather try.

And try she did. Her days were spent entirely writing music and infusing simple household potions. And finally, she had perfected a spell that helped her write her notes without her needing to. Especially big things she may not have time to write as accurately. Like her pregnancy symptoms, which had been so strong, she hadn't been able to write them down until much later when she'd forgotten details about it.

As her belly grew, so did her hope of finding a cure. And even when she got a call that her father was dead, she didn't stop her work.

Silvana didn't shed a tear for Ruben Candela. Not because she felt nothing, but because she couldn't. She had a set of conflicting emotions playing around inside her and there was no way to let it out, so she didn't cry. He had drunk himself to death, and that kind of death wasn't painless, she knew. It was long, and it sucked, and part of her felt he got the ending he deserved after everything he had put her and her mother through.

She never mourned him, not in the years after, when she had two little girls toddling around.

Roselyn was her sweet little angel at three years old, the sweetest baby Silvana would have, while Julia was a force of nature at one.

Life got busy after that. Jeanette made it into medical school and got into a serious relationship with a classmate. And Silvana, hands full, had put magic on the back burner. She still played around in her spare time, especially when Conrad wasn't around. Music bothered him when he worked at home. It was too loud and too busy, so she refrained from playing when he was there.

Life was mostly peaceful, when she didn't argue with Conrad for working too much, until one day when she went to the mall with her little girls.

She froze mid-step as her eyes focused on the man in the suit store. His hair was a little longer than she remembered, but when he turned around, his face was exactly the same as the last time she saw him while lying next to her in bed.

Across the way, Will looked up from the man who took his measurements, and his eyes met hers.

°°°

It would have been easy to avoid Will, but something in her still went to him, even after all that time and experience. Too many feelings warred inside her. Duty, nostalgia, love, anger. How could he be there in her city? Living his life as if nothing happened. As if she hadn't waited for him.

That evening, as Conrad sat in the kitchen, talking on the phone with a contractor who was going to build him a home office, she got into the shower. Adrenaline had exhausted her body. It came and went in waves.

She stood under the hot spray, suddenly in need of washing off the perfume she only wore for Conrad. When she'd seen Will at the mall, it had brought back everything. All the emotions she'd thought she had dealt with were back with a force she hadn't expected.

After, she got dressed in some of her most comfortable clothing, gray sweatpants, a white shirt, and a hooded sweater. She braided her dripping hair and left it hanging down to the middle of her back.

"I need to go to the grocery store," she said, and was sure he would know she was lying. She intended to go to the grocery store, but that was not why she was leaving the house. Conrad gave her a dismissive wave of his hand, so she made sure the girls were in bed, and left.

It wouldn't take her long. She wouldn't do any more than listen to Will, her lifelong friend. Her first love. The one who left her without a trace.

Will had chased her down at the mall, followed her to her car, where she was putting her daughters into their car seats. She'd turned to find him running toward her, and he begged her to meet him at a local park.

She got to the park and sat in her idling car for a long time. Her eyes kept drawing back to the ring on her finger, and the intensity of the emotions coursing through her. How could she not have moved on already?

A car pulled up next to hers, and Will got out.

His hair was pushed back behind his ears. The stubble sweeping across the hollows of his cheeks made him look so much more grown up. Different, yet the same. He was a man, not the boy who had disappeared from her life so suddenly, it had left her spinning and picking up the pieces of her heart.

"How are you here, Will?" she said, her voice even as they sat on a stone bench in front of a giant duck pond. She was at one end of the bench, Will at the other, as if they were both reluctant to be closer. It was spring, a little chilly, but with warm days ahead.

Her voice sounded even, but she was anything but calm.

"I just graduated and got a job at an architecture firm in town," he told her.

"A job here?"

"Yes. I moved here two months ago."

Two months in the same city, and she hadn't known. She took a shaky breath. Her jaw was so tight it surprised her she could even speak.

What would she have done if she'd known Will lived in the same city as her? She was married with two children, for God's sake. It had been years! He was her first boyfriend when she was a teenager. It shouldn't have been that important. So why did it feel like her life had taken a detour?

"What happened?" she heard herself ask. "You disappeared, and we never heard from you again. Where did you go?" She didn't care that it came out as an accusation.

His shoulders curved forward. "I was in a coma for three months."

Shock paralyzed her.

"A car ran me over on my way back from swim practice. The day after that last night we…" He swallowed. "It was a medically induced coma, to stop the swelling in my brain. When I woke up, my mom told me we'd had to move to be closer to the hospital where I was. It had the appropriate unit for cases like mine. I had to learn to walk again."

There was a ringing in her ears. She couldn't utter a word, just sat there with nausea rolling in her stomach. The night's sky seemed to want to eat her whole, and she rested her elbows on her knees and put her face in her hands.

"Who ran you over?" she asked, the image of her father instantly springing up in her brain. Could he have?

Yes. The answer was right there, though she'd never be able to prove it, she realized.

"They never found the person. I didn't see the car."

She fought nausea.

"I tried writing when I could move again," he said.

"I never got anything," she whispered, anger hot and quick inside her. She looked out at the dark water. The surrounding lamps illuminated parts of the pond, but there weren't any ducks in it. She had a lump in her throat as she stood. He stood too, towering over her in that way he did that made butterflies awaken in her.

Silvana took a quick step back and swallowed heavily. Her body was numb.

"You got married." He looked down at the ring on her left hand.

She nodded, unable to speak.

"I'm sorry about your accident." Her voice was pathetic. A whisper. "I'm glad you're okay, but I should go home to my kids."

It felt strange to say those words to him when she had once dreamed of having his babies. They would have been going home together to their kids. She struggled to keep the tears at bay; they made her eyes hot.

He nodded, at a loss for words.

She turned away, but then turned back.

"Jeanette would love to hear from you. She's really missed you."

"I've missed her, too."

But the way he looked at her told her he wanted to say those words to her. He only held back because she was married, and she knew she wouldn't say it either. She knew she should turn around and go home to her husband and children, but all the unresolved feelings she carried for Will crashed into her like the waves of a tsunami.

"Sil..." His voice was but a whisper, and he reached for her. The next moment, he held her close, and his scent, that devastatingly familiar scent, hit her and her tears flowed freely. "I'm so sorry."

She nodded and stepped back, unable to meet his eye. How many times had she wished he would come back into her life? And now that he was there, everything felt so complicated. Staving the urge to run like hell, she hurried to her car in shaky legs. Tears ran down her face freely, all the way to the grocery store, though she forced herself to stop on the way home.

She lay awake all night.

31

It took them a while to feel comfortable around each other, but one day things felt normal again, and Silvana, Jeanette, and Will fell into familiar rhythms. After a few months of co-working on the healing potion, Silvana felt comfortable enough to introduce Will to Conrad. They got along well enough, though they couldn't be more different.

Conrad was a gentleman and was especially nice after he found out Will had been dating someone seriously. He and Maggie had been together for almost a year, and Silvana found she liked Maggie. Even after the initial pang of jealousy she had no right to feel.

At least she had her friends with her, and she could work on magic with them as if no time had passed. Now that they were older, had more experience, and Will had kept up with his potion-making, they were actually making progress.

His mom, the always lovely Meredith Constantine, had cancer, and agreed to take their potions when treatments weren't working fast enough for her.

So far, it was working well, though none of the potions provided a cure. Funny how life worked.

One day, as they were finished preparing a knowing potion, which was the first time in years they had, Silvana told them that Conrad wanted her to stop making music.

"Why would anyone tell someone to stop making music?" Jeanette asked from where she was stirring the potion in her blackened cauldron.

They were in her apartment, around her tiny kitchen—Silvana had left the girls with Bonnie, Conrad's mother.

Tonight, they would record more of the music from the plants. So far, the healing potions fixed symptoms, but not the actual illness.

"He thinks I'm wasting my time." She pulverized dried leaves on a stone mortar.

"Don't you think it's about time you told him about your magical abilities?" Will asked.

Jeanette and Silvana stared at him. "That's not a good idea," they said in unison.

Will snapped his mouth shut.

"Don't give me that judgmental look, William Constantine." Silvana put down the pestle. "He thinks I should be home more."

"As if you're not home most of the time already?" Jeanette frowned deeply.

"I know," Silvana said as Will finished bottling the last of the potion. He listened in silence.

"Look, I say you tell him you need this time for yourself," Jeanette said. "We can do it here every time if it bothers him so much for you to play at home."

Silvana knew Jeanette was right, but she doubted either of her friends would understand how hard it was to get Conrad to compromise on anything. Once he got his mind of something, he made sure it happened.

Will, silent as he chopped a root, would never say out loud how much he thought Conrad Montgomery was a complete ass. He acted like a gentleman, but Will could see right through it.

"When we got married, he pushed me to play music. He even tried to convince me to change my major until I got pregnant with Roselyn and had to quit."

"And now this change?" Jeanette asked, but she had an inkling. As soon as she'd met him, Jeanette had her eye on Conrad, even when she didn't understand why she felt the way she did.

Conrad was generous, charming, successful, and well-liked. In that way that millionaires were liked because of what they could do for (and to) people.

"He's set in his ways," Silvana said, almost shyly. She didn't add that he was selfish, talked over her, ordered for her without asking her first, hired people to dress her. He'd even hired a personal trainer to help her lose weight only weeks after Julia was born because he wanted her to look good when he had functions. She was a jewel to him. Something to show off to make himself look good.

"Are you safe?" Will asked her, still not looking at her.

"I'm okay," she said, and she truly believed she was. Conrad was controlling and he could be an ass, but he had never put his hands on her. He was a good man, just a little self-involved. He loved the girls. That was all that mattered.

It didn't matter that she was unhappy, and that she'd long suspected he was cheating. Didn't matter at all.

But working around Will, she sometimes looked at him a little longer than was acceptable. She didn't want to—he was happy with Maggie. And she was committed to Conrad.

"What are you thinking, William?" she asked him when Jeanette disappeared to answer the phone. Even though they had fallen back into the same routine as before, there was still an aura of awkwardness when they were alone, right there, invisible. It seemed they couldn't just get rid of their past that easily.

He met her eyes and smiled softly. "I think you're incredible and your girls are lucky to have you."

Heat rose to her face. "Thank you."

They recorded as much as they could that night. However, the potion hadn't worked the way they wanted when Will gave it to his mom a few days later.

They hit a wall after that. When they could work, they did so at Jeanette's or Will's house outside the city. He had suitable instruments, and they had been recording the songs from the plants consistently. However, none of the potions worked as they intended them to.

They tried making that potion hundreds of times, found and sourced every single difficult ingredient, changed the order in which they added the ingredient to the cauldron. They stirred clockwise, counterclockwise, cut herbs, crushed them, dried and pulverized them. And nothing. When other simpler potions had somewhat worked, that this one didn't was enough to drive them nuts.

"I hate this," Jeanette huffed after the thousandth failed attempt. "Why isn't it working? We have tried it all."

"Except for making it during the full moon," Will said. "We have to make the knowing potion during the full moon. Why is this one different?"

"But we did try that, and it didn't work," Silvana muttered.

"Yes, but the time we tried during the full moon, we—"

"Added the ingredients in a different order." Jeanette sat up.

"And we didn't infuse the extracts with their own music," Will said, and it suddenly made so much sense to Silvana that she gasped.

"Say more of that."

"What if we make individual potions with each ingredient?" Will said. "Extracts, if you want to be nitpicky. Each extract gets infused with its own music first. Then we make the potion, using the infused extracts, but—"

"Oh my God, you're a genius!" Silvana said to Will, grabbed his face briefly, and missed how his eyes lit up when she touched him. The world paused, and it muffled, as if someone pressed a mute button. Panting, she cringed back and said, "If we infuse every extract with the music of its own plant, then infuse the potion we make with those extracts, but with the completed piece of music from all the plants..."

"That sounds like something we haven't tried yet and should." Jeanette tore her eyes away from Will. Though Silvana had not noticed that hopeful spark in his eye, she sure had. Interesting how life could repeat itself so easily.

"So now we have to wait until the next full moon to try again," Silvana said as they all stood up and got ready to leave for the night.

Will stood up and stretched, his t-shirt riding up his abdomen a little. Silvana averted her eyes and Jeanette also noticed that. She missed very little. She was going to have some tough conversations with her two best friends.

As it began getting dark out, rain clouds in the first soft stages of unloading on them, Will walked out to meet up with Maggie. Silvana left shortly after he did, as Jeanette's boyfriend, Arthur Williams, showed up for a date night.

Silvana arrived at her car, turned the ignition, and picked up the car phone Conrad had insisted on her having when it rang.

"Hi, Conrad," she said into the receiver. He was the only one with the number.

"Where are you? I got home, and you weren't here. The girls were upset, wondering where their mother is." He sounded so angry she had to swallow the anxiety that flashed through her.

"I'm so sorry. I just had a few errands to run." The lie slipped out easier than she was comfortable with.

"Let me guess," he said, something in his voice she couldn't decipher. "The music thing again? You and your friends are no longer kids, Silvana. It's about time you give up on whatever dream you have with the music."

She took in a shaky breath. She refused to let him ruin the elation from their discovery. They had worked so hard, and finally things were happening.

"I'm sorry, Conrad. I will be home soon."

When she got home, worried about a fight, she found the girls in bed, fed, the house clean, and Conrad waiting for her with roses and dinner in candlelight.

"What is this all about?" she asked, her brows tight. This was quite a change.

"I'm sorry for being a prick before." He spoke softly now, worlds away from the angry man who'd called her only a half an hour earlier. He kissed her cheek. "How is my lovely wife?"

She didn't move, just smiled. It felt tight.

"I'm fine." He didn't do things like these. Their intimacy had dwindled in the last year or two, and whenever he did this kind of thing, it was because he wanted something. It wasn't like he wasn't already sleeping with his twenty-year-old assistant. She didn't have to have concrete proof. She had seen the familiarity between him and his assistant one too many times. Silvana wasn't the most experienced woman, but she also wasn't an idiot.

"What's all this for?" She succeeded in not letting her suspicions show in her voice.

"I just wanted to surprise you." He pulled out a chair for her and she sat. The food sat under silver domed lids. "I just think we haven't spent a lot of time together lately, and I really wanted to spend time with you."

She gave him a small smile. Maybe she had been neglecting him. Maybe that was the problem. She was thinking about Will too much, and Conrad just felt lonely.

But what about the assistant?

She didn't have proof. Even if her gut screamed at her whenever she was near the younger woman.

Still, she dined with him, and made an effort to have a good time. They talked about his work and his wishes for the company, which was growing a lot more than projected. Not that it hadn't been wildly successful before. She could see his excitement as he spoke about it. It was like speaking to the Conrad she had met all those years ago at her college. The charming, sweet man who had paid for her tuition and her best friend's, even though she hadn't even finished her degree.

A few weeks after that night, she revealed to her friends that she was pregnant again. Another girl.

When she told them, her friends seemed happy. But Jeanette was concerned for her friend, more than she had ever been before, and Will... Well, he finally understood that Silvana would forever be lost to him. He loved Maggie—she was wonderful. He wanted to make her happy and could clearly see himself spend his life with her. But a part of him would always wonder what if.

Silvana stood in Jeanette's kitchen, bracing herself on the counter, nausea rolling around in her gut. Jeanette, who also had nausea rising, said nothing, and Will simply congratulated her. They worked on their magic, and their friendship never changed.

So, when three months later he announced he was also having a baby with Maggie, he was genuinely happy to be moving on at last. A part of him would always love Silvana, but he wanted to make things work with Maggie, and he would be a good father to his son.

They worked tirelessly. The potion didn't work every time, but they continued to try. They changed ingredients, swapped them for more potent plants, and continued their work. They'd started calling them the plant trials as a joke, because otherwise they'd lose their minds with the lack of progress.

Silvana took the grimoires home often, to work on them when she couldn't leave the house. Conrad still didn't like it, but Silvana didn't care. Silvana, Jeanette, and Will got together when they could, though it had to be more sporadic in those days when Jeanette finally announced her own pregnancy.

"Of course, all three of us are doing this together," Jeanette said. She'd had no morning sickness at all, which Silvana resented somewhat. "Maybe these three babies will be like we were growing up."

Will raised a glass of water he'd been drinking.

"Cheers to that."

32

Magic took a back seat again as Silvana became a mom for the third time. She had worked on the potion while heavily pregnant. She'd made it during solstices, equinoxes, in the wee hours of the morning, during eclipses—which had proved disastrous when Meredith took it and it made her deaf for six hours. She had blamed Silvana, of course, claiming she'd done it on purpose.

Old hag.

As Jeanette struggled through medical school, her baby Victoria would spend her days with Silvana, especially after Jeanette separated from her partner. Silvana had become the nanny of choice for everyone, and she loved having all the babies with her, including Will's son, Grey.

Sophia, Grey, and Victoria were three peas in a pod. Inseparable. It was adorable.

Silvana could see history repeating itself, at least partially, with those three and the way they loved each other from the time they were babies. Sophia, the oldest of the three, had put her hazel eyes on Victoria and Grey as brand-new babies, and she had been love-struck ever since.

Silvana did magic as the babies toddled around, and as things calmed down, and Jeanette finally became a doctor, Silvana continued to work on the cure.

Grey had a talent for music, was a prodigy at the piano, and Silvana taught him about music magic and the cool things it could do. He was a talented little boy. They still didn't know if he could do any magic, but that would come with time. He understood music, though, and Silvana took it upon herself to teach him everything she knew.

When Sophia turned eight, Silvana heard her speaking to a tiny cactus they'd planted together. It was in a little pot in the sunroom, as it was far too humid for it to survive outside. It was still getting too much water because Sophia insisted it was thirsty and watered it three times a day, despite Silvana's warnings that it would drown.

"Please don't die," Sophia whispered, and Silvana smiled. Her heart tugged as she watched her little girl speak to the plants. "Please, I wish you to be healthy again."

It was in that moment that Silvana saw the power in her daughter, something she had never seen before in any other witch. The cactus greened almost instantly, and as Sophia squealed in delight, Silvana swallowed a dry lump in her throat as one of her vines dried out on the other side of the room. Silvana went to it as it hung off the ceiling in its round pot. The vines became desiccated, some of the long branches turning into dust.

"Sophie darling," she whispered and held Sophia by her tiny shoulders, the little bones so fragile under her fingers.

"Mommy, I made it better, did you see? I made it all better."

"Yeah, baby," she said and bent at the waist to peer into Sophia's hazel eyes. "How did you do it, honey? Can you tell me how you did it?"

"I wished it, Mommy," Sophia said as if it was the most obvious thing in the world. "It was dying and I wished it got better and it did."

Silvana tried to swallow again, but her throat was too dry now. She hugged her little girl gently, so as not to scare her. Sophia was bright, and she saw more than people gave her credit for.

"It's very sweet for you to want to do that," Silvana whispered, unable to breathe deeply enough to speak any louder. Spots danced in front of her eyes.

Roselyn had a gentle brand of magic, all about empathy, so it was easier to deal with it. Julia had bursts of magic, had manifested telekinesis and broke a window trying to call a ball to her hand when she was about five. But Sophia and Amy had manifested nothing until now. This kind of magic wasn't common.

"Honey, there are some things I would like to teach you, okay?"

"What things?" Sophia's hazel eyes widened, already excited.

"About magic. I need you to promise me you won't make any wishes unless you ask mommy first, okay?"

"'kay," she said and went back to watching her little cactus with a dreamy expression.

Another thought occurred to her, and this one was scarier than the last.

"Have you told anyone about your wishes?"

"No."

"That's good." Silvana thanked the stars and promised she'd light a candle later in gratitude. "Don't tell anyone about it."

"How come?"

"Because it's a special thing between you and me. I can do magic too," she said, and waved her fingers and a little gust of air came out. It was a dumb trick, not really magic, but Sophia smiled anyway. She had lost a tooth, and the gap made her smile that much sweeter. "I will teach you everything."

"I already told Victoria, Grey, Julia, Roselyn, and Amy."

Oh, God. "That's okay," Silvana told her. "It's okay if they know, just don't tell anyone else. Ask them not to tell anyone else. Can you do that?"

"Okay." Sophia grinned, but took off running when Grey and Victoria came in from the garden. Silvana watched them from the window as they climbed a tree out back. It tugged at her heart to watch them. It was like seeing herself with Will and Jeanette when they were little, going up the branches to hear the music. But she worried about Sophia. She'd never heard her daughter say something like it before, and now she wondered how many wishes Sophia had already made. It wouldn't be a big deal if it wasn't for the way it worked. How it borrowed the life essence from the vines.

Amy had joined the game outside, while Julia sat on the swing with a flower in her hand.

Roselyn came to stand beside her by the window. She was a solemn child from the time she was a baby. She rarely cried or had outbursts, and as she grew, that quiet only grew with her. Conrad said it was eerie. If only he knew the things his daughter could do he wouldn't be saying that. She felt a calm wash over her when Roselyn took her hand. Her fingers felt so small and fragile in Silvana's. She looked down at her oldest daughter, her dark curls soft and glossy. At thirteen, Roselyn looked so much like Silvana's mom, except with lighter skin, that it made Silvana's heart hurt.

"You don't have to do that, honey," Silvana said, but held her daughter's hand tighter.

Roselyn looked up at her with eyes that were wiser than most adults.

"I know," she said, "but you looked worried."

Silvana tipped back Roselyn's face and kissed her between the brows, right where her little button nose met her forehead.

"You are my little sweetheart." She still worried that Roselyn would take on the responsibility of other people's feelings, which was never a good thing. But when a child had an empathic power, how did you teach them not to? Silvana didn't know what it was like to have that kind of power.

Roselyn smiled a little, but went outside shortly after. Something nagged at Silvana as she watched her oldest daughter sit on the swing with Julia.

"They're a lot like us, aren't they?" Will stepped beside her. He was dressed in a dark button-down with the sleeves rolled up to his elbows, gray slacks, and his hair, which he now wore much shorter than he ever had before, was slicked back. He almost didn't look like himself, and Silvana hated it.

"They are," she said, tearing her eyes away from him. She hadn't allowed herself to see him in that way for a long time, but sometimes, a girl was weak, and when her marriage was falling apart behind the scenes, it was easy to slip and let her eyes linger for a little too long. Conrad was definitely sleeping around, so it wasn't because of him that Silvana kept her distance. It was all because of Maggie, who Silvana had learned to love. Maggie, who knew about their work with magic and supported them like Silvana knew Conrad never would.

"Anything with the newest potion?" They had made a newer iteration of the potion for his mom, who had survived, miraculously. Or thanks to the potions they had been feeding her for years. None of them took away the cancer, but they had kept her alive, which was amazing in and of itself.

"Nothing yet. I'm hoping this is the one." He gave her a smile, but she looked away quickly. This was getting harder.

Silvana convinced herself that she was the only one with feelings because her marriage was ending. Because Conrad was absent, and he wasn't the most affectionate father. Because he had shoved her and it had dissolved the little love she had left for him.

She'd already dealt with a physically abusive father. She would not let Conrad do the same. It was easier to get her ducks in a row, given the extravagant gifts she got from Conrad, including houses, cars, and jewelry.

She just needed a little time.

33

Weeks later, Silvana sobbed all the way to Will's house. It rained as if the skies had opened, and it was miserably cold. She reached back and touched the tender spot on the back of her head. It pounded like a heartbeat.

The rain slicked down the windshield, wipers working double time. She would have gone to see Jeanette instead, but she was at the hospital.

Conrad had gone too far.

She wiped her face. Maybe she should have confronted him in a public place, or called Jeanette and Will to be there to support her. But what was she supposed to do when one of Conrad's mistresses sought her out with proof of their affair? Was she supposed to sit back and smile? She was sick of pretending that things were okay. They weren't okay.

She should have left a long time ago, even before she found out about his affairs. Now what? He had put his hands on her, and it would only get worse.

Music came softly through the speakers, and she focused on it. Music calmed her. She needed calm. She wouldn't be able to explain to the girls why she had been crying, and she couldn't worry them about this. They were with Conrad's mom, so Silvana was at least grateful they hadn't been home when everything went down.

When she arrived at Will's house, she had to sit in the car for a moment. She breathed deeply, counted her breaths until her heart slowed down.

She wore loose jeans, which Conrad hated. Said it made her look frumpy, which she resented. She had done everything for him. Going to the gym only a week or two after having her babies, keeping her hair straight because he needed her to look put-together and her curly hair was apparently offensive to him. She was sick of pretending to be someone she wasn't. Never speaking words in the language she was forgetting from lack of use. Refraining from cooking the foods her mother had cooked.

She'd forgotten her coat in her haste to get away from him, so she only wore a thin sweater she liked to wear around the house. Her hair, a pile on top of her head, was a little frizzy from the rain.

She wiped her face and went up to the house. Maggie opened the door and smiled, but her smile slipped away when she looked at Silvana's face.

"What happened?"

The house was alive with music, and though Maggie couldn't see it, Silvana did. The colors danced around as the piano played in the background, a song that was melancholy and sweet.

"Conrad..." She couldn't say another word. Her voice broke, and a sob tore through her. Maggie reached for her and pulled her into the house. They hugged at the door for a long time as Grey played in the background, oblivious to anything other than his music.

"What did he do?" Maggie asked as she pulled away.

"He slammed me against a wall."

Maggie's lips pressed together in anger. "Do you want me to call someone?"

Silvana shook her head, and it felt heavy as a sack of rice, the tender spot pounding.

Maggie nodded, but there were furious tears in her eyes. "Do what you have to do."

Silvana understood what Maggie meant, even though the words never left her mouth.

"He's up in the studio," she added, and Silvana moved forward and hugged her tightly. She had become a friend, someone who she could count on to love her daughters as her own, because Will loved them like that. That's the type of woman Maggie was.

Silvana went back out the door, headed toward the side of the house, through the garage, up the narrow set of stairs that led to Will's studio. She found him sitting in front of a desk with his mixing equipment, a pair of big headphones over his ears.

She watched him for a moment, his fingers busy on the console. She walked forward and put her hand on his shoulder. He turned and took off the headphones. His new reading glasses slipped down his nose, so he took them off too.

She couldn't contain the tears, and as soon as he was on his feet, she buried her face in his chest. His familiar scent set her off, and she sobbed even harder than before. He just held her, her quiet support throughout the years. When the tears stopped coming, she stepped back. Instant guilt ate at her because she wished so much that she had ended up with him instead. He would have never touched her like Conrad had. His hands would have always been gentle on her.

"What happened?" he asked when they were seated on the cold wooden floor, facing each other.

"I'm leaving Conrad," she said. His brows shot up, but he didn't ask why. His hair was fluffy, like it had just dried after a shower. "I have investments that have done well. I'll live in the house in the city his mother gifted me. It's rented now, but I will do whatever it takes. I have cars to my name and jewelry. That should be enough." She was rambling.

"What did he do?" Will asked quietly, his jaw tight.

"I confronted him about his affairs. He denied it, then begged me, then denied again, before he blamed me for sleeping with other women. Plural. When I told him I was done, he grabbed me and pushed me against the wall. I think I might have a minor concussion."

"And you drove here?" He looked as alarmed as he sounded.

"I was safe to drive." She hugged her arms around herself. "He said he was going to ruin me. That he'll take my girls from me."

"He can't do that."

"He can, Will. The Montgomery family is influential. They would convince a judge that I'm an unfit mother."

"You're not an unfit mother. He's barely ever home," he said angrily.

"I know that, but those things don't matter when you have money." She took a breath of courage. "I need your help to make this happen."

Will frowned.

"I need a potion," she whispered. "I need something I can use to make him do what I need to get out of this without losing my kids."

He opened his mouth to speak, but she held up her hand.

"I know what you're going to say," she interrupted him. "That it's immoral and that I should never use magic for these kinds of purposes, but if not this, then what? What is magic good for if we can't even find a cure for breast cancer?"

"My mom's been doing well," he told her.

"And I'm glad, but we haven't fixed her. It's not doing anything. The magic doesn't work." She bit her lip. "If we don't do this, I will stay trapped. I can't do this anymore, Will. He's gotten violent. How long until it escalates?" Her lips trembled. "I have to leave. I'm scared. He terrifies me. All I want is for him to let me go, and to let my girls stay with me, nothing more."

He sighed. "I'll do anything you need; you know that."

She almost sobbed in relief, as if she hadn't already known he was on her side.

"We'll need to wait until the next full moon," he said. "Meanwhile, we will get ingredients and we will write the music we need."

She nodded. "Thank you."

He walked her outside and hugged her as they stood by her car.

"Everything's going to be okay," he said, and she believed him. She would believe anything Will ever said to her. "Meanwhile, stay safe there."

"I will. All it takes is stroking his ego for a couple of weeks until we can make the potion."

"Call me when you get home." He stepped away from the car as she entered it. "So I know you're safe."

"I'll write you a note." She turned on the car. "I'll put everything under the floorboard, as we have everything else. You know the one."

He nodded, a glint in his eye.

She drove away shortly after and went home to find a contrite Conrad crying on their bed. She acted surprised, sat next to him even though all she wanted was to run away from him as fast as she could. He begged for her forgiveness, and thinking of her girls, she told him she'd forgive him if he gave her some time to process things. She didn't want to overplay her hand. Conrad was an ass, but he was smart.

For the next week, he doted on her, though she didn't let him touch her, and she played her dangerous game as if she had been born for it. Even more so when Roselyn was diagnosed only a week after that, and Silvana saw her world begin to crumble.

34

Roselyn seemed fine, even though her cancer was aggressive. It was still early, so chances were she would respond well to treatment.

Silvana hadn't fallen apart for two reasons.

One, her daughters needed her. She had to be strong for them because they didn't have anyone else to look to, really.

Two, Will and Jeanette. They were her rock, especially when Conrad was no help. All he did was bark orders at doctors, as if they could actually fix Roselyn's illness and refused to. He was so on edge that being around him sent Silvana into a panic.

But she didn't have time to panic. She didn't have time to give to anyone other than her little girls, though she would gladly stay with Conrad for the rest of her days, if her Roselyn was okay.

Silvana, Will, and Jeanette made the healing potion they gave to Meredith. It would help Roselyn, especially when she began treatments and became sick. If this was the time to find a cure, then they would do what they could to make sure it happened. Maggie came to the house often, Grey in tow, to help care for the kids. She was a gem, and Silvana didn't know what she would do without her.

"What are we missing?" Silvana asked one afternoon as they finished recording. "Why can't we make a cure?"

Jeanette, who had given it a lot of thought, said, "Maybe because cancer is too complicated for anything to work definitively." Will and Silvana looked at her. "I know this is not what you want to hear, Silvana, but even chemotherapy doesn't always work."

Silvana knew she was right, but she also knew they were too close to give up now. She said that to Jeanette, who agreed.

"I didn't say that to hurt you, Sil."

"I know you didn't, Jeanette. At least the potion prolongs life somehow, even if it doesn't kill the cancer. We're so close."

"Yes, but you still have to get her into treatment," Jeanette said with her best doctor voice. "You know you have to do that too, right?"

"And what if it doesn't work?" Silvana asked, her voice taking an edge of desperation. Her mind was on her mom all those years ago. The aggressive chemotherapy that had left her bald and sick, for her to die anyway. Now her baby girl was going to have to do it, and Silvana could not handle it. "What if it doesn't work?"

"Silvana, look at me," Will said. There was worry in his eyes, but also sympathy. She hated it. She hated all of this. "Roselyn's going to be fine."

"Is she?" Silvana ran her hands over her unruly hair. "That's what you said when it was my mom, and she died anyway. I can't lose my daughter, Will. I won't lose my daughter."

She repeated it over and over, every time louder than the last, until she was sobbing in Will and Jeanette's embrace.

Her cat, one she had found wandering outside, a golden Norwegian she'd called Sunshine, meowed at her from the floor, as if it knew. She wanted to pick her up, but Silvana couldn't move from where her friends held her up as she cried.

"What do I do?" she sobbed. They had tried for so long, had tried everything.

Sometimes someone could have the best of intentions, and still not be able to help. Silvana couldn't help. Meredith would die of cancer when her time came, potion or no. Roselyn would have to have chemotherapy, hoping to kill the cancerous cells that made her blood into a poison.

"Treatment. We listen to the doctors," Jeanette said, and Silvana nodded, even as fresh tears slid down her face.

000

DOWNSTAIRS, SOPHIA, JULIA, GREY, AND VICTORIA SAT under the piano. Amy was in her room, playing with Roselyn, oblivious to the turmoil the other children were dealing with. Julia was crying softly, but she had the heels of her hands pressed to her eyes, as if she could stop the tears from falling that way.

Sophia didn't cry because Julia was already crying, and she didn't want to make it worse. Julia had a hard time seeing other people cry. Sophia looked at Grey instead. He had pretty brown eyes that looked like the smoothest velvet, and he sat across from her with his knees close to his body, as she did.

"Do you think Roselyn is going to die?" Victoria asked, her curls bouncing around her as she spoke.

Julia sobbed harder.

"No," Sophia said with finality.

"I don't want Roselyn to die," Julia sobbed, her forehead now on her knees.

"I can make it better," Sophia told them, keeping her voice low so no one else heard them. "I'm going to make a wish."

Julia lifted her head, her eyes red and puffy and wide. "No, Mommy said you can't."

"I know, but I can help Roselyn," Sophia argued. "Didn't you hear what they said upstairs? Roselyn has poison in her blood. She will die if I don't do it."

Julia's chin trembled.

"Your mom did say you shouldn't, Sophia," Grey said.

"I don't want Roselyn to die," Sophia protested, her eyes filling because she would have thought that Grey and Julia would understand and would want her to.

She could make things better. She could save Roselyn, and her mom wouldn't be so sad anymore. Things would be better.

"I'm going to do it," Sophia whispered.

"You can't," Julia cried and crawled out from under the piano. "I'm going to tell Mom."

Sophia didn't move as Julia ran off. Instead, she closed her eyes, and resolute, she spoke the words.

When Silvana rushed downstairs, her heart in her mouth, she found Sophia alone under the piano, and knew it was too late.

°°°

THEY CLEARED ROSELYN OF CANCER THAT SAME WEEK. IT baffled the doctors, and many considered that perhaps they'd diagnosed her incorrectly. While it relieved Silvana that her daughter was okay, a part of her constantly expected something terrible to happen. She had seen how Sophia's powers worked, and she was going to have to do things she wasn't proud of.

She called Jeanette first, but Jeanette didn't answer, probably tired from her rounds. She wrote to Will, as she was wary of using the phone to call him anymore. Conrad had become jealous, even though Silvana never gave him reasons to be. Nothing had ever happened between her and Will since she married Conrad, and nothing would. Her therapist said it was projection, due to his own indiscretions.

When Will ported straight to the attic that night, he helped her make the potion that would magnify her powers for charms. She'd written the music already. He wasn't happy about it, and looked toward the door often, aware of Conrad's ridiculous jealousy.

"Are you sure you want to do this?" Will whispered. "Sophia should be trained, not bound."

"I've tried training her, Will. She wished for Roselyn to get better, and it worked. What'll happen next?"

He looked like he wanted to say more, but Silvana stopped him.

"I can't take any chances. This power is dangerous, Will. Something that works this instantly and borrows energy from other things to work... Imagine what it could do. Imagine what someone would do to use my daughter for their own perverse wishes. What will her saving Roselyn do?"

Silvana thought of Conrad finding out, and she chilled.

She went to the window, where she kept a table. Her long skirt swished around her ankles, and her hair was loose, a mass of curls she hadn't washed in a month. The large tank had a light shining into it to keep the snake warm. It was the only light in the room, save for a few candles Will had lit. The snake was a beautiful creature, so green, so pure, and it wrapped itself around Silvana's hand when she lifted it.

Silvana didn't want to hurt it, but she needed a blood sacrifice. It wasn't magic she had done before, as it was dark. Taking the life of a creature for magic went against everything Silvana believed in. But she had to protect her daughter.

She went to the scarred table in the center of the room, which she used to make her potions. The bejweled knife gleamed as she raised it.

Will looked away, pale.

"I'm so sorry," she whispered wetly when she did it, her tears blurring her vision. She put the body aside, and the blood went into her cauldron, along with the other potions and herbs on top.

Will helped her, quiet, and when it was done, he ran his hands over his face.

"Think about this, Sil," he pleaded.

"I already did."

"You already did what?"

Conrad's voice made them both jump. Conrad's eyes widened in horror as he saw the cauldron, the dead snake, the candles. "What the hell is going on here?"

Frozen to the spot, Silvana could only stare. Conrad was in his pajamas, and his face was angrier than she had ever seen it.

"I knew it," he said.

Silvana shook her head, but she couldn't say a word.

"And you were so indignant when I did the same thing you've been doing," Conrad spat, saliva spraying everywhere.

"Are you drunk?" Will asked, disgusted.

"Don't you talk to me!" Conrad came closer to Will, his face so close, their noses almost touched. Will didn't back down, and Silvana didn't think. She jumped between them.

"Conrad, you don't know what you're saying."

"I don't know what I'm saying? You think I don't know you want to leave me?" He scrunched up his face. "Are you leaving me for him? Is that what this is about?"

"I'm married, asshole," Will snapped. "We're not all like you."

Conrad's face became an ugly mask of anger, and he pushed Silvana aside. She fell hard on her side and watched with growing horror as Conrad punched Will straight in the nose.

"Please, stop!" She cried out.

But Conrad didn't stop. He jumped on top of Will, and they fell to the ground. Will rolled them over and punched Conrad right back with a force that took Silvana by surprise. There was so much rage in the way Will smacked his fist into Conrad's face.

"Will, stop!" Silvana pulled him from Conrad, and he stumbled back. "It's not worth it. Please, we have to get out of here."

"I knew you were fucking him." Conrad spat blood. It ran down his chin. "You two think I'm stupid. You think I don't see it. How long has this been going on?"

"You know fully well I have never stepped out on you, Conrad." Her voice became hard. She was sick of being accused of doing things she'd never done. "You, on the other hand, did. With several women. Not to mention your physical abuse. This has nothing to do with Will."

Conrad's face smoothed. It was eerie the way he shut it off and stood. There was an enormous bruise forming under his eye.

"You can't stand there and accuse me of doing things I never did."

Conrad stared at her, then chuckled. "It's so pathetic. You think I didn't notice that you're in love with him?" His words were laced with poison. Beside her, Will stiffened. "Why do you think I was with other people? It was your fault. You pushed me to it. You did this to us because you couldn't love me the way you loved him."

Something snapped inside her. She was like a rubber band pulled to its limit. It split her in half, smacked her in the gut, and she stalked forward until she was in front of him.

"You have some nerve," she said, her heart beating too fast. She was sure she was about to have a panic attack. "You have been sleeping with that twenty-year-old assistant of yours, plus many others, and you have the balls to accuse me of cheating with my best friend?"

"Don't try doing that—"

"What? Calling you out on your bullshit?" She stepped a little closer, though her senses went off with bright alarm bells. "You're trying to make this about me, but this is not about me, and it is not about Will. This is about you and your inability to think of anyone other than yourself."

He opened his mouth, closed it, then opened it again, like a fish out of water.

"Kylie was just a gold-digger," he said weakly. "She got to me. I don't know how she did it."

"Please, spare me the details," she told him, crossing her arms. "I'm done."

"Silvana, stop!" Conrad snapped. "I will not let you do this to me." He stalked forward, as if to grab her, and instantly terrified, Silvana jumped back, but Will was faster. He raised his hands, and Conrad flew back in the air and smacked against the bed frame on the far wall.

Conrad got up in a daze. His face was crimson with rage and fear, and before Silvana could react, Conrad pulled out a shiny silver gun from his pocket and pointed it at Will. His hand was shaking so much Silvana let out a sob. Will froze.

"How did you do that?" Conrad's eyes were wide, too wide, and he was deathly pale as he looked around the attic. "Oh, my God. Oh, my God. Stay back!" He brandished the gun wildly, then pointed it back at Will. "What the hell did you do? How did you do it?"

Silvana moved forward, her hands in front of her.

"Conrad, please, put away the gun," she cried. He pointed it at her, then back at Will.

"How did you do it?" Conrad asked again, spit running down his face. "You did a something to me! What did you do?"

"Put down the gun, Conrad," Will said and stepped forward as Conrad pointed the gun at Silvana.

That eerie calm set again, and all traces of emotion left Conrad's face. He sniffled. "I won't let you ruin me."

Silvana screamed as the shot rang out. She expected a sharp pain, heat, something, but there was nothing. When Will collapsed at her feet, the air thickened. Time slowed down, and she heard herself scream again. She threw herself over him, deaf, blind, his blood on her.

A whirring rushed past her ears.

"What did you do? What did you do?" she screamed at Conrad repeatedly as her hands tried to stop the flow of blood from Will's shoulder.

It was just his shoulder. It couldn't be that bad. The thoughts moved through her head feverishly.

"You made me," Conrad said and stood frozen in place, watching her. "You made me."

Will was shocked, his mouth open, his eyes glassy and staring into hers. Silvana looked up at Conrad, crying hysterically. He raised the gun again, pointed it at her this time.

She didn't feel the shot.

Conrad disappeared through the door, his footsteps rushed and loud as he went downstairs.

Silvana fell. She couldn't hear anything. She could only see Will, his eyes that were neither brown nor green boring into hers. He reached for her hand, and something cold went into her palm. She recognized it as the potion they had just made. She swallowed it, felt the surge of power, and she spoke the spell. Her voice broke as she finished, and the bottle fell from her hand and rolled away on the floor. A light shone from inside Silvana. It was dim at first, but it intensified as the seconds ticked by.

"Sil..." Will's voice gurgled. Their hands gripped tightly together, they whispered the spell. Her other hand went to his face as she allowed herself to touch him in the way she hadn't allowed herself to touch him since they were two seventeen-year-olds in love. When they had planned to be together forever.

Her breath shuddered out of her as she crawled closer, even as her vision clouded and darkened. Even as the pain in her stomach became so intense, it left her gasping for breath.

I'll love you until the day I die...

And when his breath stilled, Silvana howled. It tore through her like a wave, everything inside her clamoring for him.

Power exploded from her body in a column of light that reached for the heavens and beyond. It enveloped her and Will in its warmth, and as she drifted, she thought of her girls, Jeanette, Maggie, and Grey, and whispered a spell of protection.

She sobbed as she held on to Will's hand, brought it up to her dry lips, and kissed his skin one last time.

Their blood mingled together, and she looked into his empty eyes. His beautiful eyes that had always said so much, had held so much love for her. Hers were heavy now, and she felt pain no more as she closed them, and fell asleep.

35

The silence was too loud. It made her ears ring unpleasantly. Sophia sat on the floor with tears rolling down her cheeks. She did not move as her hands hovered over the last journal; the pages lay still now. Jeanette walked closer and her mouth was moving, but Sophia couldn't hear anything. She sensed Grey beside her, but she couldn't look at him. She could never face him again after everything they now knew.

After everything she suspected. Her mother's journals had been detailed, but cut short at the end, and her heart pounded and hurt at once.

"Darling," Jeanette whispered, and took the journal away from her.

Sophia let her hands fall to her lap, boneless. She was trembling all over. Jeanette whispered something else Sophia couldn't make out. She looked concerned, her green eyes glassy and sparkling with tears.

"Talk to me," Jeanette said.

Sophia opened her mouth to talk, but only a pathetic whimper came out, and fresh tears fell down her face as if someone had opened a faucet. Her face was slack, her mouth slightly open as she breathed through it.

A hand took hers and she looked down to see it was Grey's. She gripped his fingers tightly with a sob, then looked up at him. His eyes were wet, too. His stricken expression hit her like a brick to the head. He was pale, his lips set in a grim line, and finally, she let out a shuddering sob.

There was so much she wanted to say, but the words wouldn't come, and she just sat there sobbing. Lucas brought them both tea and set it in front of them.

Grey reached for her as Jeanette left the room with Lucas, and Sophia climbed onto his lap and clung to him. The crack that had appeared in her heart spread. She didn't deserve it. She didn't deserve his comfort and his arms around her, trying to make her feel better after all of that. Not when she had caused so much suffering. When her father had... She stopped the train of thought. Panic shot through her, and she breathed too quickly. Spots danced in front of her, and she couldn't catch her breath. Grey took her face in his hands.

"Sophia, look at me," he said, his deep voice burying itself inside her heart. "Look at me."

She did. His wet eyes were serene. Sad, but steady, and she found calm in them.

"I'm sorry," she said, and didn't recognize her own voice. She didn't know what she was apologizing for, the wish she'd made that caused all this chaos and pain, or that her father had killed his. Her dad was a murderer. He killed her mom and Will Constantine in a jealous rage.

He'd lied their entire life about a mother they'd thought had abandoned them. But he hadn't counted on magical journals. Sophia was both grateful for them, and hated that they existed.

Grey was quiet, obviously thinking the same thing she was. How would they ever get past this? How could they live after this? She suddenly knew too much, too fast, and she hated it. She didn't want to know any of it, wished that she could go back to knowing nothing. Blissfully ignorant to everything. She would rather think her mom had tried to run off with her lover. She would rather go back to not understanding why she heard random music everywhere. Back to singing her songs at her club and enjoying the colors on her own. Not this.

She'd wished for her sister to live and caused another disease. One that had killed Roselyn, anyway. She remembered how doctors had been baffled when Roselyn became ill again, this time with an illness they had no name for, when before Roselyn had cancer and it had disappeared out of nowhere. It had been the void. Roselyn had just been too young and fragile to carry the disease, and it killed her swiftly. Had Sophia not done anything, maybe Roselyn would have been alive.

And her mom and Will.

She pushed away from Grey. Her body had turned cold. It was as if someone dumped a bucket of ice water over her head, and she shook with the adrenaline of it all.

But she wasn't crying now.

"It's still a full moon," she said, her voice hollow. She didn't sound like herself. It was as if something had broken inside her, and she was different now. She headed to the kitchen before Grey reacted and found all the ingredients he used to make the potion for Julia and Helena. He'd been so close all his life, and now they knew what he needed to make it work for the void.

She didn't stand idly to watch him do it. She was in a trance, her movements sure, but inexpert, as she helped him make the extracts. He played all the music on his computer, using a program where he could play all the instruments. The knowing potion facilitated a perfect pitch, and they made the healing potion he had been making all along. The one that just needed a boost of music magic to work.

Once Grey had bottled the potion, Sophia remained frozen in place. Shock wouldn't leave her body that easily. How much had she done to hurt others? The witches who had died, the other non-magical humans, Julia, Helena, and the people Grey had been forced to assist in death. Victoria and Thomas. Even Aric.

Grey. She had hurt him, too.

Her chest was so tight she could barely breathe, and she prayed to whoever listened that it worked. That if she hadn't been able to save Roselyn, she could at least save Julia and Helena.

In the wee hours of the morning, the potion finished, she picked up a glowing vial.

"I want to see my sister."

Grey stepped forward, but Sophia turned to Lucas instead. Her heart squeezed painfully, but she couldn't face him anymore. Not tonight. Maybe not ever.

Lucas looked toward Grey, nodded once, and took her arm. They disappeared into thin air.

Sophia recalled the recipe she had seen for the porting potion, but infused with music to be much more potent. She made a mental note to remind Grey about it.

They reappeared straight into Julia's room at the hospital. She looked the same as when Sophia had seen her last. When was that? Days... months ago. She had lost all sense of time.

It was quiet and dark, and Amy snoozed on the bed under a window. She was snuggled in a comforter that looked a lot like one of Sophia's, and her snores were soft.

Magic still buzzed inside her, so she used it as an anchor. It would keep her sane until she could get a hold of herself. Her eyes fell on Julia.

"Sophia?" Amy sat up on the bed and blinked her bleary eyes. "What are you doing here?" Her eyes slid to Lucas, and she got on her feet. "What's going on?"

As Sophia looked at her sister, it hit her how much Amy had missed at such a young age. She barely remembered their mom, and that was most likely because of Sophia.

"I brought something that will help her," Sophia whispered, brought out the potion from her pocket, and showed Amy.

Amy's brows twitched, but she didn't look uncomfortable, and Sophia wondered if Amy had remembered something too. Maybe the spell was completely broken now, for everyone involved.

"What is it?" Amy asked.

Sophia looked down at the potion, which was still glowing brightly.

"It's a medicine," Sophia said. "A powerful extract."

Amy's eyes were wary, but she nodded and went to Julia's side.

"She hasn't woken up at all."

"May I?" Lucas murmured, and Sophia gestured with her shaky hand, to go ahead.

His long fingers gentle, he touched Julia's forehead and closed his eyes. Then, his hands hovered over her body, and Julia's eyes opened slowly.

"There you are," Sophia said with a trembling voice. All the guilt hit her at once. Poor Julia, having to work so hard to keep everyone happy and cared for, and she never had to do that. It was all Sophia's fault. Amy and Lucas helped Julia sit up, Lucas using his body to keep her up.

"What's going on?" Julia looked and sounded so weak, Sophia could have folded right then. But she didn't. She didn't have time to break down yet; there was too much to do still. She moved forward silently as Lucas held Julia up in a sitting position.

When she took off the lid from the bottle, the sweet scent hit her nostrils, and she heard the music loud and clear. She could swear that the little mist coming from the top had color to it, like when Grey had played the infusing song. She handed the crystal bottle to Julia, who took it without hesitation.

"A potion?" she asked.

Sophia nodded.

"Will it cure me?" Julia mumbled weakly.

"We hope so," Lucas said, and Julia looked over at him briefly before she drank it in one go.

As soon as Julia swallowed, she began glowing softly. It lasted only thirty seconds, but when the glow was gone, Julia sighed deeply, as if she hadn't been able to breathe before.

"How do you feel?" Amy asked, pale from what she was watching happen.

Julia yawned. "Tired," she said.

Amy placed her hand on Julia's forehead.

"The fever's gone," she said, awe in her voice. "She's been burning up all day."

Julia was already snoring and hearing the sound resonated so far inside Sophia that tears filled her eyes. This time with relief. Lucas looked down at Julia gently, then stepped to the door while Amy hugged Sophia tightly.

"I think it worked," Sophia whispered, clinging on to Amy. She had never loved her sisters more than at that moment. "But call me if anything happens."

Would she have been close to Roselyn, too?

She forced herself to not think about it, pushing that shame deep, so deep where the light couldn't reach it. Where she could ignore it better.

"I don't know what that was, but she's been barely breathing for hours," Amy said, her voice muffled. "Thank you." She said it to Lucas, who only nodded.

"Listen to me, Amy," Sophia said to her sister. "First thing tomorrow, when Julia gets released, I want you to go to my house."

Amy frowned. "Okay." She wanted to say more, but Sophia stopped her.

"I don't have a lot of time to explain yet, but I will as soon as I can," Sophia told her in a quiet tone. "Please."

Amy nodded, still frowning.

"I have to go."

She and Lucas stepped out of the room, into an empty room next to Julia's.

"I need you to do me a favor," she said to him.

"Anything."

"I need a potion that can help me reverse a spell."

"I have something that can magnify any spell you make. But you have to be specific. Spells can't be too vague or they'll backfire."

Sophia wondered if that's what had happened with her mom. If in her haste to protect her and her sisters, she had said the spell without thinking of the loopholes in the magic. Was that also how Sophia's magic worked?

She nodded at Lucas.

"I'll acquire it and bring it to you."

He did so the following day. Sophia had slept in her own bed. She couldn't fathom looking him in the eye.

Besides, there was something she needed to do before she could think of ever talking to Grey again. Before she could make reparations of some kind, though she didn't know what that would look like.

Sophia was going to pay her father a visit, and in her pocket, she carried a special potion, acquired by Lucas for her. Grey and Lucas had qualms about using magic to take away someone's free will, but she did not.

But before she did that, she wanted one more confirmation, so she ported to Maggie Constantine's house early the next morning.

She went alone. Using the potion by herself for the first time should have given her anxiety, but it didn't. She needed to have this conversation with Maggie alone.

Her sweatpants were baggy and comfortable, and she'd had the presence to wear a coat this time. She ignored her phone when it rang.

Maggie opened the door and didn't seem surprised to see Sophia there.

"Come on in."

They headed to the kitchen, where Maggie made coffee. Sophia didn't touch hers.

"What can I do for you, Sophia Candela?"

The name choked her up, so Sophia cleared her throat. There was no time for crying yet. That would happen later, when she was done rectifying her mistakes as well as she could.

"I have to ask you about my mom."

Maggie's brows raised. "What do you want to know?"

"What was your relationship like?"

"A little strained at first, given that she was in love with Will."

Sophia's heart sank, but Maggie continued.

"Yes, I knew. It was hard not to see it." Maggie wrapped her hands around her mug. "Will and I had been dating a few months when Silvana came back into his life. You should have seen his face when he ran into her the first time."

"How did that make you feel?"

"Worried at first. He was too excited. It was obvious then that he loved her and it became more obvious as time passed and they spent more time together."

Sophia bit her lip to keep it from trembling.

"I know what you're thinking, Sophia." Sophia's eyes snapped up to Maggie's. "But I trusted Will, and maybe that made me seem stupid, but I also trusted Silvana. I spent enough time around her to see her character. I never believed that they would run away together and leave their kids behind. Your mother loved you. I just don't understand the rest of it."

Despite trying not to, Sophia's eyes filled. Maggie was lucid, but Sophia didn't know how.

"You look so much like her."

Sophia nodded. "I get that a lot."

All the years of anger, thinking her mother had tried to abandon her, came rushing back. She would have to let Grey explain to his mother what happened to Will. Sophia didn't have the guts to do it herself. The truth of what her father had done would come out soon, and Maggie would surely hate her then, and wouldn't want her only son mingling with her.

After Maggie's, Sophia took a different potion before she ported to Aric's apartment in the city. It was unprotected, so she went straight into his living room. She found him on the couch, in his boxers. He looked terrible, as if he hadn't slept in a while. Despite being a shitty boyfriend to her, he didn't deserve this either.

"I'm sorry, Aric," she whispered. He didn't move.

She took the amplifying potion Lucas had gotten her.

"A wish inadvertently spoken took another's love away. Return Aric's love whence it came." Aric glowed, but only for a split moment. She ported out right away.

36

Sophia had done as she'd promised herself she would. The meeting with her father was the hardest, even in her resolution to get him to confess to what he'd done. She'd been wrong about Grey opposing it. He wanted justice for his father

The day she'd appeared at her father's house, she had been calm, as if she was living on a normal Tuesday. It had been mid-afternoon. Easy to offer a drink in which she could slip the potion. It had been easy after that. Every question she'd asked had confirmed his jealousy, his anger at feeling like he would be humiliated in front of the society pages.

Disgusted, Sophia could only listen to him confirm what he'd done, and when he was done, she commanded him to confess his crime to the police, and turn himself in. He did. She'd made sure he made it there. His lawyer was in the premises quicker than Sophia could blink.

There would be a trial, but Sophia was afraid that her father would get out of it due to his influence. Confessing would make it harder, but was there something money couldn't buy?

Sophia would not go to the trial, and she ordered herself not to care.

Good riddance.

But even in that anger, she called a therapist anyway, because she knew she'd need it.

Now, she had spent most of her time at home, burrowed into her bed. She only peeled herself out of bed to go to therapy. Julia and Amy were staying with her, and occasionally, Victoria and Helena too. The cure had worked. Helena looked better than ever, and reported no symptoms at all. Julia too, but she looked worse for wear still. Sophia knew that wasn't about the void, though.

Julia was dealing with many layers of what had happened, including her separation from Harold, and the sudden disappearance of life-long friends who now couldn't be associated with them. Sophia couldn't care less, but Julia lived for that approval.

Meanwhile, Sophia's life felt more silent than it ever had. Even her plants seemed sad.

She missed Grey.

Avoiding had both been the best and the worst thing she could have done. He'd called, and she'd tried to talk to him, but her guilt threatened to consume her. She couldn't bear the thought of seeing him, look him in the eye, and pretend like it hadn't happened. What her father had done was unforgivable. Surely, they couldn't make it work after this.

It certainly hadn't felt like they could when she got home after making her dad confess, and sat in the dark garage, her body shaking with her uncontrollable sobs. She'd cried Grey's name, her mom's. Had begged for forgiveness to anyone listening. And that terrible grief had remained with her since, as she avoided Grey's texts.

Restless, she got out of bed, taking the comforter with her. She found Julia sitting on her favorite windowsill, an unlit joint between her fingers. She looked so small and pale, her hair greasy and unkempt. So unlike Julia, it scared Sophia.

"Hey," she whispered and Julia barely acknowledged her. "What's up?"

Cold air came in through the open window as Julia lifted a silver lighter and touched the tip of the joint with the fire. A long drag, and Julia turned to Sophia.

"Remember my friend Kate?" she asked Sophia, who assented as she took the joint and brought it to her lips. "Well, come to find out she's getting a divorce."

"Must be in the air," Sophia grimaced.

"She was cheating on her spouse," Julia continued. "With mine."

Sophia choked. "Excuse me?"

"Kate was fucking Harold all along."

"My God," she whispered. How could any of this get any worse? "I'm so sorry."

Julia accepted the hug, but pulled away quickly.

"You think it's bad, and then it gets worse." Another drag, and Julia swung her feet out the side of the house, staring up at the half moon. Sophia took that as her queue to go back to the room, where she found the screen of her phone lit up with messages.

The first ones were from Victoria, whose relationship with Thomas had repaired itself as she had wished it. Sophia also hadn't heard from Aric since.

> VICTORIA: EVERYTHING GOING GREAT AT THE
> CLUB. I HOPE YOU'RE GETTING SOME REST.
> TEXT ME LATER. HEARD FROM GREY YET?

Sophia texted that she hadn't, then realized she had messages from him waiting.

> GREY: I MISS YOU.

She called him. He answered after the first ring, but stayed quiet. They'd done this before today.

"I really wanted to hear your voice," she whispered.

"Me too. Sophia come over and let's talk about this, please."

"I just need more time." She gripped her phone so tightly her fingers hurt.

His sigh was long and miserable. How long would it take for him to get sick of waiting? It had only been two weeks, though.

"I know," he murmured. He sounded miserable. She hoped he wasn't alone.

"I'm so sorry."

The silence extended. She'd made a mistake calling him. It would have been better to let him get used to the distance, so he could move on. He deserved to move on. Her eyes filled with hot tears, her nose plugging instantly.

"I'm also here." His voice was so sad, she convulsed with horrible, quiet sobs. "Don't let this define us."

"I don't know how to do that."

"Please, just think about it."

She hung up.

When Sophia fell asleep, she dreamt of nothing.

37

Time passed, and Grey didn't hear from Sophia again. He couldn't sleep, barely ate, and his work took a hit. He'd turned down several projects, unable to put his mind into it.

After a while of moping around, Lucas showed up at his house with two six packs of beer, dressed in his typical slacks, button-down, and suspenders. He found Grey sitting on the porch, looking out at the water, an unkempt beard on his face, and looking gaunt.

Lucas took a seat next to Grey.

"You'll have to shower at some point," Lucas said, and earned a side glance.

"Who says I haven't showered?"

"The greasy hair is a dead giveaway."

Grey sniffed. He wished he cared, but it was hard to when depression had hit him like it had. Not only because of finding out Conrad Montgomery had murdered his dad, but because he couldn't see Sophia. Because of course she was punishing herself for what her father had done.

"Want to talk about it?" Lucas popped open a beer.

"Why when you can just use your powers on me?" Grey picked up a beer too, drowned half of it in one go. He hadn't eaten enough to be drinking, so it would not end well for him.

"I'm not using any empathy on you," Lucas said. "I'm simply being a good therapist."

Grey finished his beer. He felt the effects quickly and welcomed it.

"I don't know what to say."

"Start by telling me how you feel."

"A little drunk."

"That's pathetic." Lucas opened a second bottle.

"Yeah, well, I'm pathetic right now."

"You're hurt. That's not pathetic."

Grey looked out at the water. It was a beautiful day. He wished he felt better, so he could enjoy it. When you felt like shit, it was nice when the weather cooperated, but that never happened.

"It sucks feeling like this."

"I know." Lucas took a pull from his bottle. "I can't say I relate to your exact circumstances, but I can imagine."

"What can I do to feel better?" He was desperate to feel better. Like a human.

"Swim in it for a while," Lucas said.

"That's stupid." He'd been swimming in it for two weeks straight.

"Works, though."

Grey's chest gave a spasm that felt like a laugh would have if he still did that.

"You can't control the circumstances of your life," Lucas said, "and sometimes all you can do is feel sad. There's nothing wrong with that. But remember, there's a difference between suffering and pain. One is inevitable; the other's unnecessary."

Grey looked fully at his friend.

"Maybe you *are* good at your job."

"You're the only one who ever doubted it."

Grey allowed himself a small smile. "Never have."

Grey saw Lucas every single day for the following week, in a therapy setting (or whatever Lucas liked to call it), and by the third week, he started feeling a little more like himself. He missed Sophia every day—he didn't think that would ever go away. He just hoped he got to see her again, touch her skin, kiss her lips. So he threw himself into his music, and wrote songs, dozens of them. All with her in mind.

°°°

WHEN SOPHIA OPENED THE DOOR, HELENA LEANED HER HEAD and did a weird cringing smile.

"Oh honey," she said and stepped into the house.

"Everything okay at the club?" Sophia hadn't been there for weeks. Every time she went, she became overwhelmed and ended up crying in the office.

"Excellent." Helena turned to her. "That's not why I'm here."

Sophia had an idea why Helena was visiting so suddenly. She looked healthy and much more cheerful than she ever had. Not that she hadn't been cheerful before, it was just more noticeable now.

"I'm here to talk about Grey," Helena said.

"Oh, thank God." Julia came out of the kitchen, where she was attempting to bake bread. She'd ruined four loaves so far. "I've tried talking to her. Maybe you can help her see reason." Julia's short hair was pinned back from her face. She was skinny, paler than she'd ever been, and her eyes were extremely sad.

The doorbell rang, and Sophia opened it to find Thomas and Victoria on the other side. Sophia's heart sang, seeing them so happy again.

"Helena," Victoria said. "What are you doing here?"

"I'm here to talk about Grey. What are you doing here?"

"That's exactly why we're here," Thomas said.

Amy came from the bedrooms, wearing a fluffy robe from Sophia's closet, and a towel on her head.

"Way too many people in one place," Amy muttered.

"We're all here to talk to Sophia about Grey," Victoria said.

Sophia pressed her fingers to her temples. "I'm already getting a headache."

"Look, I think I have a lot more to talk to her about than anyone else right now," Helena said. "Can we have a moment?"

Sophia took her back to the bedroom, where she closed the door.

"What do you need to talk about?"

"Look, I get it," Helena started, looking a little nervous. "All of this shit fucking sucks, but you can't keep punishing yourself and Grey over it."

Sophia's heart jumped at the mention of his name. Helena would have seen him recently, and Sophia was desperate to know how he was. She'd wanted to text so often, and always ended up deleting everything.

"Is he okay?" she asked, but knew the answer before Helena spoke.

"To be frank, no, he's not," Helena said. "He's miserable and so are you."

Sophia stopped when her throat tightened. She wanted to rage and scream, but so far, that hadn't worked at all. She wanted to see Grey more than she wanted to take her next breath.

"I don't know how we can make this work now."

"Sophia," Helena said, her voice firm but soft. "You are not the sum of your parents' mistakes. Your dad's a narcissistic asshole and a murderer. You are neither of those things, and Grey either."

"The only person who should feel ashamed is Conrad," said Julia from the door, which was slightly open. Julia stepped inside. "This is not on you."

Helena nodded solemnly, but Sophia's heart thumped.

"This process with Conrad is going to suck all on its own. Without you being a martyr and without you giving up a person you love. Without us punishing ourselves for sins that were never ours. It seems horribly unfair."

Sophia felt the tremble of her chin before it happened, and her eyes filled and spilled down her cheeks. Julia had married a man like their father because those were the patterns that were instilled in them.

She didn't want to give up what she had found with Grey. She just hoped it wasn't too late, when she had stayed away for so long. She put her hands to her face.

"You think he'll take me back?" she asked Helena and Julia.

"He'd be really stupid if he didn't," Julia said. Sophia knew what she was doing, and it was sweet, but Grey was within his every right to never want to talk to her again.

The door opened and Amy, Victoria, and Thomas came in.

Victoria rushed forward and pulled Sophia's hands from her face.

"Please stop touching your face. You have bacteria on your fingers."

"Is this really the moment?" Sophia demanded, her hands firmly at her side.

"It's always the moment for skin care," Helena offered and Victoria gasped, her face a mask of delight.

"I knew I liked you, but I might have just fallen head over heels for you."

Sophia looked from one to the other, then threw an incredulous look at Thomas, who, instead of looking disturbed as Sophia was, nodded with his eyes half closed.

"You're all ridiculous," Sophia snapped. "And I'm supposed to be listening to you about my love life?"

"I swear to God, Sophia." Julia's teeth with clenched together. She struggled to control her breathing and Sophia, alarmed, could only look at her and wait. "Go shower, because you stink, and go see him. You want to, and he loves you."

Julia took off from the room, red in the face.

"You heard the woman," Amy said and Sophia found herself in the adjoining bathroom. She showered and dressed quickly. She didn't care to be fancy.

She was going to go to him as she was and he would either take her that way, or he could turn her away, and she would have to be okay with that.

God, she hoped he took her back.

"Text us after to let us know how the sex is," Julia called as she walked past them. She laughed nervously but didn't stop.

She left the five of them in the living room, already chatting over glasses of wine. She took the potion right outside the living room and prayed with all her heart that he hadn't revoked her permission to come straight into his house. When she appeared in the entryway, she allowed herself to sigh in relief.

The house was dark, every single light off. Minimal light came in through the windows, and from upstairs she heard the piano play a melancholy tune. It was muffled, as if the door was closed at the top of the stairs.

She swallowed and found her way easily through the house, thankful that he was so neat. Her steps were quiet on the stairs as she went up. The door wasn't closed all the way, and she pushed it softly open. He had the drapes open and moonlight filtered into the room, partly illuminating him in silver light.

He sang under his breath, his voice soft and almost inaudible, but almost as if he sensed her there, he suddenly stopped playing and turned. His arms were bare, as he had a tank top on. His sweatpants appeared to be black.

He stayed where he was, frozen to his seat.

"Hi." She lifted her hand awkwardly, then ordered herself to put it down.

"Hi." He didn't smile, didn't move. She shifted, suddenly feeling really stupid.

"You deserved an in-person conversation after everything went down," she said. "I'm sorry I didn't give you that, at least."

She stopped, expecting that he'd respond, but when he didn't, she continued,

"The truth is, I'm really messed up right now. Anxious, depressed, feeling guilty. Ashamed."

He stood and came toward her. She took in the fresh scent of his and closed her eyes, her anxiety settling for the first time in weeks. His hair was a little damp, and her fingers itched to reach up and touch it.

He still said nothing, and she started convincing herself that she was too late. But only a beat later, he reached for her, pulling her close. She put her arms around him instinctively, burying her nose into his chest. She breathed him in, her heart beating in her ears.

"I'm so sorry," she whispered.

"I missed you." His arms tightening around her, and he lifted her against him so they were face to face.

"Oh, I missed you too." She reached up, took his face in her hands. He was looking at her hungrily, as if was seeing her for the first time.

"Things won't be easy for a while, but I want to work on it," she said. "I want to work it out with you. If you'll have me."

He nodded eagerly. "We will make it work. We can make anything work."

Her lips swept over his, and he kissed her back like a man starved. Like they hadn't kissed each other in weeks and had to make up for the time lost.

The bedroom was the most natural place to go to next.

After, she lay on top of him, her chin resting on her hands, and she bit her lip. He had a half smile on his lips, contented, with his eyes closed, and humming a tune she did not recognize.

"I love you," she whispered, her heart so full she could barely stand it. "But you knew that already."

He opened his eyes as a soft smile spread across his face.

"I love you too." The rumble of his voice vibrated under her hands, so deep and familiar.

She wanted to hear his voice every single day for the rest of her life.

He held on to her tightly, and so did she hold him too.

Not all days were perfect, but even the ones that sucked were better because they were together. A few months later, they moved in together, and they continued to see Lucas as a therapist. It didn't fix everything, but it helped heal the bruises of the past slowly and steadily, and they loved each other a little more every day.

And together, they made magic, like those who had come before them. They gave away the cure for the void, even traveled to many places around the world to help those who had contracted the disease.

Sophia never uttered another wish out loud. She made music with him instead.

AFTERWORD

Writing A Song of Magic was such a thrilling ride for me. From the moment I decided to write it, I fell in love with the characters and knew exactly where I wanted the story to end.

Like many other writers out there, I've had a project I've worked on for over a decade. One day, blocked and heartbroken that I couldn't figure it out, I turned to the internet and was inspired by a music video by my favorite A Cappella group. The story showed up so swiftly, and I instantly knew that it would be the next thing I told. I wanted to so badly to finish a story and put it out there, and here is the fruit of that. It's so special to me, and I'm so glad you're here too.

I heard recently that the brain can't distinguish between real people and fictional characters, and the way I love these characters makes that a definite truth for me. I will always have a very special place in my heart for these characters, and I really hope that they've captured your heart in the same way they captured mine.

Carolina

ACKNOWLEDGMENTS

First and foremost, let me have a freakout moment. Drumroll, please...

Picture me screaming and jumping like a lunatic

Finishing this novel has been the accomplishment of my life. I freaking did it!

Song would not be a thing if it wasn't for that breakdown I had when I realized I had to rewrite my life's work from scratch again—for the thousandth time.

In my snot-faced, ugly-cry heartbreak, I turned to the internet and discovered my favorite A Cappella artists, VoicePlay. Without that initial spark of inspiration, *Song* would have never happened, so like the cringe fangirl I am, I want to thank them for their amazing talent (especially Geoff Castellucci who has a range that makes me want to die and ascend all at once).

To my wonderful spouse, my biggest supporter. You heard me cry, rage, freak out, scream in excitement and frustration, and you stood there that whole time and told me I could do it. Thank you for supporting me in this insane dream.

To my Zoey, who thinks I'm cool because I wrote a book, and who got teary-eyed when I read her a passage. You make me feel cooler and more capable than I will ever be. I do it all for you.

To my writing partner and fellow author, Stacy Clason—you are the absolute best and I love you forever and ever and ever. Thank you so much for helping me edit this edition of *Song*.

To my amazing friends who saw this from the beginning and loved it: Lillian, Kelsey, Julie, McKayla, and my eternal cheerleader, Erin. You guys are awesome.

Love, Carolina

ABOUT THE AUTHOR

CAROLINA CASTILLO was born and raised in the Dominican Republic. When she's not writing, she enjoys reading, singing, dancing, and rewatching all her favorite funny shows and movies.

For more from Carolina, you can find her on TikTok and Instagram @creatively_unwritten

To sign up for her newsletter and for more about her books and what she's been doing, visit http://carolinacastilloauthor.com